THE LIFE OF DEATH SHOW

A speculative Novel

Mary Torre Kelly

BookLocker
St. Petersburg, Florida

Print ISBN: 978-1-64719-167-2
Epub ISBN: 978-1-64719-168-9
Mobi ISBN: 978-1-64719-169-6

Published by BookLocker.com, Inc., St. Petersburg, Florida.

Printed on acid-free paper.

The characters and events in this book are fictitious. Any
similarity to real persons, living or dead, is coincidental and
not intended by the author.

BookLocker.com, Inc.
2021

First Edition

Library of Congress Cataloguing in Publication Data
Kelly, Mary Torre
The Life Of Death Show by Mary Torre Kelly
Library of Congress Control Number: 2020922854

For John Ryland, Country Librarian, my
Flamingo, my love…

There are no unnatural or supernatural phenomena,
only very large gaps in our knowledge of what is
natural. We should strive to fill those gaps of
ignorance.

– Edgar Mitchell –
Apollo 14 Astronaut

Upon this gifted age, in its dark hour,
Rains from the sky a meteoric shower
Of facts...They lie unquestioned,
uncombined.
Wisdom enough to leech us of our ill
Is daily spun, but there exists no loom
To weave it into fabric...

– Edna St. Vincent Millay-
(d. 1950)

It is wonderful that tens of thousands of years
have elapsed since the creation of the
World, and still it is undecided whether
or not there has ever been an instance
of the spirit of any person appearing
after death. All argument is against it,
but all belief is for it.

– Samuel Johnson-
(1709-84)

Table of Contents

PART ONE

1
Near Life

April 1, SOMETIME IN THE RECENT FUTURE

On his death-day, Henry Lee Hassett missed his chance to slip the earth and instead found himself in an Atlanta TV studio watching his daughter Jessie, a network news anchor, deliver the evening news, live. He was mystified as to how this could happen and why? It was a shock to die, an outrage. So, in the absence of any absolute law forbidding consciousness after death, Henry discovered a continuing stream of probability, and he rode that lawless wave. Like the sporting golfer he was, he played through. He figured the odds of this happening were even greater than the odds of making a hole-in-one, calculated to be about 8,606 to 1, on a par 3. Still, someone made a heart-stopping hole-in-one somewhere in the world every single day.

His transition had been abrupt. One minute he was lying in bed looking out at Silver Lake, taking his last nickering of breath, and the next minute he was hovering in a television studio four hundred miles away watching Jessie deliver bad news. How was this possible? Wasn't his brain supposed to stop functioning when he died? He'd always thought religion was a caution, so he figured he hadn't been chosen. Was this God's denial? Or the effect of his own avid wish to stay alive for another round of golf? Or was it some cosmic mistake designed to tip the imagination off to what had been passing

1

for a given but was really just foolish consistency? He liked that one.

Henry found that his "I" was gone. As though he'd meshed with something bigger, something other. He'd still have to use the personal pronoun, but it wasn't the same as when he was alive. He stood outside his self now, bodiless, a virtual narrator of what he could see and hear. He had only those two senses, and thought, if you can call that a sense. The last sensation he remembered feeling was froideur: a cold that burned. Now he could no longer feel, taste, or smell anything. *Well, two out of five ain't bad.* He still had his emotions, his hearts core, and a curious mind, like another sense. So, Carl Jung and Willie Nelson, and a bunch of other guys were right about the psyche: it isn't confined to space and time. It doesn't die. You can't kill energy. It's all borrowed, and you might even get a chance to give it back.

Now Henry could see from an out-of-body distance, who he had been when he was alive, how his lifelong desire to be someone and fit in had ruled him and hindered him. Although he'd been a builder for a living, he'd always been a dreamer too. And a slow, plodding reader. Yet he had learned all he knew from books, and there were huge gaps in his knowledge. But, by amalgamating oddments of literature with science and how-to manuals, he'd become myriad-minded. He had read both with purpose, and aimlessly, always hoping to stumble upon nuggets of wisdom, those important things all but the never knowing knew. Scientific American and Popular Science were his favorite magazines. He remembered reading a quote from Carl Sagan: "Somewhere, something incredible is waiting to be known." Could this thing happening to him that no one will believe be it?

Quantum Physics led him to understand that everything changed form: subatomic particles swirled in space and could not be measured or fixed in either space or time. Come to think of it, no one had ever proven these particles didn't have thought. He'd loved his family, music, art, literature, good groceries, the natural world, electronics, radios, and the great game of golf. Oh, he'd loved life! But now he saw that he had only been an ordinary man. He was no rainmaker. And he saw how strange being ordinary really was, in the larger cosmic scheme. *I'm not even sure the world will say I have been here.*

Henry suspended his head trip to focus on the blazing television studio which looked like a mixture of heaven and hell if there were such places. Maybe he would find out. Bright broadcasting lights shone and flashed, turning the very air of the room red. The place reeked of reality, of the confusion caused by infomania, caused by television. Faint music that sounded like dying cicadas pulsed in the background, as his daughter delivered bad awful news: violent murders, car accidents, home invasions of the elderly, toxic political corruptions. Why do we default to the worst news? Why did he think Jessie could make an art out of news casting? It was because of him she was here. He had influenced her to choose what he now saw was a torturous job. *Oh, why did I do that? It's unforgivable.*

Maybe it was because he'd enjoyed watching her for half his lifetime, thirty-six years since the day she was born, and he thought everyone else would too. She had that black Irish freshness, pale skin and dark shiny seal hair, the tenderest blue eyes. Her look was unguarded and natural, in contrast to her gravitas. And her voice was exuberant, full of those feathery poly-tones females nurture babies with. He'd always told her she was telegenic, just made for TV. But now as he watched her he was appalled by how all this terrible news dark-shadowed her world, and everyone else's, how snidely

3

the background orchestral score he'd never even noticed before rose, full of treble, snare drums, a trumpet even. It was treacherous music, mockingly urgent. He looked around at the joyless faces of the crew and the producer, Eli's face, and wondered why they were so numb to it, and why it had never bothered him either, when he was alive. *No, there is no way she can be happy talking this trash. I have to find a way to save her.*

Henry thought about his younger daughter Kate and his two sons. Kate was her mama's girl. His sons had grown up to be patronizing, and distant, always fighting him, especially his eldest son, an actor, who had even changed his name. He loved them all, but he couldn't talk to any of his children, not even his wife, the way he could talk to Jessie Lee. He'd always had the strongest bond with her, and he wondered if they might somehow still connect. If this wave held.

Oh boy, everything's impossible, till it ain't.

He watched Jessie at the news desk wrapping the show and thought she looked tired. The last bit of news always had to be a tad upbeat, along with the music, he remembered that.

Above her head a glitzy sign pandered to the sweep's ratings:

MAKE GROUND WITNESS NEWS
YOUR NUMBER ONE CHOICE

Jessie smiled and brought it:

"And finally. Today a 65-year-old German woman gave birth to quadruplets. She is expected to make the Guinness Book of World Records as the world's oldest mother of quads. I'm Jessie Pettengill. Thanks for choosing Ground Witness News."

She froze in the obligatory smile until Eli called, "We're clear."

Abruptly, a production assistant was up in Jessie's face, handing her a cell phone: "It's your brother Tom, in Florida," iron in the PA's voice.

Jessie shivered. She didn't usually take a call on set, especially not one from Tommy.

Seaborn Pettengill, Jessie's husband and her camera operator, zoomed in, and just then, the producer Eli waylaid Seaborn, complaining about Jessie:

"You gotta talk to her, she has to put out more charm, we're sinking in the ratings.

Not right now." Seaborn snapped, as his camera captured Jessie paling as she listened on the phone. Real life burst upon all the studio monitors.

The curious crew watched the monitors.

Eli went on complaining to Seaborn: "We gotta talk about this—we've dropped to third in the ratings—that's so poor, so poor..."

Jessie clamped her free hand over her ear, and gasped, "What Tom? I didn't hear you," wishing she hadn't heard. What he said was unacceptable. She wanted him to say he was only kidding, April Fools.

Tom raised his voice and repeated himself, a stutter from childhood resurfacing: "He d-d died, a little after s-s-six...a h-h-heart attack..."

Jessie let out a cry that pierced the din of the studio like shot. The crew all turned away from the monitors to look at her live. Her sapphire eyes flooded, consumed the light and turned milky blue. As she listened to Tom, she swayed dizzily, a coldness seeped into her veins.

"Hey, she okay?" Eli nudged Seaborn.

Henry glimpsed Jessie's knees knocking like she had a case of the yips. He leapt forward, but the light shone right through what he was now. It was impossible to be forceful if you were invisible. He tasted Jessie's salty tears in his mind. He called out to her *I'm here! I'm still here!* but she couldn't hear him. He had no way of getting through to her. He had no way to cause anything to happen. He was just a ghost, neither here nor there.

Seaborn shut down his camera. The monitors went blank. Fresnel's reflected the Titian highlights in Jessie's hair, like a tiny fervent promise, the instant before they all clicked out. He ran to her, winding his black ball cap with white letters that said "Mr. Pettengill" on it, back around to the front of his pony-tailed head.

Jessie gazed at Seaborn, purest grief ruining her face. In one motion, she dropped the phone, her hands raked the air, her legs splayed apart. Seaborn swooped in and caught her before she hit the floor. He knelt holding her, his lips pressed to her forehead. "It's Daddy," she sobbed. She closed her eyes and thought she felt him there.

But Henry was dwindling, leaving the bad news factory behind. He took a long last look at Jessie and realized he might not always be there by her, seeing her as he did in this instant. Maybe it was just a fluke of something like luck, and he was sorely disappointed. If only he had a way to get through to her.

Now, whilst fading, he became otherwise engaged—hard to say how or where—it might be a form of sleep. If it was, he was sleeping on the very parapet of consciousness, and over dreaming. He remembered reading in Harvey Penick's Little Red Book: "The golfing area of the brain is a fragile thing terribly susceptible to suggestion."

If only, if only, if only, he chanted like a mantra, to hold back the pang of loss creeping over him. Who said don't be afraid, you won't miss yourself when you die? It's another lie.

In a flash, Henry saw his life and even his death had all been leading up to this little fable, this lore after death. But the wave wasn't holding—he was sinking fast—desperately he crooned, though no one could hear him: *Babble for her Mr. Brook... Kiss her for me Mr. Raindrop...And keep her under your roof... Please Mr. Sun...*

Henry loved songs.

2
The New Morning

About a hundred billion people have died since humans first walked the earth, and the removal of the dead has taken multifarious forms. The little drama that would be Henry's funeral began the day after his death-day. From early morning his family had been gathering, consoling, hashing out the details. Tom and his teenaged son Frank were already at the house on Silver Lake with the newly widowed Doris. They had come up from south Florida the night before. The youngest daughter, Kate, had arrived shortly after Henry passed. Henry's eldest son, Chuck-Pete Monroe—a stage name, although everyone in the family had gotten used to calling him that—was flying in from New York City, where he was a well-known actor.

Seaborn was driving Jessie the four hundred miles from Atlanta to Silver Lake in the middle of Florida where Jessie's parents lived. Down through Georgia on I-75 they tooled in Seaborn's blue Land Rover, passing stands of soughing pine trees, inter-sprinkled with blooming pink and white dogwood, and miles of plowed fields, the red clay underbelly of the Piedmont region of Georgia. Alongside the road and in the median wildflowers whirled in the wind of passing traffic. Jessie took it all in but could not reconcile this beauty with the fact of her father's death. Near Valdosta they began seeing groves of pecan trees and graphic signs for "Pecan Logs," tempting them to stop, but they didn't. Only twenty-five more miles till they crossed the state line into Florida. It would all go faster then, like a downhill course.

Jessie was grateful for Seaborn, for driving and for being willing to go through it all with her. His steadfast sense of duty was a side of him she hadn't fully appreciated until now. She lay crumpled on the seat, her woozy head resting on Seaborn's warm thigh as he drove. She was only slightly under the sedative Eli told Dr. Desmond, the station doctor, to give her. It should have knocked her out but did not. She had hardly slept at all. Her heart pined, her mind raced. She felt her father's presence glittering all around her. She shivered and turned the air-conditioning down.

Seaborn squinted when he passed the "Welcome to Florida The Sunshine State" sign, took his sunglasses off the visor and put them on. Ever-ready Seaborn, Jessie thought, watching him. Afterall, they were secure, alive—yet grief laid a pall over them—Jessie thought she could see it as well as feel it. A rain shower began and Seaborn turned the wipers on, smearing white bird shit across the tinted windshield like snow.

The light changed, began to gleam brighter, even thru the shimmering rain. Jessie fluttered her eyes, so the yellowy pink sunlight played on her eyelids. She took balm from the light, letting herself be comforted by the warmth of the April day, the way she had done when she was a child, when everything came to her through her senses. She tried to take belief in the same way, but hard as she tried, she could not believe her father was dead. There had always been a sort of current between them, and she hadn't felt any disconnect. She begged to have him back, *please God*. She couldn't surrender him to darkness. She just wouldn't. She closed her eyes, stubbornly clenching that thought.

But another withering thought entered her mind to torment her: she was at the clock-ticking age, and the scene in her OB-Gyn's office from a couple of days earlier played over and over in her mind. As she sat on the cold, paper-covered exam table, the doctor had said: "There probably isn't any physical reason, but we'll run some tests. Sometimes women in power careers like yours have trouble conceiving. You've delayed." Such a dire word. In fact, she hadn't *delayed* at all—in four and a half years of passionate sex, they'd never used any birth control at all, yet no baby. She had even quit smoking and it had been so hard to do. She still craved a ciggie. But the doctor said cigarettes killed eggs. They longed for a baby. But all that doctor could offer was: "You will just have to slow down." And now she despaired all the more because it was too late for a kid of theirs to ever know Henry, no matter how much she slowed down. Eli was going to fire her anyway if she didn't perk up. Another worry.

A tune on the radio interrupted her torment. It sounded like the key of C harmonica Henry played—he called it the happiest key—*dada da da, da da da da, dada da da da da da;* over and over again it played, lulling her, a tune she was familiar with but had never really paid much attention to until now. She hummed along. Seaborn looked down and stroked her hair. She couldn't remember the name of the tune, or the words, and this crummy unremembering bugged her. She reached over to shut the radio off so she could think a minute. But it already was off!

Her eyes grew wide. Where was this music coming from? She wondered if Seaborn could hear it. She stared at the wet sky, at the bluesy-white Bible story clouds. Clouds had such abundance, the power to disappear, reappear, and even to signify. How generous they were. Now they were delivering a peaceful feeling—but what was delivering this music?

The car phone sounded, and she picked it up. There was no one on the line. But when she hung up, her hearing felt different, changed. The tune grew louder. She shook her head and drummed her ears.

"Who was that?" Seaborn asked, his voice underwater, and she heard her own voice say "nobody" before she sank into a new tunnel of sound, with an echo, with a round resonance that made wavy light. The light made loud roiling sound waves, so scary dangerous her ears burned. She swallowed hard, coughed; her ears pop-popped, like hot oil was inside them. She was afraid to listen now, afraid even to breathe. It was hard to stay in the car.

The rain quit, or they had driven out from under it. A red sun blazed. Jessie tried to ease her panicky feelings by watching tiny drops of rainwater, like invested points of light, skitter up the windshield glass. She marveled at how into minutiae she was, how time seemed to have slowed.

Abruptly, the tune ended; she became alert then, on edge. She popped open the glove compartment and retrieved an old stale pack of Parliaments. What she needed for comfort was nicotine.

She plugged in the lighter and lit a cigarette without sitting up. Dimly at first, then clearly, she heard Henry's voice: *I thought you quit smoking?* She looked at the cigarette, then up at the sky. His voice got louder: *Yay you can hear me! It's okay. Don't be afraid. I want you to quit smoking for real, okay? It took days off my life, and when I got right down to it days counted, didn't they?* He laughed a nervous laugh, and she heard giggling too; it seemed to come from out in the universe, like children were laughing with him. She shivered. Goose bumps rose on the back of her neck and shot down her arms.

Seaborn ran his hand idly along her arm, and grazing the bumps, he rubbed vigorously.

Jessie sat up and looked at him. She could tell by his face he hadn't heard a thing. He was in his own world, driving and thinking his own thoughts. She felt groggy, dizzy. She stubbed out the cigarette.

She heard: *You have to give up the pleasure of smoking to save your own life, Jessie Lee. You'll do other things with your handles.* Jessie looked at her hands. Her father was the only person she knew who called hands "handles," and the only person who ever called her Jessie Lee. This can't be happening. *You'll mellow out, slow down to an easier pace...* The clouds were moving, and parting with each of his words. He had a rich, friendly voice, like Jack Lemmon's. She'd always thought this when he was alive too. But, oh God, what was he now?

Henry said: *Now watch this.* He made loop-d-loops with the billowy clouds and laughed wildly. *Cheer up, it's wonderful out here. Don't be sad. I'm finally free, no worn-out old body to bother with anymore, and no ego either. This light is like fresh love; that sunlight down there is only the shadow of this light. I think this is the place cats go Jess—I can hear purring.* She saw movement, like a surfer going over waves, making frothy loop-d-loops, then a vague cloudy likeness of Henry's face laughing as he sang in parody: *Don't cry for me, Argentina...*

She couldn't help smiling at that old corny song. At the same time, she began to sweat and tremble. Her mind shifted and drifted, until she had a maximum lack of control over reality while still awake. Seaborn looked over at her, dolorously, but he smiled back when he saw her smile, picked up her hand, kissed it and held it. Oh, he had no idea.

Gradually, a new picture appeared in the clouds, of a young boy in knickers sitting on a stoop holding a golf club, with his dog, a black Lurcher, settled beside him. Jessie recognized the picture from a family photo on the mantle at Silver Lake. It was Henry on the day that he'd gotten his first job as a caddy. He'd told her it was the best day of his life. She nudged Seaborn, pointing up at the cloud picture.

Seaborn tilted his head to look up, and nodded, not recognizing Henry, but able to see the foggy image of a boy and a dog formed out of clouds. "Well, I'll be damned," he said, looking at Jessie like she had something to do with it.

Ah, Jessie Lee, I don't know exactly how I'm getting through to you. It's sorta like magic. There must be a scientific explanation though. Maybe I merged with a frequency wave of some kind, latched on to radio waves. Quarks maybe—particles that interact through gravity, electromagnetism. I don't know, and I don't know how long I can stay either. I can sense a tug, pulling me up into the up where it's glorious. Remember to quit smoking if you don't hear from me again—it's a terrible hazard to your health.

"No, don't go!" Jessie cried.

Seaborn thought she meant the picture in the clouds, eroding now. He patted her leg.

For a long while they drove along in silence, but for Jessie it was a silence full of phantoms. She cast about in her mind, desperate for a way out of this overactive grief. Was she drifting into madness? She hoped it was all a dream, but she was awake. She'd once done an interview with Annie Druyan, Carl Sagan's wife. After he died, Annie finished the book she and Carl were writing together. Annie had told her: "When you love someone and are so close to him, when he dies you can still hear his voice inside your head." Jessie took deep breaths and told herself this was all it was. Or else EVP's, electronic voice phenomena—people lately were interested in listening for that. Or something incredible. Or something telephonic. She would swear that phone call had altered her hearing.

It was quiet now and Jessie slumped against the window and dozed.

After a while Seaborn switched on the radio and dialed up The Reverend Travis Thackston's Christian Crusade. He liked to listen to the cant and swagger of suck-back preachers when he drove, his idea of comedy.

The Reverend was sermonizing: "...because it says in the Bible, Mark 16: those that believe shall take up SERPENTS-AH, and the spirit of the LORD-AH will move in you. Wunst you FEEL it, you never forget it-ah..."

Seaborn grinned. "He's a born showman, you ever see him when he's in the studio, taping his T.V. show?" When Jessie didn't answer he said, "That's good, because his face is better on radio." He looked over at Jessie, expecting at least a smile, but got no reaction at all.

She was hearing from Henry again. He had cut into The Reverend Thackston's show like a commercial: *I'm back! You're gonna have lots of dangerous enemies Jessie Lee. I'm not kidding about that. So, watch out for the hazards.* He took a lob shot in the clouds and Jessie saw a golf ball sail way across the sky, hang for what seemed an eternity, and then vanish.

3
Silver Lake

By the time they reached Silver Lake three hours later, Jessie had the full-fledged creeps. She was in a hideous place, alert for signs of madness. She'd heard from Henry so many times she was weary from holding her ground against what she had begun to fear was schizophrenia. Each time he said goodbye it was as if for the last time, but he kept coming back. He tried to allay her fears by giving her the absolute assurance that he was traveling in a friendly universe, along with promises to try and return from what he whimsically called *cloud nine* and talk to her again if he could. Jessie wasn't sure she wanted that, even though she knew she didn't want him to leave her ever. How could she hear his voice so glib and witty, so normal, and yet he was invisible? Well, mostly. How could she say *no, shut up, don't talk to me?* She had never been able to refuse her father anything; they were congruent souls, each one the other's secret favorite person in the world, and now she added, *dead or alive.*

She sat up, stretched, and took deep breaths of the ripe Florida air; tasted again the wild nature of this place, hoping it would allay her anguish.

Turning into the long driveway, she saw Chuck-Pete running around the lake, the first thing he always did when he came back home. Jessie ached for him, as always. He had been both her tormentor and her hero in childhood. She'd learned about power from him, but somewhere along the way they'd lost touch. Now he was a rising actor and the pursuit

15

of fame menaced him. Seaborn said, "Hey look, there goes Chuck-Pete, working on his brand."

Jessie hadn't found a way to tell Seaborn about Henry's voice yet, despite his urging, *tell him what I am to you now, tell him you can hear me.* Seaborn hadn't gotten to know Henry very well in the four-plus years they'd been married, mainly because Sea didn't play golf. Besides that she was afraid he would think she was crazy. Maybe she was. She'd been so swept up listening to Henry she hadn't said a word to Seaborn for hours. He probably thought she'd been asleep.

Now, feeling defensive of Chuck-Pete, she made the effort to speak and her voice came out ragged, like she had been sleeping: "You like to run around that lake sometimes too."

"Yeah, but I'm not obsessive-compulsive about it."

"Oh, what big words!" He always reminded her of John Corbit's character, on old *Northern Exposure* reruns they liked to watch. "Chuck-Pete wants to keep in shape is all."

Seaborn laughed, "Yeah, he gets five pounds of adipose on him and that series he's in will bump him off."

Jessie watched her brother, feeling a yearning in her heart that Seaborn, who had no siblings, would never understand. What everyone always noticed about Chuck-Pete was his huge ego, hard to miss. It was trivial and tragic, like a broken key. She'd once had a dream about Chuck-Pete throwing away his ego, casting it off in an act of bravura. His ego had reared up and stood in the street, rejiggered into an empty white coat with the collar up.

As they coasted up to the house, a violin began da-da-ing in Jessie's head, the same tune she'd been hearing all day. To shut it out she started counting: the twelve coconut palms that lined the long driveway, the five strange cars that were parked willy-nilly on the grass next to the driveway, the gaggle of wild geese running to get out of their way. She shuddered. Why did the geese always disturb her so? She swallowed hard. *Home*. The word clutched her heart and left her wanting.

Seaborn pulled in under a white sign that Henry had made and hung high up in a big old oak tree. Clumps of Spanish moss draped the branches. The sign, in black serifed letters said: RESERVED FOR MRS. PETTENGILL. Jessie teared up, and heard the wind whispering in the old oak. She thought about the times when they had come home on holidays: Christmas, Thanksgiving, Easter, and how they would come bounding up this driveway, tooting the horn. And Henry and her mother, Doris, would run out of the house to greet them, arms flying open but then holding back suddenly, like they were afraid of revealing the suffocating loneliness they'd been hiding, even from each other. Jessie's heart broke seeing them get old so alone.

She pictured them all standing by the rich black-dirt circle admiring Henry's prize crimson glory roses. She could smell the dirt and roses mingling—then they would quickly side-step out of the burning sun, into the shade of the old barn-sized double garage, and hug, and say how good each other looked. Doris was always skeptical, never quite believing any of Jessie's compliments. Henry got sandbagged with something that stole his attention as soon as he began to get caught up. Doris said it was his angina. She claimed to know everything there was to know about her husband. Jessie was annoyed by her mother's possessiveness, and the way she always sprayed Henry right off, so there could be no doubt she owned him. But, oh mama, what are we going to do now?

It was comforting to see the old house again even though she felt a stab of pain realizing Henry wouldn't be there anymore, or would he? She loved this simple white-frame cottage, with a glassed-in porch across the front so you could sit looking out at the near perfect roundness of Silver Lake. The lake had a circumference of five miles, with a sandy shoreline, and a two-lane blacktop road that circled around the lake in front of every house. Behind the houses were acres of citrus groves where the geese lived. Directly across the lake and visible from their porch was the modest Silver Lake Golf Club. She was glad Henry got to live near a fairway and play golf anytime he pleased. Whenever he'd talked about golf, he made it sound mysterious, mystical even. She had learned the game from him, although she rarely played.

He'd once told her that golf put him in touch with all the best things on earth. It tested him physically, and even challenged him to keep his very great temper in check. Teeing off was like no other triumph—the transcendent rush of hitting a ball so sweetly sometimes he didn't even feel the impact, and then that rapt moment when the ball seemed to belong to the air. He had played the game knowing that golfers were prone to heart attacks, testing the gods, claiming it was the hill he chose to die on. He had tasted of the fruits, had hacked, duffed, and sliced his way through life, and found his paradise on the golf links. No one gets out alive anyway, he'd joked to Jessie. Although she always had the feeling he never quite believed it himself.

But after his triple by-pass he became a believer, and Jessie witnessed his once handsome features slacken; his hair turned white almost overnight. He said his body was lost to him. He sat for hours trying to recuperate, looking across the lake at the links, the memory of a good birdie shaking him like a tail. Just before sundown and again at sunrise the lake reflected light, making a perfectly silver surface, like a gigantic mirror. The heavens were like moiré, the clouds drifty mackerels in the lake. He'd told Jessie: "This is why the Indians, feather not sheet, named this water Silver Lake."

Jessie looked at the sprawling wooden garage with the rickety barn doors hanging open. Henry's workshop and library was in a big-windowed room on one side. It was full of his essence and all his collections. She loved how it was always cool, and smelled of glue, paint, motor oil, rusting iron tools, and the rosemary that grew outside under an open window. Across one wall was a mahogany bookcase holding his odd mix of books, old comics, and thirty or more years' worth of Scientific American, with little slips of paper sticking out to mark important pages. He had been a building contractor, capable of doing anything with his handles. In his retirement he'd puttered with inventions and radios, fixed broken things, made little rock people. He'd painted faces on all the cacti in the yard, and given them names like Tolstoy, Dostoevsky, Jackie Gleason. Upon the wall above his workbench hung Max Ehrmann's "Desiderata" which summed up Henry's own belief system: "Go placidly amid the noise and haste and remember what peace there may be in silence. As far as possible, without surrender, be on good terms with all persons..." Jessie had memorized the treatise without intending to.

On the other side of the garage a lean-to held Henry's golf cart, plugged in and charging. The geese squawked, strutted around it, expecting Henry. Jessie startled. Seaborn had cut the engine. How long had she been sitting there lost in thought, staring at the RESERVED FOR MRS. PETTENGILL sign? Her nose itched on both sides. "Someone's coming," Doris would say. But this time no one came out of the house to greet them.

They got out of the car and stretched, breathing in the fragrance of orange blossoms broadcasting from the groves behind the house. They dawdled through the grassy breezeway between the house and garage, and beheld the massive pheltaphorium tree, with Henry's empty hammock moldering beneath it. She felt Henry's presence acutely here. He would have rocked her baby in this hammock if she'd had one.

Just inside the kitchen door, Kate and Tom stood waiting for them. Tom Hassett was two years younger than Jessie, and already a widower. His wife had been a photographer and an aviatrix and had been killed in a ballooning accident when she was in her twenties. Since then he'd been raising his son Frank, alone, all while becoming one of the most prominent lawyers in the state of Florida. Jessie admired Tom for being a high achiever.

Kate, the youngest, at twenty, was still a student. She had come along fourteen years after Tom. Doris called Kate her "change of life" baby. Chuck-Pete had been her first born, the trailblazer, and Jessie was her middle child, the maverick.

Henry and Doris had raised their children to be competitors, to strive for power, to achieve. At an early age, they knew all the bitter games of sibling rivalry, excelling in divide and conquer and two against one. All but Kate, who was of another generation altogether, and without guile, numbed maybe by having too many parents.

Now Jessie could feel them all being realigned by their father's death, and all curiously changing, like a game of Mr. Potato Head.

She watched Seaborn shake hands with Tom, put his arms around him and hug him, while all he got from Tom was stiff compliance. Then Seaborn turned and winked at Kate. He liked attractive young girls.

She faced Kate. As they hugged, sobs lifted their shoulders in unison. The tears of one wetted the cheeks of the other. Jessie held Kate out at arm's length, appreciating how pretty she was, even in grief. She looked into Kate's big, hazel eyes, and whispered,

"Has he been talking to you, too?"

"Who?"

"Daddy."

"No?" Kate said it like a question. "Well, yes, maybe, a little, I don't know...." She looked flustered, more confused than ever. Jessie always did this to her.

Jessie waved her hand never mind, sorry for upsetting Kate, and turned to Tom, whom she attempted to hug. She looked through his strong wall and saw the little boy who used to play dolls with her so tenderly, hiding out in the car from Chuck-Pete, who would bully Tom without mercy if he caught them. She had once been close to Tom; now their relationship had become submerged under a mock maturity and they were distant with each other.

"How are you doing Tommy?" she said, immediately sorry she'd called him the childhood name he hated. He also hated his middle name, Andrews. She always had to be so careful with Tom. He was sensitive, but secretive about it too.

"Oh, f-f-fine," Tom said, like he was surprised at both the question, and his own answer. "Chuck's out r-r-running," he added, trying but failing to leap over the stammer he thought he had conquered in second grade, but was now, unmercifully, back.

"We saw him, where's Mama?"

"In the living room. Sh-she's not doin' so h-hot."

Tom's son, Frank, appeared in the dining room doorway, a shy smile on his face, anticipating his aunt Jessie, and the fuss she would make over him as soon as she saw him, and Seaborn would too. Sure enough, their arms flew out, and

Jessie squealed, causing Frank to duck, embarrassed, laughing softly.

"Oh Frank, you've grown so tall." Jessie enclosed him in her arms, standing on tiptoes to kiss his still baby-soft cheeks. "Are you sixteen already?" Seaborn wrapped his arms around them both, elated to see Frank, his favorite person besides Jessie in this family. Frank was five when he lost his mother. Seaborn's mother had died when he was the same age, and so they had this in common, shaping and connecting them.

Jessie took Frank's hand, led him quickly past the dining room table, loaded with two potted plants, a weeping fig, and a variegated Moses-In-The-Cradle. There was a pound cake oozing butter and a red Jell-o salad mold covered in blue cling-wrap, making purple. Jessie shuddered.

In the dimly lit living room, neighbors sat in a semi-circle around Mother Doris, with Henry's little black and brown Manchester dog, Ibsen, dozing at her feet. The sun setting out over the lake cast a coppery glow across the room. Jessie spotted the framed picture of Henry in knickers, holding a golf club with his black lurcher beside him, on the mantle, along with some other old family pictures. For his whole life Henry had always had a dog.

Ibsen looked so sad. He locked eyes with Jessie and gave a single loud bark.

"Shush-up." Doris hissed. The neighbors stood up and watched as Seaborn leaned down to take Doris's hand and kiss her gently on her proffered cheek.

Jessie held back, letting Sea go first. Then she knelt beside her mother and gently hugged her and was instantly repelled by the stale smell of whiskey.

Doris was angry. She sobbed, her voice high and wobbling,"It's all over. It's all over now." She looked Jessie full in the eye, daring her to deny it.

Jessie saw that Doris's usual faded-beauty demeanor had wilted—her eyes were puffy, and she looked like a weary old woman. Wads of tissues were clamped in her fists and stuffed down the front of her dress. Lines were imprinted in her swollen cheeks from the bedspread, like she must have just gotten up to greet these neighbors.

Doris gave Jessie a familiar, hopeless look that always made her feel underwhelming as a daughter, too unsubstantial, to be of any help. And Jessie waited for her mother to ask her why she didn't have any children yet, usually her very first question.

Jessie had a random memory from her adolescence of a drunk Doris wagging a finger at her: "Be yourself, just be yourself for Christ sakes." And Jessie had felt confusion about who she was and who this self was that Doris thought she wasn't being. Then Doris would seem consumed by feelings of inadequacy in her mother role, diminished somehow by her own lack of pride in her daughter, like it was something lacking in herself.

Now Jessie looked at her mother, smelled the alcohol seeping from her pores even though she seemed dully sober, and she was appalled to see Doris had on a purple dress Jessie had never seen before. Purple was forbidden in Henry's house; it was a one-man vendetta against a color. It was the one color he rejected, and he discouraged everyone in the family from ever owning anything purple, much less wearing it in his presence. Doris must have kept this dress hidden in the back of her closet, same place she hid her bourbon. Oh, she looked her worst ever, like a shriveled grape. Jessie saw she was ashamed of wearing the purple, but defiant about it too. Doris closed her eyes and laid her head back as though she'd like to go to sleep forever.

4
Doris Speaks Up

"Mama? MAMA?" Jessie was shaking her, almost hollering in her ear.

Startled, Doris remembered there were other people in the room. How long had she been staring out at that lake drowning in her sorrow? The neighbors were standing over her, saying good-byes, touching her hands, but she couldn't feel anything.

Then she was alone with Jessie and that Seamore, whatever his name was, that Indian of hers—where had he originally come from? She'd try and remember that later. She wanted to talk out loud now, to tell Jessie and the rest of them everything. Jessie was a good listener even if she never was sympathetic– not in her nature. She always had to analyze, just like Henry. Head in the clouds, both of them, high and mighty.

Doris touched her chapped lips and tears flooded her eyes. She fought her way up from a pit of disconsolate grief, and scavenged up a wobbly voice to talk out loud in.

"Get Tom in here," she croaked, clearing her throat, "and I'll tell you all what happened."

There was a scramble in the room as everyone assembled around Doris to hear her story. Jessie and Seaborn sat in the overstuffed chairs vacated by the neighbors, Kate and Frank sprawled on the floor with Ibsen, and Tom propped himself in the doorway with a drink in his hand, wishing Chuck-Pete was back so everything wouldn't have to get repeated yet again. He'd heard it all a couple of times already.

Satisfied she had their attention, Doris began:

24

"The yard men were here on their rider-mower cutting the grass. Henry and I were waiting for Kate. She was coming home for spring break. Supposed to be here by noon and it was already after two. So, we were worried sick." Doris glared at Kate a sufficient time to make her feel guilty.

"Henry had been having chest pains all morning, and he was shivering. The night before he'd spent hours out in his workshop on that damn ham radio. I begged him to let me take him to the hospital, but he wouldn't go. Said he wanted to wait for Kate. Then he said he didn't want to die in any damn hospital anyway, just to throw me off. But I knew he was bad because he was laid up in the bed watching the lake through the window instead of sitting on the porch like he usually did. He couldn't even get up, see? He had on that fancy red velvet smoking jacket Jessie gave him for Christmas, he was so cold. We came to Florida all those years ago because of the bitter winters of his childhood up on the Hudson river. He never wanted to be cold again. Ibsen was by him, looking all down-in-the-mouth. Henry said to me: 'Go out there and make sure that guy doesn't run over my roses.'

Doris suddenly bawled: "He wanted me out of the room, see? He knew he was gonna die." She fought to regain her voice, "I went to tell the yard man. I was only outside for a couple of minutes when I heard Ibsen barking and I ran back into the bedroom. Ibsen was jumping over Henry from one side to the other yelping, as if at some phantom in the room he had to protect him from. Henry had stopped breathing. I must have screamed because the yard man came running in, too. I gave artificial respiration and when I got tired the yard man took over. We kept it up for I don't know how long, until the ambulance came- who called? I guess the yard man did. The medics took over, gave him CPR, but they couldn't revive him either. He was dead already. Just told me to go outside and then died on me. My lips are so chapped from the artificial respiration. We were all so desperate just to get him to breathe again."

Doris stopped talking when Chuck-Pete came bounding into the living room through the porch door, throwing his large, handsome shadow over the coppery light. He saw everybody hushed and assembled around his mother, as he stood in the doorway panting, moving his feet in place, cooling down.

Jessie rose, tears streaming, and went to her brother, intending to hug him, but he put out his hand to block her. "I'm all sweaty," he said, shaking Jessie's hand limply, then leaning down to offer his cheek for an air kiss.

"How are you, it's good to see you." Jessie said in one sodden sentence. While her mind screamed an old heartrending question: *Why does he hate me, Daddy?* She'd asked Henry so many times when they were children. *Just because you were born,* he'd answer, or *you're too good, you make him look bad, you bring out the worst in him.* Or *you're taboo.* The answer she never did understand.

Doris glared at Chuck-Pete and Jessie both, for interrupting her. She was not interested in anything but her own story. "Then I had the priest come and give him the last rites..." Doris said loudly, recapturing everyone's attention, "whether he wanted them or not." She rubbed her hands together, making an annoying papery sound, and stared longingly back out at the lake.

5
Chuck-Pete's Letter

For the viewing that evening, Chuck-Pete Monroe walked into the funeral home through the side door reserved for family carrying a Polaroid camera and a letter. He wore a dark blue Armani suit which accentuated his thickly lashed blue eyes, and a white shirt with a band collar. He smelled of Sandalwood cologne and looked like a young James Coburn. He was about thirty minutes ahead of the rest of the family. He wanted this time to be alone with his father. For once. All his life he had shared him involuntarily, first with Jessie and then Tom and then along came Kate all those years later, about when he was ready to leave that family. Had to leave. There were too many people around for his parents to have to pay attention to instead of him. He needed a world of attention. He didn't resent little Kate, though, the way he did Jessie, that goody two-shoes-daddy's-girl.

The assistant funeral director greeted him. She was a redhead, in her twenties, just barely five feet tall, with a name badge that said JANE THROWER. Too attractive for the job, was Chuck-Pete's first thought. He smiled at her as he watched recognition cross her face.

"Great Day, you're on Television!" she clamped her hand over her mouth, nearly swallowing a wintergreen life-saver whole, and looked around quickly. "Oh, 'scuse me, Mr. Monroe, I was just so surprised to see you. Could I just? may I have your autograph? before this is..." she started to say, "all over" and quickly caught herself again. Then she blushed, as though intimidated by celebrity suddenly.

Chuck-Pete felt like something was crawling in his clothes, a feeling he always got when he was recognized by a starstruck fan. But he placed his hand gingerly on the girl's arm, looked into her adoring eyes and said, "Sure, Ms, a little later. First, I want to be alone with my father. Do you think you can help me do that?" He smiled, batting his eyes and showing off his big white perfect teeth, good enough for toothpaste ads, which he had also done– she'd probably seen them on billboards.

"Oh, of course, we are so sorry about your father. Please accept our profound condolences. she said, snapping again into her professional role, palms up, bowing and leading the way, then pausing at the entrance to the chapel, before leading him down the dimly lit aisle to the coffin itself.

As he followed her, Chuck-Pete's eyes looked ahead to the coffin, resting on a rostrum at the center of a pseudo stage, the focal point of the room. A jumble-colored assortment of flowers flanked the coffin, and a spray of all-white lilies lazed across the top. White candles the size of stove pipes, in huge, ornate brass holders, stood like Oscar statues on either side, surrounded by more flower arrangements, all sent by different people who cared. One had better be there from his agent, by Jesus, Chuck-Pete thought, anger suddenly leaping from nowhere.

He focused on a large horseshoe-shaped arrangement of red flowers on a tri-stand. Who could that be from? looked like a Kentucky Derby arrangement, bright red carnations with that heady smell. The ribbon said: "Good Lucks"– must be a mistaken delivery. Chuck-Pete felt his blood rise and looked away. He hated bungling. He stepped up and stood squarely facing the coffin, swallowing hard. His Adam's apple caught in his collar. He pulled the collar away with one finger and cleared his throat.

"Open it Ms.," he said, capturing Jane Thrower's eyes. "I want to be alone with my father for a little while. Think you can see that we're not disturbed?" He held her eyes, while he edged in closer.

She nodded and lifted the flower arrangement, the "family blanket" as it was called in the business, placed it on a nearby bench, showing concern with her careful movements. She lifted the Mahogany lid, locking the hinge in the upright position. A sweet gas immediately escaped, a puff of non-air like incense smoke filled her nostrils, and she stepped back quickly.

Chuck-Pete liked a girl who took orders well. He glared at her until she backed away and left him alone. He hardly felt the warm tears standing in his eyes, he was so calm, so in control. He didn't always know what he was feeling in the moment– usually he needed time to sort it out, and some distance.

He moved in as close as possible and began talking to his father intimately, while he studied his deadness. "I'm so ashamed of how I let you down." He muttered, his voice breaking. He swayed, feeling lost, as he tried to get used to the way his father looked dead, his skin the color of aluminum, and wearing that corny psychedelic tie he always wore. Just then the reality of death impaled him on a sword of cold fear, and he jumped back, terrified. The invincible one was dead! Anything was possible now, anything could come down, unravel, fall apart. How could they ever make up now for that big fight they had the last time he saw his father?

Chuck-Pete had a lot to be sorry for. He had written most of it in a letter– things he had not gotten a chance to say to his father when he was alive, and had trouble saying now that he was dead too. But he unwrapped the letter and began reading it to Henry, like it was a script he had to deliver. He whispered some of the parts that were too humiliating:

"Dear father, I lost my temper again and disgraced you. I was too full of pride to apologize and I should have, I know that now. I need your pardon, so I can get on with my life. This wasn't a very good time for you to die. I can only hope that you forgive me for that big fight we had. I know I didn't turn out the way you wanted. I wish I could have made it really big before you died. I didn't want you to die thinking I was a loser. I only hope that somehow you can hear me and accept my heartfelt apology for all the trouble I've caused you over the years, and you can find it in your heart to forgive me, so I can let go of this guilt..." Chuck-Pete was suddenly too distressed to finish. He kissed the letter and put it in his father's breast pocket, patting his chest, shocked at how unsubstantial Henry felt, like a straw man.

He backed away from him then, from death and from all judgment. He felt cleansed, the beginnings of being able to feel really good about himself again. He could taste freedom. He would be positive now. The enemies of death are hope and luck and he had both.

He snapped a few Polaroids while he waited for the absolution to roll, for just the right feeling he wanted, the right note to leave on– timing was everything, even here. He needed that clean slate so bad.

Jane came back into the room with her perfect timing. He had felt completion coming, like the moment at the end of a play when the lights dim, and the curtain comes down, a moment both sweet and terrible.

"Could you take a couple of pictures for me miss?" Chuck-Pete said, handing Jane the camera. He had to show her how to use it as she was unfamiliar with a Polaroid. Most people used their smart phones. But Chuck Pete liked having instant pictures he could look at and hold in his hand.

He leaned in close to Henry, almost cuddling him. "Try to get us both in it," he showed some teeth in a half-smile not meant to be mirthful, only pleasant, and positive.

After each picture, Chuck-Pete studied the results, never quite pleased. "Could you just take one from this angle now MS?" he requested, putting a dose of humility in his voice.

Jane moved around, accommodating his requests without showing any impatience with him or with doing things not ordinarily in her job description.

When they had shot up two packs of film, Chuck-Pete was satisfied, although by default– he was out of film. He had merely recorded the event, the last meeting with his father. What was wrong with that? He had taken the last pictures of them together possible anymore. So why did he feel so funny? He stared down at the pictures and tears pearled in his eyes, blinding him.

Jane took this as mounting grief or embarrassment at the sight of death's hardware. Some people got that way. She moved in to close the lid on the coffin, and start a new mood going. But before she could, Chuck-Pete separated out a couple of pictures, and tucked them inside the coffin. He looked then at Henry's hands. Builder hands. Hands that could do everything. Why hadn't he inherited these hands? Why were his own practically useless? He stepped back and let Jane close the coffin then.

What the hell was wrong with taking pictures? Chuck-Pete wondered, recovering his angry edge. He kicked out his foot and began to strut up the aisle. He knew he had Henry's walk, his exact body almost. Why, he was him now, as well as himself. He puffed up, took out a stick of spearmint.

"You want that autograph now, honey?" he said, turning around to the girl, Jane.

At the same time, Jessie walked into the chapel and passed Chuck-Pete and Jane coming up the aisle. Chuck-Pete almost didn't recognize her because she had a man's straw Panama on her head. But he turned after she passed and wondered what she wanted of their father now, as though she hadn't gotten everything when he was alive. And why the hell hadn't she stopped and spoken to him? Jessie never showed him the kind of adoration other women did, and it hurt, even if she was only his sister.

6
The Viewing

Jessie carried Henry's putter, driver, wedge, and a bag of golf balls in one hand, his harmonica, and a newspaper in the other. His favorite hat was on her head– she was hiding under it, nervous and shaky. The tune she could not identify played on, persistent, like an Andrew Lloyd Weber tune, only it wasn't.

She stopped her stride almost late, just in front of the coffin. She felt on top of it, felt it pulling her. *Come in closer* it teased, interrupting the song. She took two giant steps back and bumped into Jane Thrower who had come up behind her, all aflutter from her autograph seeking. She looked at Jane's name badge and wondered how such a pretty young redhead could be a mortician. She was too petite for the job. She seemed familiar too– Jessie didn't know why.

"I'd like to see my father Ms., if I could?"

"Oh yes, of course," Jane said, stuffing the autograph in her pocket, half wondering if this was gonna go on all night. She removed the family blanket and opened the coffin again, stifling a sigh, so as not to show her exasperation. She propped the lid and stood to the side, hands behind her, at parade rest.

Jessie gasped at the sight of Henry– she felt a sense of miracle and trepidation at the same time. Through brimming eyes, she gazed him into focus, studying him, straining to accept his deadness. He looked angelic, calm, serene, his body fixed now, permanent, awful still. He was palely beautiful, all gray and white, his face powdered, his head tilted up at an eloquent angle, his Celtic nose at last perfected

33

by a breathless inhale. He wore a gray suit and his favorite tie, a marbled pattern that resembled the flyleaf of a Byzantine book. He'd called it "psychedelic," laughing at his own goofy hipness, when Jessie had given it to him for Christmas years ago.

His hands lay intertwined upon his middle. They broke her heart. He practically was his hands, she thought, his fabulous handles, his most capable part. They had defined his whole life as surely as other people's looks or talent, character, or something else did. There was no end to what he had been able to do with those hands, from drawing a pencil portrait, to building a house, going after a splinter, scratching her back, making a pastry crust, playing piano, oh a thousand things; she saw how his whole life had been defined by what he had done with his resourceful handles. And now they were cold and still, and it was such a loss.

Jessie stared for a while at the astonishing picture, at her father's uncharacteristic stillness. She waggled the clubs one by one, and then placed them by his side. She fumbled around with the Panama hat, trying different places, not knowing exactly where to put a hat– probably not on his head, but where? She lifted his lapel and saw the letter in the inside pocket.

Jane Thrower stepped forward protectively, as though she thought Jessie might try to take the letter out and read it, or mess with the body, which was some of Jane's best handiwork.

Jessie wanted to be left alone with her father but didn't realize she could ask for that. When Jane didn't leave, Jessie placed the harmonica under his lifeless hands, and plopped the straw hat down on top of them, feeling a wave of queasiness. She tucked the newspaper under his arm. At his feet, she jammed the golf balls into the satin folds, so they wouldn't roll around.

She felt skittish with Jane watching her. She took a step back, trying to wait for the right feeling and forget about her, but instead Jane took it as a signal to wrap things up, and moved forward to close the coffin. Jessie was too tired to protest.

She heard Henry, her figment, a chimerical chuckler, as though he was keenly looking down on the scene: *I'm not in there anyway, Ha ha ha.* And Jessie understood for the first time the insular nature of a dead body; it might as well be languishing behind layers of stone doors, on an island, floating about a million miles away, giving distance new meaning. Henry had blown the pop stand of his body.

She turned and floated up the aisle, relieved, a fantasy forming and filling her with the bittersweet aura of Easter Sundays; with the grand idea of resurrection, some primal perception of it surfacing in her mind, along with chocolate marshmallows and ham, festive food to look forward to. *That's what life's about... taste it Jessie.* She heard her father's words, sweeter than advice, and the tune started up again, hounding her like an advertising jingle.

People filed in past Jessie, taking seats. Some kneeled and bowed their heads. They were mostly golfers, wearing golf clothes, come to pay their last respects. Some of them wouldn't be going to the funeral the next day. It conflicted with the opening of the Herlong Hassle, the major golf tournament at the Silver Lake Club. Ordinarily, Henry would play in it, too, and probably win. He was usually in the winner's circle with one of the best scores at the club. These fellow golfers knew that Henry would want them to be in the Herlong. It was, of course, where he would rather be.

Doris and Kate stood in the foyer near the open door, receiving the golfers and their wives as they came in. The visiting line reached out the door and down the sidewalk. Tom stood to the side of Doris, like a sentry, blanded out, detached. Frank was next to him, antsy as a colt, but endeavoring to keep himself under control, his father's son. Jessie saw how defensive Tom was about the stoic numbness he used to shield himself, an odd iceberg of feeling that kept him from blowing apart. He'd always been able to produce it whenever he felt threatened. He had used it to survive childhood, cultivated his very strength out of secret sorrows. He had needed every bit of strength he could muster too, because Tom had married young, at nineteen, and they'd had Frank while he was still working his way through law school. Then he lost his wife in that freak accident. Jessie wished she could break through his wall. She smiled at Tom and Frank as she approached, but they didn't smile back. Then she saw Frank's focus was on Jane Thrower who was coming up right behind her.

Jessie took a place beside her mother, whose face was contorted with grief. She was ashamed that Doris still had on the purple dress and smelled of sour booze. There had never been any purple within a mile of Henry as far as Jessie knew. It was a color that he took like a personal insult. Doris was still trying to stir his blood. Jessie grew disgusted with thinking about purple. She gazed out the door and saw Chuck-Pete on the sidewalk signing autographs. Jane Thrower had gone out to stand beside him. She wondered if they had a thing going on.

As people approached to pay their respects, Doris stood unsteadily, muttering bits and pieces of the story to different ones, touching her broken lips: "Hoh, my lips are so chapped... they cracked and bled. I had to give him mouth-to-mouth so long, twenty-five minutes before the ambulance came. It's all over... it's all over now."

Jessie thought it was inappropriate for Doris to mention her chapped lips, and that was her own life she was talking about being over. She looked sternly at her mother, whispered: "No, it's not over, Mama. You still have to live you know, we all do." She nudged Doris under her elbow the way Doris had done to her when she was a girl, a nudge that said, "Chin up, go out there and fight now." Doris sighed, tired to the bone. She tutted, "Oh when are you gonna come down to earth and give me some grandchildren?"

Jessie blushed, drawing her head down into her shoulders like a five-year-old.

7

Jane Speaks Up

The family of this dead man has finally gone home for the wake. They can drink and make all the noise they want to, but they won't be waking this one up. Great day I'm tired already. And this won't be over until sometime tomorrow when we shovel the mulch over him.

You know, I have a name– I don't see why everyone always calls me Ms., when my name is clearly shown on this name badge I wear throughout a funeral. Jane Thrower. I wish they would just call me Jane. Not a very smoldering name, I will admit. When I needed some fast money for the six-week course in Embalming and Sanitary Science over at the University in Gainesville, I was an escort for a brief time until I found out that's just another name for prostitute. Jane was an unlikely name for that particular job. I could have changed it, but we don't change names in my family the way these show biz people do. Now I'm just Ms. to everyone. I'm finding out no one wants to know you when you work in the death-care industry; they're afraid you'll suck them into the life of the dead, their loved one's new life. People are scared of dead bodies. They would just as soon skip death.

The escort business was too dangerous and too messy and was not my thing. You never knew if some john was gonna go crazy and cut you if you didn't put out, and if you did you felt dirty and had to clean up bodily fluids. I'm still having to do that. Golly bum, we always have to worry about leakage. Although once we drain a body, it's usually all right if all the orifices are sealed good with cotton and wax. Nobody realizes what we go through to make death palatable to the living. It's not like any dead body is ever a pleasant thing. Some of them keep on moving and farting. It's only gas, ordinary biology. I don't mind the cadaver though. It's like a dead frog to me– a rubbery shell of a thing two pounds lighter than usual, because the soul has departed. The chest sinks in– look, you can see it. My uncle says it's deflated lungs, but I have my doubts. Great day, I have gotten so morbid on this job. And I thought I could put some fun in funeral.

I don't like wearing this navy-blue uniform. It's gabardine and way too hot for Florida, and this dumb white polyoho blouse and black bow tie, I must tie with my formaldehyde chapped fingers. I can always smell the form in the fuzzy silk. Maybe other people can too. They stare at my tie a lot and turn away without looking me in the eyes. I handled their loved ones intimately, saw them naked; even worse, dead. As though it's not the most natural thing in the world. They act like they think I must know their guilty secrets, how they let their loved one down or, worse still, been let down, something witchy like that.

Jane pulled her bow tie off and slipped the white blouse over her head. Underneath, she had on a red tee-shirt with white letters which said:

I WANT TO DIE PEACEFULLY
LIKE MY GRANDPA DID
IN HIS SLEEP
NOT SCREAMING LIKE THE OTHER
PASSENGERS IN HIS CAR

This Hassett family gives me a funny feeling though, like I'm kin to them someway, and I don't know how I could be. They don't seem to like each other very much, yet you can feel how deep their heavy-hearted family love goes too. It's strange how Jessie acted like she knew me, when she's the one doing the news on television. I've never seen a family open and close the coffin as much as this one did either– makes me wonder why the wife requested a closed coffin. All of them took a turn with this poor dead man loading him up with stuff to take into the ground with him like some pharaoh; a big straw hat, golf clubs, balls; first Jessie puts in three clubs, and then the younger daughter, Kate, puts in a seven iron to tee off with, as if he'll be doing any more of that, and she puts in a pack of Jujubes, and ripe persimmons, of all things. He's got stuff piled all over him. Tom and his son Frank didn't put anything in, but they looked like they wanted to.

I never saw so many good-looking people in one family either. I'm crushing on Chuck-Pete of course, but Seaborn is gorgeous too, and Tom is a strong, silent-type, looks like he needs a good burning down. Even his tall son Frank has potential. Look me up in a few years' kid.

Tomorrow I've got to wear the chauffeur's cap and drive that big ole hearse. Great day, I can't hardly reach the pedals. I've got to learn all aspects of this business though– it's been in my family for so long, and there will always be a stable demand. But I'm not sure I like it all that much. The people can be hard to deal with. Take today. Here came Chuck-Pete Monroe, who just makes himself up as he goes, and expects you to play along, like he's the only game in town. He charms you, exerts his dominance over you, while he pretends he's not doing anything at all, it's just his natural charisma at work. But you can't say anything to break his little boy heart. He's funny, and way smarter than the glamour guy he wants you to think he is. But great day, he sure does like to make up his own truth, and just ignore everybody else's. That's the actor in him I guess. He acted so penitent with his father; he just wanted hunky-dory bygones, without too much painful self-reproach. Well now, let's see what his little letter has to say:

Jane slipped the letter out of Henry's lapel pocket, and read it, nodding her head as she read, like it said exactly what she thought it would, the usual apologia. Lots of people sent their loved ones off with a letter like this. She put the letter back in Henry's pocket, gently wiped what looked like a tear but she reckoned was just leakage off his eye, blew him a little kiss and closed the coffin lid for the last time. It was her night to lock up and everyone else was already gone.

8
Ascension

The next morning, before the funeral, Chuck-Pete was up early, doing his workout. First, he applied Vaseline all around his eyes, gently tapping the soft bags below and the bridges of the brows. Eyes had no sweat glands, so the moisture had to be held in or damage occurred. He did fifty sit-ups, some leg stretches and then went out to run the five miles around Silver lake, trying to sweat out the booze– he'd overindulged at the wake.

By the time the limo arrived at 2: o'clock to take everyone to the funeral, Jessie and Seaborn were outside the house, dressed and waiting. Tom stood at attention, with Frank in tow. Kate came out of the house pouting, giving her mother dirty looks because she still had on the purple dress. It was a tense family portraiture, a mixed bag of cored-out feelings, hangovers, sleep deprivations.

The funeral home had sent a black limo and a driver, and now they all stood beside it, with its doors standing open like bats' wings, waiting for Chuck-Pete to put the final touches on his ensemble. When he presented himself in the doorway, he was the most handsomely dressed of all, wearing a well-cut grey Armani suit, a white and grey pinstriped shirt, and a thin black silk tie. No purple for Chuck-Pete.

Everyone piled into the black limo except Tom and Frank, who followed close behind in their BMW, and Seaborn who fell in behind them, alone in the Land Rover. He looked at Tom's Dade County license plate and read the Day-Glo bumper sticker under it:

COME BACK SOON WE WEREN'T
SHOOTING AT YOU

Henry was nigh on Seaborn's bumper, riding draft, a skill he'd developed on the trip down from Atlanta. He'd lost them for a while, but now he was back for his funeral. Although he was not confined in space, it was helpful having an object to follow. He had no misgivings about Seaborn and never doubted that he made a good husband for Jessie. Henry had an Irishman's love of Indians, and Seaborn was Native American Indian on his father's side, and his mama was from an Island in the Indian Ocean, Sri Lanka. Therefore, Seaborn was half feather, half sheet. Is that P.C.? Henry wondered, like he ever cared about that. It was all good to him. Seaborn was a likable son-in-law, even if he'd always harbored hopes for one that would join him for a round of golf.

Seaborn put in a CD of Carmen Gloria and turned it up loud. As he followed Tom and Frank, he mentally replayed his morning with Jessie at the Big Bass Motel where the two of them had stayed because the house was too crowded. They had awakened after a fitful night's sleep and gotten into the shower together. In the warm, steamy bathroom Seaborn sat on the closed toilet seat drying his legs, the towel grazing an involuntary erection. When Jessie came out of the shower, he patted her down with the towel. She'd straddled him then, capturing him. They'd docked together like that for a long while, barely moving, breathing in the dizzying scent of Dial soap. It was elegiacally erotic, like an instruction in the Kama Sutra. He knew it was the most comfort Jessie had felt since Henry's death– pleasurable comfort, their bodies joined together, taking in and giving out heat and sensation the way bodies were designed to do. Seaborn realized that it was the first time they had not completed an act of coitus yet had experienced post coital afterglow. He felt as if they had stumbled upon some new, divine ground.

The family limo, with Tom's BMW, Seaborn's Rover, and Henry's ghost following close behind, pulled in front of St. Theresa's Catholic church and stopped behind the parked hearse with its back door flapped open awaiting pallbearers. Jane Thrower stood by, ready to direct everyone.

Chuck-Pete, Tom, Frank, Seaborn, and two friends of Henry's who were not playing in the Herlong Hassle hoisted up the coffin, carried it slowly into the church and set it down on a pier in front of the altar. People followed them in, taking seats inside the dim cool church, while an organ rang out, clanging, devil-chasing music. Last came Jessie and Kate, flanking either side of the empurpled Doris. The sisters had chosen to wear white, out of some Buddhist bent they both shared. Jessie had on a white linen suit with a white silk blouse and Kate wore an unbleached muslin dress with crochet at the neck, which Henry had once bought for her on a trip to Cancun. Doris was not calm and composed, but animated and coming apart. Her knees kept giving in, so Jessie and Kate had to shore her up between them by her elbows. They all had on round dark sunglasses, so they resembled the three blind mice coming down the aisle.

The priest delivered the resurrection mass all in chanted Latin as Doris had requested. Everyone teared up in the moments when he instructed the soul to ascend into heaven, by waving the smoking incense burners into the air and ringing the altar bells.

Jessie sobbed loudly. She could feel the specter of her father's soul rocketing away from her, up into the up.

Doris nudged Jessie in the ribs and hissed for her to stop making so damn much noise.

The incense seemed to drug everyone, and the bells were dizzying, so when at last the mass was over, the grateful alive followed the coffin out of the church and found themselves in the harsh glare of the noonday sun, light-headed and dopey, like they'd just left a dark theater after a hangdog matinee— eyes burned, minds went blank.

Now it was on to the cemetery.

9
The Trip To Paradise

Jane Thrower was seated atop two fat catalogs behind the wheel of the black hearse, the lead car, reading the obituaries wherein everyone died in alphabetical order. She waited while the six pallbearers grappled with the heavy coffin and shoved it back inside the hearse. Doris had picked out a coffin with no lock on it, claiming Henry hadn't even liked closed doors, much less locks, and he had told her to buy him a casket that wouldn't lock shut. And to put a flashlight in there with him too, which Jane had done, grudgingly.

Jane came from a long line of layers-out of the dead, as they were called back in the day, and it was pride in this family legacy that led her into The Mortuary Arts. It had all started in England, way back in the 1700s; first with Susannah Bliss Thrower, followed by Mary Bulfinch and then Rebecca Thrower Norton, of #6 Sterling Alley– all her kin, and also where she got her red hair from. Earthy women all. Old oil paintings hung in the funeral home, immortalizing each of these red-headed women. Rebecca had been the first to perform the undertaking tasks on her own kitchen table. After those women, and immigration to central Florida in the early nineteen-hundreds, the line changed over to men, and they called themselves "undertakers," a name that tickled Jane. It wasn't used much anymore, though; Funeral Director was the preferred title now. People didn't like to think about being taken under.

An excellent embalmer, Jane could raise an artery as perfectly as any of her cracker uncles, and she applied make-up better than them, but driving a hearse was the one job she wasn't so sure about. In being groomed as the probable successor in the family, she had to become familiar with all aspects of the funeralization of the dead, including the safe and speedy portage of the loved one to the final resting place. Surely she had a knack for this business.

She did a quick, ungraceful U-turn in front of the church, then her foot slipped, and she accidentally peeled out. She corrected though, slowing down to a crawl so everyone could catch up, and then glided along more decorously allowing time to snare the due respect of waiting cars that had pulled over and flashed on their lights while the procession passed. She wondered if she should tip her chauffeur's cap at some of the waiting cars and then decided a smile was enough.

Paradise Cemetery was a good ways out in the country she knew, although this was her first time actually going there. The only other funeral she had convoyed, went to Eternal Hills, right next to the Re-Max. She knew the way to that cemetery, but the location of Paradise was a little sketchy in her mind. Her uncle had told her to go out 17 to 441, cross the tracks and then just look for the sign. Easy peasy. There would be a green awning at the grave site. In the rearview mirror, she checked to make sure the family limo was following.

Inside the family limo, Jessie gazed out the window, her mind like a sound studio for the tune that continuously played on, as though prolonging something for her. She lit a cigarette, cracked her window, and smoked but did not enjoy it. She looked across at Chuck-Pete, and Kate, and at Doris beside her, and wondered doubtfully if they could be hearing the song too. She turned around and looked out the back window at the faces of Tom and Frank following right behind in their BMW. Did they hear the tune? Maybe Frank could hear it. Did Seaborn ever hear it? He had quieted the tune that morning, and it had been ecstasy. But now it was back, harrowing her again. She craned her neck to see out the front and keep the hearse in sight.

Jane took a wrong turn, drove the hearse down a narrow residential street, and jogged around a cul-de-sac. All the cars in the procession followed. So, for the next few minutes that cozy neighborhood got to view a rare occurrence. Barefoot toddlers stood pat in their front yards, mouths hanging open, balls, dogs and tricycles all frozen in place while they watched the strange cortege of vehicles slowly pass around the circle, headlights on in the daytime and tiny lavender flags flapping from their antennas. Once out of there, Jane dashed across an intersection trying to beat the light. A big yellow, Blue Bird school bus cut in front of the family limo and fell in right behind Jane's hearse. The limo driver had been lagging back so as not to lose the rest of the procession, which had large gaps in it. Now he ran the red light to catch up, craning his neck to see around the school bus and keep the hearse in sight. He had come over from Orlando and his instructions were simply to follow the hearse to Paradise Cemetery.

It started to rain, a Spring shower. After about two more miles of road all the vehicles had choked up fairly well and the long cavalcade was headed out into the countryside, with Jane's hearse in the lead, followed by the school bus, the family limo, the BMW, Seaborn's Land Rover, and continuing on with all the other assorted cars, including one golf cart that had come out of nowhere.

Rain began pelting the hot asphalt, slapping against rubber and metal, making everyone in the limo feel even more gloomy, and, if anyone was listening, the sound arranged itself into a rhythm and beat out the tune that haunted Jessie, *Dada da da da da da da dada...* Jessie chorused along with it, sotto voce, and Doris gave her the sucked-lemon look she reserved for all inappropriate behavior.

"Oh my God it's raining," Doris gasped, like a rainy funeral was one of the most dreaded things. Tears welled up in her eyes yet again; they were just cups to hold her glistening misery, like marsupial pouches find their function.

Chuck-Pete was having trouble getting service on his smart phone and he turned around and scowled at the limo driver like that as well as the rain was his fault. He was still so hung over, to move his head hurt, like an icepick was in his nose.

The driver slid down lower in his seat, intent now on following the school bus, ninety-eight percent certain the hearse was still in front of it, although he couldn't actually see around the bus. He had to piss bad.

Kate looked at each person in the limo and decided Chuck-Pete needed her attention the most. Even when he wasn't speared to the core, like now, he was apt to lose his temper over little things. She scooted closer to him, took his hand in hers and patted it. His face released at once.

"People forget to drive in the rain," Kate said.

"Don't you mean how?" Chuck-Pete said, "They forget HOW to drive in the rain?"

"No," she said, "they just relax and forget to drive at all. As if they're hypnotized."

Outside, the school bus with fifty screaming kids in it lumbered to a stop, red lights flashing. Its metal stop flag boinged out. The family limo and all the rest of the procession came to a halt too. Screeching brakes joined with two or three window-rattling songs blaring out of the school bus. Giggling girls and salty boys took their time skipping across the road, the boys batting invisible basketballs into baskets, oblivious of the rain and the line of funeral cars backed up behind them.

Inside the limo, Doris let out a little warning keen that she was going to go crazy if this passage to the cemetery didn't conclude real soon.

Jessie lit up another cigarette, flicking the ashes out her cracked window.

Doris and Chuck-Pete fanned the air exuberantly.

"Smoking is so uncool." Chuck-Pete scowled.

Jessie wished she could get outside like the school kids and skip in the rain. She gripped the door handle, tempted.

As soon as the bus started going again, here came Jane's hearse back the other way, shooting rain on them. The limo driver didn't hesitate; he whipped around in a wide-arcing U-turn in the middle of the road and chased the hearse. The rest of the cars did the same, doglegging around one by one and racing to catch up.

Through the driving rain, Jessie saw the other drivers' and riders' exasperated faces– some of them were laughing. Jessie felt like laughing, but she was careful not to let it show on her face since it would be too in conflict with Doris and Chuck-Pete's angry moods. She caught Kate's eye. Kate signed: *Are we lost?* and they exchanged a glimmer of a smile. Signing was their private way of conversing when they didn't want the others in on what they were saying.

Rain pelted the roof and at the same time the sun came blasting out, radiating over them, making the inside of the limo suddenly humid and hot. Doris complained to the driver: "At least turn the goddamn air-conditioning on, will you." That's when they all felt a big thump, and the smell of skunk punctured the steamy air, and mixed in with the cool air-conditioning just then circulating through the limo.

"Jesus Christ," Chuck-Pete yelped, gnashing his fine teeth, cupping his sensitive nose.

"Sorry," said the limo driver, speeding up, nearly crashing into the back end of the hearse.

Jessie heard Henry laughing that goober laugh he had sometimes, and she couldn't help it, this time she laughed out loud, startling everyone anew.

Chuck-Pete and Doris glowered over at her. "Get a grip." Chuck-Pete said.

Abruptly, Jane's hearse pulled into a Sonoco station, the first sign of civilization they'd seen for miles. So, the limo and all the other cars stopped too, pulling off the road every which-a-way, sending the alligators scurrying for the ditches. Some cars idled in the middle of the street, truth or dare style, their engines steaming and snorting vapor in the pouring down rain.

Jane ran into the gas station to ask directions, leaving the hearse, with its big motor idling, in Henry's charge. Emissions of lilac smoke shaped like Casper the Friendly Ghost came whorling out its chrome tail pipes.

The limo driver slid out too and headed for the bathroom. "Hey, where you goin'?" Chuck-Pete called after him, and Doris wailed, "You're leaving us out here in the middle of nowhere."

Jane was back in two minutes and did another wide, whipping U-turn, dislodging the golf balls so they rattled around inside the coffin. She gunned the hearse back down the road from whence they had all come, irked that her plan for gracefully repairing to the cemetery was shot all to hell.

The limo driver, still tugging on his fly, scampered back out to follow her. The other cars had to wait for him to go first, so they stood dead in their tracks, with their engines revving, spitting, and rarin' to go.

Finally, all the cars were bumper to bumper again, following Jane as she headed back out 17, crisscrossing her old path; but this time she made a left at 441 and when she saw the railroad crossing on her right she turned and crossed the tracks onto a little black-top country road that sent the smell of creosote up everyone's noses. The road ran in a parallel arc to the tracks, winding and snaking through acres of live oak trees and overgrown weedy bushes– the boonies. Everyone avidly followed Jane's speeding, wild-looking, rain-spitting hearse. But the road curved back out to the tracks and Highway 441 again.

Jane stopped dead on the tracks. "Shit!" She pounded the steering wheel. She had to think a minute. She straddled the tracks, looking right and left. All she needed was a train coming now. She had gone too far and missed the Paradise sign, that had to be it– nothing to do but go back and find the durn thing. She held her breath, feeling the color drain from her face as she executed one more lumbering, golf balls rattling U-turn, closing her eyes this time as her hearse slinked by the family limo.

As she passed the cars that hadn't turned around yet, she heard a lot of bellyaching and saw fists out in the air shaking at her. The smell of skunk and creosote mingled, causing People to have hankies tied around their noses like burglars. She watched the bushes; the sign should be just a lick and a jump beyond the mobile home park; all this overgrowth was why she'd missed it.

There it was Great day! PARADISE CEMETERY, such a tiny little blue and white sign.

Color came back into Jane's face as she made the turn. At some point the rain had stopped or they had driven out of it. The sun was a-blaze again, no sign it had rained at all in Paradise. That's Florida weather for you, Jane thought. She steered into the cemetery, spotted the green awning, and brought her charge to a grinding halt behind the golf cart which had somehow beaten them all there. A few people were standing around the sunny grave site like they would like to have been at a funeral, only nobody showed up.

The limo pulled in right behind Jane's hearse. The driver jumped out, snapped open a black parasol and held it to shade Doris, who looked like she would fight a circular saw if somebody turned one on. As she climbed out of the limo, she knocked the umbrella away, and said, thrumming her chest: "Jesus, Mary and Joseph, I feel like kissing the ground."

Elegant sable palm trees and old mossy live oaks grew in the grassy landscape, randomly spaced, with life-sized statues of the saints mingling amongst them. The flat expanse of Bermuda grass was not interrupted by any jutting tombstones or real flowers growing anywhere, except the wild fuchsia periwinkle which could not be controlled. This was one of those memorial park type cemeteries where the gravestones had to be flat to the ground, so they could mow the grass on a rider-mower. Except for all the saints, it looked more like a golf course than a cemetery. You expected to see a ball coming.

As Jessie got out of the limo she closed her eyes against the sight of the neat rectangular grave hole that was banked with a hellishly bright green astro-turf.

She heard Henry say: *Look at this beauty-full place Jessie! In death, as in life; location, location,... and I forget what comes next.*

10
The Nineteenth Hole

Jessie and Kate sat on either side of Doris, in folding chairs, at eye level with the coffin, which was straddled above the Astro-turfed grave. Chuck-Pete stood beside Kate, his hands clasped together. Tom and Frank stood behind Doris, and Seaborn was behind Jessie. All the men had worn catholic-navy-blue except Chuck-Pete, who was a standout in the light grey Armani. Cousins, aunts, and uncles merged behind them, establishing the family tableau under the low green awning. Around the edges, golfers' wives, neighbors and friends, funeral faced and whispering, completed the punk of mourners. *All in all, a good turnout, Henry thought.*

Jessie stared out into the cemetery at the flat gravestones which had little built-in urns that could be pulled up to hold flowers. Some of them held bunches of artificial flowers, presumably because they lasted longer than real ones, basking in the Florida sun, baking, and fading until they looked deader than any real ones ever could. She turned her attention to the gorgeous spray of flowers that rested upon her father's coffin. She had seen Doris's order for "The Family Blanket" when she went to the florists: white lilies named Journey's End and Naked Lady, with sprigs of purple heather mixed in. She could smell the heather. Two crossed golf clubs had been added to the arrangement and were peeking out from under the demure lilies– a concession on Doris's part, who thought of golf as the other woman. A wide sash of purple ribbon which said "Beloved" in silver letters festooned the top.

Jessie heard her father chattering in her head: *Periwinkles are from Madagascar. Manhattan is an Indian word meaning hilly island. A hammock is a tree or a forest island.* In life, Henry had been forever plying her with facts like these, and she hoped she was only just catching flashbacks. No one else seemed to hear him. It was only grief, she decided, so profound it took his voice in her mind. Trying to ignore him, she gave her attention to the arrangement of flowers she and Seaborn had sent. It had been placed at the foot of the coffin, upon a tripod; a triangular-shaped fairway flag arrangement of white roses, with the number nineteen configured in red roses. The final hole, the one that came after the end of the game. She was proud of it.

The priest began the service, making the sign of the cross a couple of times, which everyone hurried to duplicate. He intoned the liturgy solemnly: "Who reasons death any more than they can weigh the earth or the heart of beauty? Nature has insistent pride; there's no shame in death, for it is the entrance into immortality." He made the sign of the cross in the air with his crucifix and everyone bowed their heads except Jessie who was staring at the coffin, fixated on a little space between the box and the lid. It leaked. It wasn't any kind of tight fit at all. She stared at this space with disappointment, besotted with it. That crack would allow worms and dirt to get in. It struck her suddenly that everything leaked, humans and machines and everything in the world. Her father had been fixing leaks all his life and here he was stuck with one he'd have to go into eternity with. She wept wretchedly and Seaborn held onto her bucking shoulders.

A butterfly kept swooping down, playing in the family blanket. It was black, orange, and white, and looked like it had a set of piano keys along the bottom of its hind wings. Jessie heard the tune tinkling in the soft wind, like on a child's piano. She watched the butterfly dip and soar and fly all the way behind them, so that she had to turn around to follow it, halfway lifting from her seat.

It landed on the chauffeur's cap atop Jane Thrower's head. Jane was smiling at that moment because she was remembering her long dead grandfather who had also been in the funeral business and had lived to be ninety-seven and told her his secret for a long life was root beer and Fruit loops. Jane could still hear him laughing, only now it was accelerated and rich, like other people were joining in, laughing with him.

Jessie heard the laughter too. She had the strangest feeling about Jane as she studied her, like she was a long-lost soul-sister, all five feet of her. She could feel people looking at her, turned around in her seat like she was, but she didn't care. Tom finally had tears in his eyes, she was relieved to see. And Henry's only grandchild, Frank looked at her so intensely, but when she returned the look, he looked down, shy, his eyes uncapturable. What was he thinking? Hearing? Jessie wondered. In his hands he fiddled with two small magnets. She saw that he had Henry's handles. It was amazing. He was smart like his grandfather, eccentric too. She turned back around, just as Doris perfected the dirty look she was giving her. Anger love was all she'd ever gotten from Doris and she knew her mother didn't like her very much, neither did her brothers. She felt a stab of pain at how alone she was in this family now, her best ally was dead. But there was Kate, dear Kate, and Frank, yes Frank liked her too, she hoped.

The butterfly, which had ascended high up over the gathering, did a low, scooping dip, producing a rainbow in its wake for all to see, if anyone besides Jessie was watching.

She heard Henry again: *Now, look here Jess; remember the order of colors in a rainbow: red, orange, yellow, green, blue, indigo, violet. This is valuable information. Did you know rainbows can even appear at night? They're called moonbows.* Jessie smiled, giving in; rainbows always made her smile. She sighed. What was a smile but a feeling of happiness?

The priest caught her smile before it faded and directed his words more in her direction. He had seen people smile at funerals before, but it always unnerved him. Jessie watched the priest's lips: "Life is changed, not ended. Have faith in eternal life, do not let bitter grief rend your heart. Doubt is only self-pity. Let death deepen the wonder." He made the sign of the cross and switched to chanting in Latin: "In nominee patris, et filii, et spiritus sancti, holy, holy, holy." He held up both hands, signaling to everyone: "Let us pray," He bowed his head, and all was silent for a long moment, except for an uproar of butterflies in the palms.

Nevertheless he prayed, his voice grandiloquent: "Dear God, resurrect the soul of your child, Henry, cleanse it, purify it, for all is clouded by desire as a mirror with dust, so the soul is clouded. . . "

Inside Jessie's head the priest's voice trailed off, as if she were drifting down into a long, watery tunnel, out of hearing range. She stared straight ahead at the coffin, watching light leach through the crevice from one side to the other. It seemed to be in those little intensities of light that Jessie heard Henry again: *Ah, Jessie, my soul is not clouded by anything anymore. That other part is right, though, eternal life is a safe bet. That's why you've got to live as if you will die tomorrow, but study as if you will live forever, because you bring it all with you— all the intangibles, like the order of colors in a rainbow. Stop all this crying and believe your own ears. I'm gonna get this show on the road. Watch this!*

A sudden wind whipped up out of nowhere and lifted the blanket of flowers, clubs and all, a few inches in the air, held it there for five seconds, then let it drop back with a thud. Jane's cap blew off, and she went running after it. Then as swiftly as the wind had come, it was gone, and thunder boomed in the heavens, bolts of lightning streaked along the horizon– the one element in nature that can officially stop a golf game.

Frank dropped his magnets like they were hot.

The mourners all grew restless, talking and moving around, expecting a million-footed rain, but instead the sun blazed out, shockingly bright, and it was dry as a sand trap. The priest had finished and was leaning over Doris, giving her the crucifix he'd blessed, holding both her hands in his, whispering. Then he stepped away and began working the dwindling crowd.

As Henry was lowered into the ground, Jessie heaved a big shimmering sigh. It was over. Now he would be put to rest. He'd stop haunting her. She looked at her wrecked mother, who smelled like whiskey, and put her arm around her in a protective way. A few people came up condoling: "Was it sudden? It's good it was fast. He's lucky."

Doris said, interacting with each one: "I'm worn to a frazzle, I can't make a fist," and "hoh... my lips, my lips are so chapped." She touched her mouth pitifully and shrugged her shoulders to brush Jessie off. She was uncomfortable with being touched.

Jessie didn't know how to comfort her mother. Had she seen the gap in the coffin? The butterfly? The rainbow? The wind lifting the flowers. Anything that could rival that final scene when despite all her artificial respiration her husband died and left her with chapped lips?

If the trip to Paradise Cemetery had been a vexation of spirit, the ride back to the home place on Silver Lake was endured in crushing silence. Everyone was rung out. There was still the feeding part of a funeral to go through, possibly to enjoy, so people came back to the house now, most carrying food. In the center of the table, a chocolate ice cream cake shaped like an Easter egg quavered, melting from the inside out. There was a baked ham with pineapple rings, a plate of comforting deviled eggs, tomato aspic, warm cheesy casseroles, finger foods, lots of good groceries, just like Henry liked. But no one was looking after the table, so the food sat where it was plopped, halfway unwrapped. China plates were stacked with silverware, but the food was only picked at willy-nilly. Looking after the table was probably Jessie and Kate's job, but they had gone out to Henry's workshop to seek his essence. And now they were hiding under the lean-to, sitting side by side in his golf cart, smoking a doobie. They sat very still, hoping to catch whiffs of their father's scent, a combination of machine oil, the herb rosemary, and the pencil eraser smell around his ears. Right after the funeral, they had gone and stood in his closet, inhaling, while his scent still lingered in his golf shirts, not giving a damn if anyone caught them. They found the joint in one of his pockets, probably bounty from a game, a bet won. Most of the golfers at the club were old rascals, often playing for outlawed, joke prizes. Jessie coughed, and passed the doobie over to Kate. Geese strutted up to the golf cart, attracted by the smoke, and caused Jessie to tense up.

11
Invisible Love

It had turned into a pretty, sunny day. Small planes whined low over Silver lake, headed for the municipal airport off 441. While the women sat inside with Doris, the men milled around outside smoking cigarettes, drinking beer, enjoying the smell of fresh-mowed grass. The yard man had come back and finished the mowing while everyone was at the service. The men leaned on their cars in the driveway, and talked about sports, mainly golf, straining to find things to laugh about. Tom, Frank, Chuck-Pete and Seaborn stood around in a semi-circle, obliged to listen to stories about Henry: how he had been a 75 shooter, and he always had to have a little action on every game; at last finding humor in a bet lost to Henry, because now he couldn't ever beat them again. They told about the time Henry had hit the ball 178 yards with a seven Iron and come within an inch of acing hole No. 4. How he'd leaned down and blew the ball in.

When Kate went into the house to check on their mother, Jessie wandered into the groves behind the house. She felt Henry's absence there and was relieved. She was ready to get used to his being dead, to not hearing his voice ever again. She knew it was the way it had to be– the only way grown children were able to come into their own after their parents died was by accepting death. Hearing Henry's voice alienated her from real life. She had to let him go. She drifted among the grapefruit and orange trees, long ago planted in casually eye-balled rows, some of them older than Henry was, trees that had survived the brutal freezes of central Florida, and hardier varieties that had been planted to replace the casualties. He'd nurtured all the fruit trees, a lone key lime, and a few persimmon trees. Every year he would box up a variety of ripe fruits, and jars of jelly he made from the persimmons, and send it all to Jessie. She'd never get another box now. Doris wouldn't go into the groves—she was afraid of snakes. Jessie realized that during the closing years of his life Henry had come to love the groves almost as much as the golf links. It was nature he loved, and wasn't that really the point of golf, being out in all that natural beauty? Henry had walked these groves daily, swam in the warm air leavened with fragrant citrus blossoms, listened to the transporting sounds of bug industry, and honking geese. What was it about geese, Jessie wondered again, that made her so anxious?

A couple of hours later, everyone but immediate family was gone. The light changed into the descending shades of twilight when the lake was most reflective. Jessie took the grieving Ibsen for his walk, down the long driveway, and across the street to the lake bank so he could prowl at the water's edge, and pounce at the flirty movement of fiddler crabs the way he liked to do. But Ibsen just sunk down in the grass and whimpered for Henry, who should have been the one walking him.

Jessie paced around, kicking seashells and pebbles, having a poor run of thoughts, mostly about how selfish dying was. She looked askance at the shells which had always struck her as incongruous here in the middle of the state, miles from the oceans. Once Henry had told her about a time in history when all the lakes had been connected to the sea and almost all of Florida had been under water; the seashells were a legacy of that time thousands of years ago. It was the kind of information he twinkled in telling. Jessie thought that if Florida could rise up like that, out of the water, it could sink back down again too. Now that she had gotten used to the mountains and put her roots in the dense red-clay earth of Georgia, being in Florida was like being out on a diving board; it always felt like water was right under her feet.

She looked back at the house, listened to Kate plinking out notes on the piano with one finger, not playing anything the whole way through, watched Seaborn in the side yard doing Tai Chi to Kate's music. She saw Frank go on tenterhooks into Henry's workshop.

Jessie had something bothering her. Henry had never once said 'I love you' out loud. And she'd only said it to him once when he was being wheeled in for his by-pass. She had called the hospital and gotten the nurse to hand him the phone, and she'd said, "I love you daddy," and he'd answered: "yeah, me too." That was the closest he ever came to saying it. Yet she'd felt loved. Hadn't she? Now she wasn't sure. She felt abandoned, even though he talked to her, maybe despite that, as if he were mocking her need of him, trying to drive her crazy. He was a rascal; that she knew. It was astonishing how he seemed to have no sympathy for the people mourning him. He was without malice, but without mercy too.

"Why didn't you ever just SAY it?" she asked the sky. Ibsen looked up and barked once.

In a moment, the answer came: *Jess, you got that idea from the movies. You never had to doubt my love. I showed it to you all the time. Love survives death; it's the immutable part of our being, so stop worrying about it.* Ibsen wagged his head and tail, as though he heard and understood. *I'm gone from you physically, twenty-billion lousy cells, de-animated, but I'm still with you. I'm an intangible now, that's all. So, c'mon, we've got work to do.*

Why are you haunting me like this? She raised her arms imploring the sky.

This isn't a haunting. I need your help. All my life I wanted to transcend myself, but I never knew how. Now I have a second chance. I'm surrounded by wonderful spirits who tell me who they were in life, and what they want to tell their loved ones. I can be an invisible avatar and deliver their messages. I'd just as lief be at rest, but I can't. I have to do this.

But why me?

Because we're a twosome Jessie, and you're so open to it, and besides, you have the skill set: you're on the air, and you have a readymade audience.

Jessie grew quiet as she thought about this, furtively examining her own mind. Was it open? Or was she deranged? What were these messages? She thought of a game they used to play when she was a young girl. They would write messages on each other's back, five words or less, and then they'd have to guess what the message said before it could be the other ones turn. She could still feel the tickle of the words on her back. She'd loved that game more than anything.

She looked out across the lake and made out Chuck-Pete in the distance, loping along on his nightly run. He looked so lonely, so outcast somehow. She felt pent-up love for him, like she did for her mother, love that never saw the light of day. When they were kids, Henry had been embarrassed by Chuck-Pete's mountainous ego; it was like a deformity to him. Jessie had seen in Henry's eyes the fear that ego would be his son's downfall. The two of them had fought about ego all the time, always disguised as fights about something else.

Now she heard: *Ego is an oily thing Jess, like an involuntary muscle in people who have too much...* She looked up at the opalescent clouds, astir like melting butter. *And you always gotta forgive selfishness because it doesn't go away, and there ain't no cure for it either.* Jessie wondered when Henry had become this champion of Chuck-Pete's ego.

After his letter, Henry answered her thought, *I never knew how to be a good father, only how to be myself and how to think and learn. I never understood my own impact on my sons. I was different with them Jess. I had too much anger. I was really mad at my own father for dying on me when I was only nine. Learning how to love took me a lifetime, and finally the only way you do it is by forgiving. You'll have to learn to forgive your brothers, Jessie, for whatever they do. Even if they're not sorry– and you'll have to accept an apology that you may never receive. You have to be the strong one.*

Jessie's eyes began to glaze over like a person getting too much advice. She was exhausted. It was all too much to think about, on top of her raw grief. Henry whistled the familiar tune all the way through; she'd always been soothed by his whistling. Her ears grew keen on the sound now, and she stopped fighting it. She felt the sound more than heard it, in the light evening breeze on her shoulders, heady with the scent of early orange blossoms. She stood very still, and time seemed to stop too. The hair rose on her arms, and she shivered.

Henry said: *You don't feel that breeze in death, touching you– that's what you miss when you die, touching, and a few other things, like food, ha ha. Not that I'm hungry. Amazingly though, you can take all your emotions with you, they endure. Trust what you're hearing Jess. Can't you believe the preposterous, marvelous, mind-whirling possibility that my consciousness somehow operates independently of my body?*

Ibsen began running around in a circle, squealing.

Jessie stared up at the sky. And then all was underwater quiet. She had the sensation of swimming in a watchful tenderness, assured of Henry's love even more than when he was alive. Presently a new sensation began for both her and Ibsen, like they'd been washed, wrapped up in warm towels and were being held aloft to receive the warmth of the setting sun. They seemed to float side by side, looking skyward, and drawing deep synchronized breaths.

Jessie couldn't be sure how much time had passed, but in a while she felt grounded again, and knew that Henry had gone, in defiance of gravity, out into the universe without a grave. Would he come back? She knew he'd try.

From the house, she heard the cords of the tune that had been playing in her head. Her blood rose. So, Kate knows the tune. She picked up the leash. "C'mon boy, let's go home." They ran up the driveway, buoyed, exultant.

Frank lay in the hammock under the Pheltaphorium tree, his eyes closed. Jessie saw that he had changed into his recalcitrant clothes. She planted a hand-kiss on his forehead, and hooked Ibsen's leash over the post of the hammock. Ibsen whined, and curled up underneath the hammock, to sleep and dream the way he used to do with his master.

Jessie headed into the house, in a hurry now to question Kate, to find out the name of that damn tune that haunted her.

12
Frank

Before he came outside to lie down in the hammock, Frank had been watching Jessie through the workshop window, saw her flailing her arms like a crazy person, and wondered who she was talking to, besides herself. He'd gotten tired of repairing all the little things he found broken in the house that his grandpa hadn't been able to keep up with after he had the by-pass. He wondered how Doris was going to manage living alone in this old place where things constantly busted? He ached for his grandpa who had taught him how to fix everything, how to think about life. He looked at the radios lined up on the work bench waiting for Henry to scan the frequencies, his favorite hobby. Into the tabletop microphone he'd say: This is WD4LLB, over. Anyone? Contact thrilled him. He'd told Frank bouncing a signal off the moon only takes 8 minutes. After a while Frank had gotten chills being in the workshop– it felt sunken in on itself, haunted. Even this hammock was possessed with the indentation of Henry's body. But Frank was covertly enjoying that.

He knew the real reason he was tired was from holding his pain so tightly, and he longed to let it go. With Henry's death, his deepest wound was reopened, as though his mother had died all over again. Maybe he'd never stopped grieving her because he hadn't ever been able to grieve it out with his father; it wasn't allowed in Tom's move-on world. For years Frank had cried himself to sleep, alone.

His mother's death when he was five years old was a recurring memory he couldn't shake. Unbidden it would play out in his mind, silently, except for his own heart's thumping: first his mother gave him a big red balloon on a string, then she knelt and hugged him. She smelled like vanilla and oatmeal. She took a breath and filled her cheeks with air like the blowfish they had watched on the beach that morning, and they laughed together, puffing their cheeks. And then she walked across a field, her camera bag swinging, waving goodbye. He watched her climb into the gondola of a huge red balloon/airship with some other nice, smiling people. He watched the balloon launch up, up, until it was just a tiny red dot in a beautiful bluey sky. But not away; not up and away. No, instead it exploded. He'd been quickly yanked off the field, led away by adults he didn't even know, though he understood they were trying to shield him. He kept looking back in shock and horror, at what had to be pieces of his mother falling from the sky, his heart kept stopping and starting up again, like somebody had it in their fist squeezing it.

Frank lurched forward in the hammock, almost falling out. Ibsen jumped up in his lap, pinning him, licked his tears, circled, and settled down so Frank would too. Frank stroked Ibsen, tried to relax. He gazed out into the orchard of trees and let their deep tranquil essence flow into him. It was easy to love nature. Natural science was what he had turned to when he lost his mother. It was the comforting subject he studied to concede himself a future after he lost the one person he thought he couldn't live without. Then he'd found electronics, computers, and the internet, where untold worlds were uncoverable, and electric science, as well as the cosmos became his orchard.

Frank felt the sun and air honey-combing his skin, healing him. He dozed off in a dreamy inertia. As he drifted, he heard words inside his head, like from a half-recalled Hamlet or something: *Only barely a thread holding you 'tween this world and the next. You afraid of soaring? Is that why you ignore me? To keep yourself grounded?* It was his grandpa, talking to him in that patient voice he'd used when he was showing him how to solder: *You see these two wires? watch this now: ZZZTTTT... Listen up Frank: here's how I died. The pain was crushing my chest. I was cold and couldn't get warm, couldn't stop shivering. I went down in my hopes. Then I saw an opening, like a peek through the flap of a stage curtain, at a fresh audience all waiting for me, only this was even better; it was an opening into a no-time place, intensely bright and appealing. My mother was standing there with open arms, the grandmother Jessie always called her archangel, and Jesus, she was wearing that purple velvet dress we buried her in, but this time it was beauty-full, and I wasn't afraid, you know, of purple.*

In the air, Frank tasted the burnt smell of the soldering iron. He shifted and sunk deeper into the hammock to make sure he could still feel his body. He had a sensation of towering above it that was great. He pictured in his mind his grandpa in his red smoking jacket, parked in his old La-Z-Boy recliner, holding forth:

Ibsen was jumping over me, barking wildly. As soon as I accepted the cold feeling, it went away, every feeling did, so did the pain. There was no sensation except of drifting up, but that was purely mental. The essential me was immaterial. I was out. Then nothing but sound, lots of sweet sounds like baby giggles, coming and going, and screams too, but I got away from them. Somehow, I knew I had to listen softly, uncritically, and hold back my judgment, because the angels needed me to do that in order to help me out. It was hard— I had to go against a family trait— judging is probably coded in our genes for Christ's sake. But I had to drop it to progress.

Once I did, the sounds stopped, and the light began, like the very heart of light, older than earth and of such a purity that it was locked away in my primal memory when I was alive. I saw shafts of rainbow, lunar rainbows, then the clouds, Jesus, great heaps of them, soft and summiting, and I felt intense, soaring freedom, no gravity holding me down anymore.

Frank felt the invincible happiness that comes from thinking interesting thoughts, with the promise of more to come. He dared not awaken, fearing his grandpa was only a dream. In an act of will he kept himself floating above his body, the better to listen and imagine.

The clouds were like whipped-cream dumplings my body makes indentations in, only I had no body, though I still had the memory of one. I could make it happen with just my mind. Everything is possible, like in dreams and art. Chance and luck and randomness are very real things. Chambers of my memory are all here, lined up waiting for me to examine again, to go backwards and forwards in, and this time no clock. It's pure rapture. I've waited all my life for this chance. So, how could I not go? When you're young you outgrow the world but when you're old the world outgrows you. I'm telling you all this Frank because you are endowed with the seventh sense of the imagination. You are a scientific wizard standing at the cusp of human knowledge. Hidden technological forces are changing everything. Your generation will be the artisans of the future. Electronics will open up more possibilities, and knock down more boundaries than anyone ever dreamed possible...

13
Kate

"What were you just playing?" Jessie demanded as she came bounding in the door.

Seated at the piano, Kate looked up dreamily. "Beethoven?" she played a few bars.

"No, no, the other one." Jessie panted, out of breath.

"You mean this?" Kate picked out the keys.

"That's it! What's it called?"

"Hmm, I don't know... I just heard you humming it. Daddy used to play it sometimes."

"Yeah, like it was his all-time favorite song, but what the hell's the name of it? It's been driving me crazy."

Kate plunked out the tune again, trying to remember. "I don't know, really– I'm sorry."

Jessie started riffling through forty years of old phonograph records, tapes, and CD's, jolting Doris out of her daze. She was a damson lump in the chair– Jessie hadn't even noticed her. Taking care of her husband had supplied a shape to Doris's life, and now that the shape was gone, she appeared shrunken, almost invisible. It hurt Jessie to look at her.

"What are you looking for? You're making a big mess," Doris suddenly crabbed, like her old self, rattling the ice in her high-ball, taking a big swig.

"Do you know daddy's favorite song? Do you remember the name of it, or the words?" Jessie pleaded, da-da-da-ing the tune for her mother.

Doris glared at Jessie like she was crazy, inappropriate as usual. She heaved a loud, hopeless sigh. Song? His song for her was Always, I'll Be Loving You Always. She sang a few bars quietly for Jessie, tearing up.

Then she said, "Don't you want to know my favorite song?" and looked wall-eyed back out at Silver Lake when she got no immediate answer.

Kate picked out the chords to "Behind Closed Doors," and aped a wicked grin.

"You were always such a daddy's girl," Doris complained, glaring at Jessie, stating what she believed was the real problem here.

Jessie piled on a stack of ancient, scratched records to play, slamming the arm down on the old stereo.

"Cast Your Fate to the Wind" played first. "This sounds sort of like it?" Jessie prodded Kate, doubtful herself.

"It's close. But that's not it. I think I know where we might find some answers..." Kate hesitated, looked over at their mother. "Casadega," she whispered, too loudly.

"Oh, that's a lot of hooey," Doris said, batting her hand at her daughters, not looking at them, not wanting to take her eyes off the jack rabbits that were feeding on the lawn between the house and the lake. The rabbits did this every evening at sundown, halting, listening, and quivering, then hopping off. She and Henry had always watched this together, sucking their teeth, discussing what they were going to have for dinner.

Kate felt a little funny making her suggestion; she was stepping out of the child's role with Jessie for maybe the first time, even though she was twenty-one. As the baby in the family all her siblings had been her parents too– she'd had five parents bossing her– and now she was daring to lead her big sister somewhere. And of all places, Casadega.

In the middle of the night, when it was quiet and dark and everyone else had been asleep for hours, the disconsolate widow Doris, tearing her hair, yelled at the top of her lungs: "I want my husband back." Her voice echoed across Silver Lake like a light plane crossing of an afternoon. Kate ran in to her mother, held her head while she threw up in the toilet. "Oh God," Doris moaned, "it's all over for me Kate, find some nice guy and get married and give me some grandchildren, will you? Jessie's never gonna do it."

14
Casadega

The day after the funeral everyone disappeared, except for Kate and Jessie, who were staying to keep an eye on Doris. She was volatile in her grieving, angry, drinking too much. Seaborn wanted to get back to work, so he left in the Land Rover. Jessie planned to fly home to Atlanta within the week. She hoped her job would still be there. She knew if she stayed away any longer it might not be. Kate would stay at Silver Lake and watch over their mother until spring break was over, when she'd have to get back to school.

Doris was finally sleeping. She slept for two days straight, and on the third morning, Kate and Jessie fixed her a big breakfast, and invited her to ride with them to Casadega. But Doris said she just wanted to sleep some more. They'd been relieved. Her leery eyed skepticism would have put a damper on the trip.

Jessie had searched for the song's title, and for the words, playing every bit of music in the house, even going out to comb the music store in the mall. The identity of the song still eluded her. It must have been a song Henry hadn't collected but had heard and carried around in his music-loving head. He'd done that a lot, obsessing over songs he liked. When Jessie had been an investigative reporter for the Miami Herald, and she had hold of something like this, she couldn't let it go; it would bug her until she solved the mystery. She was so tortured by it, she was beginning to believe it was some kind of grief psychosis working her over. She didn't consider herself musical, yet every melodic note played perfectly in her head, and on different instruments! It was such a little thing, surely, the name of a song. Why couldn't she find it?

They took Doris's Oldsmobile, a vintage Delta 88 convertible, and headed east on 441. Kate drove with the top down. It would take a couple of hours to get there. She knew the way because the year before she had attended a spiritualist's camp meeting at Casadega. One of the psychic readers had impressed her, a man named George Vogel, and it was to him that Kate was taking her tormented sister now. She had called ahead for two appointments and made a pact with Jessie not to tell Vogel about their father dying, not even that they were sisters. Let him guess. He was supposed to be the psychic.

The song in Jessie's head no longer played on violin or piano but had deepened down into a string bass. With the car-top down and the whipping wind she had a cottony view of Henry, morphing in cumulus clouds, cavorting as though he was accompanying them over the greens to the next hole, Casadega. She did not know what to make of how they talked back and forth. It made her so nervous she smoked three cigarettes in a row, without enjoyment, without a thought.

Out of the blue, she asked, "Do you still hate the color purple, Daddy?" She looked over at Kate; even though she'd spoken out loud, with all the wind it hardly mattered. Kate was concentrating on her driving, chewing gum, looking out the window, in her own dream world. Jessie wondered what Kate's world was like, what she was thinking, hearing, seeing, feeling. Sometimes Kate appeared to be preoccupied, and she wondered if the great gap that could form between them was common among sisters, or was it just their fifteen-year age difference? She felt protective of Kate, and proud of her little sister. For now, here Kate was, leading the way.

Well, do you? This time Jessie only thought the question. Henry had assured her that telepathy was real. It's invisible, yet you can hear it. And invisibility is greatly underrated, like joy which is also invisible.

She had to wait a few minutes for Henry to answer:

Huh? Purple? . . . nah. How can you hate a color? Death's not like that. Everything's the same now, equal. It's not about what you like or don't like, or choices. You need time for all that. This is timeless. The same as love; love is a golden light, the penultimate color, Jessie. People have a terrible fear of love. That's why they kill and do bad things. It's harder to love than to hate. People have careless relationships with one another instead of possessiveness because they're afraid to love. There's a dangerous preference to be in power rather than in love. But when you die, this love light absolutely owns you.

Yes, but did you see the purple? It was all over the place. The dress Ma had on, the color of the ribbon on your coffin?

Yeah, how 'bout that! Henry laugh-slapped his knee. Jessie could just make out his form before it dissolved into drifty cloud again. *Was a time that woulda bothered me.*

He waxed on happily about the quixotic simplicity of death and the capacious universe, chock-full of spirits longing to communicate, to stay in the game.

And when they got to Casadega, Kate had to shake Jessie out of a deep sleep. As Kate drove down the streets Jessie smelled jasmine and couldn't believe her eyes. Casadega was storybook real. A whole cozy town full of spiritualists living an intuitive life, plying their sensory talents. On the little paved lanes, a mailbox outside each modest cottage bore a name and a specialty. She read them off as they passed: Psychic Reader, Channeling, Healer, Aura Readings, Past Life Regressions, Astrology, Palmistry, Astronomy, Animal

Readings, Mediation, Massage, on and on. A whole town of serious seekers; it was their culture, as well as their livelihood. They passed a grocery store, a big old, white-washed inn, The House of Charm Beauty Salon. Jessie was amazed that such a place existed, so congenial to the supernatural, so new-agey. It was only slightly off the beaten path, in the hot heart of Florida's citrus belt– glowing with good health and weather– a wondrous village where extraordinary senses were held in the same esteem as gold. Jessie was grateful to Kate for finding it. In her current frame of mind, she wanted to move there. It felt like a true home, a wonderland, and a place for answers.

Kate was happy to please. Casadega had been her secret from the rest of the family, especially Tom, until now. In the whole town there was not one, (whom Tom would consider,) reliable witness. Everyone in Casadega had felt or seen spirits, ghosts, angels, or aliens of one kind or another and talked openly about it. Tom would label them all wackos because he didn't allow himself to see, feel or believe anything that couldn't be proven by logic. Law school had taught him platonic thinking, and he was locked in that mode. There was no place in his fiercely rational mind for such nonsense as ghosts. He'd stopped taking Henry seriously long before his father died, and called him a crackpot, and a kook, behind his back. Kate had often been Tom's sounding board. She wasn't about to tell him anything that would cause him to ridicule her too. She lived in fear of her older sibling's judgements.

George Vogel's mailbox said, "Psychic Reader." They flipped a coin to see who would go in first and Kate won the toss. Jessie sat on a log bench under an oak tree, across the gravel road from Vogel's house, to wait, while Kate went inside for her reading.

Jessie craned her neck upward, basking in the warm sun swirls filtering through the old oak trees, swaged in Spanish Moss. It was a beautiful day– Florida in April was perfection. She stared at the ground and dug around in the sand and gravel with a stick, idly looking for acorns that weren't broken yet. The birds were loud and flat sounding, as though they were waiting for inspiration. A black cat sidled across Jessie's path and she laughed. She heard Henry say: *Are you kidding us, cat?* Squirrels spiraled up the trees and down again, chasing each other. Jessie wondered why they didn't just go straight up, instead of spiraling like that. Her thoughts seemed to breathe a life of their own: *It's the motion of the Universe built into their genes– the Universe loves spirals.* The answer popped into her head, from Henry. His voice came and went. There was letting involved, she had to let him in. Only she wasn't sure how she did it. It felt involuntary, like sweating in the Florida heat, like his voice bedewed from her own mind, unbidden. Now she heard: *Don't reject me, Jessie. I did that once. I have a confession: we didn't really move to Florida just because I was cold. It was my mother's ghost I was running from. I'd seen her coming down the stairs the day after her funeral, wearing that purple dress we buried her in, and it scared me so much I shut my mind down. She was trying to get through to me, but I wouldn't let her. I never wanted to see the color purple again. I thought it meant death and darkness, and I ran from that, to the orangey Florida sunshine.*

This revelation made Jessie feel more beleaguered by Henry's voice, like her life had taken a turn she must follow even though she didn't feel strong enough to go. She was bogged down with grieving for him; wasn't that enough?

And don't be afraid of dying. I arrived in the afterlife as overwhelmed as when I departed the earth. But oh, very soon, it got rich. An invisible plane supports that visible one. And just imagine not cycling on a crumby twenty-four-hour day anymore? Desire trumps time Jessie.

Henry broke into a corny song, one he'd made up himself, she was sure, like he used to do when she was a child and needed cheering up. But it was to the tune of the song that dallied in her head, and there was a sob in his voice: *There's no picture I could give you of a heart as luxe as yours, no song that I could sing to you could match your precious pulse.* Then he whistled the whole thing, trilling the sound, like birdsong, the way she'd always loved.

Hang onto Life, he hollered, so loud Jessie looked quickly around to see if anyone else heard him. *To YOUR life, Jessie. See, it isn't really the middle of it, because you can never know when the middle of something is until it ends, and then I didn't even end, Jessie, ha ha! I thought my destiny had ended before I died, but it was only my destiny on the ground. There's more!* He laughed wildly. *Now, ax me any questions you like. C'mon, fire away...*

And Jessie sat on that stump and asked him what the hell was the name of the song he kept haunting her with? Immediately she heard it, this time on an ancient-sounding stringed instrument—a harp?

She got up, and walked towards the sound, as though she was being pulled down a gravel road until she came to a big white-frame Victorian house with long windows that came clear down to the foundation. She Cupped her eyes and peered into one of the windows and saw a young girl perched on a stool plucking the strings of a beautiful harp. She was playing the song, and singing the words too: *"Like a circle in a spiral, like a wheel within a wheel, never-dying, never-fading..."* People sat around the girl enjoying the lovely music.

In the twinkling of an eye, Jessie knew the name of the song: "The Windmills of Your Mind!" In a flash of recognition, she knew all the words, and everything she needed to know for messaging, too. She looked back at George Vogel's house just as a bevy of peacocks crossed in front, fanning out their lovely tail feathers, fairly taking her breath away, like omens always do.

It was simply a clue to hold your attention, to keep you interested, to sort of break your fall. Henry said, as Jessie floated back to Vogel's house. *You know, never-dying, never-fading, it's in the old Bible I think, who knows where? Besides, a tune is so much more memorable than anything else, don't you think?*

Kate came out of the house beaming. She shook her head to signal Jessie that George Vogel hadn't guessed Henry's death on her. She looked happy because even though he had taken note of her sadness, he promised her a serendipitous future.

Jessie met Kate's smile with a radiant one of her own. She felt high. She practically levitated into George Vogel's house then, curious to hear what he would say, a giggle bubbling up her diaphragm. She had never felt happier in her whole life, and it was because of that one moment of recognition when she had named that tune and a new seamless road opened up, like her grief had just been so much fodder, like the rational world was a delusion.

George, who was in a state of wonderment himself, shaded his eyes from the radiant light surrounding Jessie, and said the first thing that popped into his head: "Did someone close to you die recently? In fact, let me see here, I'm counting... one, two, three, four– four spirits came in with you. One of them is very fresh, an older man you loved very much... your father, is it? And one is an archangel. The other two are women, one is Asian. She has a little dog... no no no, it's just a fur stole... They're dimmer, but they're accompanying you. Goodness, any idea who all these spirits might be?"

Oh, George could see all right. Jessie wasn't even seeing all this. She could feel it though, the radiance bedazzling her. The room was crowded. Her tongue was thick. Colors glowed fantastically. It was like the time she'd dropped LSD in college, only she was fearless now. Language was too solid to use– all she could manage was a huge smile, and a universal giggle. Her thoughts danced. Her sapphirine eyes flitted around the room like lightening bugs.

George Vogel smiled back, his eyes crinkling. He waited expectantly for Jessie to speak.

With effort, she overcame the paralysis and words staggered out of her mouth while her head bobbed affirmatively, "my father... yes... his mother, my grandmother, she's my archangel. The others, I don't know. I've been trying to identify a song since last Thursday, the day after he died, and I just did!"

Oh, what a triumph she was feeling– George could feel it too, as well as see it. Even if it were only to do with a song.

He said, "You're lucky. Lots of people on the other side want to make a connection with a loved one, but it's too hard for them to get through. Something must have greased your wheels, heh-heh, because it looks like you're an open portal. Nothing can deter you now."

Jessie heard the words, *grease your wheels,* repeating over and over in her mind like an unbridled echo, like it was the grease itself soaking her brain, liberating her from concerns on the ground and loosening her up for the radio dynamics to come.

George leaned forward, whispered, "What did your father tell you?"

Jessie thought a minute. "It wasn't morbid or anything. It was so natural, just told me about what it's like being dead. He just spoke to me like he always did. He told me to quit smoking, for one thing."

George looked a little disappointed.

"And that we have messages to deliver," Jessie added, nodding.

George's face lit up like a meteor. Then he looked worried for Jessie.

Little did she know what she might be in for.

15
Breaking Form

Jessie was relieved to be back home in Atlanta, in Seaborn's comforting arms, back on set, the realm where she belonged, even if the grind of trying to stay atop the news anchor arena was difficult. The high velocity atmosphere of the television studio was her real life, the job she had worked so hard for. The time she'd spent in Florida for the funeral was like a tribal family limbo she wasn't used to anymore. Except for Casadega, which had been a wonderland, a delivering experience. After that, she told Seaborn all about hearing Henry's voice and about the song. But it distressed Sea—he was skeptical and found it all too hard to believe. He couldn't help being suspicious of Jessie's mental health, so it became a sore subject they didn't talk about, like her failure to get pregnant.

Jessie had earned her anchor power and found it heady stuff. Yet now, back in place, she grew anxious again about not having any children, the one thing she felt she was biologically put on earth to do. She'd never even had a miscarriage. The words *slow down* haunted her. Had she fed her soul to her ambition? Did she want this desk or a baby? She knew the answer, but not how to abandon the career she loved so much. And now she felt the crimp of time racing, the more so because of Henry's death.

She sat at the news desk feeling antsy and restless amidst all the hubbub of setting up to deliver the six o'clock. She was high one minute, low the next, as though she was struggling to uncover some new middle ground to exist in. Yet, in her pale blue linen suit, and wearing her favorite Vetiver scent, she looked fresh, if you didn't know. Her mind wandered back to childhood, the way she supposed a parent's death caused a mind to do. She had lots of wacky thoughts, and of all things, she found herself thinking about Brenda Starr, a maverick reporter in old comics. Henry had saved comics from when he was a boy and shared them with Jessie when she was old enough to read. She had idolized Brenda Starr—she was her first role model. She'd be embarrassed to tell anyone that now and kept it a secret. She had told Henry though, back then, that she wanted to be like Brenda Starr, and he'd said: "everything you need is already inside you. You can never be more than what you are, so build on that." Now she remembered this vividly. And how she'd always loved telling Henry about her dreams for world peace, for an end to poverty and hunger and racism, unafraid of exposing her naive idealism. She never had to hold herself back with him. He was just as wild a dreamer as she was, wilder even. They had glowed together, imagining things. "Television," he told her, "Television is the way."

Sure enough, on tests, her aptitude had shown up in communication skills, confirming the natural calling she'd felt. She remembered how she had begun by taking liberal arts courses at Florida State University. Because of Henry she was a great reader. Counselors at FSU helped her map a career path. First, she had earned a bachelor's degree in political science, with a minor in journalism. Then she'd served a tough internship at the Miami Herald, one of the greatest newspapers in the country. She cringed thinking of those days at the Herald, when she'd been a laughingstock because of her naivete, earning the scorn of cynical, seasoned journalists. She'd had to fight for any respect at all. But it toughened her and taught her that she was no journalist. So, she set out to read the news instead, on national television.

She came to work in Atlanta, at Ground Witness News because it was the only network station that offered her a job, and by now, TV was her destiny. She admired all the pioneers like Jane Pauley, Diane Sawyer and Cokie Roberts, who advised aspiring female reporters to "Duck and file" when things got messy. "Just do your work and get it on the air." She had grown with the station and it had been hard working her way up to first anchor, without stepping on any toes that she knew of, sensitive to that. Gradually she came to love the changing seasons of the middle south, the classical yet casual quaintness of Atlanta, still ghosted by the civil war, and "Gone With The Wind." The red-clay earth and the piney Piedmont got into her blood and rooted her. And when she became best friends with Seaborn Pettengill, her camera operator, and then, to her surprise, they fell in love, well that was it, Atlanta was home.

Jessie watched Seaborn setting up his camera. She often thought their marriage was like a long date. People called him the man behind the woman, and he didn't mind, he even seemed amused. He had passed over work opportunities that would have taken him out of the country to exotic places. "Are you sure? This is your chance to see the world," she had urged him. But he wasn't interested in travel, said he never wanted to leave her side. He claimed he'd already achieved his life's ambition, to be a cameraman, and he only wanted to be a wiz at his craft. Even so, he was distrustful of perfectionism, calling it self-abuse—he was never one to sacrifice good for perfect. If people thought she was obsessed with her career, they found Seaborn to be the opposite: easy going and laid back.

Jessie was in love with Seaborn's innate goodness, a rarity in the world. He was a kind, and true gentleman and she knew she was lucky to have found him. Women adored

Seaborn, and boldly flirted with him, but if he was tempted, he hid it well. She knew Seaborn liked to be around women more than men, and sometimes it was hard not to be jealous. He was so good looking, playful, smart, domestic even, and a couple of years younger than her, although he didn't look it. Nobody thought so. She even took his name, Pettengill, and got a razzing for it. The producers thought it sounded uppity. Feminists thought it was retro to take a husband's name, so 20th century. But she countered saying "All the names are men's names anyway."

Jessie felt she was well-liked among her co-workers; she surprised people by keeping her sturdy ego in check. She'd learned how from Seaborn, who had a bodhisattva nature he inherited from his Indian mother. The interns found her accessible enough to ask her advice about their own career goals. Last month the evaluations had described her as "steady and real," and Seaborn told her: "You can't fake steady and real in front of a TV camera." The notes further said she was "an equalist, humane and savvy." Just what she expected a news anchor should be in a news and information culture. On the critical side though, it was noted that she was not perky enough, sometimes her voice squeaked, she showed a vague passivity, too subject to the whims of others, was too liberal, too laid back and a tree hugger." She agreed to work on all that.

Now there was a hushed atmosphere in the studio, out of respect for her bereavement. She was grateful for the sympathy of the crew and tried to reassure everyone with her smile that she was fine. She didn't say that she knew the name of the tune now, and she'd experienced a transformation upon discovering it. No one would understand. She was grateful for everything and found it impossible to be sad and grateful at the same time. She had been distressed grieving Henry, who told her the antidote for despair was a purpose, and then he gave her one. She didn't want to hurt Seaborn, but she knew her purpose was going to have a large impact on him.

It was also tensely quiet in the studio because the pictures of the brutality of ISIS coming out of the muddle east, as Henry called it, were so depressing. More explosions were killing the innocent. The security of the world was under a dark threat. It made Jessie ache inside. It was like everyone was forced to witness the unraveling of civilization. (She was on in one minute) Sometimes life seemed only about pain and loss, and human beings were doomed to suffer. She had come to dread the all-terror-all-the-time-news that she was duty-bound to report.

The lights came up and Jessie was on. She reported the middle east carnage, and other bad news, in seven minutes of rapid-fire sound bites. In the commercial break, she drank warm tea to soothe the squeak in her voice, and recited Dylan Thomas's poetry softly to herself, trying to retrieve an equanimity with language:

The conversation of prayers about to be said / Turns on the quick and the dead, and the man on the stairs / Tonight shall find no dying but alive and warm.

She had been experiencing aphasia in small doses; the cat had her tongue. Profuse and repetitive news bytes sometimes caused that, and there were so many—there was so much hype, and it was the opposite of the natural world she felt a simple longing for. There was earth, air, water, fire, and then there was hype, like another element, oceans of it, always advancing.

On the floor director's signal, Jessie looked up, gazed again into Seaborn's hot camera, and continued reading copy from the TelePrompTer:

The mood in Cairo is sorrowful as thousands continue to mourn the loss of the Nobel prize-winning Egyptian writer, Naguib Mahfouz. Today is the anniversary of the day he died in a cafe in Cairo when he was ninety-four...

Seaborn was operating camera four, aimed at Jessie, his red tally light a beacon for her. He had on a headset over his black ball cap which was turned around to the back as usual. Upon the bill was perched a live, yellow butterfly; Jessie saw the butterfly. No telling how it got in the studio; she had never seen bugs in the studio. Nobody was looking at Seaborn's cap. All eyes were on her as she continued:

In other news around the world . . .

Tears suddenly choked her; the camera captured her looking distressed.

My, my father. . .Mah-Fouz, Ma-Fooooos...

She stared into the camera, breaking form. The air went dead; the silence as variously shaded as speech would have been. The crew collectively held their breaths. The yellow butterfly swooped into view and landed on Jessie's script right in front of her. She looked down, and a single bubbly teardrop fell, just missing it. She sneezed then, a juicy one.

In the control booth at the same time, six people wearing headsets, including the producer-director hyphenates, Eli and Smithy, stared intently at Jessie's face on their monitors. Was she having a sneezing attack?

Eli said cautiously, "Ready fill . . . take my cue."

But Jessie recovered her composure, wiped her nose with the back of her hand and began speaking again. Only this time, it was in Arabic:

بنفـس .ومتعـاطف سخي الفـن
مع بهـا يسكن الـتي الطريقـة

البؤســـاء تهجـــر لا ،السعداء
وســـيلة سواء حد على يوفــر فهـــو
في يتضخم مـا عن للتعبـــــير مريحة
قلـــوبهم.

She immediately translated into English:

Art is generous and sympathetic. In the same way that it dwells with the happy ones, it does not desert the wretched. It offers both alike a convenient means for expressing what swells up in their heart...

She paused only a second, then her eyes locked on the camera and she said: *Death is a soft landing. Be comforted. Stop all this obsession with violence and concentrate on eliminating the hate in the world. We are underestimating the weakness of evil. Good and evil are not equals...and love and kindness are in short supply...*

Every headset crackled with Smithy's sputtering, "What'd she say? ...the hell's going on?"

A flustered Production Assistant answered him, "I think that Arabic part is from Mahfouz's Nobel acceptance speech; it isn't in the script though. I don't know where that other came from. She's supposed to be talking about the quagmire in the Middle East..."

"Cut the audio, go to black," Smithy roared.

The set lights went down. There was a chaos of sounds. P.A.'s scurried around, eyes wide.

The floor director called out, "We're in a commercial."

Jessie lowered her eyes as she always did, to rest them from the lights.

Seaborn looked up at the control booth in amazement, (where had Jessie learned to speak Arabic?) "Man, those Arabs love spontaneity," he said into his headset, trying to laugh it off. But He had begun to recognize their ruin. Ever since Henry died, Jessie had been on the brink of going rogue. This was her bizarro Irish father's doing.

Smithy said to Eli, "Get down there."

Some of the crew were already beside Jessie, comforting her, touching up her make-up, whispering, "You okay? What's wrong?" A make-up person dabbed at her teary eyes with his own monogramed handkerchief instead of tissues.

The Reverend Thackston, whose show would be taped next, stood grinning in the shadows where he had been watching. He was the only one truly enjoying Jessie's form break.

The floor director called, "Thirty seconds..."

Eli held her wrist, like he was taking her pulse. "You need some more time off Jessie? Maybe think about the sponsors?" He didn't even smile at his joke.

Jessie ran her fingers through her hair, looking spacy. She said, "No, no, sorry, I'm okay, just a little queasy...I'll be okay now."

Eli studied her, "Just read the copy, no additions, okay?"

Jessie nodded, pasted a smile to reassure Eli as he backed off, anxious, on shpilkes, "and keep it perky," he added, his usual last little piece of advice.

Over the headset, Smithy's voice croaked, "Down in five, four, three, two. . .."

The lights came up and the floor director signaled Jessie with a descending arm. Cameras two and three were tight on Jessie, who looked fresh again, as if nothing had happened.

Seaborn on camera four had been redirected. He was now pointed at the weatherman, who was poised in front of a map, ready to fill.

Jessie read the rolling script:

In Rio, the Earth Summit has reconvened. The focus is on what commitments governments must make to progress in the twenty-first century on an ecologically sound path. Environment is at the center of economic decision making for governments, industry, and the home. To make an enemy of the Earth is to make an enemy of your own body. We don't know the limits of consciousness, nor the boundaries of knowing. Your next life begins during this one.

Up in the control booth, Eli flinched, "Jesus, she did it again; that ain't in the script."

Smithy yelled, "Ready four, go to weather, go to weather."

Phones were ringing in the control booth. They had an anomaly.

The weatherman began giving his forecasts into Seaborn's camera, but Seaborn was watching Jessie. Her eyes gleamed with precognition. She stared straight ahead, as if entranced. Seaborn saw she was about to speak again, so he whipped his "hot" camera around on her, close. What the hell, they were gonna get fired anyway. The floor director waved his arms wildly, but Jessie, interrupting the weather, said over the airwaves:

Knowledge, like the order of colors in a rainbow, that's what's important. Color is eternal, the memory of color can harbor in your soul and become a part of you for all eternity. And you CAN take it with you. Whatever feeds your soul becomes a part of it, like an implant...

"Hey! the hell's goin' on here? What's Seaborn doin'?" Smithy was rapping on the glass, hollering, "What're you doing? You're outa here. He's fired!" Both his thumbs stabbed the air.

On the monitor, a rainbow made traces of color across Jessie's face like a winged mythological annotation.

Where had that come from?

Smithy, seeing it, went pale.

Everybody's cell phone was sounding off a different ringtone. Eli, listening on his phone and scribbling on a pad, said to Smithy: "They love it! The calls are running ten to one in favor of hearing that crapola she's spouting, 'steada the news."

The studio monitors showed the weather broadcasting from camera two.

Seaborn's tally light was off, but even so he kept his camera on Jessie, and she kept right on going:

...You can take your playfulness with you, a sense of humor, hope, integrity, good character. You can take a couple of million thoughts with you, whatever you collect on the micro disk that is your mind. If you let your heart and soul decide its better stuff...

Everyone in the studio had stopped what they were doing to watch Jessie, live.

The Reverend Thackston ogled her from the shadows, his usual calamine complexion flushed to a deep organ-meat red.

Smithy roared over the headsets, "Jesus, she's crazy as hell. Someone get Doctor Desmond, and get her the hell out of here"

PART TWO

16
Jessie's Fugue

Dr. Desmond waited in his office at the station for the anchor girl. Sure, he wanted to have a look, but she was lost he knew already, dissociated from reality. He'd seen the tape of what he was sure would be her last newscast for some time to come, maybe forever.

He combed his hair, a full pompadour in front and a marine trim, sides and back. He wished it weren't such a mummy brown color, shot through with aging gray, but he drew the line at hair dye. His shirt was pima cotton, the jacket Scotch wool, a foxy-brown hounds-tooth. He prided himself on being a natty dresser, always ready for anything or ready for just being. He enjoyed how he looked. He straightened his bolo tie, studying himself in the full-length mirror mounted on the back of his entry door. The clasp on his bolo was his own private trademark, a silver coil he gave patina to by constantly fingering. He used it for hypnosis. The psyche was a coil and when you left a patient feeling good and fine they just went away from you and took up with their demons all over again, spiraling right out of your control. It was discouraging. He was helpless before insanity. He couldn't reason it away, but he was damned if he was going to let himself be victimized by it.

He'd taken the classic Erhard Seminars Training and reamed out most of his unproductive personality, relieved to learn that he was responsible only for his own actions. EST internalized his ambitions, affirmed them, and quelled his overly maternal tendency to nurture and attach. He'd been a guilty nurturer. Then after he went through primal scream therapy, rebirthed, and confronted his own demons, he knew, by God, (wasn't it obvious all the time?) what life was all about once you rose above survival. It was about creating revenues. Money. With money you created realms, a personal lifestyle. Everything always came back to money; it was the bottom line. He knew that was cold, but he was tired of having to be warm just because he was a doctor. What warmed him up was money. He'd studied the passages of life and knew what his forties were for: amassing wealth. He remained ever vigilant for that opportunity.

After the two years of Primal Scream Training, Dr. Colin Desmond changed his name to Dr. Padgett Desmond. He'd been teased all through grade school and now he wanted a high-concept name with no nasty double entendres. He wanted to recreate himself now that he was clean, and he wanted a fresh arena. That's when he came to the television studio with a proposal to service the egos at Ground Witness News, tall promising in his vitae to always put the crew as first as possible, right behind the producers and sponsors.

Desmond had built his practice by word of mouth, and pampering outsized egos was his specialty. He used his own knack for high drama with his patients, inviting them to act out, scream if they wanted to. He could take anything they had to dish out, and then he translated their fears for them. It was always that: anger, depression, everything was a symptom of fear. Oh, he had a nose for it. Then, naturally, he brought everything back to the central issue of God the father. People needed a God to fill up that black hole caused by fear, until he could think of something better to offer. He had teamed up with The Reverend Travis Thackston, sometimes doing a guest appearance on his TV crusade when it suited his own purpose. Sometimes it suited his purpose to report The Reverend to Eli and Smithy, who produced Thackston's show, as well as Ground Witness News. Like when Travis acted deranged and went around his office bum rushing young Christian groupies and tearing his clothes off, exposing his rod or staff, whatever he called it, and his tight, disgusting pink anatomy. He thought Thackston was foolish—he felt sorry for him. But he knew that the Reverend also made people feel good.

Desmond grimaced, checking his teeth.

Jessie opened the door while he was looking intently in the mirror and the door knocked him in the head.

"Oh, sorry Dr. Demond." she said.

"DESmond," he corrected her, rubbing his head, "PADgett DESmond." He gave her a limp-fish handshake, irritated already.

Jessie scanned the room and sat on the appropriate couch for her first experience in a psychiatrist's office. She helped herself to a couple of Hershey's kisses from a dish on the coffee table. They tasted a little funny, but she ate them anyway.

A few minutes later, Jessie began crying softly she didn't know why. She had assumed the therapeutic reclining position, and Desmond had begun hypnotizing her with his silver coil.

Jessie could hear the now-familiar tune playing softly on a flute, or was that the Muzak? Something held her back from asking Dr. Desmond.

For his part, Desmond was running videotape of the session with Jessie in case he needed proof to support his findings, which he feared might be unpopular, since Jessie herself was so popular. He swung his silver coil back and forth in front of her and began:

"What thoughts are you having in your mind, Jessie?"

After a pained silence, while she was trying to decide which thoughts might be appropriate to tell, Jessie shrugged and said: "There's been a paradox in my mind, for weeks now, whether to believe in death as an ending, or...this miracle that is happening to me."

"Mhmm, and what miracle is that?"

She mewled, "The one where I'm hearing from my dead father... from the other side."

"Oh...mhmm...Desmond rolled his eyes, caught himself then quickly continued, "and what does he say to you?"

Jessie seemed to be searching a jumble of thoughts in her mind for a safe answer. Finally, she said, "He really wants me to quit smoking."

"He must have cared very much about you. Has anyone else heard this voice?"

"Not as far as I know." she said. "Also he wants me to be a sort of conduit, to help him deliver messages from other departed spirits. He says we have been given a gift."

There it was, out in the open now, what the hell. It was a load off. Jessie felt some better.

"I see...mhmm... and have you also SEEN your father Jessie?"

"Only in the clouds." she answered. Then she remembered Sea had told her not to mention seeing Henry in the clouds.

"Mhmm... and what is your most frightening thought about death, Jessie?"

"Well, since my father died, I'm not afraid of death anymore, but let me think, I used to be afraid of nothingness. I don't know why, since if there's nothing, I wouldn't be feeling anything at all, would I? But that void where there is nothing used to terrify me."

Dr. Desmond said: "Just think about all those void years before you were even born? They weren't so bad now, were they? humm?" He smiled wisely, stroking his silver coil clasp.

Jessie smiled too, through her tears. Then she said: "I believe in reincarnation now too. It's really resurrection. A line has been blurred that can't be unblurred."

"What line is that?" Desmond asked.

Jessie answered, "The line between death and consciousness."

She sat up, smoothed her skirt, wiped her eyes, reached over to the coffee table and took another Hershey's kiss, peeled it and popped it in her mouth.

Desmond was derailed. Why, she hadn't even been under. He released his spell anyway, saying, "When you wake, you'll feel good and relieved and will remember nothing..." and so forth, all the right words. But Jessie was chewing with gusto and hardly seemed to hear him. Next, she offered him a piece of his own candy, aweless. Then she began to cry again for no reason at all that he could see. He handed her tissue after tissue.

Later, when Dr. Desmond reported back to Eli and Smithy, he suspected he'd been trifled with. He fingered his coil and talked rapidly about Jessie, who he considered at the very least pixilated.

"Talking to the dead and hearing them talk back is really sad, really really sad, except to the person it's happening to. She can't accept death. It's too painful for her, so she concocts this story about hearing from her dead daddy, while he's in some sort of bardo between death and rebirth. Her wits are addled, she's exhausted, and she's also cognitively dependent."

"What the hell is that?" said Eli.

"She's in a fugue, in her own mind too much, delusional, addicted to wrong thinking..." and chocolate, he started to add, but held back.

"Jesus," Eli said, "she don't want nothing to die and she's a pseudo-intellectual. We got grounds to fire her for that?"

Desmond said: "Well she wants to deliver messages from the dead on the air."

Smithy jumped up: "What! Are we supposed to believe the spirits of the dead are sitting up there in the clouds mocking us?"

Dr. Desmond smiled, "Mhmm, that's so highly improbable, gentleman, that it's quasi-impossible. We can choose to refute superstition or succumb to it."

The three men looked at each other.

"Bottom line, can she work?"

Desmond spoke easily: "Not right now. Believing in the afterlife is a coward's way of course. But I wouldn't trust her to give this up too easily. She has a strong emotional need to converse with her dead father, who knows why. While it's not exactly schizophrenia... it's not a casual mysticism either. Something else is going on here. This could take a while."

17
One Wing Flapping

After they got the boot from GWN, Seaborn packed up the Land Rover and they headed for their log cabin in the Blue Ridge mountains. "Be a good boy and get her into therapy," Eli had bellowed in the studio in front of everyone, "and get yourself some help too." Seaborn had noticed strange cars parked at the curb outside their Morningside house and he was afraid they were being stalked. The newspaper, radio and TV stations had all reported what Jessie had said on the air; she roused lots of interest with her aberrant statements, even though the station called her form break a simple nervous breakdown.

Their cabin was about two hours north of Atlanta on fifty or so acres atop Cowpen Mountain, the highest point in Georgia. They had named it "One Wing Flapping" for a wooden duck whirl-a-gig which had only one wing and had come with the place. Every free weekend they drove up Cowpen mountain to One Wing, to taste the mountain air, to witness the majestic Blue Ridge Mountain range from their wide front porch and enjoy the unadorned beauty of the trees of the Chattahoochee forest. Jessie loved trees. Seaborn was counting on the place to heal her. All she needed was a long rest.

In the darkening bedroom, Jessie sat in an old Brumby rocker, with a notepad in her lap. Seaborn sat on the floor beside her. For a long while they were quiet, as they looked out the window and watched the sun setting over the Cohutta wilderness. Jessie received a message, the first of many from G.O.'K.: *Everyday give greetings to the sky and the mountains and the sun and the wind...* she wrote it down, determined to record every message now, no matter what.

"We'll take a little time off now and rest," Seaborn said, trying to comfort Jessie, who had been disheartened, but now wore an expression of angelic hardness, like a marble statue. He read the message she was writing down from someone named Isaac: *Don't believe for a minute there are no genuine mermaids, merwomen, or mermen—they thrive in the dark like celery.*

She touched Seaborn's face. "This isn't time off, Sea, we got fired. I got you fired."

He moved his head about like a cat as she stroked his hair. She hadn't touched him like this in a while, she'd been so griefy, so out of it. He loved her touch. He loved her like his own life– that was all he was sure of—and the certainty, an apprehension really, that his love was going to be tested.

"You'll see, we'll come back Jess. You'll be your old self again."

Jessie grew silent, took her hand away.

"You okay?"

"I'm not crazy, Sea. I'm just the only one who can hear these messages."

She told him it was like she was looking out from newly formed Montana's in her mind. He wished he could crawl in there with her and hear it all too. He wished it was him Henry was talking to—he'd send him packing. Then he realized that's why it wasn't him.

"We're always at our best in the mountains." he said.

He rose and led Jessie over to the bed and lay her down on the feather pillows. He began kissing her, stroking her. At the same time, he had a funny feeling; he couldn't help wondering if he dared to make love to a channeling woman. But Jessie responded to him, to the balm he brought to their loss. And in a while, they were making mountain love in the warm sea of the featherbed and, as they always did, they visualized making a baby.

In the middle of the night, Jessie got up, sat before her computer, and tapped out messages as fast as they leapt into her mind. She was distant from Seaborn then, and from ordinary life. Henry told her not to worry about rational vs. irrational. *Use another system of reasoning: no logic—without logic it's indisputable. Science and art and the spiritual world are all the same thing in the universe, and the U is always moving towards becoming more complicated. The computer is sentient. Here, let me show you.*

The messages flowed into her mind; and slid onto her turquoise screen like glycerin: *I was only a pencil in the hand of God the artist,* Mother Theresa chortled. And somebody named Be Full bubbled over: *God is an active verb, connoting the vast harmonic reordering of the Universe from unleashed chaos of energy. Nancy here, I died in 1955, but to pinpoint the moment of death is erroneous, for time is a bubble—Your birth and your death are a long time coming.* And then a message from Mrs. Houseworth of Albemarle County, who said she was a plumber's wife, telling her husband: *Read that Proust you was always trying to get to Herbert because it will round out your plumbing knowledge, and die sober so you'll be alert, I'll be waiting for you.* Jessie loved how everyone was equal in death. The somebodyism that caused people in life to be constantly competing and othering each other was apparently absent in the afterlife. Death aligned every social difference. And while interracial communication failed on Earth, it was the ticket in the great beyond. As the printed-out messages piled up she realized that spirits were color free, status free and had the same weight and value—there was no hierarchy at all in eternity.

In the days and weeks that followed, Jessie continued the work of gathering messages. Swept along the watery, glassy currents of shewing, she was like glass herself, a mirror reflecting the incandescent Henry who roamed the universe culling messages, touching them up, refining language and syntax, using accents, and subtle mannerisms of speech that would clue in the loved ones still on the ground. He was a mimicker, a mockingbird messenger. He tried to keep it light, like he was just entertaining her. He relished being this harbinger, this go-between, a role he had always wanted in life, but hadn't gone for. He'd been way too timid when he was alive, he now realized. It was because he'd quit school in the eighth grade, and it had always shamed him. It was why he'd never had any real confidence. *Imitation is a strong form of love,* he told Jessie. And a torrent of messages followed about love; *T. Lyman, d. 2-6-92, Love is anticipating another person's needs and then trying to meet them. Huxley, d. 11-22-63, There isn't any formula or method You learn to love by loving– by paying attention and doing what one thereby discovers must be done– If two people do this, well, you can see they make love. Arias, d. 9-11-01, The thing about love is it's close to death... it's ferocious like death. T. Wolfe, d. 9-15-38, Loss is made endurable by love and love echoes through eternity. O Lost!*

Jessie was enchanted. She especially marveled at the messages that she recognized as quotes from famous people. Most messages attempted love in its many forms, as though a message could only be driven if there was benevolent energy behind it. Sometimes, unresolved anger, if tinged with understanding and overriding love got through. Even in languages formerly unknown to Henry and Jessie they were facile, often translating out of curiosity, as simply as turning over leaves. Somewhere, someone awaited these messages.

Strangely, there was no malice. What happened to the spirits of the violent, the evil and mean-spirited? More and more Jessie wondered. It was as if violence did not have a part, and bad people didn't make it to wherever Henry was. "Are you in heaven?" she asked him. *I dunno. If this is heaven, it's like your thoughts—it's a thought filled place. I'm out in the universe, still in the Milky Way Galaxy, I think. I'm close to God though, every day I see the hand– God is boundless energy, so much bigger, wider, all-encompassing than any puny religion has it. All this technology put in the brains of humans is the work of God, Jess, and Jazz and Rock n'Roll preceded it, ha ha. All art is God's hand.*

But where are all the bad people? She wondered. "Where are all the common killers?" So far he hadn't found any. Finally, he said: *Ah Jessie Lee, I see now there is no center in violence, never was. It's dead-end. If you do murder, you murder your own spirit, you destroy your soul. I see the banality of evil now– the violent inhumanity of the world that I lived in. The constant sharpening of swords that goes on all across the planet. But war is obsolete. The revolution causing war to be obsolete is already happening. The power is in pacifism now. The reality of nuclear weapons is that they can lay waste to all of life on the planet. So far as I can tell, everything here where I am consists of undiluted love. Its power exceeds the power of evil. Love is the pathway to an eternal summer of the spirit of life—at least I think it must be... and to tell you the truth, I don't look for bad people or bad news. Never liked either one..*

Names were important to Henry, nicknames, pet names, and all other identifying nomenclature. He attached the greatest joy to name-dropping and date-dropping death dates. Sometimes an old phone number or a place identified someone. Sometimes a spirit could remember none of its earthly numbers or names or didn't care to. Henry named these messages Anonymous, or A., and they kept cropping up, along with gurgling babies, and extraordinary sound fragments that were not even words at all in any language that Henry knew of. The babies were angels Henry told Jessie; all dead babies had a place in a covey of angels like in a fairy tale.

Spirits were not always in agreement– there were lots of cosmic arguments, and Jessie found herself intrigued by metaphors and ambiguities. Like: *James Stephens, d. 1950, You must be fit to give before you can be fit to receive. Knowledge becomes lumber in a week, therefore, get rid of it. The box must be emptied before it can be refilled. A sword, a spade, and a thought should never be allowed to rust. Never lay tools on lace.* The next day James Stephens sent another message: *A secret is a weapon and a friend. Man is God's secret, Power is man's secret, Sex is woman's secret. By having much you are fitted to have more. There is always room in the box. The art of packing is the last lecture of wisdom.*

Jessie was beginning to believe that holding opposing views simultaneously was valued in a capricious universe, as well as humor, irony, the simple, the complex, contradictions, and much more that she might not have expected: *Michael, d. 9-11-01, I have the feeling that all that matters is being good, you know, dying with integrity and honesty, because it's like who do you want to be when you're dead? How many people can you cause to think kindly of you when you're dead? But be careful not to be pious, because that's too hard, and you'll be constantly tempted into corruption. Self-righteousness is piety's evil twin.*

Don't get me wrong Jess, I haven't found any murderers that I know of, but the standards aren't that high. Lots of ordinary sinners here. Liars that consider themselves creatives. One spirit told me he pilfered a lot. I myself used to clip things that weren't nailed down. Stealing is my shameful secret. My conscience always bothered me. Haven't found any really bad people here, no haters though, lots of contrite old sweethearts, mostly penitent spirits.

Seaborn moved a comfortable wing chair in front of Jessie's workstation, where she often fell asleep, a cigarette left burning in the ashtray. She told him that even in her dreams she got messages. He would wake to the sound of the printer spitting out reams of messages, as constant sounding as the hither and thithering waters of the mountain spring that brought fresh water to them. Spirits were scanning their mysterious sparks of consciousness into the computer. Was the computer sentient like Henry claimed? Seaborn wondered how that could be possible.

Great stacks of printouts accumulated on the floor of the cabin. E-mail from eternity constantly filled her screen in the exact words of the spirit Henry was relaying: *A., Woo-Woo, some of us can trance. But off-hand, I'd rather play the course. J. Nicolas, d. 2000, me too. Happily, I returned to my peak after I died. Glick, d. 9-11-01, I did a little judo on them, next thing I know the really bright lights came on. Williams, d. 9-11-01, Hey I'm still your father. Give that cell phone the old heave-ho. Use your brain cells.* A lot of cryptic messages came through from the 9-11-01 date, a tragic moment in time never to be forgotten.

Seaborn saw that the fax machine seemed to work of its own volition– Henry had tapped into the phone line. He could beat the time it takes a microwave to bounce off a satellite and return to Earth. He told Jessie: *It's pure radio out here. I operate in cones, moving from the wide end, right down into the narrow, funneling to you, sphere after sphere, words from people who all once walked on the ground. To tell you the truth, I might be hearing from some strong spirits still down there, bouncing back at me. you know, like reverb.* He tried to take the sting out of death as they worked together, sharing the same skull. I'm closer than your skin. *Don't think of me as dead. That's the best thing you can do,* he whispered, and Jessie shivered.

If Seaborn had any doubts before, and he did, the outflow of messages alone was enough to show him that the computer and Henry, or whatever was driving the computer besides Jessie, was etherealizing their existence. Seaborn had relied on a prescribed, preestablished collection of certainties all his life. Now he had to look obliquely at life, with wonder, not knowing.

Jessie's nerve ways were open to every sensation, and the possibility of sudden new intensities. She went around barefooted, saying shoes blinded her feet. She wore inside-out sweats and mismatched clothes in color combinations resembling the Good Will's supply of lost socks. For the first time since he'd known her, she was able to tolerate messes, disarranged furniture, piles of laundry and dirty dishes. Seaborn, always a believer in lost causes, began to believe in ghost epiphanies, and when he dared, in e-mail from eternity. It was better than believing that what Henry was doing was driving Jessie mad, and she was truly insane.

"You sure you want to do this?" he asked Jessie nearly every day, regarding her doubtfully, but he always got similar answers:

"I have no choice. I can't hear AROUND these messages. I can't go blind to my e-mail."

Seaborn had lots of time on his hands to work on the cabin and property, doing all the deferred maintenance he'd never gotten around to before. He grew to like doing laundry, washing dishes, and straightening up. The mindless organization of housework was something he could control. They had a pantry and a freezer full of food and he loved to cook, but he lacked fresh produce. He poked the hard red-clay ground with a shovel, turning the redolent soil over, wishing for a plow and seeds. If April and May had been their cruelest months, he hoped June might not be too late to start a garden. One of the messages had been: *The Earth is a Mother that must never die.* He wanted to reach into the earth for the desert places in his own self, try to recapture that calm peace that he'd known in nature when he was a child. In rooting the food they needed to survive, he hoped to recover his own roots as well.

In early June, he left Jessie alone for a while and went down the mountain into the town of Mineral Bluff to get supplies. As he drove, he thought about his Indian connections, sheet, and feather, as Henry used to say. Seaborn's own father was a native of Georgia, half Creek Indian on his mother's side, half Welsh on his father's. The grandfather, who he never knew, John Playfair Pettengill, had emigrated from Wales to Georgia, and married a Creek Indian woman. They produced Seaborn's father who was also named John Playfair. Young John Playfair had been sent to Oxford to get the Indian educated out of him, but it didn't work. Before he came back home to Georgia, he married a Sri Lankan girl he met at Oxford, Seaborn's mother. She gave birth to Seaborn aboard ship on their way back to America and named him for that defining moment and place.

And then when he was five years old, his mother died suddenly of an aneurysm. He remembered sitting on his grieving father's knee, feeling heartsick as he looked way up at the white lacquered coffin that held his mother. She was so still—what to do with all this fullness of love he felt for her?

He swallowed it, kept it inside like a sweet secret. He'd done something then that soothed him, but whatever it was he didn't remember it. Only that afterwards he'd been set free of his pain. It didn't jive with popular sentiment, the way he'd gotten over his grief so easily, and grownups were suspicious and looked at him and wondered. But Seaborn was too young to tell them, and now he still couldn't remember.

He'd inherited his Father's panther-like body, and shared his interest in all knowledge, though he'd never been a scholar like his father, and had only gotten by in school, was bored by it, and liked to do things with his hands. He hoped he had his grandmother's American Indian instincts. He knew he had his mother's skin, a color between peanuts and curry, and her nature too, which included a relaxation of self-interest strivings and a belief in the limits of ego. At an early age he knew instinctively that "I" misrepresented the infinite. He thought of how often this had been mistaken for humility. Egotism and machismo were expected in the American male, and when they weren't there people were thrown off balance. He could always see when someone decided he was a wimp. But he didn't care.

Down in Mineral Bluff, at a second-hand shop, Seaborn found an old hand plow, and an old pitchfork, the wooden handles of both worn and smoothed by many hands before. He thought well used tools with a good vibe might help him, since he knew nothing about gardening. He also found some old golf clubs, a driver and a putter, and a sack of balls. Why not whack some balls to relieve his stress and maybe appease Henry. At the Farm store, he picked up the Old Farmer's Almanac and read about lasagna gardening, layering peat moss, compost, newspapers, and planting the seeds in the middle like cheese. He bought a hoe, a spade, and Burpee seeds: lettuce, peas, corn, shallots, cucumber, radishes, butterbeans, arugula, watermelon, and a huge bag of sunflower seeds for the birds. He studied the flowers. The roses looked like bundles of sticks, so he chose flats of baby's breath, snapdragons, Foxglove, Lilly-of-the-valley, and sprouted sweet peas for Jess, and stinky marigolds for bug control. He would not use pesticides. He bought garlic and multiplying onions, beds of sprouted tomatoes, strawberries, raspberries, and asparagus plants. He whistled as he drove back up the mountain, his Rover loaded with loot and smelling like a hayride after a June rain.

He was so excited he forgot how long he'd been gone, leaving Jessie all alone. He sped up the mountain, suddenly afraid of stalkers, and as he crested the last ridge, he saw them. Despite his NO TRESPASSING sign, a white media truck from a station in South Carolina with a satellite dish on top was in the driveway, and three stranger vehicles were parked in the clearing in front of the cabin.

Jessie was up on the porch looking pale and wearing a false smile. A carload of hippies, high on something, was chanting and dancing around the clearing, banging on tambourines and goading Jessie to join them, moving in closer and closer. But they didn't scare her half as much as a group of stern women all dressed in black and standing outside their van scowling as if they came to crucify her. It was messy and she was terrified. All she could think of was "Duck and Cover." Then she saw Seaborn, and she waved desperately.

The guy with the satellite dish was getting ready to film it all when Seaborn walked up to him, blocked his camera, and yelled: "Get the hell out of here, all of you!" Behind Seaborn came a Forrest Ranger, hidebound against trespassers. He helped Seaborn run everyone off, threatening to arrest them if they crossed the NO TRESPASSING signs again. He advised

Seaborn to block the road with his Rover until he could get a fence put up. Seaborn had known this ranger for a long time, ever since they'd bought One Wing, but it was the first time they had been saved by him and Seaborn was grateful. As they shook hands, he wondered how much the ranger knew about Jessie. The ranger gave Seaborn the name of a fence builder, his own cell number, and said to call him if he had any more trouble. He wished Seaborn good luck with his garden and waved to Jessie as he drove away.

Jessie went inside the cabin and collapsed on the couch. Seaborn hurried in to see how she was; it seemed like he was constantly asking her if she was okay. He was sorry for staying away so long though, and he sat with her until she was calm again, and she could sink back into her obsession for gathering messages.

The next day, in the warm spring air he began the backbreaking work of clearing a patch of ground. First, he had to battle the kudzu and fierce weeds, long established. He chopped and dug with the hoe, mindful of the roots, then giving up and hacking away at them. He was out of shape, physically unused to such strenuous work. He pulled his white shirt off and worked out his aggressions in a lather of sweat. What am I so mad about? he grumbled to himself. He knew it was Henry; the dead were supposed to desert you, not tyrannize you like this; you give them a chance, they hold on to the living. Seaborn believed in an unseeable plane, in reincarnation, in souls leaping boundaries, at least in theory. When you are in tune with the unknown, the known is peaceful is what he liked to believe. But Henry's fantastic domination of Jessie was too much. He had no way of understanding it and he felt left out. He had no way of avoiding feeling jealous; the green devil he despised. Against his own better judgement, he was envious.

He labored and brooded, turning the fragrant earth over and over, dropping to the ground and sifting it with his bare hands. He loved the ripe smell of dirt. He thought about his own father, the brave man who'd raised him alone. He was a cosmologist at Emory University now, and he worked on spaceships. Always gone, but very much alive. He had been an Oxford hippie in the seventies and had given Seaborn good hippie values: a love for atoms, an awareness of the interrelatedness of all matter, living things, and occurrences. He wished he could talk to him now about what was happening.

After a couple of hours with his face to the earth, Seaborn looked up and studied the shape-shifting clouds. He saw expanding billows of information in them, tactile knowledge, not words or pictures. He saw the difference between the way nature works and the language man thinks in; working a garden with his hands was showing him that paradox. If the nineteenth century was an age of river seekers, and the twentieth of planet seekers, surely the twenty-first would be the age of reclaiming the earth, of coming home. All nature would be new to art all over again, and this time with respect. Space and consciousness exploration were alike to him.

He planned to garden by the moon, 238,000 miles close— sow seeds that produced their yield above ground on the new moon, and sow root vegetables that yielded below ground on the full moon. Or was it the other way around? He'd check the Farmer's Almanac. His Creek Indian grandmother had planted by the moon, in ground not far from there. He wanted to place himself and Jessie in ecological harmony with an awakening world. He believed the next century would show the last that it had endured a dark and meager consciousness. As he put his back into it, using muscles he'd never used before, he felt the hot sun purifying him.

The rich voice of Nat King Cole came wafting out the window and spread across the garden like warm rain: "Unforgettable...in every way...unforgettable though near or far...how the thought of you does things to me...," Seaborn sang along, it was wonderful. Who turned the radio on? He looked through the window and saw Jessie gazing at the computer monitor, oblivious to the music that was coming out of it.

At sundown, Seaborn quit, exhausted. He wiped sweat across his beaded forehead, picked up his white long-tail shirt and hung it on an upended shovel he'd stuck into the ground, making a scarecrow. It looked like a ghost fluttering in the breezy shank of the evening. He went inside and soaked in a tub of warm water and Epsom salts, moaning. He could still taste the earth; the nose piercing smell of it was in his head. The next day he could hardly walk, and he was sun-burned, but he got back to work. The moon was three-quarters full, and he had to have the ground ready to plant on the full moon, and then again on the wane.

In the droughty days and weeks that followed, he hauled up buckets of water from the spring, trying to keep the ground moist so the seeds would germinate, and prayed for rain. They sprouted finally, although many of them keeled over.

That same night a torrent of messages fell like ripe peaches into the fax lap. When Henry said: *listen to me, let my mood dominate,* Jessie obeyed. The mouse began a movement of its own on Jessie's computer, clicking through programs until it found a way to draw the Earth on the screen and a diagram of the summer solstice. Jessie showed Seaborn the phenomenal pictures. Then came the words: *Fertility is hooked up with the whole cycle of life, with the Earth, the solstice, the harvest, food. It's all about agriculture. For food to flourish... food flourish food flourish food flourish...* the words were stuck, blinking on the screen like a neon sign. But Seaborn felt Henry was talking to him, finally.

A few minutes later, Jessie received a message from a John Burroughs, no date, to his beloved Lisa Marie. She tapped the message out on the keys: *I found my angel twin, and we want to guide you. The best thing you can do is try to save the land. Try and stop the poisoning of the land. If you don't have good pure agriculture and water, the Earth is going to die. I know how important art and race are to you sweetheart, but they won't matter if there's no Earth.* Seaborn was amazed. He looked at a pile of printouts with the initials J.C. on them and read: *As a white candle / In a holy place / So is the beauty / Of an aged face / Her brood gone from her / And her thoughts as still / As the water / Under a ruined mill.* He recognized Joseph Campbell's poem. "Some of these characters said these same things when they were alive so why are they disrupting our lives by sending these messages again?" he asked Jessie.

"I don't know," she answered, "Maybe the ego doesn't die. Maybe because the times are dire, and people didn't listen before. I don't always get a name or a date. It's like once you're dead no one needs to do anything for money or power or ego anymore, so why bother with a name? Some of the ones that give a name or date want to reach a loved one, is all; they want to offer reassurance."

"Seems like your father hasn't lost his ego."

Jessie just shrugged.

As the weeks went by, the day came when Seaborn started to worry about money. They had bills to pay, and the severance as well as their savings was nearly gone. Although they had closed up the house in Morningside, it still had a mortgage; utilities and taxes to pay. They would probably have to sell it. He knew he could go down the mountain and get a job, except he was afraid to leave Jessie alone, even though the high fence was up now. What was happening to her was miraculous and immense, yet it also hobbled her. He could see that Jessie, formerly his liberty, was now a prisoner of Henry's indomitable spirit. She'd been sucked into the lives of the dead and had been ever since Henry died. They were being held captive by something bigger than both of them, and he couldn't see any way out.

Seaborn suspected that Jessie was no longer bound to her physical frame; she seemed free, roaming out there with Henry, on to the next tee, like they were playing a round of golf. So far, she had always come back. But what if she didn't? She had refused therapy with Dr. Desmond, saying he had nothing to offer but chocolate. Seaborn had found a nice female therapist in Blue Ridge, who was willing to come up the mountain and pay them a house call. After one session with Jessie, she told Seaborn that auditory hallucinations were common; when your loved one dies, you want to hear them, so you do. And that hearing the voice of God, or feeling grace singling you out, descending on you, was evidence of an unstable temporal lobe. But Jessie countered, "Henry is not God." And she maintained that no one could possibly understand this. Like so many Irish, she was impervious to psychotherapy.

Jessie's state of being had begun to encompass Seaborn utterly. For what was marriage if it wasn't living inside another person's insanity? Even if it was only mundane. But he didn't think Jessie's insanity was mundane; it was mystical and other worldly and most of all not entirely under her control.

Seaborn had never felt so helpless before. He practiced Tai Chi daily. He whacked golf balls into the Forrest and made a smooth grass mound with a hole in it for a putting green. He fished for trout, picked apples. The garden kept him going, confounding him too. How did farmers do it? The deer ate the corn, birds drilled holes in the tomatoes, the asparagus would take years to produce something edible. Every day he weeded and fought off the rabbits and squirrels for the few meager vegetables they left him. After a while, all they left was garlic and onions. If a family was depending on him for food, they'd starve. He felt like the worst farmer on the planet. In the back of his mind, he plowed a space for the day when Jessie "finished" this obsession, and they could return to Atlanta and their broadcasting careers. He longed for the ordinary things, like his job, supermarkets, his Gym, going out to dinner and dancing, plays and movies, back when they had been normal people. How long could he continue on like this? What about their dream of starting a family? How could they do that now?

18
Angels Spotted

Seaborn brooded in the pantry surveying their stores. They had long since eaten everything he'd harvested from the garden; the lions share went to the bugs, rabbits and deer. He wanted to get some Geese- they were good watchdogs- but Jessie was adamant, "No Geese!" Growing food was so much harder than he had ever imagined. The only vegetables still going were Arugula and onions. They liked cold weather. He found an unopened jar of Henry's persimmon jelly from year before last, but nothing to spread it on. He'd run out of all the ingredients for making bread. There was oatmeal, three cans of soup, a bag of dried navy beans and a pack of Turkey-Jerky. He put the beans on to soak. Jessie loved beans. They'd been out of work for seven months, and after he paid all the bills for the month they were down to their last fifty bucks. He slammed the lid on the pot. One thing they did have plenty of was crickets and he'd perfected a cricket stir-fry with arugula and onions that was tasty as well as good protein. Jessie loved it. He didn't tell her she was eating crickets.

He could hear Oprah Winfrey wrapping her new show which featured mediums and psychics, and he sidled over to the TV to watch as Oprah said:

Ever since Ground Witness News Anchor, Jessie Pettengill had a spiritual breakthrough, or breakdown, depending on your point of view, the question has been: Will your own ancestors talk? Tune in tomorrow when my guests will be famous

116

psychics who claim to have the answers, and the doctor who diagnosed Jessie. Here's a clip. . .

Dr. Desmond came on in a segment from his interview with Oprah:

The classic case of death denial is a form of narcissistic self-absorption. Nobody knows what death is, except perhaps the dead and they aren't talking, heh, heh, not out loud at least. Who wouldn't want to be a bridge between the living and the dead? But we must be careful of these delusions when a loved-one dies. Mystical dementia is an international plague in our time... when one seeks to change reality, one usually self destructs.

Dr. Desmond fondled his silver coil, and gave his best know-it-all smile, while Oprah's theme music came up and the credits rolled.

"You're full of shit, Desmond!" Seaborn leapt up fuming. He felt like a ball of lead was in his stomach. His anguish swamped the room. He changed the channel.

Just then, Jessie came floating out of the bedroom. With her was an elderly archangel in a purple frock, with huge white wings tucked behind her, and a pleasant face, like Shirley MacLaine's. The two of them sat down on the couch in front of the TV.

"What's the matter, Sea?"

"Nothing," he snapped.

"I heard you yelling."

"It was just something on TV. You've got to eat more Jessie. You're looking skinny."

"I'm not hungry."

Jessie was a bit bedraggled, tired, unsmiling. She rested her hand atop the archangel's sitting next to her. But Seaborn sat down right on top of the archangel, who vanished, and

Jessie realized he couldn't see her. Jessie looked at her absence on the lumpy couch and Seaborn thought she was looking at him.

He stared back at Jessie lynx-eyed. Was she all there? He couldn't help doubting. Was he, for sticking around? He had to do something. How could they just go on like this?

She patted his leg as if she could read his mind.

Ground Witness News was coming on, their old show—they hadn't watched it since...quickly Seaborn started to change channels, but Jessie stopped him, "Let's watch okay?"

There was a new, attractive news anchor who spoke with breathless impatience:

> *Today six Russian cosmonauts reported sighting a spectacular band of angels with wings as big as gumbo—uh, jumbo jets...on their...*

"She can barely talk," said Seaborn.

> *...on their one hundred fifty-fifth day aboard the orbiting Space Station. Here's the report...*

Seaborn frowned. "I suppose that's under-appreciated in an anchor."

Jessie put her arm around him and drew him closer. They watched as the screen showed a satellite picture of the interior of the space station where six cosmonauts bobbed for face time in front of the camera. One of them spoke in English with a Russian accent:

> *We saw seven giant figures in the form of humans, but with huge white wings and misty halos, like the classic depiction of angels in ancient art. They were smiling as though they shared in a glorious secret. For us, it was proof of life in the hereafter.*

Jessie whooped, "It's Sukeroff."

"How do you know?" Seaborn said.

"He's come before. I've seen him in his angel form, just like my grandmother takes. I don't know how they do it.

"Yeah, and why do they want to?" Seaborn grumbled.

"Because angels admire the living Sea. We're the lucky ones." She smiled, trying to cheer him up, "Sukeroff is restless though. He wants to help the Russian people so much. His love is strong. He's been advancing toward incarnation and he's almost ready to be released into life again. He said he hoped his death was only going to be a slight hesitation before rebirth. I'll show you the message if you like."

Seaborn stared at Jessie like she was crazy, guilty of magical thinking, as usual, while he had to contend with the realities.

His stomach growled.

At the same time, a delightfully impossible idea began to take shape in his mind. The idea grew, slid, and hopped, like a banana foot, a rabbit peel. It was so over the top of anything he'd ever thought of before that in the novelty of the moment he began to look at everything differently. Mystical dementia looked like an arbiter of chance. His mind shifted and drifted, as boundaries slipped. Hopeless diversity looked like opportunity. The smile on Jessie's face that was vacuous and irritating to him a minute before now looked right, so right.

From limbo, he had been delivered to the crest of a wave, by a simple, inevitable idea. It was kismet. He could barely contain himself.

Just then Jessie received a message from Henry: *You don't have to try to think outside the box Jess, you have to think further inside it than you ever have before. Here's one from Theodore Roethke: What we need is more people who specialize in the impossible.*

19
The Pitch

The next day Seaborn was up with the sun, ready to go. He felt uneasy about leaving Jessie alone, but he had no choice. The new fence was in place now and he called his Forrest Ranger friend and asked him to look out for Jessie while he was gone. He left her barefoot at the computer, with a big bowl of navy beans, and drove the ninety-five miles to Atlanta, going over in his mind the whole way how he would present his idea, the utter logical justice of it, the beauty of a divine impossibility rendered. He was jumpy, scared, but exuberant.

At the station, Seaborn joined Eli, and Smithy in the control booth as they taped the Reverend Thackston's show. He found the producers hostile, reluctant to make time for him, defensive as hell. He was willing to wait. He hadn't called ahead for an appointment because he was afraid they'd turn him down or give him the slip with their rotary phone menus. When the Reverend's taping concluded, Seaborn made a racket unloading Jessie's printouts onto a table from his backpack, hundreds of messages. Some were too long, would have to be edited. Henry wasn't choosy and didn't care a lick about time. Seaborn would edit them later– he had to pitch his idea now, as is.

Eli and Smithy glanced at the huge, messy pile indifferently. Their eyebrows said NO.

Seaborn stayed standing. He didn't know where to start, so he took a deep breath, closed his eyes and plunged in, gesturing wildly:

"Maybe there are things, that with all the information we have, we still just don't understand. The problem is... is that everybody's always trying to be rational, but rational thinking is too limited, it's this box that doesn't serve the whole truth because it lacks the roundness, ambiguity, and mobiusity of the universe."

Eli and Smithy looked at Seaborn with interest, like he was crazy.

"Look at these names!" he continued, "Ordinary people all mixed together with famous people. The mighty and the obscure, all alike out there, just trying to get a message through." Seaborn fanned the messages out on the table and swallowed hard.

Smithy said, "Jesus, what do we look like, Western Union?" Idly he read the message on top of the heap from a guy with two front names: "Tell the boys to follow, to be faithful, to take me seriously." Henry James. d. 1916.

"All I'm asking," said Seaborn, "is we test the water. You guys know that anchors need immediate gratification. She'll die up there on that mountain without an audience."

"Yeah," said Eli, "what I know is you want us to dance with wolves like you do." He glanced at the messages and shoved the pile over to Smithy. "I'm taking my exercise now." Eli left the booth, muttering, "all I need– a mouthpiece from beyond." He went outside and galumphed around the building, to get his cardio-vascular up.

While he was gone, Seaborn worked on Smithy even though it appeared hopeless. Getting the right words out was like eating hairs. He had never pitched a show before in his life, never thought he'd have to. But he had to make Smithy see the whole big picture. "We get it out of the news atmosphere, start small, see if the demand is there." Seaborn was saying, when Eli came back in, all sweaty and wheezing.

Smithy said: "I don't know, it's kinda thin," he felt like humoring Seaborn, "How is Jessie different from any other weird sister popping up for the new millennium?"

Seaborn danced around the table, his energy mounting, "because by god, she names names! death dates! Everyone knows someone who has passed. The audience of the dead is a vast untapped demographic, a potential goldmine. The living will watch with bated breath. Don't you get it? She has to deliver these messages. This is the real thing. If you guys don't do it, someone else will."

"We got a few letters, some of its hate mail," said Eli, huffy. In his mind, he opened the door of the closet where they crammed all the mail they'd received, and got bombarded with thousands of cards, letters, and checks; boxes of ashes even, remains. Lot of crazy's out there.

"People are afraid of what they can't believe, but they're also curious as hell." Seaborn argued. "We could call it..."The Life of Death Show." He swept his arms wide to help them visualize the name in lights.

"Oh, Christ, that sounds perky." said Eli.

Smithy was busy reading the messages. "Hey, listen to this one, 'Give your money away. Use it. Make beauty with it. Help someone get comfortable,' from some guy named Turner, claims he had unspent millions."

"I like the concept," said Eli, "give your money away, but like, who's gonna do that?"

"Lots of people," said Seaborn, "once they know they don't need it anymore, once they see there's someplace else to go where money is not the currency, where it's worthless."

Smithy guessed, "They'll give it to Jessie? so they can keep on hearing from their dead loved ones?"

"Right! and death gets a life." Seaborn said.

They all laughed heartily.

Seaborn lowered himself into a chair and exhaled. He knew he had them then. Eli said to Seaborn, "You're a pretty smart guy, lot smarter than I took you for." "Yeah?" Seaborn grinned. "Let's talk about money."

Back at One Wing, Jessie sat at the computer wearing the headphones Seaborn had fixed her up with, listening to the tune, in a version performed by Sting, although other sounds layered and crisscrossed it. Utterances joined in and rose to a pitch causing Jessie's face to go from rapture to agitated. She snatched off the headphones and held her throbbing head in both hands. Waves of nausea rocked her. She hardly had the strength to read the messages coming off the FAX: *Fore! You're blocking again. Soon as you let the messages FLOW, you'll be okay. Anything dead coming back to life hurts. Don't waggle so much you forget your purpose. Here's some psychic grease; Open open open open open open open open open* ...The "opens" trailed off the page like oily snails, soothing her, like standing under a waterfall. She felt as though she was in training for something rigorous like an Olympics, and it was costing her.

Henry tried to keep his voice steady and real for her, so she wouldn't be so distressed. He had started using a loud fore! to signal when he was coming through. She wanted to duck. Other Henry's played in his messages with a wry wit: *Henry, d. 11-29-01, What's all the fuss about? It's not bad being dead. I miss the Earth and all the people though... Ut oh, here comes a ball, or is that the sun?* She thought of a message she'd gotten earlier in the day from Joseph Cambell: *You must be willing to get rid of the life you planned, so you can have the life that is waiting for you.* Sometimes she thought Henry was drawing from <u>Bartlett's Familiar Quotations,</u> one of his favorite books. That would be just like him. He'd always been a plagiarizer, an impersonator, claiming everything was derivative anyway. She felt Cambell's message was meant especially for her. Would she comply?

Jessie sunk to the cold pine floor, tucked her head in her arms, shut her eyes and shivered. It was winter already, and dark. The wind howled outside, rattling the windows. She was alone but the room was morbidly crowded. She missed Seaborn so, he'd been gone for hours.

"Oh, where are you Seaborn?" she muttered, "I'm so hungry and there's nothing to eat. Are we living in some kind of a fool's paradise?"

20
The LODS

And so, at a time of horror shows, of vampires and zombies and viruses, genocide and the diversity of terrorism, Eli and Smithy mounted THE LIFE OF DEATH SHOW. It was November 1, All Saints Day. There was a makeshift set; the budget was small, so Seaborn had to do everything: he was creator, director, and camera operator. Two loyal P.A.'s from the news show had volunteered to help. The first few broadcasts would be taped, to preview both the material and Jessie's stability, planning to go live if everything worked out. They'd test the show in a limited market, and then take it national. It would be a wild card to play, but a feather in Eli and Smithy's cap if by some miracle, it caught on. If the wave held, was how Henry thought of it.

Jessie sat at a computer, strumming away, THE LIFE OF DEATH SHOW emblazoned in neon lights above her desk, while Seaborn leaned in behind a robotic camera, his eyes aglint with mischief. He was happily back in his element. No studio audience, no one in the studio at all, but them and a skeleton crew. Jessie was once again happy to be back on set. She wore her mountain clothes, blue jeans, and a cream-colored blouse, and forgot about make-up. When the set lights came up, and the neon faded, Jessie looked up from her desk and began talking, casually, in no hurry, unlike the news. Even on that first show she exhibited none of the backsliding that was expected from six months' absence in front of the camera. None of the nervousness common on the first tee, not a tremble, not a yip. She was relaxed, not perky.

She didn't force a smile. She didn't try to duplicate Henry's impersonations either, she was just herself.

She looked with intent and purpose straight into the eyes and hearts of her viewers, and brought it home:

This first message is from Harry Rotenberg, who died on the twenty-second of October,

(Jessie looked at her calendar watch) *only ten days ago. He wants his wife Toukie Rotenberg to listen up.* (Long pause) *Toukie, are you listening? Harry has figured out the formula for charm and he wants you to have one last crack at it in your old age. Now here's his message: Nothing matters but DRAMATIC BENEVOLENCE. . . Did you get that Toukie? dramatic benevolence. Now here's the key to CHARM: Charm is the absence of excitement, it's COOL. Excitement uses up too damn much natural energy, Harry says. You burn it up getting excited, and you haven't any energy left to project charm. If you don't get too excited, you'll have TIME to be charming– he wants you to try it. Okay Toukie? He wants you to find another husband. You're too good to spend time alone.*

A tear rolled down Jessie's cheek, not of sorrow but of joy– not really her tear, but Henry's, or maybe Harry's. She tipped her head as if listening, and continued messaging.

And listen—what was that tune backgrounding the show? another one of Seaborn's ideas: "The Windmills Of Your Mind." This wonderous version playing was by Dusty Springfield.

The commercial value of the show was undetermined. Eli and Smithy didn't think advertisers would be willing to align with a cockamamie seer, so they encouraged a subtle hint for donations, and Jessie agreed if the suggestion could be construed from Henry's messages. She knew everyone always had to make money. Life was about commerce. How else to live? Henry of course knew it too. One of these early broadcasts produced a bundle:

You can take with you: love, beauty, truth, honor, and stupidity too, so watch out; your integrity, character, a sense of humor, a good eye for measurements, says Einstein, who also says, Time is love. That's why you can see something happening before it does. It already has happened in the recent future of this dream on Earth. Forget about power and fighting over Real Estate. Go after beauty like it's a food group– don't worry about what it is anymore, a waste of energy, you'll recognize beauty if it feeds your soul, alters your mood in some good way. When you find beauty, absorb it, hang on to it, enjoy it. And give your money away. If you are not going to use it now, when are you? Make poetry with it. Move information. That's from a Mr. Turner, more or less, and some others, who want to remain anonymous.

Henry had messed with that message quite a bit. The show had to be monetized. And so it began. Jessie charmed her audience, transmitted oceanic love. Connection with spirits was better than most condolence. She held nothing back, as though she was filling from beneath, like well-water, and the source was unlimited. She was engaged in the rarified luxury of smoothing the bed of cruel death. And Henry had convinced her she had a gift for it. *Our task is to let the soul rise from its prison into the light.* He told her, and she acquiesced. People loved hearing from a recently passed loved one, the sooner the better.

Then when Eli and Smithy could easily have found sponsors, Seaborn insisted on keeping a noncommercial status instead, supported by donations, and paying them all salaries, based on a percentage of the money that came rolling in. Also, they would sell DVD's and CD's of the shows, and transcripts bound into books. He knew commercial sponsors would start making requests, and then demands, and Jessie was not of a mind to obey anyone but Henry.

Eli and Smithy faded more and more into the cyber-ground, watching the monitors for messages, not sending any notes themselves, the way producers usually do. For one thing, they could not reach Jessie. "Keep it perky" meant nothing to her anymore if it ever had. When she required silence, she stopped and stared like a cow into the camera for whole minutes– producing that dreaded, dead airtime that was anathema to broadcasting. She sometimes giggled about it, while Eli and Smithy cringed. Jessie would allow no fill. It was like she was insisting upon a new appreciation for space and time, showing an openness to the unknown which might appear at any moment on a live medium. *TV momentum is an artificially created heartbeat. I am here with you in real time.* She said, giving everyone a chance to catch up and digest what they were seeing and hearing. *Speed is a greatly overrated concept, and technology, while wonderful, is often too fast. For some reason, and it strikes me as bizarre, people try to prove themselves by going fast. Speed makes a soul rancorous, it's not satisfying. Slowness is. Hesitation is intuition's chance.*

Everyone knew Henry was talking through Jessie; she was his "mouthpiece." Eli and Smithy worried constantly that Henry might at any time stop talking to Jessie. And it was Henry who put the idea into Seaborn's head for another neon sign. It flashed: THERE IS STILL TIME.

Jessie had her own little sign to remind her to keep it funny and graceful. She'd written it on a yellow post-it note and stuck it on her P.C. It said: Elvis is watching you.

The LIFE OF DEATH SHOW was gaining an audience at the speed of light. In late December, affiliate stations nation-wide picked it up, and all sorts of wonky cult groups glommed onto the LODS, as the show came to be called. People had begun gathering on the sidewalk outside their Morningside home and Seaborn had to hire security. They were glad to be back in the city, but they couldn't just go out to a restaurant anymore without being accosted. The newspapers, magazines and TV Networks all loved the story of Jessie's entrancement or possession or whatever crazy name they chose to call it. Sometimes there were days when Henry was silent, dormant. Once for a whole week. Then they had to rely on the stacks of accumulated messages to fill the show. This made the producers antsy. Seaborn told Jessie, "There are about twenty-five billion embedded chips in the world– about the same as the number of cells in a human body. We have to be vigilant about our e-mail, make sure it's all really from Henry.

Fore! The business of Apocalyptic prophesy is the oldest profession, not prostitution. It's as old as religion itself, debuting around 200 BC. The word APOKALYPTEIN comes from the Greek verb, "to reveal" and the Greek Delphic Oracles were all women. So, watch out for the sand traps Jessie, and don't forget who you are.

"The End Is Near" people were bustling about: the cover of one of their magazines had a headline: "FOR GOD SO LOVED THE WORLD THAT HE SENT HIS ONLY BEGOTTEN DAUGHTER" Under the headline was a picture of Jessie, looking indifferent. So, a crown of laurels had been airbrushed on her head. Jessie laughed when she saw it. "Who dreams this stuff up?" she asked Seaborn, who shuddered, not venturing a guess.

Not for a second did Jessie believe herself divinely instructed, whatever that might be. She knew she was only a conduit, and a handmaiden to her father, as she'd been when he was alive. In fact, messaging seemed to her to have very little to do with God or religion, although she believed in a God, the designer and master architect of the Universe and everything in it, the original audience, creator, and holder of all secrets. It was her constant awe of God's creativity that was her faith. There had been a message that made her laugh from Luis Bunuel declaring *I am an atheist still, thank God.* And a spirit named Peter had quipped: *It is the final proof of God's omnipotence that he need not exist in order to save us.*

On the next LODS broadcast, Jessie said: *I am the daughter of God in the same way that you are the daughters and sons of God. There are 10,000 religions in the world, and Gandhi said God has no religion. God gave us free will and he's watching what we do with it. Going to church doesn't make you a Christian any more than standing in a garage makes you a car.*

Most of what Jessie said did not sit well with some Christians; they sent letters to the LODS, threatening Jessie. Religious news organs condemned her in print. Churches grew agitated. Sermons became interesting again, with a new enemy of righteousness. But there were many more Christians who loved Jessie's messages and believed in a spiritual afterlife right along with her.

Jesus might come back as a magician, Seaborn figured, like that David Blaine guy who was so amazing. Seaborn loved magic. There was a dance, with magicians entertaining, at the Biltmore's Georgian Ballroom on New Year's Eve, and he wanted to take Jessie. It would be their first appearance in public since the LODS began. Seaborn also loved to dance. But Henry put the kibosh on it, sent a warning not to go: *It's too dangerous right now. Stay home and read a book; reading is a gateway to deep time. I was so crushed by clocks when I was alive that I rode a golf cart around the course, in a big hurry. That's the very opposite of what golf is about, and life too. You're not in a hurry anymore once you're dead. Start the new year slow. Every day is a special occasion in the universe.*

Henry claimed to be embedded outside of time now– it stood still for him. He'd rushed around all his life, trying to beat the clock. The messages that came through on New Year's Day were all about the same subject, not the end of time, but the end of the domination of time: *Time follows, imitates you. When you get in a hurry, time flies. If you slow down, time goes slower. Look at life as a marathon, not a sprint—you can do everything over a lifetime, but not all at once. Dividing time into hour and half hour segments is not natural, it ruins time. That's what's wrong with TV. No name with that one, sorry. Oh, here's a name, R. Frost, d. 1963: Time walks by your side unwilling to pass.*

Then for days afterwards, all the messages that came to Jessie were about time, as though Henry had given an assignment to the dead. *Morales, d. 9-11-01: Time is what I didn't have enough of. Now I don't need it. Tell my niece she's nice, and I went to Mexico. Adam, d. 9-11-01: I saw my fate. I jumped while I still had time to get away from that greasy flannel smoke. The last thing I saw was a beautiful troika of red fire engines. W. James, d. 1910: Common sense and a sense of humor are the same thing, moving at different speeds. A sense of humor is just common-sense dancing. Elizabeth Rosemond Taylor, d. 2011: The shorter our time, the greater our capacity for waiting.*

The terrorism of the new century had brought with it a boom in spirituality and religion. For years, ordinary people had half-expected to find Jesus or Elvis in some form or another walking the Earth again. Because lots of impossible to believe things had happened, it became easier to believe the fantastic, the improbable. Many people who had vowed when they were alive to "talk" from their graves when they died did not come through. A Houdini fan club of thousands was continually hounding Jessie for Houdini's promised messages, but so far, he had been mute as a mud puddle.

Sometimes Jessie's messages were thought to be outrageous, inappropriate, risqué even, and the FCC would threaten to shut them down. Only a mounting viewer demand for the format, as it was, kept them on. People showed a hunger for spontaneity, for recovering history and values in this random, unscripted way, and even for the inappropriate. The rich tried to "buy" messages from their deceased loved ones, but Jessie refused, saying on the air: *I have to be unbought and unbossed, and besides, messaging is a voluntary thing; not all dead people want to do it.* They donated huge amounts of money anyway, just in case, and because they couldn't take it with them, and they were getting increasingly convinced there was someplace else to go. Jessie didn't give personal readings, but there were lots of clairvoyants and mediums who did, and she gave them audience and airtime on her show like invited guests. She wanted the LODS to be like a library of thoughts channeled from the dead, through the living.

Jessie's mother called late one night in a rant, demanding to speak to her daughter. Jessie had collapsed, exhausted from delivering a long miscellanea of messages, so Seaborn took Doris's call.

"Listen Seamore, let me talk to Jessie. I wanna give her a piece of my mind."

"I can't do that Doris, she's asleep."

"Oh you are too good to be true. When are you gonna do something about this?"

"What would you have me do?"

"Can't you shut her up? this is dangerous! She's just acting, making all this foofaraw up, and everybody knows it. She's always been such a damn dreamer. It's a disgrace!"

Seaborn could tell Doris was toasted, so he spoke gently: "Why don't you come see us Doris, see how Jessie is. She misses her family. She has messages for you too, I bet."

Doris snorted, "Oh PLEASE, perish the thought!" and hung up on Seaborn.

Doris always called when she was drunk, and usually talked to Jessie who would be upset afterwards. They had invited her to visit before, but she never came, claiming she didn't like the state of Georgia, all that rain and red dirt. She acted like messaging was an injury Jessie was inflicting on her personally. She didn't really believe Henry could send messages. He'd stopped talking to her a long time ago. Both of Jessie's brothers had called the station to complain that Jessie was slandering the dead and violating their privacy. Tom wouldn't even speak to Jessie but gave all his vitriol to Seaborn to pass on, which he never did because it was so hurtful. Chuck-Pete was more forthcoming. He was on a speaker-phone the last time he called lambasting Jessie, and she heard it all: "What the hell are you doing? Are you crazy? You're a sick puppy! You're not my sister anymore, you got that?"

Jessie was stung. She cried and sunk into a depression. The condemnation of her family always made her feel sick, wretched, ashamed.

To Seaborn it was like her family had chosen to stand apart from her, isolating her, and themselves, like a small nation made up of grumbling factions.

As the LODS grew in popularity, it began to put a serious dent in the profits of internet commerce. People were being unwittingly weaned away from consumerism, which had not really filled their voids the way messages from spirits had. Lots of spirits advised their loved ones to stop buying "things" and instead to "behold" the wonders of the Earth, and each other. Jessie had relayed a message from a spirit named Stine, with no death date, who was eloquent on the subject: *Is there not more to life than getting stuff? And then getting more of it, faster, and then stuffing what you can't use now somewhere so you can use it later. If this is so... what a SAD routine. How really very very sad. On the other hand, know for sure that you are rich, when your hunt for alternatives becomes sincere.*

Jessie's viewers appreciated a revolutionary idea when they heard one. And they read God's intentions into Jessie's utterances, even though she didn't claim that. Every day, more people abandoned home shopping networks, and various religious programs, because they preferred hearing whatever came from a blissful and mischievous hereafter, over hearing what the televangelists had to say about life on the ground. They'd heard all that before.

Now they heard from Henry: *Death and life are not the opposites I thought they were when I was alive. Life has no opposite. The opposite of death, if it has an opposite, is probably birth. Life really is eternal. There is more to life than life. Think about it. It's too easy to believe in the nothingness of life and death, and in the nothingness of life after death.*

Some of the home shopping shows folded. Iceland banned American televangelists, declaring them a public health threat. The televangelists soldiered on, most of them trying to ignore the LODS, although their resentment of Jessie was growing. She was denying heaven and hell, as well as robbing them of their rightful audience, and their revenues. They all agreed that someone had to stop her– but how to stop Henry?

21
The Reverend Redhead

The Reverend Travis Thackston considered himself an important Man of God. He was the hottest religious mogul in television, besides the Bible mavens Ruth and Esther, who had enjoyed many years in his reflected limelight, until Jessie Pettengill came along to rock the ark. Ruth and Esther might be willing to ride out a dignified fade into martyrdom, but The Reverend Thackston wasn't. He was indignant about this usurpery. On one of his shows he trumpeted; *This woman is not of God! She is wild and blue, receiving messages from out yonder somewhere and dependent on COMPUTERS-ah. I receive directions from GOD-ah. I am his humble servant whom-ah he has appointed-ah. God speaks to me DIRECTLY...*

Eli and Smithy also produced The Reverend's weekly television and radio shows, THE FUNDAMENTAL CHRISTIAN CRUSADE. He had the backing of a powerful alliance of elders. Up until Jessie appeared on the scene with the LIFE OF DEATH SHOW, The Reverend had been Eli and Smithy's biggest moneymaker, and he liked it that way. He'd gotten used to it that way. Now though, his security, and his very livelihood was threatened by THE LIFE OF DEATH SHOW. Every day, he saw huge sacks of mail with letters, checks and cash, "donations," rolling into THE LODS. Most of these contributions would have gone to him, and other televangelists, if Jessie hadn't stolen so much of that audience. He feared he was no longer on solid footing in the ratings either. He'd lost viewers and advertisers. His own wife was divorcing him. He had no choice but to punish

Jessie's evil secularism, and to blow things asunder. And he felt his mission growing: he was the one chosen to take her down.

Sometimes he aligned himself with Dr. Padgett Desmond, who wanted very little to do with him in public, shrugged him off like dog do-do on his shoe. A different story in chambers though, when the Reverend sought the comfort and council of the doctor. After all, as the station shrink, Desmond was obliged to lend his ear and pathos, in full confidentiality of course. And although The Reverend knew Desmond considered him a hothead, he also knew his mixture of religion and madness entertained and thrilled the Doctor in an unsound, forbidden way that they both secretly enjoyed. Besides, Desmond was a little unpopular himself for not having made a $mart call on Jessie the way Seaborn had, even though nobody knew how long all this could possibly last. In Vegas, they were laying odds.

The Reverend decided he would have to help himself. What Jessie was doing was an outrage to Christendom. How dare she make a fool out of him and his whole industry? She was the fool. Why couldn't all the other fools see that? Everyone out there was a thief or a whore of one kind or another, and everyone had a sacred right to make a living, including him. He had an offshore bank account he needed to keep plumping for his old age. Jessie was a leprosy on his retirement plan. Now there was gonna be alimony to pay. He had to shut that cunt down before she ruined him altogether.

One day when Jessie was in the middle of a broadcast, The Reverend Thackston led some of his followers on a "Raid for Christ," staging a mock robbery, with no weapon but The Reverend's own tongue.

The set of THE LIFE OF DEATH SHOW didn't have a decorative backdrop; the space around Jessie's desk was white, to reflect her changing auras, most often turquoise. And behind her, twenty feet of open white space she called holy ground created a luminous habitat for the comings and goings of images that might form and float, ghosts, angels, duendes that might appear to someone in the audience open enough to see them. Jessie's archangel was said to hang out back there and lots of people claimed to see her: ancient, winged, translucent, tinct with purple.

The Reverend's hair, an outsized shock of red, stood on end, as he stepped into that white space and walked right through the angels like an exuberant clown. He never could resist a microphone, and so he leaned into Jessie's where she sat, violating her personal space and interrupting her messaging. He was so close to Jessie she could smell the liquor on his breath, but she let him go on delivering a bitter-lipped sermon of his own improvisation, surprising even himself. Jessie looked frightened and amused at the same time, as he twanged over the airwaves:

"Even today, JEEsus comforts the afflicted and afflicts the comfortable-ah. Why have you forsaken ME, his humble servant-ah? This woman Jessie is NOT of the BIBLE. She is immoral, kinky—she is a paraphiliac-ah. She takes chocolate and other foodstuffs to bed with her-ah. She TRANSGRESSES over God's laws and carries you right into PERDITION-ah. She perverts the WORD-ah, she oozes carnality. I am raiding her coffers in the name of JEEsus Christ. I need for all you true Christians-ah to send your money to me, your humble servant." He gave an 800 number for donations and finished with: "Pledge as much as you can to ME, and God-ah will bless you with abundance and riches!"

He raised his fist and scowled down at Jessie who chose that moment to squirt fresh cream in The Reverend

Thackston's face from a canister of Redi-Whip she happened to have on hand. There was a look of vexed disbelief on his creamed face. He couldn't stop licking himself, lapping it up with his long pink tongue, and wiping at his eyes with sticky fingers, all of it caught on camera.

In the wings, Eli and Smithy looked appalled at what was happening, with no chance for a do-over; they were LIVE ON THE AIR!

Seaborn watched in disbelief too— it boggled his mind—but he never called CUT.

As the Reverend escaped with his bandits, who had all grabbed sacks of donations, bound books, and cases of DVD's of the LOD's shows, for bootlegging, Jessie remembered a couple of messages she'd been saving for the right time. Now giddy, she said to the camera like a sassy rebuttal:

This is from Norma Jean, d.1962. Have an orgasm, that's your own little thing you can have, it's a gift, a reward, a way to transcend your SELF. You deserve that, don't you?

Jessie smiled benignly, swung her dark shiny hair over her shoulder and continued, on a roll:

Any girl that can see a spiral nebula gets a big bottle of scent, with a playful invitation to come again and really explore the moon; embossed with a coronet and signed, Yours very affectionately, A. Huxley. Oh, I accept, Norma Jean says...

While Jessie continued messaging and giggling, (she had developed a new giggle,) one of the cameras followed The Reverend all the way out the door and zoomed in when The Reverend flipped them all the bird.

After this outburst on Jessie's show, high-ranking members of the Christian alliance came down on the Reverend, conveying their disapproval and outrage. He was filled with remorse, fearing he'd made a very bad tactical mistake. For days, he had a biblical hangover. He had to regain lost ground, to improve his standing, and his ratings. So, his next show a week later was special, a great revival, from the super altar of his grandiose CATHEDRAL FOR THE LORD set. He went all out, and with Eli and Smithy's help, a huge, live audience was invited.

Flanked on either side by his Muscle-Men-For-Christ, who had buff weight-lifting bodies and held iron chains they effortlessly snapped in two, The Reverend Thackston preached a sermon of forgiveness and thanksgiving: *Our Heavenly Father from-whom-ah all mercy flows-ah, blessed-ah be your loyal followers in ME-ah...* He offered a long litany of heartfelt apologies for stooping to the Devil's own level, for acting the fool, *today my friends-ah, I am a sadder and a wiser man. But God-ah is forgiving, even when mankind isn't. God has a plan for us all that is-ah encouraging. Let our grateful songs before thy throne arise!* He smiled big, raised both arms to the heavens, and a large lady sang "God Bless America." The choir picked up at the end of that with, "America The Beautiful," as six members of the United States Air Force in full dress uniform, padded in and lined up on the altar. Then the whole choir sang, "From The Halls Of Montezuma" as six decorated Marines, their chests swathed in golden cord, marched down the aisle, and stood at attention alongside the air-force men. No separation of church and state for The Reverend Travis Thackston.

America was founded-ah in the name-ah of JEEsus Christ! He trumpeted, thrusting his fists in the air in a wide arc, opening his palms and tilting his head way back to catch the wild rain of applause, to feel that sting of glory he needed and loved best.

After that first robbery, The Reverend's bandits came peacefully by themselves for money every week. It was understood The Reverend sent them. If guards started to arrest them, Seaborn stopped the guards and declined to press charges. Seaborn was a fan of The Reverend's in a campy sort of way, often listening to his radio show. He called him The Reverend Redhead behind his back because of his big marcel of bright red hair. But Seaborn felt sorry for him because he knew red-headed kids always got bullied and picked on in school, and he was sure Travis had suffered that fate. In fact, it had probably formed him. But he liked how the Reverend could muster up great, bombastic charisma, even though he looked like a fresh-scraped carrot. Seaborn was the only one who cut The Reverend any slack, sending over large donations regularly. But it was never enough.

"Anyone who steals does not know his father," Seaborn told Jessie, "they're stealing what they think they have coming to them." Seaborn didn't mind a little Robinhood, even if it was skewed. He believed in keeping his enemies close-by and well fed. The Reverend and his flock needed the money to live, and if they didn't get it from the LODS, they'd take it from somewhere else and just increase the enmity in the world.

For his part, The Reverend Thackston was insulted by Seaborn's charity. He scorned him in his sermons and denied taking anything that wasn't his. "How dare that Seaborn patronize me." he told his assistants, "This is all his fault. Who does he think he is, Jesus Christ?"

In only ten months, a groundswell of viewer interest had boosted the LIFE OF DEATH SHOW to an international format, as Jessie shewed more and more in different languages. There was always an English translation provided, and they added one in Esperanto, and someone stood beside Jessie signing for the deaf. Jessie was no longer fringe and marginal; she had moved to the center, and her star was still rising. The LODS was a brand. The DVD's, CD's and bound books from transcripts were hot sellers. Jessie appeared on magazine covers: <u>REALTALK, PEOPLE, DETAILS,</u> even <u>INTERVIEW</u>. She was featured on <u>TV GUIDE</u> in a cover story with the headline: "RATINGS WAR: THE TELEVANGELIST VRS. THE TELEVISIONARY."

The foreign press followed her mushrooming popularity. A big syndication deal was in development for the LODS.

Then, just short of a year after Henry died, Doris passed. Seaborn booked a small private plane to take Jessie down to Silver Lake for the funeral. He wondered, like everyone else, if Doris would message. Jessie's parents had been ordinary people, substantial, yet mystical, full of Irish power and pathos. They made him think of the Griffons on Notre Dame Cathedral, although he'd never said that to anyone. He knew he had been unusual to them as well. He'd never had brothers or sisters and found sibling rivalry peculiar; there was an ungratefulness to it. Jealousy and power trumped love.

Kate was the exception, but then she was a whole generation removed. It was Kate who called to tell them that Doris had gone into the hospital in a hepatic coma and died- it was liver failure, bleeding esophageal varices, same thing that killed Jack Kerouac.

Chuck-Pete called Jessie with a verbal assault: "See what you've done? It's your fault she's dead. You killed her with that phony show." Seaborn grabbed the phone and hung up on him.

But Jessie was shattered by her brother's words.

Seaborn knew it was an unspoken rule that Jessie's fame must never eclipse Chuck-Pete's. He was the big brother, the leader. Doris's death even more than Henry's seemed to stoke the fire of their lifelong brother/sister rivalry.

Tom didn't call at all.

Even Henry was silent for a change.

22
Laid To Rest

Once again, Jane Thrower handled the funeral, and once again she drove the hearse, only this time she knew the way to Paradise Cemetery.

Unmanageable crowds gathered for the funeral, everyone expecting Doris to cotton to messaging like Henry did and give a performance from her coffin that would make big news. Helicopters blighted the sky– it was a mob scene, a circus. Jessie was shocked that Doris's funeral was the focus of so much media attention. Because of it she had been asked to stay away from the church and was only now catching up with the funeral at the gravesite. The night before, at the wake, the press had trampled over the yard at Silver Lake and gotten Tom so mad he hurled empty bottles and beer cans at them. Jessie and Seaborn had escaped through the groves in Henry's golf cart, to their motel, on 441, between Silver Lake and the Municipal airport. Henry's silence felt like desertion to Jessie.

It was a warm, spring day, just like the day on which Henry was buried. Jessie was suspended in a droopy daze, postponing her grief, with so many people, mostly strangers, gawking at her. Seaborn had hired two big bodyguards for protection. Their eyes whirled like gyroscopes at the dangerous crush of people– impossible to tell friend from foe. Jessie saw her brothers standing together, glaring at her, and she almost felt afraid. She tried to break their frozen stares with telepathic love, but it had no effect. A current of shame ripped through her. And then there was Kate weeping so sadly it broke her heart to look. She reached out for Kate, but there were too many people between them. Frank? Where was Frank? She couldn't find him in the crowd.

The noise was a din. Photographers shouted, music blared from one of the vans, "Everywhere you go I'll be watching you..." The blitting sound of helicopters rose and fell. Jessie couldn't hear the priest's words. She tried to read his lips. What she did hear was a loud reporter broadcasting from inside a media truck parked nearby, on the cemetery grass:

"Social scientists now say that requiring firm physical evidence of
phenomena like flying saucers and ghosts is just a failure of the imagination, an inability to believe in the invisible..."

All at once she was swamped with reporters and realized the priest had stopped talking, and the funeral was over. Where were the bodyguards? She saw the paparazzi scrambling towards her, popping off pictures, jockeying for position with their microphones and video cameras. Seaborn was being pushed further and further back. She saw Chuck-Pete get shoved roughly out of the way, and Kate signing f-a-r-e-w-e-l-l to her with tears streaming. The pressure was suffocating. Microphones were thrust in her face, one grazed her tooth– a conflagration of shouting voices all attacked her with the same mocking question: *"What is your mother saying Jessie? What's she say Jess-ay?"*

In the fracas, she saw Jane Thrower coming towards her, and she took Jane's outstretched hand and Jane pulled her through the crowd and pushed her into the hearse; whereupon Jane slammed the locks, climbed over to the drivers' seat, laid on the horn, gunned the engine, and sped off. Across the urn field she raced, narrowly missing the media-vultures, running over grave markers like cobblestones, giving Jessie the ride of her life, and jettisoning her to freedom.

Jessie kept her eyes peeled out the back window looking for Seaborn. Where was he? She couldn't see him anywhere.

On the ground, on his butt, Seaborn watched helplessly as Jane whisked Jessie off. Right then he realized a few things: The news people had no respect for Jessie, or anyone else, not even for the solemnity of a funeral. Besides the money in news making, they had latched onto the idea that they were performing some sort of service for mankind, so anything goes. It was as if they were inured to death, not only by their arrogance but maybe now by the possibility of an afterlife. He had been unprepared for the onslaught and realized he needed more than a couple of bodyguards to protect Jessie. He knew that he had to get someone like Jane Thrower, whatever it took, someone who could handle the unexpected, even if her driving skills were somewhat lacking.

That afternoon, with Jessie safely secluded away at the small motel on 441, Seaborn went back to the Funeral Home hoping to have a private talk with Jane Thrower. He found her seated behind a desk with her feet up, eating a green apple.

He tapped on the open door and stepped into the office. He was grim, unsmiling, and he came right to the point: "I like your style."

Jane, who was already beaming at the handsome Seaborn, gave a wink, "Don't worry, I billed you for it."

"No, really, that was a brave thing you did rescuing Jessie like that. I really appreciated it. I don't know what would have happened...if..."

Jane popped one shoulder up in a flirty shrug, revealing her joy at what she also felt had been one of her finest moments. She said, her brow knitting: "To tell you the truth, I felt someone overlapping my grip on that steering wheel, like when someone tries to show you Sam Snead's swing, you know?"

Seaborn nodded. He stood there wondering how much Jane knew about Henry and Jessie. He felt admiration for her; she was tiny, vulnerable, and yet so strong. She exuded an attractive mix of common sense, soul and sass. The whole room smelled unexpectedly fresh, like green apples.

He said: "I need a good f-f..."

Jane held up her hand, shook her head: "Sorry, as tempting as that is, I don't do sex work anymore."

"..factotum." Seaborn said, slapping his cheek. You know, a good girl Friday.

Jane howled. She whacked her knee, "if I didn't laugh on this job, I'd be ill as a hornet."

She motioned for Seaborn to sit down. Would he have a drink with her? She took out two delicate glasses, a bottle of Henry McKenna Bourbon, and poured them each three fingers, neat. They drank a toast to Doris's passing.

Seaborn relaxed then and looked around Jane's office with unbridled interest. It was chock full of butterfly collections, mounted on the walls and lying about in cases– dead, yet beautiful, butterfly and moth bodies.

Jane explained that she believed as the Buddhists did, that human spirits, newly dead, inhabited butterflies during their short lives– why they flitted about so happily.

Seaborn took it all in, as well as the casual order of everything. She was an organizer alright, but not overly fussy about it. She didn't think death was fearful or intimidating and that alone was remarkable.

"We need someone like you to come work for us, a Jane-of-all-trades, pardon the pun. Jessie needs help, a personal manager to look out for her. She's so isolated in this thing she feels like she has to do."

"I thought you were her manager." Jane said.

"I am, but she still needs someone who understands her, you know, from a female point of view. She needs the support and protection of a woman friend."

Jane liked a man who knew this.

Seaborn put his head in his hands; he was painfully silent for a long moment, nearly in tears. He looked up. "I need help," he admitted, "it's getting out of control. I need another person to rely on, someone smart, who I can trust. I need you."

Jane thought about her life, all the thoughts a summary replay of what had been bothering her for a little over a year now. She believed that having a small, tidy life in this town where everyone knew her, even if they didn't want to, was an attempt at an authentic life. Isn't that what everyone wanted? She believed, at least in theory, that a progenitor ought to carry on a family business. One of her aunts had deeded over a house for her to live in, and she had saved up almost enough to pay cash for the ruby red 4-wheel drive pick-up with a sunroof she wanted. But great day, she still couldn't help feeling like she was getting ahead by taking advantage of other people's losses. She thought about the need of her job, how necessary it was, and how few people could manage it. She knew she had a special connection to death. But there was still something rearwardly moldering about the job that bothered her— putting people to rest was too all-the-time sad. Although she wanted to be of service, she suspected that she really was unsuited for the funeral business. She just didn't like it. Lately, her uncles had to keep telling her: "stop smiling, not so cheery, be more somber." It was an acting job pure and simple, yet she wasn't so sure she relished the role. To be somber was at odds with her own nature.

Seaborn pulled her out of her reverie, "You're compassionate as well as brave; you're resourceful, and down-to-earth. You're the perfect person for this job, I'm sure of it. I think Jessie would learn to trust you, and she's tough."

Jane poured them another drink.

Seaborn saw he had piqued her interest, so he went in for the kill: "We'll pay you double, no triple, what you're making here, plus moving and living expenses, anything you want, just name it."

Jane imagined she was the one being rescued now. Her compassion should include herself right? Otherwise it was incomplete. But she didn't want to appear too relieved, or over eager. She simply nodded, and a big bourbon smile gave Seaborn her answer.

23
Frank's Ostracism

Frank was at the home place on Silver Lake taking care of Ibsen, waiting for everyone to come back. He'd skipped the cemetery to stay with Ibsen, sensing the dog was too distraught to leave alone; he'd lost both his owners in the course of a single year. Frank was counting on seeing his aunt Jess and uncle Seaborn when everyone came back to the house after the funeral.

His father Tom was the first to return, glum and in a big hurry.

Frank had decided: "I want to take Ibsen home with us and take care of him."

"The dogs got heart worms." Tom said.

"So, they have medicine for heart worms."

When the media trucks started coming up the driveway, Tom made Frank get in the BMW quickly. He locked up the house and they left, taking Ibsen with them. But a feud had begun, an argument that would rage for years, polarizing them.

Frank was disappointed. He wanted to see Jessie and Seaborn. "What about all the people coming over?"

"That's cancelled."

"Why?"

"Ask your aunt Jessie."

All the way back to Miami it rained, and Tom sped, corked up and angry. Frank recognized his father's style of grieving. He'd grown up with it; a punishing sadness would permeate him, and all the space and everyone around him. Frank sighed. What would he have done without Luke, his neighbor and friend? another house to escape to. At first, he'd been teased at school for talking about electronics, instead of sports, but now in high school, kids called him a nerd, or a geek, and it was a high compliment. He felt at home in the digital era and knew he was destined to be a technophile.

He was learning so much from Luke, who had a degree in engineering from Georgia Tech. Luke had moved into the house right next door, back when Frank was five, right after he lost his mother. Over the years Luke had taught Frank everything he knew, becoming his mentor, and truth be told, a surrogate father. They shared a keen interest in all the mechanical workings of the world and in all the realms of extreme possibilities. Together they built computers out of parts scrapped from industry waste, adding their own spins. They scavenged for small electronics, slowly accumulating great stockpiles of parts. There was virtually nothing about electronics or the programming of computers that between them they didn't know or couldn't find out. Frank became a hacker of the first order. He had the capability of accessing information on a quantity level with encyclopedias. His goal was to invent, create, develop. He liked to go to new and better levels of what was already out there. He would be graduating from high school in two months and was getting ready to go out on his own. Funny, although he was seventeen, in some ways he still felt like the five-year-old boy he'd been when his mother died. He wondered if he'd always feel that way no matter how old he got.

They'd been back home from the funeral for one week, when Tom came into Frank's room and announced: "You have to go to college soon and you can't take the mutt."

"I'm not going."

"What do you mean you're not going?"

Such a small decision had come to Frank ready-made. He hated school. He always had, so he'd faked it. Most of the time he skipped out around second period and spent the day at the university of Miami library doing research on one of his own projects. He felt alive outside of school. When he was eleven he'd built an oscilloscope in his room from a Heath Kit. In the year since his Grandpa Henry's death, he'd taken apart an old Renault Gordini and put it back together again. It was Luke who was his teacher, and who constantly challenged him to learn everything there was to know about how things worked in the world. No college could equal that.

Tom could never understand why his smart son got such indifferent grades. He'd had to enroll him in a junior college, the only place that would have him.

A week later, when Frank was out of the house, Tom took Ibsen to the Vet and had him put to sleep.

That was the first time Frank ran away. He drove the restored Renault to Atlanta where Seaborn and his Aunt Jessie had a new television program with a funny name, The Life After Death Show, or something like that. He never watched TV. He'd felt an incompleteness about not seeing Jessie and Seaborn after Doris's funeral. It had all been over too fast, and left him with a dull, unfinished state of mind.

When Frank arrived at the studio, he broke down and cried about Ibsen and Doris, and about his father whom he had begun to fear. "He's so cold I had to leave. He doesn't believe that a dog has the ability to feel what we're feeling."

Jessie and Seaborn comforted him, telling him Ibsen was old and couldn't live much longer anyway. Frank could see that they were happy to see him, as always, but they were distracted by the enormity of the new show. Jane, from the funeral home, was working for them now, and she took an interest in him. He liked Jane. She took him out on the town, and he spent a couple of contented days on his own at the Georgia Tech library. After a week, Jessie told him: "Every heart has its secret sorrows which we can't know anything about, and sometimes we call a person cold when he's only terribly sad. I think your father really loves you, and he needs you. And you have to go back and graduate from high school."

Reluctantly, Frank went home, to live once again on his father's lacerating edge of loneliness. But he vowed to leave again as soon as he could.

Tom bribed him with a new BMW for graduation and continued bugging him about college.

Frank balked. "I don't want any institution owning me, telling me what to learn and what I should do in order to become a cog in the wheel of some wasteful industry or bureaucracy that I don't even care about."

"Bullshit!" Tom slammed his fist down on Frank's worktable sending circuits and computer chips flying.

"Where'd you get that bunch of bull from? That wing-nut Luke you hang out with? Long as you're under my roof..."

So Frank placated his father by taking courses at the junior college.

Tom kept on forcing the issue; he wouldn't drop it. One day while nosing around Frank's room, flipping over parts on his worktable, he challenged Frank: "In this world, you've got to either conform or inform; which is it going to be?"

Frank thought a minute, looked up from his soldering iron and feeling playful, said, "Well, I see more than those two choices, but I'll take inform."

Tom thought he had him then. "Okay, so you have to move on to a good four-year college to do that and learn something you can inform us all about."

His father's condescension stung. He tried to pass it off lightly, as he usually did, "Nah, I don't need college. I like to study on my own like Grandpa Henry did."

Tom hit the roof, threw up his arms, and began hollering, "What are you gonna do? Turn into some old hippy full of weirdness? Cadge off your friends?

Frank couldn't understand this—his Grandpa hadn't done that. He'd been a self-taught man, and had done fine for his family, never cadged off anyone. Frank was tired of feeling worthless, the refection he always got back from his Father. He felt rage, tears bubbled in his eyes, and he let loose: "I'll tell you one thing, if I did need a buck, I'd ask a hippie in an old, splattered truck for it, that's who I'd ask. Because he'd give it to me, no questions asked– he wouldn't mind because it wouldn't be an instant what's in it for me thing, will I turn a profit? does this insure my B-M-W-ness? They don't think that way. It's just a buck man, is how they think. I don't give a crap about your money-grubbing world!"

Tom hawked and spit on Frank's floor, and stormed out, his blood-pressure pumping abnormally high.

Frank pressed the heels of his hands against his eyelids; his tears ran in defiance of gravity up and disappeared back into his eyes without falling. That's when he knew he had to get out, and soon. But it would be another two years of trying out different schools and fighting with Tom before he could break away for good.

24
The First Move

Everything was broadcast. THE LIFE OF DEATH SHOW went to-and-fro in time, layering requests for reruns with new messages, as they came in. Most of Henry's messages were everyday household communique, even cooking tips and recipes. Yet somehow, they were transformed by the sphere they came through; like when a simple truth hits you and sounds like something new. *Ted Kelly, d.2014: Always cook your grits in half n' half and put a sunny-side up egg on top, then mash it into the grits.*

Planet Earth was in a swirl and things were changing at a dizzying pace. Climate changes, viruses, early puberty, gender confusion, a rise in Downs and Autism and mutations of genes in everything carbon based. The war against terrorism was worldwide– persecutions and genocide were unraveling whole cultures. Climate change had reached a crisis state. The woman's #Me-Too movement expanded to include men who claimed to have been seduced against their will, and some who had been beaten bloody by angry women. The movement was exposing all the unfair job discrepancies that were harming women proportionately more than men. The nuclear hayride caused by loose nukes was a constant threat. As licenses expired on nuclear reactors, the regulatory commission imposed harsher standards to extend them. From a flock of hovering helicopters, the artist Christo, wrapped the Sarcophagus at Chernobyl in Mylar so that as it continued to crumble, the radioactive dust was contained in the package. Radioactivity was a real disease, a disease of matter, and it was contagious as hell.

Magic was rampant in the land; imagination had crept to the forefront and was becoming as important as logical reasoning. Attention was the new commodity, and Jessie's meteoric rise drew everyone's attention, especially because she was egregiously illogical.

Infomercials and news broadcasts intersected the LODS:

In age quake news today, the army of the aging is growing again. Medical deaths and resuscitations are on the rise. Twenty-five million people have died and returned to tell about it. That's enough to swing a presidential election. Meanwhile, those that come back are requesting their bodies be wired for sound when they die for real.

Norma Jean was back, relaying messages: O*n the other side the sexes have all mingled, making soul-love. Sammy Davis Jr. says to savor the moments that are warm and special and giggly. Nabokov says to caress the detail, it is divine, the SEED. Sally Xavier Brown, d. 2001, wants her family to go to Alaska. Space is Love. She said a mouthful. Jack K., d. 1969: Of what use would Jesus be to us if he didn't have to have a mother's care?*

Fore! It's like I'm omniscient Jessie. Always dreamed about this, but I thought I wasn't good enough, I didn't have enough confidence. Isn't that always the showstopper? I can't find your mother, Jess. She's playing hard to get.

Many messages overlapped. In the biosphere of the dead, the repetition of messages was highly valued; restatement and paraphrasing were complements liable to occur at any time. Imitation was a complement, and the plagiosphere contained a happy coincidence of ideas, all in the ether. Everything was derivative after all, including facts and alternative facts. Some people complained that the messages were so ordinary, and Henry said the ordinary is just as important as the profound, all things being equal in the universe.

Drolleries mingled with the energy of outrage people felt at having died:

Bob Jones, d. 12-18-71, I'll never forget my mashie shot on the 71ˢᵗ hole. What do people do on Sundays who don't play golf? Sam, d. 9-11-2001, Why the hell didn't they do this on a Sunday instead of on a Tuesday, when we all came into work? Lieutenant Bobby, d. 9-11-2001, I miss life, but no matter how bad it looked, my death was a soft landing. Spinelli is here too, and Clark, so thanks for the cake. I'm with you kid...

And for the deaf, there was Jane Thrower signing right beside Jessie—no end to Jane's talents. She dressed in flashy Versace, no more navy gabardine for her. The clothes always had to be altered since they were designed for amazon models, and Jane was barely five feet tall. Jessie had delivered a message from Versace telling his sister, Donatella, to create a new line for petits, a miniature palette. Jane was anticipating it.

Meanwhile, Jane enjoyed dressing Jessie in softly hued, gossamer gowns, and jewel-toned silk-velveteen capes, gorgeous with her dark hair and pale blooming skin. Jessie's clothes came from a variety of designers, living and dead. Both of them loved to wear art, and at the same time they went around the studio barefooted.

"Jessie is not transcendent," Jane explained to new assistants she hired to help them, "but in closer touch with her senses than most people are. She possesses special powers. The practicalities of living are hard for her." The only thing familiar that Jane could liken to Jessie's enlightened state was LSD, where the senses were at full throttle. "But" Jane assured them, "Jessie isn't on any drug at all. Shewing is exhausting. That's why she gets so tired, and why she sometimes seems drugged. Also, we're weaning her off cigarettes which makes her grouchy."

Jane didn't trust The Reverend Thackston, who grew more ruthless as his power declined. He'd called Jessie the anti-Christ on his show, and rejected the live-and-let-live attitude she and Seaborn, and even Henry in his way, tried to foster around the studio. The Reverend was out to prove God's power by surrounding himself with passionless muscle men who could bend pipe and break iron chains, all in the name and service of his God who, according to him was a vengeful God; it said so in the Bible.

So, in the beginning of its third year, when the LODS audience had grown to forty million viewers, Seaborn decided to move to New York City; to get away from The Reverend and the religious extremists who pilloried Jessie at every turn. In the city he thought it would be possible to live a more liberal life, with doormen and limos and New Yorkers' oxymoronic love of both celebrity and anonymity. The South had been too friendly. Privacy in Atlanta had been as scarce as skunk in New York City.

Eli and Smithy mounted a more expansive show. They bowed down before the mystery. And the stakes had been raised in the evermore global community of the LODS audience. So as the polar ice caps melted, and the earth churned towards extinction, the LODS had on guest speakers, experts on global warming and ways to save the earth. They were mostly scientists not interested in the supernatural, but anxious for any platform they could get to spread the alarm.

The new LODS studio was in a lavish old art Deco building on east fifty-seventh street, and despite layers of renovations, Jane found it still had a tangy, arty atmosphere. It included a bed-sitting suite, bijouly decorated by Jane, for whenever Jess and Sea wanted to stay over, which was often.

Their fan base had grown. Photographers, most of them just stalkers with cameras, hung around outside waiting to ambush them. Even though they kept a separate apartment, they found it increasingly difficult to go between the studio and the apartment– a risk to their tranquility, and even their lives.

The LIFE OF DEATH SHOW neon sign was curvilinear now, baroque, and huge. THERE IS STILL TIME scrolled as before, right above Jessie's desk. Eli and Smithy spared no expense, raising their own salaries with the same largess they extended to everyone who worked on the show. Seaborn had ceded the management of the money over to them, with certain controls of his own still in place. All they had to do was sit around thinking up $pin–off items to offer with the LODS licensed logo, and count the money that poured in from donations, the sale of books, DVD's, CD's, and whatever else they came up with. They worried constantly about Jessie, either running out of Henry's messages, or getting murdered; without Jessie, the show would be over. They fretted that the show was too soft, and thought people really wanted to hear dark terrifying stuff from sinners, about greed, corruption, and wickedness. All the movies and TV shows were obsessed with the dark side. But Jessie couldn't deliver it. The LODS broadcasts were all videotaped, and compiled in books in different languages, and also in braille. The deaf and blind were great receivers. Messages were streaming on-line, in bloggers chatrooms, on Twitter, and in offices and homes where the computer had become the new bright kingdom. Lots of people could hear their loved ones talk after they died if they were open enough to it. But very few spirits maintained a dialogue, like Henry and Jessie did. There was a great resurgence of seers in the land. But so far none of them had been able to mount or sustain a hot TV reality show like the LIFE OF DEATH SHOW.

Funeral homes still prepared the dead, although now they were like mini newsrooms, where coffins of the newly dead were wired for sound, since it was believed a spirit could hang in near its body for an indeterminate length of time. Cremation became unpopular in the mistaken belief that a body was needed for messaging. Old crypts also were wired—teleradiophones were installed randomly. It was a super-sensitive switchboard; the slightest sound caused radio waves, and little sensors tripped the recorder. Then THE LIFE OF DEATH SHOW picked it up and played it back, broadcasting the messages with Jessie's narrative aid. A number of people were in the new business of capturing/storing lightning bolts for electricity, which conserved energy for the LODS increasing needs. The LODS owned million channel receivers and hired technicians to sift through the stray noises out in the Cosmos. They picked up some great spirits, long dead, like: *W.B. Yeats, I am pure joy in the center of my magical life having abandoned intellect completely...* and Susan Sontag who said: *Prioritize emotional responses over intellectual judgments.*

Eli and Smithy came to the conclusion that the Evangelists shows and the LODS were going after the same audience, people who were looking for easy answers. So they severed ties with The Reverend Thackston when they made the move to New York, selling him off to another network. Although the Reverend still had a large audience behind him, compared to Jessie he was a losing proposition, and the two together were no longer copacetic.

The Reverend felt so rebuked he wanted to rip Jessie's face off. Now he understood why the apostles carried swords. He began working on a book deal, writing plaintive letters to

Jesus. "Who the hell else would I write to?" he'd screamed at his agent when she had the gall to question him about it. But writing a book didn't satisfy him. What would his idol Falwell think of him if he were still alive? The Reverend heard a menacing whisper: *your duty is undischarged.* He scratched at his ears, his head, his blazing red face. Such heat he felt rising in him. "Amen" he said out loud, which means 'so be it.' "Amen, Amen, Amen." His skin itched like hell.

25
New York New York

On New Year's Eve, for the first time in nearly three years, Jessie and Seaborn were headed out on the town like an ordinary couple. They had been invited to a Masked Ball at the Plaza Hotel, to dance the night away, sub rosa. Henry warned Jessie not to go, but she ignored him this time mainly because they would be going in disguise, and nobody would recognize them. Jane was an expert in make-up and masquerade. Besides, Seaborn loved to dance and so did she. They disserved this.

Jane dressed Jessie in a vintage lavender-blue Randolph Duke gown to which she had added feathers, and a begilt peacock feather mask, all sprinkled with stardust. Seaborn displayed over his bespoke tuxedo the full train of iridescent tail feathers of the male peacock. His mask was a gewgaw of male pride and frippery, and his ponytail and all the feathers were speckled with the mystical eyes of Argus. Jane smuggled them out of the apartment in between racks of flamboyant costumes, into a limo, and they were safely away.

The costumes worked well– the peacock feathers kept everyone else at a safe distance and gave Jessie and Seaborn a feeling of incognito. They moved gamely through the crowded Grand Ballroom to sample the buffet of exotic foods arrayed on big round cloth covered tables, before hitting the dance floor. They had two bodyguards, one at their table, and one in a nearby room, watching the party on a closed-circuit surveillance system.

"The Big Fish Ensemble" played an old Hoagy Carmichael tune called "Skylark," and the lead singer

162

sounded exactly like Aretha Franklin: *Is there a meadow in the mist, where someone's waiting to be kissed?* It was a slow dance, and Seaborn held Jessie under his feathery veil of privacy, enjoying their blissful moments of anonymity together, as the singer crooned: *Strange as a will-o-the-wisp / crazy as a loon / mad as a gypsy serenading the moon...*

"You look gaudy," Jessie whispered.

"Fly pride, says the peacock," Seaborn answered, whirling her around the parquet floor with a flourish.

"It's odd how every generation rediscovers the tail feathers of the peacock," Jessie said, "over and over again," she gazed around the room, "despite technology."

Against the gilded mirrored walls, twenty-four big video screens encircled the room, one for each time zone around the globe. Each screen showed a different New Year's party in progress, all linked together by satellite. The New York screen showed Times Square, where huge crowds earnest with new year's resolutions waited to see the ball drop, a tradition since 1908. This ball, in use since 2,000, was a huge prismatic crystal.

The New York screen kept cutting to parties covered by different broadcasting stations, so that all the satellite-linked parties from around the planet combined with cyberspace technology for a virtual reality experience on a global scale.

As they experienced all this, Seaborn felt Jessie shudder. "Hold me tighter, or I'll lead." she said. He held her tighter and felt her release in his arms. He said, "I know. It's like being in a room with five billion people." He kissed her through his mask. She looked gorgeous, all her brunet anima to the fore. She was more with him this night than she had been in a long time. They circled the dance floor with romantic brio, and he began to notice that no one was taking their eyes off them.

"I've got a joke for you," Jessie said, "know how a ghost gets to be a ghost?"

"How?" Seaborn kissed her ear.

"By making PEOPLE believe in her."

Seaborn suddenly whirled Jessie around in a swathe of feathers.

"Wait, there's more," Jessie giggled, "know how a ghost gets to be an archangel?"

"How?" said Seaborn.

"By making OTHER GHOSTS believe in her."

Seaborn laughed, dipped Jessie low and nibbled her sweet-smelling neck till she giggled again. She was like his regular Jessie. He was reminded of simpler days when they'd gone out dancing, or to a movie and dinner with no hassle. That was so long ago, before messages became their reality, before the panopticon took over their life. Oftentimes he felt he had lost Jessie, first to Henry, and then to the world.

He felt the dry shot whiz past, even before he heard the thunder-like discharge.

Seaborn's hand automatically went up to cover Jessie's head, as he dove with her in one confluent motion under a table. A hellish chaos of screams and stampeding began. The lights went out, the electricity cut off, the video screens went blank. A burning metal smell whiffled in the air, more screaming, then moaning; someone had been hit. Sirens sounded immediately, off in the distance.

Seaborn peeked out from under the tablecloth, and in the light from the candles still burning on each table he made out an exit route. He wondered where his bodyguards were, and if the limo would be in the same place, waiting, or if the driver would have been chased from the entrance. He decided they had to take the chance; the longer they stayed in place the more dangerous for them. He removed their cumbersome masks, and his heavy fan of tail feathers.

"On my count, we'll run for that exit Jess, see it? you ready?

They crossed the dance floor in seconds, flew down a hallway, and out into the brightly lit lobby. All heads turned as they hit the revolving doors running. It was like this part of the hotel didn't know anything had happened, so what was the big hurry?

Their blue-black limo, iridescent as the peacock, was still there. They leapt inside, and the driver sped away. Jessie sobbed with relief. Seaborn panted, "It's okay, it's okay now baby." They headed straight for the studio/suite, where they had planned to spend the night because Jane was having their apartment painted. Seaborn was distraught wondering: did someone know their plans? Was that bullet meant for Jessie? He had a flash of insight about how very dangerous the masquerade actually was; his own security team was hampered by all the masks and costumes. Who was the enemy? Closed Circuit Surveillance had proved useless.

Getting into the studio on East Fifty-seventh would be an ordeal, as always. When the limo pulled up, fans who were passively sitting on the pavement suddenly sprang to their feet. Cameras came clicking to life as Photographers jammed into each other, strobes flashing.

Seaborn braced himself and held onto Jessie as they leapt from the car to run the gauntlet. Fans swarmed and bristled in a mad frenzy, shouting things, trying to touch Jessie. The stalkerazzi's bazooka-sized camera lenses flashed only inches from their faces. Jessie leaned in close to Seaborn, covering her face with her long hair. Once they got inside the building, they went straight to their bed-sitting suite, through double doors that had porthole, one-way windows in them. Seaborn bolted the doors, and leaned against them, panting. Jessie threw herself on the bed and buried her head in a pillow.

Outside, in the wide hallway, cater-corner to their room was another set of double doors with porthole windows and inside was a vast studio, and a brightly lit technical room where twenty-four hours a day technicians sifted through migratory sound waves out in the Cosmos culling for messages.

This night on their million channel receivers they struck pay dirt. A spirit, d.1926, said:

Stop copying flowers, make your own like God does– original designs– invent them. Forget about leading-edge art. That's only an economic game. Wank . . . Fame is Wank too, WANK . . .

After a hail of static, they heard:

Oh, go paint a saucer of sagebrush. Beauty is an expression of the artist's spirit; the web comes out of the spider's nature. The pearl is the oyster's autobiography.

Then the airwaves were overcome with galactic static.

"Who the hell was that?" one of the technicians asked.

"A woman named G. O'K, and that art guy named Money," another techy answered.

"You mean Monet?"

"Yeah, that's him, the guy that's always arguing with Picasso about the light. Him and G. O'K fight too and hang out together."

"Yeah, I heard them a few times, Jessie had 'em on. They're strong, still coming on after all this time. They must have latched onto some antenna, maybe one of them Voyagers."

"They still out there?"

"Went against all predictions."

They heard a crackling that almost sounded like laughter if a shark was laughing. Then music, The Brandenburg Concerto, and another voice, raspy, coming through a hailstorm of musical static. After they filtered, they heard it clearly enough:

Damn right, they're still out here. One, two, three and four. Let me put Voyager into perspective for you boys. Oh, my name's Delong. I was an artist in the fifties in Florida. Did a lot of space work, heh heh. Anyway, Voyager is an object of art now, not science, because its function is to reveal radiance, not prove facts. See? Voyager transcended Science.

Baldwin, James. d. 1987: Flowers? Radiance? Nice, but the purpose of art is to lay bare the questions that have been hidden by all these answers.

Carrie, d. 9-11-01: Flowers? Look at those fat new blooms bursting on the snapdragon. They're like the faces I sketched on the subway– reasons to live.

The voices went silent then, like a plugged bottle.

"Jesus, artists are running everything these days,"

In their bed-sitting suite, Jessie and Seaborn listened to the messages the technicians were capturing while they helped each other out of the costumes. When the talking stopped, they heard the Brandenburg Concerto playing, strong and endlessly, coming from Voyager. Seaborn walked around the room lighting scented tapers and turning the lights off. The room glowed, perfumed with Fleurs de Amour, thanks to Jane who was a big believer in the sacred power of scent, as well as candlelight. They needed both this night. Seaborn wondered if it was ever worth trying to go out on the town.

"C'mere birdman," Jessie said from their bed.

Seaborn leaned into her kiss, then lifting her deep into the feather bed they crashed together, stressed, and yet oddly stimulated by the near miss. Jessie's fingertips roamed over Seaborn's sweetly familiar skin. She stretched him out on the bed and rubbed his limbs the way he liked, until she felt him release tension. She kissed his eyes and his cheeks, ears, neck, moving slowly down his body with delicate kisses, and her keen hands. His penis reared up like an exquisite animal in the bed with them.

"Sit on it." Seaborn coaxed her.

Jessie teased him just a little longer with her tongue, until he was wild-eyed, and she felt an aching desire for him. Yes, now, oh... They moved with Bach's music, deep inside the music, and each other, their spines pitching in sync with the violins, drums throbbing inside them, matching their hearts, beat for beat, as they reached the crest of orgasm and miraculously slipped the Earth.

A shrill alarm sounded just at that moment and they sprang apart. The room lights automatically blasted full on, destroying the slant of delicious candlelight that had been shimmering with them.

"Goddamit!" Seaborn roared. He grabbed the remote, dropped it, and it bounced a few times, changing channels like slides. Instead of the universe on audio, they got the west side of the building on video, where security police were wrestling two people away from the door. Ugly sounds intruded into their bed-sitting room.

Finally, the alarm quit.

Seaborn picked up the remote. Standing naked and shaking, he clicked, achieving three other views of the studio exits on a bank of surveillance screens overhead. The break-in attempt was only at one door, he was relieved to see. God, something evil was after them tonight.

He watched the security police search and cuff the two interlopers, a man and woman whose press badges identified them as partners in a photo enterprise. On the ground their cameras panted like held-off pit bulls. Seaborn had a full dose of the anxiety of the hunted. He and Jessie were prisoners, not free to go in safety, and stalked even in their own cell. How would they ever escape this?

He looked at a monitor which showed the front of the building where media Jackals slumped on car hoods waiting to spring; it was their whole wretched life. Pugnacious Fans argued, pacing back and forth in front of the surveillance camera, looking up at it like guppies. Some had on t-shirts with Jessie's face printed on them, a crown of thorns around her head—unauthorized, pirated.

Seaborn said, "Look at this! eventually that mob is gonna find a way in here. We gotta find a safer place."

"Somewhere up high," Jessie said, dazed and dreamy, like grateful-to-be-alive-sex had anesthetized her to disregard the fear emotion. She got up, slid on a silky kimono, walked over to her computer, and started reading e-mail from eternity. She'd always loved the way language came back after lovemaking, with a whole different quality, as if it were informed by going to an ecstatic place without words. She read: *You don't choose who you love, real love chooses you. T. Capote, d. August 25, 1984.*

Seaborn watched Jessie, wondering how she did it. One minute she was one with him, the next minute she was absorbed in a bliss-field of messages. But it was her intense calm that always precipitated his best ideas and now he thought, yes, up high, with an escape route into the under populated sky, his favorite frontier. He'd been taking helicopter flying lessons and was enthralled with flying. He'd ordered two of the best Personal Helicopters ever made. The

P.H. had not been safe or practical– they'd often bumped into each other– until advances were made in neural networks. As Frank had explained it to him: the simple concept of bear right and up had to be genetically engineered into the collision avoidance mechanism as an artificial intelligence algorithm for safe flying. Just as a flock of birds don't bump into each other, even when they're startled. The anti-aircraft missile shield around Manhattan had been adapted to accommodate the P.H. There was a corridor only for P.H.'s, above the trees, buildings and Drones, but below the airspace for planes. Like Drones, they had their own Air Traffic Control System. And P.H.'s were clean, they ran on hydrogen, super conductivity, or on ethanol, and they reduced road traffic.

The ground was overpopulated, nearly everywhere. Crowds were the biggest problem, a world problem—people were multiplying and gobbling food almost as fast as the Brown Tree Snake. Johnny Carson, who died in 2005 had sent a message to remind everyone that during the thirty-year period that he hosted The Late Show, 1962 to 1992, the worlds' population had gone from 3 billion to 5 billion people. Where was all that going to end?

Seaborn walked over to see what Jessie was up to. Over her shoulder, he read the messages coming in:

Fore! The Babe says: Women are more calculating than the most calculating man; they have the power, the speed and the line, although not the same compulsion to get the ball in the hole. Women tend to pick up lost golf balls while they are still rolling. This is John, d. Dec.6, 1980 A red lettuce day. Know what the definition of a big fan is? Someone who would blow you away Ha Ha Ha, Woody prophesied everything in "Stardust Memories."

Seaborn thought about how the dead say all the things they might have said when they were alive, except now it was filled with latent metaphor.

He stretched and yawned like a cat, "c'mon back to bed Jessie."

"Wait a minute, this is rich, listen, from *Nam June Paik, I died in Miami on January 29, 2006. But I discovered a channel of communication unlike the thingness of art, utilizing a threshold of perception called synthesizing man with his technology. The intricate architecture of these common proteins is gradually being revealed...it's a cosmological mystery, and there are many...*

Seaborn said: "I remember him. He was a dynamic New York artist ahead of his time. A Buddhist, I think. His images were otherworldly, and he loved television."

26
One World Trade Center

One afternoon, a few weeks later in lower Manhattan, Jane, Seaborn and Jessie, emerging from their limo were mobbed like Elvis. Bodyguards scrambled out of the lead and tail cars and held back the TV news crews and fans that were already on the scene waiting, having been alerted somehow. Jessie had on jeans and a cashmere twinset in virgin Mary blue, while Jane was a standout in a red-orange Versace outfit that accentuated her wild russet hair– she believed in being fabulous in the face of danger. Nobody noticed what Seaborn was wearing.

Henry watched on the TV set inside the vacated limo (he also loved TV) as a news anchor reported:

Yesterday another attempt was made on the life of Televisionary, Jessie Pettengill. Lots of speculation about the would-be assassin– police suspect it might have been someone close to Jessie. The Life Of Death Show is moving up to safer quarters...

Jessie and Seaborn had been leaving their studio/suite, on the way to ABC for an interview with Barbara Waters when the shooting occurred. The interview had been cancelled and postponed, until they could gain a new level of security way above ground. The police were investigating Tom and Chuck-Pete, as well as other leads they had from the shooting at the Plaza Hotel. Jessie felt sick when she heard this. It was impossible to believe that her own brothers might shoot at her. Henry didn't believe it either, but he couldn't know everything after all, especially all that was happening on the

172

ground which he grew less and less interested in. At first, he had tried to make a joke of it:

Fore! A Mulligan! Not permitted in the rules of golf. No second chances allowed!

Ah Jessie Lee, I may joke but the truth is this really pains me. I didn't do my best with your brothers and I can't make it up to them now. I wish I could have a second chance. I went off the rails with them more times than I care to remember, and worse, I held back love. God, I even gave Tommy the middle name of Andrews, after a great golf course. How self-absorbed is that? I didn't take them out on the links enough when they were boys. I took you instead. I didn't trust them enough, so I didn't give them self-trust. I was a bully, and now they're bullies. If only I could go back. Even dead, I'm better with my grandson Frank. I get him, and he gets me.

Jessie didn't want to tell Henry, it would hurt his feelings, but the truth was she had never liked golf that much. She wasn't interested in spending that kind of time getting a ball into a hole. She'd already decided not to think any more about who was shooting at her. She wanted to reassure Henry and distract him from his painful memories. So, she asked him: "Do you miss playing golf Daddy?"

Every day I play an invisible game. The best part of the game was always concealed. Now it's like being the ball. The ball knows where it's going.

Then he'd launched into a whole stream of messages from old dead golfers.

Now the bodyguards blocked the paparazzi roughly, while Jane hurried Jessie and Seaborn into the building, One World Trade Center, which was to be their new home. In the lobby a long, horizontal, color filled mural, "A Union Of The Senses," made by Jose Parla dazzled everyone.

Reporters screamed out questions: *"Jessie, who do you think is trying to kill you? Are you afraid? Why are you moving here?"*

Jane zig-zagged Jessie and Seaborn through an immense airy atrium, past gigantic marble columns, one of which featured a brass plaque engraved with the words:

THESE LIVES LOST WILL NOT BY SIMPLE DEATH BE UNDONE.

An elevator stood ready to carry them 104 stories to the top of the tower. Jane had been helping the guards hold back the jam of people and just managed to squeeze herself into the elevator before the doors shut.

What should have been a quiet, smooth elevator ride was for Jessie a torture chamber. She heard human voices howling, sharp yells, moaning, and soft words of comfort, along with endless numbers. It was like gaining access to a spirit gulf stream. She yelped softly and shook her head. Jane and Seaborn were clueless.

In less than a minute, they emerged from the elevator into a bright phantom space, Jessie clutching her temples. She felt the full power of this highly charged area, where human atoms had so immediately become part of the atmosphere. She was unsure of herself suddenly, shaky; the intensity here was almost too much to bear.

Their new living and working quarters were under construction. It was a huge daunting project still weeks away from completion. The framing was going up; the sounds of the workmen busily hammering away drowned out the numbers Jessie was being bombarded with. She and Jane milled around the vast sunny spaces fragrant with fresh-cut wood, while Seaborn walked over to meet Detective Cosgrove, who had just arrived. He was a big man with gray peppered black hair and a Rosacea complexion.

As they shook hands Seaborn made eye contact trying to determine if he could trust Cosgrove. The Detective looked steadily at Seaborn while he talked about evidence he'd gathered from the shooting on the previous day: "It was a high-powered rifle– according to ballistics, either an AK47 or a deer rifle. You know anybody has one? it knocked this off." He handed Sea a brick-sized piece of their building on east fifty-seventh.

Seaborn hefted it, recalling the smell of cordite, and the boom from the shot that missed Jessie by inches. He shook his head. He looked to make sure Jessie wasn't listening before he handed over an envelope that had been delivered to the LODS that morning. It contained a page torn out of a Bible with a circled passage.

Cosgrove opened the envelope and read slowly: John 16:2, Whosoever killeth you will think that he doeth God service. Scribbled in red ink was: Sorry I missed. A Big Fan.

"Someone doesn't mind desecrating a Bible." Cosgrove said.

Abruptly, they were interrupted by a commotion across the room. Two Police officers struggled to hold onto a teenager, six feet tall, in funny clothes.

Jessie came up behind The Detective and Seaborn, who were hurrying over. "Frank!" She ran to him, excited.

Detective Cosgrove said, "How'd you get in here son?"

Frank said, "Freight elevator. Hey Jessie."

As he and Jessie hugged, Jane wrapped her arms around both of them too.

"It's okay, we know him, our nephew." Seaborn said.

"Her brother's kid?"

"Her brother didn't do this." Seaborn said.

Frank said, "That's why I came. The note, from a Big Fan..."

"How'd you know about the note son? I just read that note myself." Detective Cosgrove looked peeved.

"Someone put it on twitter last night and it went viral." Frank answered.

Jane looked way up at Frank and smiled. He'd undergone another growth spurt since she'd last seen him, he needed a haircut, and he had an angry case of acne. "Great Day," she teased, "where are your little magnets?"

Frank blushed. But then he raised one brow, said, "Where's your little navy-blue monkey suit?"

Everyone, except Cosgrove, laughed.

For weeks, Seaborn and Jane had been diligently working on the new quarters they had leased atop One World Trade. Yesterday's shooting pressured them to be in an even bigger hurry. The construction phase was at the place where they needed a trustworthy and knowledgeable contractor for all the electronics. The bids had come in, but Seaborn was afraid to trust anyone with the job, especially with the parts that would secure their complete safety and privacy.

Providence, (or Henry,) intervened that day, when Frank showed up, looking for his Aunt Jessie and Uncle Seaborn. Frank had become an electronics wiz, a genius in electrical and computer engineering, a habitué of digital culture. And because of the computer he was savvy to an eclectic mix of the world's knowledge. Henry had been following his grandson's progress and growing capabilities, while he also wished Frank would take up golf.

In the days and weeks that followed, Frank, who looked to all just like a big pimply-faced kid, showed extraordinary expertise in leading a team of master electricians he cherry picked himself, to wire the new penthouse. The studio/home was being built especially for the LODS, custom in every detail. Frank was ingenious, and completely self-taught like his grandpa. His mission was to create and solve. If he hit a snag, he discussed it online with his encyclopedic mentor, Luke, who had moved to the Florida panhandle, on a new job. Luke was by nature in service to the moving along of information, and still generous with all his knowledge, and his time.

To Jane, Frank confided that he'd realized he had to face who his father was and get on with his own life. Through angry tears, Frank called Tom counter-intuitive, dog mastic, rad-hardened. Jane had laughed, but it was no joke. Frank said The Life Of Death show angered his father more than anything else Frank knew of, even him. That was why he had finally decided he had to leave. And because he was worried about the recent attempts on his aunt Jessie's life.

"Dad can't feel with other living beings, not people, not even a dog. Or if he can he doesn't want to show it. Him and Uncle Chuck-Pete won't even talk about Jessie. They've banished her; it's like she's dead in their minds. They think she's crazy. Whenever I try to talk to them about her they tell me to shut up, I'm talking treason. They don't like being investigated either. Do you guys think they did it?"

Jane thought about it, "Well, neither of them would pay a ransom on Jessie, but I don't think they'd shoot her either."

Jane let Frank vent all he needed to, then she applied some healing modalities, which she'd recently learned about from Russian peasants; the laying on of hands, accompanied by strong positive thought charges, and bright colors. She told Frank about how, during the communist regime in Russia, Khrushchev had closed two-thirds of the orthodox Christian churches and religion was forbidden, so the people developed spiritually by practicing healing. They became excellent psychic healers and there was much to learn from them. She gave him Dong Quai and Ginseng, in addition to Russian Gypsy Moth Tea.

Jane arranged Swedish body massages for Frank at the end of every workday. She made a big fuss over him, working her magic, until he hummed with happiness and felt like a new man, even though he was barely twenty.

Frank understood why they all considered it a gift to be in such a sensitive place, it was a beacon of history. The world had awakened to a nightmare on September 11, 2001 and crossed the Rubicon of horrific terrorism. And when the towers were gone they were like ghost limbs– everyone could feel them even though they weren't there anymore. Like the spirits of the dead, the spirit of the World Trade Center came roaring back. Frank thought it was an echo of the resurrective inclination of the universe.

Frank believed something truly grand had been rebuilt on those sixteen acres at the south tip of Manhattan, upon piles of consecrated ashes; in fact, a sacred burial ground. It took ten years to achieve a Memorial for soothing the searing loss that people experienced when loved one's bodies couldn't be found. And a masterpiece of architecture married with engineering produced a vast pair of abyss-like pools foot printing the foundations of the lost twin towers. First, the scale was overwhelming, and then the three-story deep waterfalls cascading over the granite sides of the pools, water forever recirculating, gave him the sensation of vanishing into nothingness, of abject invisibility. When he first discovered the names, nearly three thousand of the dead, engraved in a beautiful script into the continuous rim of bronze that tilts for your eyes all around the pools, he was shocked. He wanted to read each name, and he intended to go back and do just that. And where World Trade One and Two once stood, a new tower, One World Trade Center, and five shorter skyscrapers rose resolutely from the ashes, reborn martyrs, iconic, elegant. Frank was dazzled by all of it. There was no more sacred site in all the world. The tower was called One World Trade Center out of homage and affection. And lines of business and finance were still conducted there, befitting those who died while working in these pursuits. He knew for everyone, there was a fearlessness about the place, a sense of resurrection, of light returning from darkness.

Frank stayed on at One World Trade for as long as it took to wire and program it, and then perfect the suave electronics that would connect it intimately with One Wing Flapping, where he intended to go and live. Seaborn and Frank were close, despite their age difference. They all felt an abiding tenderness towards Frank, and were in awe of his mind, and their good fortune to have him with them, on their team. He opened up new worlds, brought in computers that shipped billions of bits of data per second, so that complete encyclopedias of knowledge were laid open. He connected them to the whole world, also having a crackerjack knowledge of satellites, another one of his special interests. Frank could access any information on the planet that they might ever need. And because of his competence, they were able to move to One World Trade weeks earlier than expected.

Jane ordered a new limo for Jessie, bullet-proof, like a Pope's, which Frank found for her on-line. Jessie laughed, calling it a coffin, giving everyone the chills, except Frank, who laughed along with his Aunt Jessie. They had the same sense of humor, Henry's.

Once they were in residence at One World Trade, Jessie was bombarded with messages from those who had died there. Essentially, it was a place where thousands of spirits lingered. One of Henry's Fore's! had begun with his stark observation: *Nineteen Suicides stand in eternities unmarked grave of discarded lives. They are mute. But their victims are here all the livelong day: Todd, d. 9-11-01, I don't know where those guys went. I saw them on the plane, and then boom, I'm on another plane, I believe I'm invisible—still got my mind though. Tell my wife I love her.* More messages poured in, all the same: *Tell my wife I love her, from Mark, Jeremy, Tom, Joseph, Chris, Roger, Christopher, Kevin, Clark, David, Leonel, Michael, Lenny, Al* ...on and on. Jessie had printed out pages and pages of the same message from different men. And from women to their men: tell my husband, father, brother, sister... It was a continuous stream.

She'd gotten messages from the spirits of 9/11 before, in other locations. But now she was overflowing with the current of a post-traumatic resonance that was way more forceful. She received litanies of survival skills that had been useless against the inferno, endless stock tips, and hundreds of numbers, cell phone numbers? along with desperate pleas for communication, and expressions of anguish at premature, sudden death. She was in the ether like never before. She appreciated that One World Trade had been built with imagination, love, and power. But late at night, and especially in the early morning hours, she felt haunted and suffered the worst despair she'd ever felt; it visited her in dreams, blitzing her unconscious, and even when she was wide awake. Henry began to grate on her with his ongoing barrage of pained messages. She struggled to find some peace but for her there was little to be had.

One afternoon Jessie was late for a broadcast and Jane went looking for her. She found Jessie passed out on the bathroom floor lying in a pool of blood. Jane brought her around with a cold washcloth and helped her to sit up on the toilet. Jessie clutched her abdomen, "Oh my back," she moaned. "I'm so dizzy." She saw the gelatinous mass and rubbed her belly. "What's happening to me?" she cried out to Jane who did not want to tell her. "I'm so sorry honey, but you've had a miscarriage.

Jessie hadn't known she was pregnant. She felt like her body had turned against her, another enemy. It was a cold hard whiplash in her long struggle to conceive. She thought she would never trust her body again. She had failed and she was miserable. She made Jane promise not to tell Seaborn until she felt unashamed enough to tell him herself.

When Frank moved to One Wing Flapping, he had two new double-wides hauled up to the top of Cowpen Mountain, hid them in the trees, and gradually filled them with electronics and all his ongoing experiments. He chose the trailers, because he could easily keep them dust-free, and he could move them around if need be. The Internet was the promised land for anthropologists which is what Frank and Seaborn both aspired to being. And they were both avid river keepers, beekeepers, environmentalists, and earth preservationists.

There was enough money to supply anything Frank needed. Seaborn was glad that someone would use and appreciate One Wing, where he hoped one day to return himself. "Once I had a garden there..." he told Frank, homesick for his roots, and the long-gone days in Atlanta, when he was a simple camera operator and Jessie was just a news anchor, and they had trekked up to their mountain home nearly every weekend for R and R. It was so beautiful and peaceful in amongst the trees, with their own clean spring water, high above the suppurating waters of polluted rivers and estuaries which people were finally now in the long process of reversing the damage. Seaborn's activism and contributions to environmental organizations helped, and Frank joined him in that cause and others.

Frank promised to resurrect the garden. He had help from a spirit named Rodney, who'd died on 9-11-01, and offered gardening tips for Jessie to relay in hopes of getting them relayed to his wife. Rodney knew a lot about growing watermelon for one thing and told Jessie that the Bradford melon was the sweetest watermelon the south has ever known. Frank googled it and discovered he could order the heirloom seeds from the Bradford family in Sumpter, South Carolina. Now Frank's patch was thriving– it was his favorite fruit, besides Rhubarb. Rodney said: *Surround your garden with rhubarb to keep the deer away– the leaves have oxalic acid and are poisonous– the deer won't touch it.*

He and Seaborn both wanted what everyone wanted: to live a simple, authentic life. They found it interesting that it was modern technology that allowed them to enjoy the simple life: old-fashioned pleasures, like staying home and working around a place, while still remaining connected to the world electronically. Frank wired One Wing with sophisticated surveillance and created an impenetrable fortress of invisible electrical force fields which activated at the sound of an alarm. He feared someday this might be needed. Instead of geese, he took ten baby pigs to raise into fierce hogs. They were good protection, and Jessie would never abide geese. For companionship, he had a young kitten he'd found on the streets of New York City, and named Baby Beast. He partook of all the kingdoms he loved; animal, plant and electronic, just as his grandpa had, and he felt happily surrounded by the psychic element he found in all these kingdoms. He was a champion of Arthur C. Clarke; whose third law was: "Any sufficiently advanced technology is indistinguishable from magic."

In one room of the log house, Frank built bookshelves, and set up a library for all Henry's old books and magazines. He read avidly in Henry's old Scientific American's and kept a subscription current.

When Tom found out Frank was at One Wing, he was furious. He brought his legal power to bear, spearheading a class action suit against Jessie and the LODS, for libel, slander, and making defamatory statements about dead people on TV. It was easy to get people to join in the suit. She had lots of enemies.

Tom changed his will and cut his own son out of his life. Now, like Jessie, Frank had been shunned, and completely disowned.

27
The Interview

A picture of the new LODS penthouse was on the cover of <u>Newsweek,</u> and then on the cover of <u>O.K.</u> and other popular magazines, sparking new waves of controversy. Mainly featured was the LODS "living lobby" where people were allowed to visit, up to a hundred at a time, while being closely watched by guards armed with stun-guns. Jessie herself had insisted on the lobby, which was up an escalator, refusing to be ruled by fears for her safety. She said, "if the fans can get close, they won't be so obsessed, they'll feel included and respected." She envisioned a combination of visiting the White House and falling UP a rabbit hole. All visitors had to proceed through a body scanner, and a search. They had nose dogs, bomb detectors and other kinds of unintrusive security that had become available from Homeland Security.

Barbara Waters came to them this time for the postponed interview. Some time had passed before the "get" could be rescheduled. Waters and her network considered Jessie a clever mentalist, a personality, someone to be reckoned with, since she had everyone's attention.

Jessie had grown distant in her new rabbit hole, withdrawn. She had changed, Jane claimed, maybe because of the place, the attempts on her life, or the miscarriage. She slept too much and did not seem interested in anything. She was not even what Jane considered a regular, everyday person anymore. For one thing, she didn't seem to have any appetite and wouldn't eat; it took lots of coaxing. On her own, she'd eat a chocolate Hershey bar with almonds or canned whipped cream. It was as if sorrow had driven her temporarily insane. She seemed to be losing her personality, as well as weight, drowning in a sea of messages mostly from the September dead that were ever more pressing on her. Some days she hardly spoke to Jane and Seaborn– she was in a fugue state. Her eyes stayed focused on her TV audience, just looking to make that spiritual hole-in-one. Or she would completely withdraw, and they had to air reruns.

Jane felt sorry for Seaborn. His wife was hung up on her father. It was all so hard to understand. She tried to console him, he seemed so lonely, especially at night, when Jessie was apt to leave their bed, and stay up for hours tapping out messages from Henry. Jane didn't mind being Sea's go-to. He could unburden his existential woe on her anytime. She considered it part of her job to take care of him too.

Before the interview began, Jane led Barbara Waters and her crew in a walkaround of the private living area. Every room had one curved wall, and Jane had chosen a theme of Elysian opulence in the colors and textures of the rooms: soft blues, auric-yellows that glowed, fresco-pale apricots. By their combined radiance they created a calm, ethereal air. Jane dressed Jessie in these misty colors too, although Jessie hardly noticed and didn't seem to care what she wore anymore. Jane always wore vivid jewel tones to reflect her personality. The marriage bed was round, and Jane piled baby dolls on the pillows, trying to comfort Jessie, as she would a little girl. Anything she could think of that might bring Jessie back to herself, back to the living.

Waters was enchanted, as though she'd found herself in a beatific castle. The huge windows looked out on the sky, the Hudson Bay, and the twinkling illusory city that never slept. Jane explained to Barbara that their picture windows were one-way; on the outside, they were mirrored tiles. She showed her the Bucky-ball draperies for drawing across the windows, which looked like linen, were the color of flax, yet had the strength of carbon 60. She impressed Barbara with many unique devises, most of which Frank had a hand in engineering.

Barbara picked up an object d'art and said for the camera: "The place is serious. It lends itself to soul-making by its very beauty. You feel full going through these rooms, nourished. There is a dimension of magic here." What she really thought is that it was all an elaborate ruse.

The camera panned rooms where employees were packing up DVD's, and bound books of transcripts, a cottage industry kindled by the growing demand for the afterlife. It traveled around the gorgeous gigantic "living lobby" as it was called, where fans and proselytes were snagging a chance to stay a while in something close to celestial comfort. It peered down an escalator to the floor below and held on a big neon sign that said in rainbow colors:

THE LIFE OF DEATH SHOW THERE IS STILL TIME

Interviews were at the top of their form. Everyone loved them, privately fantasizing what they would say in their own interview; what questions they would like to be asked. Ordinary people rehearsed a startling revelation, the bon mot that would "make" the interview—the world craved new utterances. People were fiending for social interaction. The interview had endured to a classic form, pervading culture like the opera, or rock n' roll, and it was even sometimes credited with displacing some of the violence on television. People would rather gossip. Juicy gossip, not made tedious by morality, brought about a certain kind of intimacy, without the necessity of contact. And talky interviews were like little novels, inviting the audience to identify, and take a rooting interest in the characters. They created ebullient melodrama, even romance. Once the interview form merged with the talk-show form its ascendancy on the airwaves was rivaled in popularity only by The Life Of Death Show. People were slightly more interested in hearing from the dead than the alive.

In her intro, Barbara Waters said: "It has become a talk-show world, and perhaps the greatest talk-show of them all has on, as its guests, spirits from another realm, visited upon one earth angel named Jessie."

The interview with Jessie that followed was not a success, not a keeper. Waters broke down and dissolved in tears right at the beginning, when Jessie gave her a message that popped in her mind on the spot from a departed relative with a glass eye: *If you don't have a temple in your heart, you'll never find your heart in a Temple.* Waters remembered hearing her Father say this in her childhood, it was his mantra, and in a moment of sudden self-awareness, she made the discovery that she had built her personality on that simple philosophy. She had a nirvana experience right on camera, smiling and crying at the same time.

So, Jessie had been the one to interview Barbara Waters, murmuring reassurances to stop her crying, and urging her to talk about her memories. Waters life-long conviction that there was no afterlife had shattered while her guard was down, and she was in a state of shock, infected with belief. Jessie took no pride in conversions though. She simply tried to be a friend to Barbara, like she supposed a regular person would do.

The network thought the interview was compromising for Waters, she was too vulnerable, and that it gave Jessie the upper hand. Barbara had even begun (uncharacteristically) quoting Wordsworth of all people: "Faith, that lodestar of the ghost..." she'd mumbled on camera. It would all have to be done over when Barbara was her strong self again.

Jessie agreed to meet at another time, and in another place. The network ran a back-up interview instead, not bothering to let Seaborn in on what they were running. When Seaborn saw it on the air he was outraged. He felt sorry for Chuck-Pete. It was one more thing that he would have to make sure Jessie never saw.

The interview had been taped a few weeks earlier. It featured Dr. Desmond, safe in his studio-office setting, with cutaways of Chuck-Pete Monroe talking and lounging in a limo as he traveled to see his agent, or some important director, it was unclear where he was headed. Chuck-Pete felt flattered by having been asked to do a prime-time interview, even if it was with some shrink he didn't know. He hired the limo to look hot, and busy. He was both. He currently had the lead role of McMurphy in a Broadway revival of *One Flew Over The Cuckoo's Nest*. A perfect role for him. It was a big hit. Besides, he felt safe from stampedes inside a limo. His fame had grown, and he lived in constant fear of being assaulted. He'd shown a flair alright, yes indeedy. He could play a romantic actor, a villain, and a comic hero, his favorite role. He hoped his versatility would be the thrust of the interview and get him new and interesting parts. He supposed, as always, he would be in charge of the Shenanigans, humor being one of his long suits. He had a few good jokes lined up. He gave himself one final mirror face in the rearview and put his insecurities to rest with an encouraging wink. Then he had waited, and waited...

There were problems with the video feed, and delays, one after another. So, he had a little drink while he waited. Two, three drinks. By the time the interview began, he was fiery with liquor. He felt disrespected and was anxious now just to get it over with.

But right from the get-go this Dr. Desmond's snarky questions were about HER. Who wrote this script? He thought he had successfully distanced himself from Jessie— after all, their names were different– hardly anyone connected them. Chuck-Pete couldn't seem to change the subject though. *"Was your sister intuitive as a child? Did you get along? What do you think of her sudden fame?"* Who was this guy? Chuck-Pete fumed and lit another cigarette. He'd taken up smoking recently to calm his nerves. After about the tenth impertinent question, he felt ambushed, no question about it; his patience flew right out the window with the goddamned smoke.

From his secluded studio, Desmond hammered Chuck-Pete with the edge of a guilt-feather, (he knew how competitive the sibling relationship could be,) until, at last, Chuck-Pete lost his ego-bearings altogether, and started raising Cain: "Who do I look like? her keeper? I thought you wanted to talk about ME! She's just a silly goose, she's looney tunes."

So, then Desmond asked him how he felt about being under investigation in the shooting attempts on her life. That was it, Chuck-Pete's ire was now full blown: "You call that proof of anything?" He stamped his feet, an unusual sound in a limo, and started fiddling with the video feed to Desmond trying to disconnect it. He yelled: "Jessie's crazy; we've got the damn papers that say she's crazy!"

The camera zoomed in on the vein in Chuck-Pete's neck which was bulging dangerously. He looked like he'd been had. Then it cut back to Desmond's self-satisfied face, and thence to a commercial.

After the interview, Reverend Thackston who happened to be in the studio watching it patted Desmond on the back. "That was good! It's juicy news when family members renounce each other, shameful, biblical stuff."

Of course, Desmond knew all about the papers saying Jessie was crazy, since he had been the one who drew them up for brother Tom. Chuck-Pete just hadn't made the connection. Tom had asked Desmond for a diagnosis on Chuck-Pete also, so Tom could hold onto damning papers for him too, in case they were ever needed, on condition that Chuck-Pete never know about it.

The network noting Chuck-Pete's displeasure with the interview apologized and promised him a do over sometime in the future that would go more to his liking.

Desmond had gotten a book deal based on his close and personal examination of Jessie's family of origin, a gene pool like no other. He'd thoroughly researched it: her father Henry, the messenger, was a blood cousin of Eugene O'Neill, and her mother was a Doyle, related by blood to Arthur Conan Doyle. Both were Irish madmen. The publishers hadn't given the go-ahead yet. There was the question of doctor/patient confidentiality. But Desmond contended that Jessie and Chuck-Pete were not his patients. Lawyers were still looking into whether the material in his book might be inflammatory, litigious, etc. Desmond hoped this interview would clinch the deal. In his opinion, Jessie and Chuck-Pete were BOTH certifiable, even Tom was suspect, not to mention Henry. What kind of proof was required? He was the expert, a Doctor of Psychology. And this was the century of the psychiatrist's couch, just as the nineteenth century had been the age of the editorial chair. Marshall McLuhan said so. She had quoted him, from the so-called other side.

Desmond's pitch was that this was not the time for a second-coming sister or daughter-savior, whatever she was. "Next thing you know, she'll be lacing Kool-Aid in some stadium," he said to the publisher's legal department and whoever else was listening, all young people, too young to get his historical references.

Still, Desmond had speaking engagements booked up for the next year at fifty grand a pop. He was doing okay. He had a new coil on his bolo too– solid gold.

28
Scoffers

And so, at a time when the word "vibe" was commonly
used, and people were all about feeling vibrations, the
shewing grew more wondrous; there was a richness and
necessariness to it. Jessie was an app now, entwined in social
media, and her messages went out into all parts of the world.
On twitter hate was still more viral than love, but caring
kindness was catching up. There was in the world a hunger
for goodness. Jessie made it more attractive with her
messages. She was sometimes called the Daughter of God.
The door was open to believing she was sent by a higher
power; the times were elastic. But Jessie wouldn't claim a
special connection to God or heaven; she refused a ride on the
coattails of any religion. Religion was a ground game. The
Zen Napali's believed she was a goddess come to save the
world. But Jessie said she was no goddess– she wished she
was. She found it hard to talk about herself; lately she felt like
she had no self. And anyway, she had the cool conviction that
everyone was sent by a higher power.

Although she was loved by a large audience, there were
lots of scoffers. She couldn't figure out why some people
were so upset by messages from the afterlife and it pained
her, since she knew that she was just an instrument. She was
wounded by charges that she was an actor, and a plagiarist,
and the LODS was just another fake reality show, she was
just a "short-lived meme." Where exactly is the afterlife?
people wanted to know. Like asking where is the internet?
And where are all the wicked people anyway? People were
demanding to hear from them. People wanted to hear some

contrition once in a while. Henry couldn't help. He said he was telling her all he could tell her. *I don't get to choose, it's all random. Still, I try to find spirits. There seem to be huge no-name cosmic intelligences that like to collaborate. But bad energies just aren't around me I guess. I'm not saying there is no evil. It's still there on earth, but it's not here, wherever I am. I'm saying death isn't the end. If there is this afterlife, this realm I'm in now, there has to be some sort of God. But I haven't met it yet either. Unless...*

Jessie was criticized for claiming a false intimacy with death, for being cold and insensitive to the living and the departed alike. She'd been called everything from a wacko, to neurotic, hysterical, mad, and Jane's favorite: pixilated. It hurt. Why were people so cruel? All she ever wanted was to be believed. But was that really all she wanted? She felt more and more isolated and alone with this *gift* weighing so heavily on her. She felt argumentative. What kind of life is this? She wondered. This is not my life. This is Henry's life after death.

When the show raised questions Jessie couldn't answer, she said, *love all the questions, the universe isn't stingy. There are unguessed possibilities. What we know is a cup of water from the oceans. Think of deep time. Everything is impossible, till it ain't.* Henry's words, as always. He loved the up-swelling current of the singularity, finally declaring: *The singularity is God, Jessie, although God isn't singular. God's an infinite multiple. And technology is sentient. It unleashes the supernatural. Light is Gods language—he manages the universe with it. I've been looking for Stephen Hawking but haven't found him yet...*

The Reverend Thackston, along with other religious zealots, accelerated their attempts to malign Jessie because she refused to partner with them, or even to acknowledge them. She never listened to them on the radio, or watched when they were on TV, the way Seaborn did. She didn't feel anything in common. They were not her family. Jessie's TV audience was her family now.

One day Henry was troubled: *Fore! I can't find my father, Jess. When I try, all I get is a memory of the taste of rhubarb pie, that pungency and sweetness mingling, and how my mouth used to water anticipating it. My father loved rhubarb and so did I—must be genetic. Also, I get the memory of mustard. Why was there always plenty of mustard? We were so poor we took mustard sandwiches to school. Memory is a funny thing, like dreams. When I was a little boy I couldn't stop wetting the bed, so my father tied a bottle on my penis and made me wear it to sleep. I ache with shame thinking about that. Lots of spirits have memories of childhood shaming. Still if I could, I'd find my father. I can't find Farnsworth either. He comes after Emerson when I'm drawing from the chambers of my memory. He first got the idea for television in Utah, at the age of 12. Did you know Farnsworth's Image Dissector went into space? `the Eagle has landed...' TV unleashes the supernatural world. I'll keep looking though. Found Hogan, who told me: Great champions do not come out of the pack; they don't play by conventional rules. Tell them this from Emerson: Nothing can bring you peace but yourself. The only way to have peace is through integrity, through the triumph of principles, through forgiveness. Ursula d. 2019 says freedom is a sweet invention, cherish it. Try to remember it when the hard times come. Harriet d. 2017 wants to tell her daughter: you don't have to set yourself on fire to keep other people warm.*

A couple of days a week Seaborn went to real estate closings with lawyers in New York, New Jersey and Connecticut, where he bought, and then reconveyed houses

Jane had picked out on the Internet and elsewhere. She had good taste in houses, as in everything, and she believed rightly that price was only ever an issue in the absence of value. In faraway states like California and Florida, they participated in closings by phone, FAX, and the internet. The money to buy the houses mostly came from stock profits, from the tips Jessie received from the World Trade spirits. Seaborn acted on lots of these tips and made money. The idea of posthumous insider trading tickled him.

He always took Jane with him to the closings and they went in his Personal Helicopter, which he'd learned to maneuver expertly. This was their favorite activity. It kept them from going stir crazy holed up inside One World Trade. Their aim was to help homeless families, Indians, Latino's, people of color and other minorities to colonize. All the groups that were behind in owning homes. Real estate was the basis of wealth and self-esteem on the ground. They "sold" homes to families that expressed an earnest need and desire, "for one-dollar and other valuable consideration," which was a handshake, and a promise to take good care of the property, as well as their families.

Jane picked out the best houses from among those listed on the MLS market, Zillow, FSBO's, and bank foreclosures. There were always plenty of families applying for homes and she kept a running list. And when they were going to a closing, Jane called a caterer. Seaborn had recognized a spiritual aspect to "the closing table," both secular and mystical. The way everyone gathered together to formalize an agreement for shelter, for a "home," reminded him of The Last Supper. So, he liked the table at the lawyer's office to be groaning with lots of good food and drink. They made a celebration out of each closing.

All sorts of people were tuning in to knowing in a precognitive way, like intuition, knowing before knowing. Psychokinesis was the bliss mode. Even TV play-by-play golf announcers used it to try to move the ball and influence the outcome of matches, speaking in quietly hushed voices into microphones: *I channeled with him for that miraculous birdie at number seven.*

Mr. Rodgers, who had died on a snappy new day in February of 2003 sent a message: *Dreams prove the world is really transcendental. Do you know what that word means, boys and girls?*

Art was another up-swelling current of the new century. Art was taking over not only among spirits, but on the ground too. It had proven to have value beyond money; it was the highest form of hope. More artists, poets, intellectuals, and creative types were being elected to political office everywhere around the globe. They had as their model a deceased architect/poet named Havel who believed that lost culture could be redeemed by writing poetry and making art. He was one of Henry's strongest spirits, coming through often, determined to open the door for poets and artists to seek public office and run the world on a preservationist platform. He'd left a legacy in his own son, who was a politician and wrote poetry that was lapped up like soul nectar.

On the LODS, Jessie said: *All the Art of ancient Egypt springs from their belief in the afterlife– il faut cree' = YOU MUST CREATE. Emerson says to speak wildly with the flowering of the mind. Ginsberg says flowering is where it's at. John Peeple Tarlton, d. 2008 says to Learn why the world wags and what wags it. Iris Murdoch here: I died in 1999. All the best people are dead. Perhaps the living can always outwit the dead. But theirs is a hollow victory. The work of art laughs last. Oscar Fingal O'Flahertie Wills Wilde, d. 1900, my real name– isn't it beautiful? G.O. 'K., Just call me Georgia. The secrets of life are in art. A color sense is more important in the development of the individual, than a sense of right and wrong, because if you develop a color sense, you instinctively know right from wrong.*

One broadcast featured dying words. Jessie said: *Henry's last dying words were "go out there and make sure the yard man doesn't run over my roses." From Tim Leary, d. 1996, My dying words were "why?" then, "why not?" still good questions. Ibsen: My last word was "but." Shakespeare's dying words were "love denied blights the soul." And Kabir said: "do you think that the same power that gave me radiance in the womb would abandon me now? It is I who turns away and walks alone into the darkness." And O. Henry's last words were: "Turn up the lights, I don't want to go home in the dark." And Linq, d. 9-11-01, said: I knew it was time to go, but I had no time.*

One day the fax spewed pages of nine-elevens, with more dying words. Jessie was pelted with the terrorist furies again and seized with the comprehension of how all the living had also died a little on that long-ago day in September. She was tormented, catching blow-back that pierced her heart, and went on non-stop. And being indoors day after day, she longed for nature, trees, grass, silver lakes. She didn't even know what season it was. She could only vaguely remember a time when she used to be sunny and happy out in the world, the great outdoors. Now she was filled with anxiety and a biological loneliness. She had not told Seaborn about the miscarriage yet, it was a surreal blur to her, and she did not want to put that on him. And too much time had passed.

Then a quiet period set in, and Jessie became enervated, limp, like a prisoner released from the throes of the rack. She read some of Allan Grossman's poetry hoping for energy: "Deep in the brain's cave is the world set right; a great house: warm, intelligent, alight." Henry tried to sooth her. Instead of his own voice, he brought the yearning voice of a Wedding Singer who crooned: *Someday my happy arms will hold you and someday I'll know that moment divine when all the things you are, are mine...* love songs. Henry knew music stimulated oxytocin. What she needed to continue.

She slept for days. Not true sleep though, her body was restless. She thrashed and tore at her gown and flung the baby dolls off the bed. Messages poured into her minds core, which was now just a stream of mortal consciousness. There weren't even any Fores! Henry had been overwhelmed too. When Jessie awoke, she delivered a barrage of nameless, 9-11 messages: *It's hard to get anyone's attention when you're alive but it's not so important when you're dead. / Pay attention to the children. They need certainty, and there is none. You create it for them. / There is a need for greater ingenuity in the world. / You saw steel smelting and buildings full of people plunging to the ground; when my body began to avalanche down, my soul took wing. / I saw our baby take her first step. She drew me right to her. / I took my shorts out of the dirty clothes basket that morning because they had become relatively the cleaner pair. / look for a strongbox full of gold hidden in the attic under the rafters for this rainy day. / Getting old is the hardest thing I was unprepared for anyhow. / My lovely pregnant wife don't worry. I see our baby. I get to examine the nature of unborn awareness now, the bud of innocence at the heart of all persons. The sun shone as it had to. Ha Ha the joke was on us. There never was any security at all...*

In the weeks that followed, Jessie became despondent, uneasy, and adrift. She felt confined, locked up in the studio day after day, remembering the beauty of the world that she was being deprived of. She woke up every morning now in a dull depression. She realized she was merely subject to the whims of Henry, with hardly any claim at all to a life of her own. She was a slave to Henry's wishes and what's darker than slavery? Nothing. She'd become the darkness she abhorred. Death ought to be an alien. Was it fame that was so heavy and burdensome, or was it Henry and her own passivity before him? He claimed to have no ego—that was a lie. He had plenty of ego, even dead. She thought of Mathew from the Bible: What do you benefit if you gain the whole world but forfeit your own life? When she looked back she saw she had given up everything, her own life, and Seaborn's as well for Henry. What they were doing hurt Seaborn. He was a good man and what the world needed most was good men. They wanted a baby. Tests on both of them had shown nothing. If I don't have a baby, I'll die before I die, she screamed inside. She wanted a family, friends, a regular life again. Was there really still time? She had reached the land of now or never. It came down to messaging or motherhood. A subversive idea began to take shape, of resisting Henry, of escape. It filled her with fear, dread, and hope, all at the same time. She would have to conquer the fear somehow to get free of this ruinous gift. She would have to go against Henry who had become her demon, her tormentor. But how could she do it? She'd never once defied him. She knew the lengths he would go to, to exist. He'd never turn her loose. She would have to kill Henry to live.

Back at One Wing Flapping, Frank kept abreast of everything that went on atop One World Trade. It was a major part of his day. He had created the enabling program himself, one that could not be accessed by anyone else on earth, not even the Russians. It was a unique network, capable of shipping enormous amounts of information back and forth at gigabit speeds. He communicated with his "family" unsurveiled by outsiders. He saw all the broadcasts, the transcripts, witnessed the studio and household functioning, the behind-the-scenes workings. When he wanted to talk privately to Jane or Seaborn or rarely to Jessie herself, he turned the scrambler on so no one else could make out what they said. And when they wanted to leak information to the world press, they left the scrambler off, went off-book, and word spread.

Frank was worried about Jessie's recent slump, and her distraught state of mind, which he probably knew as much about as anyone. He was what his father Tom would call an eyewitness. Seaborn was busy shielding her from the death threats that were now multiplying daily, as well as insults from Tom and Chuck-Pete. He had all but given up on having a regular family life with kids of their own. Jane was doing all that she could: hiring more guards and beefing up security around the penthouse. But to him, Jane voiced her fears about Jessie's instability, her profound restlessness and discontent, her erratic consciousness, her jangled nerves, her lost appetite.

Frank felt a turning coming.

PART THREE

29
Midnight Conception

The large bedroom was warm and moist like a greenhouse. Amber light cast a paradisal glow in the round outreaches, where live tropical flowers silhouetted the rococo botanicals painted on the curved walls. The bucky-ball draperies were drawn across the huge picture windows, around which kudzu was trained in loop-de-loops because Jessie loved the scent of its bloom. It smelled like the grape Kool-Aid from her childhood. A round bed was moored out in the middle of the room, sitting in owl's light, like an airboat parked in the foreverglades. Encircling the bed from ceiling to floor was a white, gauzy canopy of veiling. And within this veiled Eden, Jessie and Seaborn were making love.

At the moment of an intense orgasm, Jessie was transported inside her own body, to the snug fallopian folds of her womb where she witnessed with a kinesis of all her senses, the champion swimmer sperm in a cast of thousands, make the egg, lash it with its tail rotating at 8 rpms in a love dance, then burrow through the protoplasm, and go for the wall. Witnessing this miracle exhausted her, and she fell asleep and forgot it, cradling a plump baby doll in her arms.

Seaborn luxuriated in the afterglow, satisfied of his need for love and fullness at his heart's core. He knew love was only ever as good as the lovers and this night they had been good. Jessie had been all his, they were one. Wasn't that the magical goal of lovemaking?

He held her loosely while he enjoyed the rippling warmth of sated sex, and he soon dozed off, with Jessie dreaming in his arms.

After a while Jessie separated from Seaborn, buckled like a slinky toy, and rolled off the round edge of the bed. Her head hit the floor last, with a hard whomp.

A cat's nap later, Jessie woke on the floor, and couldn't remember how she got there. She sat up, sniffing the air like a frightened animal, a strangled scream caught in her throat. Her head ached. Her heart pounded. Her hair was a damp tangle across her face. Naked, she hugged her knees to her chest, desperately trying to recapture a dream as vivid as real life. In the dream, she saw her mother Doris, in her bedroom, slumped over in a chair, dying. She saw her soul, a tiny little light, disjoin from her body and jerkily ascend upward, like a strobe walking. Then she saw Doris lying in a hospital in a coma, but that hadn't mattered; the moment when she left the Earth had been in the chair. It horrified her that the soul could be gone from a body that was still alive. How could it ever get back?

Jessie caught movement in the room and saw through the gauzy veiling she was all twisted up in, a woman in a thin red dress, looking at her and smiling. She had the unsubstantial look of a balloon. She began to float around the room lighting candles– she filled her mouth with air like a blowfish, and with a *poof*, she lit candle after candle, just with her breath.

Jessie gasped, "How'd you do that? Who are you?"

The woman smiled again. She floated around to the other side of the bed where Seaborn lay sleeping, faded back into the shadows, and disappeared, like a minor actor leaving a stage.

Now the room was all alight in candles. They were casting crabbed shadows, like aspersions from her dream. I was at death's door, Jessie thought. She looked around the room and felt a dislike for it. I like my bed up against a wall for one thing, with square corners and a headboard. What is this veil thing? She swatted the gauze, crawled out from under it and stood up. But she was dizzy, and she leaned back against the bed, grabbing hold of the covers.

The room seemed an outlandish scale. She drew her long hair around her face for some protection. A chill feeling of rootlessness filled her. She trembled and rolled her head to scoot away all the shadows that she might be taking for substance, for ghosts, like that was a common possibility.

She saw she was still not alone. Another woman, small and Asian, wearing a golden sari and swaging a ruglet of animal fur round her neck, moved, buttery-smooth on the other side of the bed. The woman seemed to be messing with Seaborn, who was asleep, or maybe he was awake. She batted the face and tail of her pelt trying to fascinate him; causing Jessie to abruptly yell: "Okay, get out of here whoever you are—go now!"

Jessie rubbed her eyes with both hands. When she looked up, the woman was gone. She had an overwhelming desire to speak, as if the words were coming up from some dim, stored engram for de-devilments, for laying ghosts. She trilled: "Go. Go in peace, all of you. Requiescat in pace." and didn't recognize her own pip-squeaky voice.

She crawled back into bed and scooted close to Seaborn who had awakened and had propped himself up on pillows, with his hands behind his head, laughing softly, but trying to hide his mirth. Jessie could see him in the dim light grinning, as though it was only an everyday ring of familiar fairies visiting them.

"You saw them too, didn't you?" She said. She jabbed him in the ribs so he couldn't hold back his laughter any longer. "That really happened, didn't it? Didn't it?" she jabbed him again until he laughed freely.

"Okay, okay, take it easy," he said, "take it easy, they're gone, probably Jane's little helpers just looking in on us."

Jessie was so relieved she whooped and jumped on Seaborn, straddling him, "Oh, thank God, for you, Seaborn. I thought I was going crazy. I love you, love you, love you." She bussed his mouth with kisses.

But there was something smeared on Seaborn's hairless chest and Jessie snatched her hand away and looked at it.

"Ay yi yi," she said, her face a moue of distaste, "You've got something all over you." She smelled her hand, surprised, "uuumm...it's chocolate!"

"Of course, it's Hershey's—your favorite—you frosted me a little while ago with a chocolate massage, don't you remember?"

Jessie did not remember. She stared blankly at Seaborn's chest.

"When we were fooling around...hey, what's wrong?"

Jessie backed off the bed frowning, shaking her head. It was like coming out of a fog. She pulled on a flimsy robe she'd never seen before which was crumpled on the floor, and moved uncertainly around the room, with a ravening curiosity. She turned on lamp lights and picked up objects d'art that were lying on tables. In the light, she became enthralled with the lavishness of the place, the painted trompe l'oeil effect on the walls, vaguely familiar, like a page she might have seen in <u>Architectural Digest.</u> She thought it must be a posh hotel. She crept lightly, arms folded, hugging her elbows. But when she came to a place in the wall painted cleverly to hide a door, she found the knob, opened the door, and peeked out into the adjoining room. She saw a hallway of people she didn't know lying around on banquettes. She shut the door quickly and ran back to Seaborn.

"Who are all those people?"

"Most of them work for us." he answered, lazily drawing rivulets on his chest, and licking the chocolate off his fingers.

"Doing what?"

"They take care of us sweetheart, protect us. What would you like right now? Name it. Anything in the world you want, I can get it for you." He winked sportively and rang for Jane.

Jessie slid back into the bed close to him, pulled the covers up over her head, and murmured, "I'd like to know where I am and why I feel so damn empty?" She raised up, flopped the covers over in a fold and looked out, "how long have we been here? Is this a hotel?" Her voice trembled.

"Jessie, this is our penthouse, our studio–home." Seaborn said, taking her face in his hands, looking into her eyes, beginning to feel sorry for her. She looked small and endangered.

He felt her head, "What's this bump? You're burning up. Why are you so hot? How did you get this bump?"

She released a big sigh, slapping the mattress, "I fell off this platter of a bed. I don't like round beds. "How did we get here?"

"We got this penthouse with the money from the show, the DVD's, the books you wrote. And thanks to Eli and Smithy's super-management and overarching greed."

"What books? I couldn't write books. That takes years." She pulled away from Seaborn.

"Well, at least you remember me. Glad you haven't clean forgotten everything."

"Of course, I'm married to you." She felt cranky, and doubtful though.

Seaborn shrugged, looking puzzled.

"I dreamed... I don't know what now." Jessie swiped her hair back off her face. "It felt like a dream that was buried inside my real life."

She shook her head, bewildered, on the verge of tears.

"I don't know this place. This is all very strange to me, all but you. You're the only familiar..."

There was a knock and then Jessie saw a petite red head standing in the double doors to their bedroom, holding out a bowl, like an offering. She knew her, from somewhere. Two girls appeared on either side of her, holding out...is that bags of popcorn? She wondered why they all stood in a row, watching, smiling, as though they were waiting for permission or something.

Seaborn called out: "Jane, we need an ice bag, Jessie fell off the bed. She's got a big goose egg on her head." He lowered his voice, mumbled, "and a big gap in her memory."

Jessie got up and walked over to the Jane with the bowl. Her eyes lit up when she saw that the bowl held black-eyed peas with pieces of crispy streak-o-lean, and corn bread on top.

"Is that for us?" she asked, feeling suddenly like she was starving to death.

Jane nodded and handed the bowl over to Jessie who began eating hungrily, while everyone watched, in amazement. Then they applauded. Jane hurried off to get the ice bag surprised because it was the first time in many moons that Jessie had asked for food.

Jessie, puzzled by the applause, snatched a bag of popcorn from one of the girls and closed the doors in their faces, surprised by how cranky and rude she was getting away with being, but her head was hurting bad. She had a vague memory that her deepest instinct was to be nice, but she just couldn't live up to it.

"Why were they all clapping?"

"Because you took the beans. It's a challenge for them to find something you'll eat. Did you recognize anyone?"

"Jane... Jane, I think. But where do I know her from? Who were the others?"

Seaborn grinned, "GOG's. Jane hires all the staff, mostly good ole girls, she calls them GOGs; most reliable sort of girl on the planet, Jane says, if they aren't too Bible-whipped. Some people think you're just a good ole girl too, Jessie Lee—it pops up in your language sometimes. Like you called me your Hill William, said I was a Hillbilly with class. Remember that?"

Jessie frowned. She looked down at the warm bowl of peas and bacon. "I love these beans and I feel like I'm starving to death." She ate ravenously, scraping the bowl, glad there was a chunk of cornbread to sop up the juices with. Her headache began to ease some.

"You love me too?" Seaborn asked.

"Like my own life." She answered automatically, and their eyes met acknowledging the answer they always gave each other.

"Only, this place... it's like a foreign country."

She put the empty bowl down and got back into bed with Seaborn, snuggling him. They began to fool around under the covers. Seaborn gripped his penis and said it was only half-hard.

Jessie whispered: "The other half is hiding and won't come out until all these strangers leave."

"Oh, I don't mind the people anymore," Seaborn said.

But Jessie heard weariness in his voice. "Well, I do," she declared, and leapt off the bed. She straightened her robe, tied the sash, and charged out through the faux-painted door to the outer room, ordering everyone she saw to leave.

"Whoever you are, go. Get out of here," she sang out crazily, not sure they would accept her authority. She was at the point of not caring. People giggled at her but began moving along anyway, as if they might be leaving; some of them went to find Jane.

Jessie barged through double doors at the far end of the hall and entered a large screening room. Media pundits watched monitors and spoke into voice-notebooks, about Jessie Pettengill, calling her names, like, "Firebrand Priestess" and "North American Channeler." They strained for tag lines. When they saw her, Cameras began clicking and questions started flying.

"Jessie, do you think nuclear FUSION is the greatest invention of all time?" someone asked, and then there was a buzz of nattering questions, while Dragon Dictate voice processors printed out every spoken word.

"Do you like neural networks? Do you object to the mapping of your genome? Is it true the attorney representing all those people suing you for using their dead relatives' names is your own brother?"

"I don't know what you all are talking about, so would you please just leave." Jessie said over the din, feeling bewildered and ineffectual, like she wasn't even being heard. She shrugged and ran out of there, down the hall. This must be a studio, yes, she was a news anchor, that's who she was, she remembered that, sort of.

The media people ran after her. Then she bumped into a whole new horde of people. They were coming up a ramp into a gigantic living room, all of them thrashing to enter. Some were dressed in costumes. The room full of people made Jessie feel angry, argumentative. She raised her voice:

"What are you all doing here? Don't you people ever sleep? It's the middle of the night."

She saw a huge neon rainbow sign:

"THE LIFE OF DEATH SHOW @ THERE IS STILL TIME"

"It's a tour, lady. Hey, you're Jessie! Wow!"

Every eye in the room locked onto Jessie. People rushed to surround her, putting their hands all over her, shoving each other out of the way, which resulted in shoving her too. Murmurs of appreciation mounted to catcalls and screams, as they got rougher and wilder.

Jessie screamed, "Get out! This is crazy. I don't want company right now." Everyone in earshot laughed and hooted—that Jessie, she never could resist making a joke.

Guards rushed over, led by Jane, horrified to see Jessie nearly dishabille, totally vulnerable. They shoved the fans away from Jessie, who was mauled and shaken, but still standing, struggling to fix her robe which had nearly been torn off.

The crowd began chanting: "Autograph...autograph, gimme skin...hair...relics...Jess-eeee.

Jane moved in front of Jessie protectively, and handed her an ice bag, motioning for her to get going, pointing the way back to the room.

A bunch of moaning, whining women wearing purple-hooded capes spotted Jessie and all at once advanced like a swarm towards her. Jessie felt a word, *Jeremiads*, enter her mind; she had the memory of an old fear, of being overrun by these piteous women. She turned and made a break for the bedroom, her own, hopefully lockable, quarters.

Jane and the guards blocked the Jeremiads. Death groupies is how Jane described them. They complained loudly but moved back to their own corner in the big "living lobby" where they watched LOD'S reruns on the big screen plasma TV and ate sweets.

Seaborn was still lounging around on the bed when Jessie burst back into the room. She slammed the door and locked it. "How long has this been going on?" She demanded, breathless.

"let's see..." Seaborn looked at his watch, "It's October fifteenth... it's almost five years now, since Henry died..."

"Henry? My father. Who's the President?" Jessie didn't wait for the answer. "Oh, my God, I've lost all those years?" She paled, wreathed in sweat and confusion." This is an awful place—there's no privacy—strange people milling around, touching me." She swiped her arms.

"It's exactly what you wanted. You said it was impossible to be alone anyway, what with all the latent spirits roaming around everywhere like satellites."

Jessie plopped the ice bag on her head. "How on earth do we live crowded in with so many people?"

"I don't know, but we do. It's crowded everywhere. Now look at this!" Seaborn drew back a shoji screen, exposing a workstation with a menagerie of aural word-processors, computers, a bank of video-screens. There were caddies of video-archives, DVD's, piles of books with Jessie's name on the bindings.

"You sat in front of one of these Dragon Dictates for hours at a time, enchanted. We had to take you off it, to feed and bathe you and put you to bed. All your broadcasts are taped and transcribed in books too."

Jessie pulled out a book, opened it and read randomly: *Nothing matters but dramatic benevolence. Excitement uses up too much natural energy. If you don't get too excited, you'll have time to be charming.*

"I don't care about being charming," she said, "I'll be charming once I figure out what the hell is going on."

She sunk down at a Dragon Dictate voice processor and punched in a couple of keys and magically a bright blue screen lit up with stars blinking in it. "It's the Universe!" she chirped, and her words appeared floating in the blue.

"Frank designed it, along with practically everything else we have. Remember Frank?"

Jessie tapped out F-R-A-N-K and immediately an image formed in her mind of a young, teen-aged Frank, and she said with relief: "My nephew Frank, yes," and her words came up on the screen.

"You said you had to create from out of the known Universe, so Frank simulated a Universe. We've learned to take you literally, like a child, and we always try to provide whatever you ask for. You mainly write with your voice; but sometimes you still tap the letters out. And usually you intermingle the senses. You're a synesthete. You use all your senses including a couple that most people don't have. They think that's how you get Henry's messages. It's a cognitive fossil in some people. You use Esperanto too, and got everyone else using it, the universal language, and someone's always signing for the deaf. I can't believe you don't remember any of this."

Seaborn knew that time could wear down even the sturdiest of mystics, but he was afraid to hope that Jessie had actually been released from Henry's iron grip.

"How's your head?"

"It's better. Tell me, what did I write about?"

"The essence is of death, the life of death, the death state itself, all gleaned through messages from, uh, the dead."

He saw Jessie's face drop, so he hastened to reassure her, "Really great dialogues– you name names– that's why you're so popular. People never know when they're reading along if someone they knew will turn up talking, you know, like from a LODS they might have missed. They read and watch avidly, hoping for some communication from a loved one. At first everyone thought you were making it all up, but then it was impossible because way too much strange personal stuff was coming through– there was no way you could have known about it."

Jessie stared listlessly at all the computer hardware. "What is LODS?"

"It's short for The Life Of Death Show." Seaborn said. Then hastened to add:

"A Crow Indian named Chester Pretty On Top who all the Crow remember and revere, sent messages. And a Blackfoot Indian Chief who said: "Life is the little shadow that runs across the grass and loses itself in the sunset." I really like the Indian messages. The oldest spirit so far was a woman about a thousand years old who couldn't figure out why she couldn't come back yet– of course nobody knew her. Einstein's still out there waiting to come back, full of regret about the last time, wishing he'd become a watchmaker."

Jessie turned pasty. Holding onto her stomach, she spotted the bathroom, and made a run for it.

"God, you don't remember?" Seaborn called after her, "We have the biggest show on the air. We've got archives of videos; everybody loves the reruns. You talk about death without sorrow. People have parties in cemeteries, and marriage/funeral combos, with barbecues and balloons, even night funerals, dancing, lots of post-mortem pastimes. We televise a lot of it. Dying has become the act of disappearing– a lot of the dread has gone right out of it– and don't you know it's all because of you?"

Jessie retched over the toilet, and Seaborn never stopped talking. Lost the beans. She ran the water, splashed her face, brushed her teeth, breathed weakly. Shocking to look in a mirror. Who was that skinny woman? She heard Jane come into the bedroom bringing more ice. When all you want is tea and a piece of buttered toast, it's lovely to have it. She wished she could have that now but didn't have the sense to ask for it.

Seaborn's enthusiasm did little to lessen the disorientation she was feeling, still she let him go on and on. She had to know. She sat on the bed and listened, while she ate popcorn, chewing it slowly, piece by piece to settle her stomach. He'd always been a long-winded talker, fifty-dollar words. She remembered that. Her face showed her utter bewilderment though. She put the ice bag on her head and tried to understand, tried to remember.

"People don't even care so much about money anymore, you know? They always knew they couldn't take it with them, but now that they know there's someplace else to go, they don't hang onto it so tightly, because there's nothing to spend it on in the invisible realm." Seaborn laughed at how impossible that still sounded after all this time.

"So what DO people care about?"

"Well let's see, mostly they care about fat databases filled with good memories, they're after straightforward love, beauty, knowledge, wisdom, kindness, integrity, character, charm, generosity, talent, a sense of humor, stuff like that; whatever makes a person lovable can go with them you said. People are going after art and beauty, like it's a food group. You told everyone we were coming into a walking-through-walls era and we should prepare."

Jessie shook her head, confounded. She wished she could see herself in all this, but she felt like a stranger in her own life. Seaborn looked slightly older, although his beautiful Indian skin was still tawny and tight. How did she remember his skin? Why were some memories so close, so grounded? Tears began to bubble.

Seaborn hopped back in bed beside her and took both her hands in his. "Hey don't cry. Everyone lives in hope of bridging this world with the other one, like you do."

"What other one?" Her tears streamed now.

"The one you're always off in, with Henry."

"My Father? He's dead though, isn't he? But I'm not. Can't you see I'm right here, and I don't know about any of this!"

"Good, you remember that Henry died at least, that's good..."

Seaborn took her in his arms, but she squirmed loose, batted the veiling out of her way, jerking it back on both sides of the bed, exasperated, "This is smothering me."

"I thought you liked it, for a little privacy. You love this beautiful room, all of Jane's decorating ideas."

"I like screened-in porches, not beds." Her hands dropped to her lap where she absently held one of the baby dolls.

"How much does this place cost, anyway?" she suddenly wanted to know.

"Eli and Smithy handle it."

"Oh yes, my producers." Jessie was surprised that she remembered them, "But exactly where are they? and where are we?"

"We are on top of One World Trade Center, in an observatory penthouse, outfitted especially for us. And they are in an office of their own downstairs. You wanted to be up high remember?" Seaborn took her over to the window. He drew back the drapes, exposing a blue-black sky spiked with stars.

"Look at this amazing view."

"Oh my God," Jessie said, taking it all in, looking down what looked like miles to the ground. They lived in a glass house with clouds lowering down on them like fat butts. "I'm getting a splitting headache. How do you stand all this?"

"I manage. It's a job with no description," Seaborn winked a playful wink at her.

"I want my ordinary life back," Jessie said faintly, "I need the ground under my feet."

"But you have it all now, honey, everything anyone could want. You are loved and you're famous. You live a magical life. People are saying God so loved the Earth that he sent his only begotten daughter."

"Oh sure," she scoffed, "so what are you doing having sex with God's daughter?"

"She likes sex," said Seaborn, wrestling Jessie down on the bed and tickling her until she giggled wildly despite everything.

Suddenly she was pummeling Seaborn's chest with the doll, beating him to a fare-thee-well, yelling things she didn't even mean, crying out all her frustration.

Seaborn held onto her through it all, until exhausted, she surrendered and let him hold the ice bag on her head. The cool felt good. The room was candlelit and dim. Someone had turned off the lamps. She finally stretched out and began to relax.

"Rest now Jessie, the doctor will be here in a little while to look at this bump. You must have bruised your hypothalamus or campus region, whatever it's called, the part that controls your memory, that's all."

But as she fell asleep Jessie was thinking about something else. She had an idea. It came from Merlin: "Fate can go begging, destiny has to be won."

30
The Dream Speaks

Most of the candles had burned out, and they had both fallen asleep again. From the darkness around the bed the dream came back to Jessie, the dream the two ghost women seemed to have come out of, the dream of her Mother dying. She had to finish this dream. She knew she had paid the price of her memory for it. In the re-dream, the two ghost women were sitting with Jessie's mother, Doris, and her archangel grandmother, under interstellar arches made of gases and what-not, chatting in the foggy jasmine scented mists. Four chairs, four women, all seemingly with one heartbeat. Or was that her own heartbeat? Time was away and somewhere else. Doris was unhappy about something, as she had always been in life. She had always let her powerful discontent loose in the house. Now this inner friction was out on the table airing, like it was something solid that could be dealt with.

In a river nearby, Jessie sat in a little dory boat, afloat in oystery, cloudy water, avidly watching the women. She smelled wet wood and felt small, like she was invisible. Henry drifted up beside her, playing his harmonica under water. Jessie knew the tune well. *Dada da da da da da da...* It was bittersweet to be with people she loved who had been dead for a long time.

Henry said, *don't get excited now, you're here and you're still there, and everything is accomplished... well, maybe not exactly everything...there are always new messages...*

Jessie felt him pulling her closer, trying to magnetize her all over again into his world of messages. He wanted to keep her with him is all. She opened her mouth to holler, to signal to someone outside the dream to help her, but no sound came out. She didn't want to risk frightening the ghost women away by calling out to them. She still needed the ghosts, her archangel, even Doris, she didn't know why. She looked with longing at them, her eyes entreating...

You are made of star stuff Jessie Lee. Henry said, and drew the boat closer, towards the grandmother he knew Jessie looked up to and loved. He had a choice now. If he let her get away, his role as a light-fingered avatar of messages would be over. He would be neither here nor there. Was the gig up? Might he find companionable silence among the stars?

Jessie looked deeply into her grandmother's eyes, saw her rapt soul, a pure bounty of eternal love and support for all her life. How could she not join her, if that's what she wanted?

But her grandmother cautioned in a whisper: *Love is the most power... the source of true power is practiced love... Love your life now, and do not speak of this anymore. You can live a lot of life before you come here. People who love themselves as Gods creations live the longest.*

Jessie grabbed the oars and began to row hard, leaning with her back to where she was going. Scallops of smoke parted the air, and always there seemed to be one more river to cross. She looked back at everyone, saw Henry reaching for her, his arms extending out in a long rubbery s-t-r-e-t-c-h. He called out: *Come back Jessie Lee, there's still time...*

But the wave wasn't holding.

"No, I don't want to do this anymore. You're dead!" Jessie yelled, desperate to breakaway, to choose life. Isn't that what everyone had to do when a parent dies, in order to become their own true self? Chuck-Pete had done it, and Tom and Kate. Why hadn't she? She watched the band of women ghosts slowly fading; they couldn't function in a state of no affirmation. Jessie's imagination had been exhausted to the point where it wasn't strong enough for them to enter anymore. They were moving up into the up, away from the misty arches, out into the boggling heretofore. She rowed harder and harder, her arms aching from the exertion of dream-rowing backwards, until finally she was propelled awake.

She shot up in the bed and cried out, "Oh God, I got away, I think I'm free of Henry."

Seaborn was startled awake. He wrapped his arm around Jessie and held her.

She was shaking, full of questions, babbling: "How did I remember love and not my own mother's death? There must have been a funeral—did I go? There was something disturbing about it, not what a funeral should be. Was mama in a coma?"

"For a couple of days, Jess, and then she passed."

"Oh God Seaborn, the dead go out into the Universe to atone, not to any heaven or hell. I saw it all. They have a soul like a gene, invisible, but packing a load."

"I know honey, it's okay."

Jessie nestled her head against Seaborn's chocolate scented chest. She pulled the covers up over both of them, and kept her eyes wide open in the darkness, afraid to close them again. Seaborn held onto her.

"I wish we could stay like this forever," she whispered, "you're all I need in this life or any other." She sighed: "Oh Seaborn, you could do so much for me if you just would."

"What, Jess? what do you want me to do?"

"Get me out of here. Take me back to where this all began. It feels like I've been frozen and now I'm thawing out. Where is my sister Kate? Is she okay? Where are my brothers? Why would Tom want to sue me? What happened to our life? I have to find it. I have to get our regular, normal life back."

31
Reruns

Early that morning, a neurologist brought in a portable scanner and examined Jessie. He found some swelling around the bump, but no concussion, no signs of stroke or seizure. There was no bleeding.

He asked Jessie, "Were you deprived of oxygen at any time?"

Jessie shook her head.

"Has there been an emotionally stressful incident? A recent traumatic event?"

Jessie nodded, but found it hard to say just what– her mind fogged at the prospect, and she felt tongue-tied. He would never understand.

After a minute or two, when nothing was forthcoming from Jessie, the doctor turned to Seaborn and asked if they'd had sexual intercourse just prior to the memory loss episode. When Seaborn said yes, the doctor gave his prognosis as though Jessie wasn't even in the room:

"I think she has TGA. She's able to forget her troubles, whatever they are, by forgetting who she is; it's anybody's guess how long she needs to do that."

Jessie blinked, amazed at his candor.

"What the hell is TGA?" Seaborn barked.

"Transient Global Amnesia. It's temporary, she'll probably come out of it, given time."

"How much time?"

"Days, weeks, maybe months."

So, with Seaborn by her side, Jessie began watching old reruns of THE LIFE OF DEATH SHOW, hoping to recover her memory. They started at the beginning, when she had suddenly broken form right in the middle of the evening news. One minute she was speaking English, then she sneezed and started speaking in Arabic, a language neither she nor many other Americans knew, even though it was the primary language of three-quarters of the people around the world.

Jessie mouthed the Arabic words she somehow still knew.

"You remember, yes!" Seaborn declared, shaking a loose fist in the air.

He was still such a young fledgling, Jessie thought. How old were they, anyway? A number that had surely lost its meaning. Seaborn would always be young to her, and then she remembered he was three years younger, just enough to make him her best friend and champion.

The video had advanced to a message from Satchell Page, d.1982: *How old would you be if you didn't know how old you are?*

Jessie said to the TV, "I like nineteen."

On the set, above her head, she saw the neon sign: THERE IS STILL TIME

She remembered it had comforted her in a strange way she hadn't really thought about.

Jane came into the room wheeling a cart piled high with breakfast. She was hoping Jessie's appetite had returned for real. Her homeostasis had been out of whack for a long time. She had never expressed hunger, nor had she concerned herself with the unending succession of human motivation-reaction units normal people had, like a need for fresh air. To Jane's dismay, Jessie had played with her food like a child, and probably would have died of starvation if Jane hadn't found clever ways of getting her to ingest something besides chocolate and Pepsi Cola. "Great day, she's skinny as a magazine," Jane complained in a dither, feeling responsible for Jessie's condition. Now though, Jane saw, something was different about Jessie.

Jessie got a whiff of scrambled eggs and sausage, and bounded over to get some, almost colliding with Jane and the heaping plate she was fixing to hand Jessie.

"Great day in the morning," Jane caught the plate before it flipped in the air.

"Oh, s'cuse me." Jessie backed up, blushing. She couldn't think how to gracefully cover the nakedness of her hunger.

"That's okay, here, eat! eat!" Jane was tickled pink.

Jessie gulped down the eggs, grits and sausage and started in on the buttermilk biscuits, heaping them with peach preserves. Oh God, it was all so wonderful. She was aware of the good ole girls peeking at her, whispering, and she felt suddenly self-conscious.

Seaborn had put in another video so she could watch while she ate. He went over to a far corner of the room to talk privately with Jane, who turned often and stared at Jessie, who sometimes caught her and stared back.

Jessie wondered idly where the kitchen was, why Seaborn was spending so much time with Jane? Why did she get close to him like that, with such familiarity? She forced herself to turn back around and pay attention to the video.

A segment was running about someone complaining about the flowers not being profuse enough, and another artist saying *painters should begin by cutting out their tongues.* Jessie laughed out loud when Picasso messaged: *I always wanted to be a window dresser, but I didn't know how to go about getting the job.*

She watched herself on television, a startling experience, the more so because of not knowing what she was going to say next. A woman named Putnam sent a message: *A good cabbage has a hard heart, or is it that hard hearts are for cabbages? It's confusing. What I really mean is good people have soft hearts. Why take sentimentality as an accusation when it's really a natural resource? The truth is the entire sum of existence is the magic of being needed by just one other person.*

Jessie's voice changed, went lower: *John Updike, d. 2009, ...the truth is, the world keeps ending but new people too dumb to know it keep showing up as if the funs just started.*

Jessie remembered now, like a movie she'd once seen and forgotten about; when she was messaging, it was like watching another self in motion—she had opened her mouth and gone blind to her own thoughts, the words coming to her on greased wings, fluidly, her eyes pearling with moisture at the flight of words that ran glycerin-like through her mind and slid easily off her tongue. It had been blissful. And afterwards, exhaustion, sleeping deeply for long periods, and dreaming dreams like visiting pasts and going to futures, all unknown and supernatural.

Of course, it was her father who got the messages through; Henry had the grease, he was the messenger. She was just his conduit, a receiver and transmitter in one human being. He had inhabited her mind; he possessed her in a way no one ever had. She had recognized his distinct voice, his sense of humor coming through, then his Fore! Jessie missed him now terribly; and remembering made her feel bereft. Tears brimmed her eyes as she watched what she still hoped was now all over and done with.

At noon, Jane was standing over Seaborn and Jessie waiting for the right time to ask a question. The video had advanced to a sequence about Carl Sandburg, who had stuck little pieces of paper in the pages of books when he was alive, to remember passages he thought were salient. He wanted his successors to read these passages because they had supplied him with points of wisdom he had felt compelled to not repeat in his own work. This had made his own output very small, which he apologized for. Unlike the universe, he didn't like repetition. In the tape, Jessie got bogged down reciting titles of books and page numbers that Sandburg was supplying instead of the actual passages. What a bore, Jessie thought; even the dead could be boring. Sandburg said he had, like the trees, been reduced to numbers because they were purer than words. Jessie hit fast forward.

Jane took her shot: "Eli and Smithy want to know when Jessie will be ready to go on again," she tried to sound casual, upbeat, "they're asking for new messages."

Jessie turned to see the producers lurking in the doorway, a worried look on their faces.

Jane frowned and waved them off. She signaled for a GOG to close the double doors.

Seaborn took Jane aside. He whispered, "Look, I don't think she'll be going on anymore, but keep it on the DL." His hand sliced the air. "She's got some selective amnesia, and nothing new is coming in." He gave Jane a wink and a cool-it smile, squeezing her arm, "Stall them, tell them she bumped her head, make something up."

Jessie watched Seaborn with Jane and felt oddly excluded.

"Okay then, what would y'all like for lunch?" Jane piped, pretty sure that nobody could possibly be hungry again already, but trying to put some cheer in the room, not ready to think of the consequences of Seaborn's little revelation.

"Fried chicken! Pack us a picnic. Let's go to ride. I need nature, animals, plants, fresh air, the ground." Jessie said, hitting the power-off button and standing up, in a burst of decision making new to her.

Jane laughed, covering her mouth, trying not to howl.

"Jess, you can't just go out for a ride anymore," Seaborn explained, "it isn't that simple. If we leave here, there will be lots of people chasing us, running us down." He pressed some keys on a remote, and all sides of the building at the street level came on across a bank of TV monitors. "Take a look at this." People milled around, some of them already in Halloween costumes, some were mourners with flowers, tourists, paparazzi, and crazed fans waiting to catch a glimpse of Jessie. They wore t-shirts that said: "I'M FOR THE AFTERLIFE." They held cameras, urns of ashes, wrapped-up presents, suitcases. Hooded Jeremiads mingled among them.

Jessie looked but did not really connect with what she saw. "Can't you please get me out of here some way? I've got to get back to our home." The word home caused a sudden hot emotion to swell in her chest.

She started pacing around the room, running her hands through her hair, restless and petulant about her captivity. "I'm like a tape that has to rewind, play from the beginning and then maybe I can go forward. I can't sit and watch these old shows forever. They don't tell me how this all happened. This place is a beautiful tomb, but I'm alive. I need to go back to the north Georgia mountains, and old Florida." She suddenly looked afraid, "they're still there, aren't they?"

Jane and Seaborn nodded. But they exchanged a private look, not lost on Jessie.

She sunk down in a chair. They couldn't know how hard she was trying to control a strong desire to just run full tilt. But she knew she'd never make it. She was like a bright red target; her fame was a stranglehold.

Seaborn said: "We've got to get her out, Jane."

Jane pondered a minute, then said quietly, "Okay, I'll work on it." She wished she had a handle on the extent of

Jessie's memory loss, and whether Jessie remembered her or not. She'd been distant, like she didn't know her or trust her either one. Jane was a little put out by that.

"I'd just like to see a tree, one tree," Jessie muttered, "there have to be trees? I want to hear birdsongs. Where is my nephew Frank?

"He's at One Wing Flapping. Do you remember that place?" Seaborn asked.

Oh, yes– please, let's go to One Wing, go see Frank."

"Well, at least she remembers Frank." Jane said.

Seaborn took Jane's arm and led her away from Jessie where he could reassure her that Jessie would remember her and trust her again too, and soon—he was sure of it.

Jessie watched them, feeling jealous about how close they were.

32
Artscience

After a hearty lunch, they took a nap. Seaborn had shoved their round bed up against the wall at Jessie's request. She fell asleep right away. He lay beside her ruminating, too keyed up to sleep. He could feel her emptiness, her sense of displacement. Because she was who she was and he never knew when she might be different, he had found himself always adapting, like atoms and molecules. Atoms knew how to change, they had instincts, intuition, they were his model. If when people died, they went to other realms, and invisibility was another state of being, then humankind really was in a walking-through-walls era and the minds of people had just not caught up yet, as Jessie's had. Huxley was woke and his prolific messages were some of Seaborn's favorites: *What was one day a sheep's hind leg and leaves of spinach was the next part of the hand that wrote, the brain that conceived the slow movement of the Jupiter Symphony.* Everything Seaborn did was an effort to wake up.

Before they could leave World Trade, he had a few important things to take care of: P.O.A.'s to execute for real estate closings in New York and surrounds. Someday it would all come out, where the money went. Seaborn liked playing the stock market with the good tips he got in Henry's messages. He'd developed a knack for creating recurring revenues in the marketplace. Then he plowed the money into houses for the homeless, playing a little game of Monopoly with agents, and lawyers, trusting in their confidentiality. He didn't want what he was doing to come out until he was ready. And that time might be coming soon. Another one of his favorite messages had come from Henry Miller: *I have no money, no resources, no hopes. I am the happiest man alive, only I'm dead.*

Two closings were scheduled up in the Bronx for that afternoon, and one over in Brooklyn, but they couldn't go to them now. Ordinarily that would have been his and Jane's outing for the day. But he saw their old routine was finished. A lot of things were going to change now, and he felt anxious. He needed to talk to Frank.

He and Jane had helped Frank grow up since he'd been living at One Wing Flapping. They had given Frank the stability and balance he needed, although not in person. Instead, they talked on FaceTime every night over dinner, like good friends, filling the night side of their lives with news and speculation about the magic, drinking good wines together. Now, even all that was going to change.

Frank's indifference to money was a joke among them. He hadn't wasted ten minutes of his life on the pursuit of money. Instead, he did everything for the LODS that was asked of him and more, and in return Seaborn paid all the bills and gave Frank carte blanche for whatever he needed in his research. He had his own bank account as well, and a salary. Frank had become their most valuable player, and Seaborn and Jane both knew it. They considered him a natural resource it was their job to preserve and sustain. Jane teased Frank, called him a maverick and a bright-collar worker, and he told her: "I'm just a tinkerer with no collar at all."

Seaborn remembered the time when Jessie relayed a long message from Mr. Noyce and Mr. Kilby. In life, they had invented the microchip, which proved to be the backbone of the second industrial revolution in the nineteen-seventies. He knew it was Frank's all-time favorite message. Noyce and Kilby wanted the world to know that they had both flunked the entrance exam at MIT, and they laughed about it. They wanted to convey how unimportant failing someone else's test really was. The important thing was to keep on with your own work and outlast the failures; failure was simply a temporary state.

Both Seaborn and Frank thought highly of Jane. They admired her empathic nature, and how she stayed grounded and remained intuitive and open. She had a special gift for relieving anxiety, and she had relieved theirs many times when they needed it. Seaborn wondered how much, or if, Jessie even remembered Jane; she was almost hostile towards her. They needed Jane now more than ever. He blessed the day he'd found her and hired her, in spite of those five U-turns to Paradise Cemetery. He laughed remembering. He'd wanted Jane to be the person who helped him protect Jessie, and she had never let him down. Her strength was disguised in a flashy sort of femininity. But he knew she was capable of being as shrewd and calculating as any man in the highest secret service office in the land.

Jane had taken on Frank, six years younger than she was, as her special project, and taught him the practical details of living he somehow missed growing up. She helped him kick a burgeriferous diet, in favor of fish, fruits and vegetables. Seaborn had witnessed all this. If it weren't for Jane, Frank would still have acne. She had reminded him to shower, brush, clip, and floss, as he had been apt to forget about the daily care of his body. She looked after Frank in a subtle way, with just her voice mainly. On FaceTime, she rarely looked directly into the phone while she talked, preferring to move around the room, gentling Frank, with a nurturing matter-of-factness, like chuffing a cub. She had gradually habituated him into taking care of his body, in order to free his mind for its HLD (highest level of development,) Frank's own favorite concept.

And now Frank was in charge at One Wing, and Seaborn had to trust that he knew what he was doing. Frank's two trailers, behind their big log house were jammed full of the latest state-of-the-art electronics, satellite technology, computers, surveillance, and his own little single bed. Frank kept the news and events of the world closely monitored, for all of them, believing culture to be the family of the family. He'd faxed big themes to One World Trade, in the arts and sciences, more and more linked together. The constant genetic developments that he intercepted were first priority to Seaborn, as well as artificial intelligence, and weather and environmental themes, especially the inexorable changes caused by radioactive pollution. They were kept abreast of everything thanks to Frank and Seaborn felt good about getting the chance to go see him at One Wing.

An hour later Jessie woke up, and Seaborn settled her down to watching old videos again, even though she protested. He got on the phone and plotted with the lawyers and real estate agents, faxing them specific P.O.A.'s, so the closings could take place without him. He'd miss the handshake, an important part of the deal, and the table groaning with good food. There were more closings scheduled in Florida that he had to take care of. He'd always thought it was a shame that Tom had been too hidebound to join them. He could have done all the closings in Florida where he lived, but he didn't approve of anything they did, and would not be up for giving away houses.

Seaborn next called Frank and had a long conversation with him, all the while keeping a close eye on Jessie who sat on a floor cushion, wearing a white terrycloth robe, looking like a stranger in a hotel room.

Jessie scanned the taped shows with a haphazard curiosity, afraid of getting too close– wanting only to work up to the present, to the day she awoke, without getting hung-up again in the mania of her entrancement. She wanted to know how all this had been possible, how she and Seaborn had been able to manage it. But the answers were not in the messages, although she found a wealth of other stuff there. Cokie Roberts sent a message saying that she also loved Brenda Starr and she was her role model too. How had she known Jessie's secret?

The interview with Dr. Desmond had been aired. There she was, lying on the couch sobbing, while Desmond in a houndstooth jacket sitting in a brown leather chair attempted to hypnotize her by swinging a silver coil. It was murky in her mind, but she remembered it now. He had given her a drug, maybe in the chocolates, that had sent her into a fugue for hours afterwards. She hadn't known the session was being recorded either. Whatever happened to patient-doctor confidentiality? Was privacy utterly gone?

Jessie quashed the Desmond video. She saw that the date was way back in the beginning. "Mama" was the sound that emitted from her throat. She smeared away tears with the back of her hand, thinking of her haunted dreams and feeling again a sharp stab of grief.

Dr. Desmond had looked so reputable– how could anyone not believe him? Then it struck her that there must be a whole lot of people out there who did believe him and thought she was insane and waking up would only confirm it. She felt tired, limp, not strong enough for what lay ahead. It was like melting, this waking up. She felt like a piece of ice on a hot stove, riding slipshod over her own downfall.

She went through a dozen other videos, trying to lose the aura of Desmond, and finding The Reverend Thackston instead, his pink demeanor making her shiver with dread: *Jessie is a heathen jingoist coward who cannot be allowed to cross our borders. Stop her now before it's too late...* Jessie couldn't hit the fast-forward button fast enough.

She noticed in the tapes, she mentioned that spirits had spotted Voyager I or II. They called them spacewagons, maybe because they were about the size of a Volkswagen. *Oh-oh, there goes that spacewagon, plowing through dust, sending out its beacon, a fossil slogging through eternity, beautiful . . . a dazzler . . .* Jessie sang out on the video, excited. And Jessie felt elated too. Realizing that her entranced self enjoyed the same things as her awakened self gave her hope. There was color in space too, aquamarine, and lines like the rings around Saturn, ice, plumes and gravity and roundness. The same God that created eggs and sperm created all this too, and more.

Seaborn came over to explain what was going on: "See, the spirits provided an antenna relay on occasion, and scientists on Earth couldn't figure out why in the chorus of natural radio noises there was a never-ending, strong signal, 30 or more times stronger than galactic noise, coming from both Voyagers, even though they should have gotten weaker years ago. Scientists are still not willing to concede that spirits even exist in the Universe, much less that they can help relay signals."

In the same video, Jessie delivered a message from an artist named DeLong, who said: *Voyager's function is to reveal radiance, not facts.* At once she remembered the night that message had come in. Excited, she said to Seaborn, "That was New Year's Eve! and we had been out dancing, and then..." she stopped, squinted, "...and then we went home and went to bed, but it was somewhere else– in a different bedroom."

"Yes, in a studio we had on east 57th street, on the ground floor," Seaborn encouraged her, "it wasn't safe." He waited, wondering if she would remember all the attempts on her life. He wasn't going to bring it up unless she remembered herself.

But Jessie only gave him a spacy look and hit fast forward.

The videos reflected changes in worldly politics and were actually a history, because, thankfully, no one had bothered to edit out the news reports that intersected the Life of Death Show. There was Marianne Williamson in one, calling for an end to bombing: "Bombs are archaic. Why doesn't NATO indict the BULLIES who are guilty of crimes against humanity, hunt them down and bring them before a tribunal, punish THEM, instead of destroying property and innocent people's villages? If the worlds predilection is towards naive idealism, why can't we have a little of it? Why do we let evil forces call all the shots?" Jessie high-fived Marianne.

She was bemused by many of the news items about artists getting elected to public office. As culture became more throwaway, and forgettable, there had come a mass movement to get it back, to resurrect it, hoist it back up there in the public mind. Art was the highest form of hope. She liked that idea, and the closer she got to the present in the videos, the more it prevailed. What a jaw-dropper! She'd always believed the world would be run better by artists, there would be an end to wars, and the planet would be preserved, the universe would be taken into account. Creativity would drive people instead of the lust for power and money. She hoped it was true. She felt a new excitement to be alive in such a time and was ever more anxious to get out of the building.

33
Jane's Plan

After almost two weeks of watching reruns, Jessie was anxious and more than ready to go. The plan had fallen to Jane as she knew it would. Once in a coon's age Seaborn and Jessie went out in the world together, and then it was her job to run interference for them. She had to come up with disguises, and mastermind the low intrigue that would distract the reporters and crowds, who were at all hours interested in any little move Jessie made. The Reverend Thackston's Fundamental Christian Alliance constantly monitored Jessie's movements. All and sundry stood ready to pounce in the exits from the cozy Eden she had created for Jessie and Seaborn in the "Ivory Tower Tomb" as it was slanged in the media. Every way that Jessie might leave the building was covered, including flying off the roof. Helicopters were parked atop nearby skyscrapers, ready to leap and follow.

Seaborn could move around, almost like a free agent. He came and went all the time, bouncing high, a quiet dare on his face. News hounds followed him sometimes, like they got the scent of Jessie off him, as though she might be jammed down in his pocket or something. The pocket idea intrigued Jane, but so far, she hadn't come up with any way to shrink Jessie. As soon as Seaborn stepped onto the roof garage of One World Trade, where he kept his Roto, as he called it, his Personal Helicopter, plus a second, spare P.H., which she was learning to fly, the scalding glare of search lights from the roofs of nearby skyscrapers assaulted him. Pictures were instantly digitized to see if it was Jessie. Mere disguises didn't work. Lord, she wasn't even entitled to go out for a bite to eat in a nice restaurant once in a while. She couldn't go anywhere without being hounded and harassed? No wonder she lost her appetite. It was inhuman the way she had to hole up just to stay alive.

In all the world, there was no normal enjoyment for Jessie, and very little for Seaborn. So, Jane had tried to provide it as much as she could; tried to make the penthouse a world all their own. She and Frank and Seaborn were Jessie's family now, and they were close. But Jane felt fearful for Jessie. While she had been entranced and her mind was moving out in the Universe she hadn't wanted anything Jane couldn't provide. But great day, now she was awake, acting like a normal person, rocking her own world, aggravated to be trapped on top of a building, however beautifully decorated, and Jane didn't blame her one little bit. But Jane's job had expanded overnight. Not only did she have to protect Jessie from the world, now she had to protect her from her own self, too. Jessie had no idea of the danger that was out there, of how many enemies she had, of how even the well-intentioned fans, people who loved her, could hurt her. She may be finished with messaging in her own mind, but people would not easily believe it, and the Goliath of fame would still be stalking her without mercy.

Jane had been developing a scheme to get them out, and it had begun to take shape in solid scenes in her mind. Seaborn had once called her a risk-capitalist of the imagination, and she'd laughed at him. Now he was going to have to trust completely in her imagination. Because one thing she was sure of: they could not use his P.H. on the roof to escape. It was too obvious and dangerous. She'd probably have to fight Seaborn on this. But having decided, her mind was free to focus on a ground route. She was thinking deeper into the box because no one would expect them to travel by ground.

Seaborn kept his car in perfect condition, although they seldom used it. Sometimes to go to closings or to shop. It was parked in a garage over in Hoboken.

The Jeremiads carried those old-timey wicker baskets with their depressing foodstuffs inside, things like blackened bananas and ostrich jerky. Who knows what all? The baskets sometimes smelled worse than a four-day-dead rabbit. But they could be useful for carrying disguises for the second phase of her plan. She had to create a major distraction though, and a reason for the Jeri's to have to leave the building all at one time.

Maybe those two salt-of-the-earth ghost women who the Jeri's claimed kept blinking in and out, appearing out of nowhere when they were least expected, like they came right through the durn walls, would be helpful. Jane couldn't see them, but she suspected they had helped keep the Jeremiads under control a time or two. When the Jeri's saw them, they'd hush and move along. Otherwise, the Jeri's hung around in that lobby, just crying themselves blind. Jane always treated them like mourners, feeding them, although they ate without hunger, like a meal after a funeral. The one thing they would devour was sweets. The Jeri's were sure enough live women gone off the deep end feeling sorry for themselves. Nothing new about that. They were afraid of the darkness of death, of being trapped underground in the cold earth. They couldn't imagine shedding their bodies, their souls soaring up into the Universe. Most people were like that, but not everyone made an obsession out of it the way the Jeri's did. They had stopped living because the thought of death paralyzed them worse than death was going to. They acted like ghosts with those long black dresses and purply hoods up all the time, reminded her of those suffocating burqas. Why would anyone choose to wear such things?

Gave Jane an idea though. Lordy, patience and tolerance paid off every time. At last she had a good use for the Jeri's and her plan began to jell. There were details to work out, disinformation to spread on thick, some things she'd have to go uptown for, and then she'd be ready to put the escape plan into action. She was certain she could get Seaborn and Jessie out of New York City, and if they could only make it safely through the Bible Belt, Frank would be there to catch them at One Wing Flapping.

Jane left the building to obtain a drug called SAC, a Suspended Animation Capsule. She knew about it from her days at the University when she'd studied pathology, long before Seaborn had lured her away from the funeral directing business. The drug's true versatility had been discovered by accident. While it was still a new drug, intended to slow the heart down for surgery, a few people had been overdosed and presumed dead, only to wake up hours later on the cooling board, surprising some undertaker.

Keeping up with Scientific advances was another hobby of Jane's, and the Internet, plus Frank, made it easy and fun. So she knew that researchers had taken SAC to its highest level of development, and now it was being used to simulate a death state in experiments in physics and medicine. SAC would never be allowed on the open market because it could enable insurance scammers, and allow people to wantonly "play dead," among other flimflams.

Jane Ubered up to Columbia University where she scored the SAC from a researcher she knew. Then she went to Bloomingdales and bought wigs and some neoprene body gloves and leather jackets. She had decided on the nineties aerobic-bimbo look for Jess, and old eighties high-Harley for Seaborn, urban guerrillas with some wild-card current fashion touches thrown in, an amalgam of street and chic– sort of like

Dragon Con costumes. This type was the least approachable. She'd layer their disguises, so they could peel in a hurry. Halloween would help.

When she returned, she found Jessie all alone in the big kitchen baking a pound cake from scratch. She must have shooed all the good ole girls out.

Jessie muttered: "A pound of butter, three and a half cups sugar, four cups flour, ten eggs, how do I remember this?"

"That's good you do." Jane said.

Jessie was concentrating hard on memory retrieval, and hardly acknowledged Jane. She had wanted to be alone in the kitchen– hoping to recover something on her own by cooking, strange as that might seem. Baking used to be a meditation for her.

"Anywho," Jane said with a shrug. She didn't much like being ignored, but Jessie's baking gave her an idea. She began lashing together a batch of fudge Brownies.

She was beginning to like this new retrograde shape their life was taking, the idea of going back, and retracing. She didn't know why, except it fulfilled a need she had, right along with Jessie's need to close a circle in time. She liked being of service and being useful to other people, but truth be told, she was tired of the hermetically sealed life they all had to lead, up so high above the ground. She missed nature, watching things grow. She was in the mood to welcome any change at all, even a dangerous retrograde one.

"I love to go somewhere with a cake in my arms," Jessie said, aware that Jane was watching her. Every time she looked at Jane, she had odd feelings about her. She thought Jane must know everything about her and Seaborn there was to know, and Jessie found this humiliating. She was vaguely aware of having trusted Jane over a long period of time. Maybe too much and for too long. Was Jane in love with

Seaborn too? she wondered. She was counting on her to get them out of there, and she couldn't help wondering what was in it for Jane, who was now smiling at her so agreeably. Jessie smiled back, quickly put her pound cake in the oven, set the timer for one hour, and went to find Seaborn.

Jane took her brownies out of the microwave, cut them into squares and inserted a SAC into one of the squares. The heat would dissolve it. On top of each brownie she placed an orange candy jack o'lantern. When everything else was ready, she would bring out the brownies and work her plan. For now she hid them in her staging area.

She hoped those two phantom women would help her succeed, but she was not going to make the mistake of counting on them. The trouble being, she couldn't see them herself.

It was time to call Frank and run all her plays by him for his input. Seaborn would not make a move without Frank's okay. And Frank was going to be the catcher in the rye.

Jane turned on the scrambler and punched in the sound bites that would alert Frank that it was not an ordinary call— they had an anomaly, which he already knew— but she thought it best to confirm it. She spoke a series of passwords into the phone: "Seek higher ground," followed by a "great day" to signal it was her. Each one of them had their own personal expressions for passwords, more specific even than their names. Frank had no careless relationships. If you were friends with Frank, he found ways to possess you, and allowed you to do the same with him.

"I guess you know who's anxious to get moving." Jane piped into the scrambler.

A picture of Frank mugging a horrified face blinked on the screen, and then it went blank. "Yeah, Seaborn filled me in. It's about time you called."

"I've been working on my plan to get them out and I'm ready to run it by you now." Jane went over all the details and waited for Frank to come back with suggestions.

"That wig and leather disguise sounds a little tricky. Are you sure about who they will appear to be?" he asked, fearing for their vulnerability out among the public.

Jane's mouth curled. Maybe she should have chosen the generic business look. She thought for a second. It flustered her if Frank questioned something because he was usually right. But she'd been out on the streets and seen people dressed like this, and he hadn't, so she tried explaining what the disguise meant, running her mouth enthusiastically: "They will appear to be nihilists, super-rationalists, obsessed with the wipe-out of humankind, beyond personal history, a scary, unapproachable sort. They're into the tragi-comedy of a world concluding, urban guerrillas, for heaven's sake, the mask of choice, where have you been Frank?" she said, tickled to be challenging him.

"Just checking," Frank said, "I don't keep up with fashion trends as you know. But I'd hate to see them reduced to a photo-op out there if they were recognized."

After a short silence, Jane said, "It wouldn't be that nice. Jessie could get torn to pieces by the very people who idolize her."

Frank was a scientist/creator. The fundamental reason for science was to learn about new things. He thought it was time the world stopped trying to draw a line between the real and the supernatural. He didn't believe in Jessiolatry, although Henry and Jessie were heroic figures to him. Privately, he believed in Henry's ghost, in his techno-rapture, in the singularity, and sometimes he could swear he heard Ibsen's particular bark. He'd gotten messages in his mind too, stray thoughts that were not his own. But he had no call to put himself on TV like Jessie did. He liked living simply, without motive, mission or bias, the way animals and trees did. Animals were smarter than people. They never fouled their own nest unless they couldn't help it. Trees talked to each other, even did simple geometry– that was a known fact now. They lived longer than people too and were far wiser. People were a destructive threat to everything else alive.

Frank voiced his confidence in the plan and made suggestions about what they should carry. He favored the use of aromatherapy and supplements: "Give Jessie rosemary, Gotu kola, Bacopa and Ashwagandha to help her relax and get her memory back. Add anise and basil for Seaborn, so he'll be alert and awake for the long hours it will take to drive to One Wing."

To Jane's surprise, he even agreed that coming by ground was the best chance they had of getting through. Frank said, "She would be easily spotted on the roof, even in a disguise, and once word got out, the New York sky would be full of P.H.'s and interception dangerous and inevitable. It will be up to you and me, Jane, to keep a smoke screen going as long as it takes. We can play ground games with the media dogs and fanatic fans, ya know? I've got a few ideas."

Paranoia was a natural, accepted condition to Frank, because it really was true that everyone was out to get them, especially the lunatic fringe, and religious extremists. Frank had mapped out routes of escape years ago, should they ever be needed. He had always been ready to cross her back over, if or when she came out of it.

Frank had practiced accessing satellite pictures of all the roads in a direct path from One World Trade to One Wing Flapping, with interim relaying satellites. So they were not wholly dependent on U.S. satellites parked out in space in geosynchronous order. He would be guide. He was beginning to pick up on Jane's enthusiasm. At the same time, he had sympathy for how confused and disorientated Jessie must be; how strange everything must feel to her, without memory bearings. She had to be desperate for any vectors of identity she could find and was probably experiencing the kind of despair you felt when someone you loved died.

Next Frank talked to Seaborn, who had just come into the kitchen. He told him: "place all your faith in the masks Jane has for you, move stealthily out of the city by car, make your way south, to One Wing and I'll be waiting for you."

"By car?" Seaborn balked. "You gotta be kidding."

"It's your best chance. You'll make it man. Jane and I will help you. I have a lot of moves. All we need is a little random luck and some heavy magic." He laughed, but he knew the promise of magic always reduced Seaborn's anxiety. Belief in magic was a cognitive fossil, and they all seemed to have it to some degree.

"It's unbelievable that we'd go by ground, when we have the great P.H." Seaborn said.

"We're counting on everyone thinking that way." was Frank's answer. He promised to stay in contact with Seaborn all the way, to run interference and guide them home. He went over the details of the plan again with Seaborn, laying out the strategy, along with advice: "Always use the passwords and scrambler to eliminate cellular spying. And no pictures, they have great lip readers. And watch out for the hard-shells, and your old pal, The Reverend."

Jessie came into the kitchen to check on her cake. She could smell that it was done.

"Now let me just say hello to Jessie." Frank said.

34
The Escape

It was four p.m. of a cool and crisp All Hallows Eve, the best time to commune with the dead, when Jane went out into the living lobby with her fresh baked brownies. She offered the brownies to a cluster of Jeremiads who accepted them eagerly. Chocolate was an unexpected treat amidst all their suffering and denial. As they ate the brownies, they watched a LODS rerun on the big screen plasma TV.

Jessie said:

Although anyone, at any time can lose his life, no one can EVER lose his death. Death is safe and secure to each of us, and therefore, a gift, every bit as much as life is. Only mind what you do on earth because you'll be stuck with it in eternity too.

Twenty minutes later, one of the Jeri's collapsed, and all the other Jeri's screamed and scrambled around her, fretting, and crying. Jane rushed over and made a big to-do of checking her pulse, then her heart with a stethoscope. Finally she announced: "I'm so sorry, she's gone. Her heart must have just gave out." Jane wrapped the "dead" Jeri in thin veiling, and four guards lifted her gently onto a Gurney with wheels, and stood by, awaiting further instructions. All the Jeri's surrounded their dead sister, weeping and carrying on. Some were in shock, numbed by the unexpected transformation from life to death.

While this commotion was going on, GOG's, possibly assisted by the two ghost women, tapped two Jeri's, and bid them follow through a door into the private quarters. They went curiously, grateful for entry into the hallowed inner sanctum. Their baskets were promptly poached, their heavy purple capes were snatched off their backs, and their long black dresses removed. They stood wide-eyed, in their grayish underthings, shivering, but still more than willing to be handmaidens to these nice girls and phantoms, who gave them warm blankets to cover up with and locked them in a nice room of their own with chocolates.

Minutes later, two Jeri's stepped back out into the lobby in black dresses and hooded capes carrying the baskets. They joined the wailment in motion, if not in voice. They had been well prepped and knew their safety depended on minute details Jane had carefully thought out. Lots of people were in costume outside– the high spirits of Halloween prevailed. Jane had also factored in the rush-hour traffic as cover. Thousands of people worked in One World Trade and the surrounding skyscrapers, and most of them would be going home between four and seven. A rushing crowd could be both the best cover and the worst trap if they were recognized. Jane had figured on about two hours of daylight to get Jess and Sea out of New York City and on the road; then they'd have the protective cover of darkness. Now she wondered if they would ever come back to The cloudland Eden of World Trade that she had created.

The guards wheeled the Gurney with the "dead" Jeri on it into the big freight elevator, and all the Jeri's scrambled to get in the elevator with it. Jane stood by looking worried, as the doors closed, and the elevator began its decent. Seaborn and Jessie kept their heads down, inside the hoods, almost cheek-by-jowl with the other Jeri's. They descended one-hundred and four floors in fifty-eight seconds. To Seaborn's horror, the wrapped pound cake Jessie was carrying inside her basket oozed a buttery perfume. He shuffled his feet nervously. Just in the nick of time the doors slid open.

They trailed the flock of griefy Jeri's who were pushing the gurney out into the open atrium between the buildings, and stood huddled next to a marble pylon, while the Jeri's performed a sorrowful keening in the wind that attracted a crowd.

Silently, Jessie read the words by Paul Valery that were engraved on the pylon:

I give myself up to these brilliant spaces
On the mansions of the dead my shadow passes
Reminding me of its own ephemeral hour

She drew a breath. It was beautiful. She lifted her head and peeped at Seaborn, on whom their safety now depended. How funny he looked as a Jeri. She drunk in the taste of New York City air, grew dizzy with it, so grateful to have her feet on the ground at last, even if it was concrete. Memories of their first move to New York years before, came flooding back to her.

The wind between the buildings was creating a Venturi effect, causing the veil covering the Jeri's "body" to flutter wildly. Jeri's clasped the veil, holding it down, lest crowds of strangers see the face of a Jeri in death, a dreaded funk to them. Jessie saw that the Jeri had been covered with the veil canopy off her own bed—Jane must have thought they wouldn't be needing it anymore.

Seaborn saw Jessie looking longingly at the Sabrett Hot-Dog truck parked at the corner, sending mouth-watering aromas across the square. Before she lost interest in food, Jessie had loved a good crunchy hot-dog with mustard, relish, and onions, smothered in kraut. He took hold of her cape, afraid she might run over and try to get one. He was fairly certain Jeri's didn't eat Kosher hotdogs. Jessie felt the tight hold Seaborn had on her and frowned at him.

Finally the Jeri's had gleaned enough pitiful attention, and they began wheeling their corpse down Church Street toward Battery Park, where they would put her on the Staten Island Ferry and take her home for burial. The cult of Jeremiads in New York mostly lived on Staten Island, in a bazaar compound, close to a garbage dump. They grew a lot of their own food using what some considered questionable obsoletes of composted garbage.

Seaborn and Jessie took up the rear, walking slow and numbly, imitating the Jeri's.

Jane had calculated the SAC dosage, so the Jeri would wake up about midway on the boat ride across the East River, well before they put her in the ground or the sea, or cremated her, whatever Jeri's did with their dead. Jane had no idea.

At Wall Street, Seaborn and Jessie dropped back, and Jessie saw for the first time two phantoms, twirling above all the Jeri's, like the two ghost women in her dream. Seaborn quickly steered Jessie down some steps, into the frenzy of rush-hour in the subway. It would be a quick ride. They would get off at the first stop near Chambers Street.

They sat low in the subway seats with the Jeri hoods covering most of their faces. Jane had warned them that to be recognized in the subway was a ticket to stampedesville. Seaborn clutched his basket; it held two measly sandwiches and he wondered what they'd do for food now that Jessie's appetite had come roaring back. The simplest things were made complicated by fame. The baskets also held their next disguise: the look of masses of people that would render them safe retrogrades, according to Jane. She had pointed out that there were thousands of throwbacks to the eighties and nineties all wearing this mask. "The best disguise is the same one everyone else is using." She'd chirped, selling it. He just hoped Jane was right about this, and all her other calls too.

While the subway smells assaulted her, Jessie glimpsed an advertising sign overhead for Pepsi Cola. It pictured someone with her own face, a lookalike, smiling. She remembered Pepsi Cola and wished she could have a cold one right now. "Pepsi comes alive," the sign said in English, and below it, the slogan was written in Chinese:

百事可乐把你的祖先从坟墓里带回来

She translated it as "Pepsi brings your ancestors back from the grave," wondering where she had learned Chinese. In another lifetime?

In fact, no language was unknown to her suddenly, and she easily translated the conversation in Yiddish between two Jews sitting beside her: "We kept company for ten years before we got married. We hada fine out about each other." Then she realized the last part was in English, heavily accented. Languages began melding together in her mind, along with accents. She was confused, mentally whirring. She clutched the pound cake, inhaled deeply of its comforting aroma and closed her eyes, letting the noises and smells fill her up so she could stop thinking for a few seconds. She was losing something, she didn't know what, didn't know if she was coming or going.

The bullet train they were riding in shot through the tunnel and screeched to a stop at Chambers street. The doors flew open. Seaborn yanked Jessie out into the station before he remembered that Jeri's never moved very fast, and hardly ever touched each other. "We have to get rid of these clothes, that's for sure," he muttered, under the hood. "I can't act like a Jeri. Stay close to me now, until we find some place to change."

If Jane's distractions were working, they were probably not even missing yet. You could only give the public so many reruns and then they wanted fresh messages. Eli and Smithy would be the first to discover their absence. Seaborn wondered how long Jane could keep them at bay. Once they realized that he and Jessie were gone, Jane wouldn't be able to keep it from the staff, and eventually all the dogs would get the scent.

He looked toward the exits trying to spot a place where they could change. He remembered how barbarically scarce public bathrooms were in the city. There were none in the subway stations, and men were known to piss against the walls like dogs. He had to find a place, and soon.

Seaborn watched Jessie sheepishly chewing her knuckles as she walked beside him, not out of character for a Jeri, so he made no move to stop her. He could see it had been shocking, going from the tranquility of their penthouse into the stinking subway at rush hour. He led her up the concrete stairs to the street, where it would be a short walk to the Pier on the Hudson.

At that moment, a couple of boys on hover boards came barreling by, twelve inches off the ground, and missed Seaborn, but Jess was a touch late in her movements and they knocked her down.

Seaborn threw his hood back and yelled, "Why the hell don't you watch where you're going!"

Passing people stared at him—transvestite Jeri's were unheard of. He hoped he hadn't been recognized; they would have to get out of there fast just in case. He helped Jessie up while she protested that she wasn't hurt, just surprised is all; she had never seen a hover board before.

Seaborn went off on a tangent: "They're new. Nearly a whole generation of kids, mostly African American, had been killed off by guns and crack before anything had been done about it. When they took the drugs and guns away, they had to give kids a replacement, so now they were trialing with hover boards. But the incidence of mid-air collisions from "hieing," as it was called, was climbing, even though the injuries were usually minor. The kids easily learned flocking behavior and didn't bump into each other much– it was pedestrians that got in the way, that moved when they shouldn't, anticipated too early or after hie-time, as Jessie had. I'll tell you more about this when we get to Hoboken okay? C'mon now, let's get out of here."

But just then the boys came back, surprising Seaborn. He hadn't expected them to take responsibility for knocking Jessie down.

"You okay, lady?" one of the boys asked. "We're sorry,"

Being talked to like this and seeing these fresh, young faces unlocked something inside Jessie and she smiled, happy.

To Seaborn's astonishment, she asked the boys for a ride, hopping on the back of one of the hover Boards before he could stop her.

"Hey!" he called after them, as the boys whizzed her off, "take her to Pier 21." He ran behind, trying to keep up. Jessie's cape purpulated behind her. Jeremiads never rode hover Boards, and there was a big grin on her face. He'd never seen a Jeri smile. Jesus, Seaborn felt exposed– he looked around quickly. He ran faster, passing a newsstand, and spotting Jessie's digitized face plastered on magazine covers, reminding him of some spooky Shroud of Turin.

Jessie was waiting for him on the pier. He could see for once she had the good sense to keep her head low inside the hood. Crowds of people hurried past her, heading home from work. Seaborn led them inside the station. He scanned the waiting area, spotted a door marked MAINTENANCE ONLY. It was unlocked and they ducked inside and Seaborn exhaled a sigh of relief. Quickly they both started changing clothes in the tiny semi-dark space, dank with the smell of sour mops.

Under the dresses and Jeremiad capes, they had on body suits. Jessie's was white, Seaborn's was black. He wore black leather boots. He tucked his own short brown hair inside a black and blonde streaked fade wig and put on a black leather jacket and solar glasses with a neb piece, his Blue tooth earpiece attached to a long dangling key chain-compass-phone that crossed his chest and tucked into his pocket. He laughed as he glued a moustache in place—which was so unlike him— he hated facial hair and Jane knew it. Jessie's long dark hair was hard to cram under the strawberry-blond glamour wig, and she left some tendrils dangling out. Her huge glasses also had a neb-piece which completely altered her looks, so that she resembled a cat more than a woman. Her white jacket was long and flared out, made of feather-weight pleather, thin as a nightgown, yet opaque and warm. It swished attractively and smelled of patchouli. Her shoes were spike heels. As she applied red lipstick, she walked in place, trying to practice, she hadn't worn high heels in years. She put on the white gauntlet gloves that completed her look. Did people really dress this way she wondered.

They gulped down the turkey sandwiches and oatmeal chocolate-chip cookies Jane had tucked in the basket and swigged a flask of sweet tea. Jessie clutched the wrapped pound cake, and, on Seaborn's signal, they took deep breaths, opened the door and bounded out into the fray.

Jessie went down almost immediately, shushing across the slick floor, dragging Seaborn, who had hold of her hand behind. A baby carriage stopped her when she plowed into it. The surprised baby started howling. He wasn't hurt, just surprised, but his mother snatched him up, patting him, and holding onto him tightly as she glared at Jessie and Seaborn.

"Oh my God, a little baby... I'm so so sorry," Jessie said, "we didn't mean to...." She hadn't seen a baby in years, and it was so fresh, new, and beautiful, she wanted to touch it. But the mother pulled back protectively. Jessie felt a tinge of envy. Tears bubbled in her eyes. She reached down to rub her burning ankle.

The baby was dressed in a pumpkin costume and the mother, now glaring at Jessie was dressed like a scarecrow. Jessie's ankle was awkwardly twisted under her and the heel broken off the shoe. She wasn't sure she could stand up, but she decided to try. But where was Seaborn?

Seaborn had run back to the maintenance room to retrieve her flat slippers, grumbling about Jane's weakness always showing up in the field of transportation. How could Jane imagine Jessie walking in stiletto heels when she'd been mostly barefoot for years? He was back in less than a minute and examined Jessie's ankle. She pulled back, in pain. He placed her old flats on her feet and helped her get up. She was rattled, but she could stand. She took a few wincing steps, leaning on Seaborn. He just hoped she hadn't broken anything.

Jessie picked up the pound cake, which was stove in on one side, although the wrappings had not come apart. She patted the cake, to restore its shape, and straightened out her crooked wig, taking a last look at the sweet little baby.

"You okay Jessie?" Seaborn looked around quickly. He shouldn't have used her name. The scarecrow mama looked at them suspiciously as they hurried away, leaving Jessie's broken high heels behind on the floor.

Seaborn said as they went, "Sorry, so sorry," nodding his head in uncharacteristic politeness, and at the same time remembering his type never apologized– "never explain, never complain," was one of their stoicisms. This disguise wasn't going to be easy either. They'd have to be more careful and move slower. It was hard for Seaborn to slow down. His adrenalin pumped like a teenagers. "Try and get in the mood of these clothes," he said to Jessie, who limped along beside him, her ankle throbbing painfully. "We're supposed to be the darkness and the light, the smartest of the smarts, tough lovers in a world we believe is concluding. We're environmental guerrillas when we feel like it, and most of the time we don't care about nothin' but each other, you got it?"

Jessie nodded doubtfully, as Seaborn yammered on, gesturing wildly like he imagined motorcycle intellectuals did, trying to get in character himself. He wished he had a big ole Harley under them right now.

They took the Hydrofoil to Hoboken, which skimmed across the river to New Jersey in two minutes. They sat together facing the fiery autumn sun setting in the water, casting a rippling reflection over everything. Jessie became mesmerized by a sign on the Jersey shore, flashing on and off: "WHEELS OVER INDIAN TRAILS." An old stray memory popped into her mind: A tableau from a couple of hundred years before, of the Algonquin Indians in their slim dugouts, paddling across the Hudson river, and being swamped by big old sailing barks. She saw the proud feathered Indians natural and at home on the water, and recalled Henry telling her at his funeral that Manhattan was an Algonquin word that meant "hilly island." But the hills were gone now. They had all been leveled for skyscrapers. Did Henry know they would live in Manhattan? Where did history go? It went nowhere. It was always there. Another invisible.

Seaborn took her arm at the Hoboken pier, snapping her out of it. She almost didn't recognize him. His Booker T. Washington wedge made him look like a black Indian. Then there was the wily way he moved, from somewhere else altogether. She felt full of people herself and wished she knew who she was and why she felt so lost and helpless. She sighed, exhausted already; it felt like her personality kept filling up and draining out. Now she was empty again.

"It's okay, we're going home," Seaborn whispered, "stay by me, only a short walk to the car now. I want to show you something good on the way."

35
Bae Bae's Kids

Jessie saw that it was a beautiful autumn; the trees still held their leaf's, all turning gorgeous colors before falling. She saw windmills tucked hundreds of feet high over the skyline of Hoboken, ticking as they turned. They looked like gigantic Legos, storked against the crimson-golden sky. It looked as though New Jersey had turned into a modern Dutch landscape.

"What are those?" she asked Seaborn.

"For wind power." He churned his arm breezily through the air. "Ten percent of our energy is generated by wind turbines. It's abundant, if unpredictable, renewable, and doesn't pollute. Energy-making is a venerable craft now. We've got sea-wave energy, hydrogen, ethanol and lots of other excellent methods for generating electricity and empowering machines. And fusion where it's practical because it turns matter into energy with nothing left over, no waste products. Fossil fuels are on the way out."

"Is that why the air is so clean?"

"Thought you'd never notice. Looks like everything's been hosed off, doesn't it?"

"The trees look really happy," Jessie was cheering up. She wanted to hug one the way she had always done when she was a young girl. The trees had not always been so happy, she remembered that; they were threatened like every other living thing on the planet.

"Oh, boy, they found out about trees, Jess. Trees count. They actually do geometric progressions with each other. Bio-scientists are studying them, writing down the numbers.

Trees are part of the pure geometry of Earth. Frank can tell you all about it."

Seaborn's excitement made Jessie feel good. Trees had always been comforting and heroic to her. How she had missed them. Now she remembered Henry relaying a funny message he claimed was from a tree: *Tell a story from my point of view.*

"Another reason why it's so clear is that we don't use as many chlorofluorocarbons anymore. Remember CFCs?"

Jessie thought a moment, "They made holes in the ozone?"

"Right. Penetrated the hemisphere, and the sun's ultraviolet rays could have killed everything on Earth if we kept on using them at the rate we were. The holes were getting bigger and bigger, so we had a worldwide ban on CFCs. There are still pockets of pollution, called POP's, and clean-up is a big-ticket item worldwide, called MOPs."

Seaborn thought about the new field of bioremediation which used microorganisms to convert hazardous carbon-based waste to an environmentally benign form. They brought the organisms into a waste spill and grew them. He decided to tell Jessie about that later. Instead he said, "It's been exciting these past few years; and you were a part of it Jess, you're new age."

"What does that mean?"

Seaborn looked over his shoulder grinning, and whispered, "It doesn't matter, you're it. But a whole bunch of people don't like us, and that's who we gotta watch out for."

Jessie's cat-faced bewilderment kept him talking as they walked.

"You gave people a purpose under heaven, and ideas, woke them up. You took an ax to the frozen sea of death and gave value back to life. Everyone who dies learns the value of life and lots of them are anxious to tell about it. You were an open channel. There are others who can do it too, but you had television and a natural-born ability." Seaborn lifted Jessie's chin, "How did you do all that?"

Jessie didn't know. She couldn't do it anymore, that was for sure. Who was she now? That's what she had to find out in order to feel okay. It was baffling to be back in what felt like a new world; like she'd missed too much school and would never be able to catch up.

Seaborn led her down the street toward a public square with a monument which he had commissioned to a famous New York artifactist, as a gift to Hoboken. Artifactism combined art and futurist geology. It was the current, stable trend in art, if an art trend could ever be called stable without insulting it. Seaborn loved art, and secretly wished to make it; tie his own ideas and images down in a material way that would stay on Earth after he was gone.

"Where are we going?" Jessie struggled to keep up, her ankle throbbing, her neb glasses slipping, wig askew.

Seaborn slowed the pace. "Here, hold onto my arm." He was so excited, "You're going to love this Jessie." He'd wanted to show it to her for a long time.

As they approached the end of the street, the public square dramatically opened to them. Suspended on end, in its very center was Seaborn's gift: a thirty-cubic-foot, transparent Lexan cube, bulletproof and impregnable. It was chock-full of revolvers and pistols, gun parts, broken up shooters of every caliber and kind, floating in solid plastic, frozen, forever.

"It's ultra-art, Jess, art with an idea that rocks; on a par with your need to see it."

A flock of young kids on hover boards came circling round the cube like it was their own creation. They listened to Seaborn; they had seen him before on that spot.

Jessie thought what a good teacher Seaborn might have made. She studied the cube, but a time gap prevented her from totally understanding. She read the bronze title plate out loud: THE LAST DING-DONG OF DOOM * HOMAGE TO WILLIAM FAULKNER AND MARTIN LUTHER KING JR.

She had a feeling of nostalgia. Then she remembered and called out to Seaborn: "That title is from Faulkner and King's messages– they're palling around together."

Seaborn nodded. "Faulkner said that once he escaped the visceral level he could see the absurdity of racism."

"Yes, and King said: We are all tied to the same garment of destiny—whatever happens to one of us happens to us all." She felt triumphant, remembering the day those messages had come from Henry.

"And Faulkner said we are a huge species, race is a tiny detail." Seaborn held his thumb and first finger up a quarter inch apart, squinting.

"Yes, and King said for people to get involved in saving the environment of the world; forget about race and colonize Earth, not as a race but as a species."

"Evolution is circling back to the primitive, Jess. We've got cognitive fossils we aren't even using because we got hung up on appearances. Remember the drug wars? Crack cocaine, and all the shootings that were killing off thousands of children?"

Jessie nodded vaguely. He'd started to tell her about that at the station.

"Something had to be done, not only about the crack, but about the guns. There were two-hundred-fifty-million firearms in America, enough for every single person to have one. They had become more prolific than bicycles and just as easy to get."

Seaborn circled the cube as he talked, "There have been a lot of changes in a short period of time. But lots of firearms are being hoarded and hidden away like pornography. So we flush them out with bartering, with trade-ins. You can trade a pistol for a ride, say a good bicycle, or an electric hover, or a hundred pistols for a motorcycle, or a thousand for a P.H., or a car. Most of the firearms are melted into scrap metal and recycled to repair the bridges and infrastructures; it's the business that gun manufacturers have gravitated into."

Jessie peered into the Lexan cube at the slurried firearms, frozen in suspended animation, transformed into a sort of fascinating radiance. She looked across the square and saw a band of little kids sitting around a campfire roasting marshmallows on sticks. They looked skinny, nervous and misbegotten. She started to walk over to them, but Seaborn stopped her.

"Those are Bae Bae's kids," he said, solemnly. "They have a different drumbeat in them because they were born crack addicted. They're second and third generation crack mutants, survivors. Some of them are the failures of cocaine being used as an abortifacient."

Jessie winced. She couldn't believe what she was hearing. And it didn't jive with the wonderful smell of s'mores wafting in the air.

"It had been going on for years before anyone did anything about it. They're not like these other kids, Jess. They're a different breed, very unpredictable. They live mostly in large cities, abandoned by crack-addicted, or dead mothers and fathers. So we take care of them, and they're called Bae Bae's kids."

Jessie took a couple more steps, but Seaborn stepped in front of her.

"You have to look out for them, Jess. They get violent and destructive really easily. They can't help it. At their best, they sit and stare, maybe in some kind of mental anguish we can't even imagine."

Jessie shook her head, still feeling drawn to them, feeling a maternal tug new to her. Seaborn held her back. People were beginning to stare at them.

"See those two pretty girls on the bench?" he said, "They're caretakers. They have this band of Bae Bae's all settled down around that fire, and it would be disruptive to go over there, Jess. Bae Bae's are paranoid as hell. One break in that circle and chaos would rein until the girls could settle everyone down again. There's nothing you can do for them anyway, you have to be trained." He turned Jessie away, but not before she saw both the girls on the bench wave at Seaborn who had lifted his neb piece, so they would recognize him. One girl blew him a kiss. Jessie wondered at this familiarity, how they knew him so well?

"We donate money to the training of good caretakers. We support a group called The Bedrock People, who take care of Bae Bae's kids. We're not abandoning them anymore Jessie."

She was crying now. She took her neb-glasses off, blew her nose and her disguise.

"Hey lady, it's okay, they living large now. You shoulda seen 'em before." one of the boys on a hover board said. More boys gathered around Jessie. They all began a rap-ride, hei-ing and snapping in the air on their hover boards to cheer her up– building a rap-ballad about the Bae Bae's in the sweet timbre of their changing voices:

We the boys
Lookin' out for
the Bae Bae's

This our ride
take us high...

A crowd began to gather. Seaborn hustled Jessie away
fast.

36
Out of Hoboken

They cut through old deserted, burned-out buildings covered with vines and graffiti, and hurried down a neat residential street next to the mess, that was brightly painted like a street in Disney World. Off in the distance, they could see Manhattan and all the skyscrapers. They came to a bean-sprouty looking restaurant, but to Jessie's disappointment, it was closed. Behind it stood the garage where Seaborn kept his car. He unlocked the door with his thumb print, raised it up, a light went on, and before them was the Land Rover.

An instant look of recognition crossed Jessie's face. She patted the shiny Clearwater blue hood, remembering a bond with this good car that years before had carried them around Atlanta, to weekends at One Wing, and to her fathers' funeral. It had been a secure and comfortable ride for them once, and now, she saw it could be again.

Seaborn kept the car in cherry condition as a personal hobby. Frank called it "a fortuitous concourse of atoms." Not many Range Rovers that originally had internal combustion engines were still on the road. Seaborn never wanted a new body, even the paint job was original. He had converted the old engine to hydrogen fuel cells. A single solar-cell farm one-fourth the area of New Mexico supplied enough electrically produced hydrogen to replace most of the fossil fuels in the United States. He could go long distances without refueling, and it was clean burning.

When he had also been considering a magnetic field engine Frank was adamantly opposed. He thought it might cause cancer. Frank had them all wearing wrist wave rectifiers which collected electromagnetic radiation and converted it to a direct current field like Earth's, to protect them from other destructive electromagnetic fields. It was Frank's bite of the dog theory, although he hadn't had time to actually prove that it worked.

As they pulled out of the garage, bolts of lightning streaked across the sky, rain pounded them, and thunder cracked in a sudden atmospheric tantrum. Along the horizon, the setting sun had turned a purple-grey shale. But they were dry and safe, inside the old Rover.

Jessie yawned. Her ankle ached. She was tired, and hungry.

Seaborn patted her leg, took her hand. He hoped going by car would prove to be a good decision. But he was worried. Birds flew at night, birds flew even in rainstorms. He knew it would be simpler flying in his Roto and faster, though maybe not as stealthy. In the sky there was speed, emptiness, but no cover. Anyway, he had always liked long-distance driving and didn't get to do enough of it anymore. That was probably why he had given in so easily when Jane and Frank chose the car.

He frammed it down and headed south, out of New Jersey, while an old song played on the radio: *"Skyrockets in flight, afternoon de-li-a-ite,"* past honey wagon camps and two-story town-trailers and a full landfill.

After the first burst there wasn't much rain, just enough to wet the bird droppings on the windshield. The wipers smeared it like white shoe polish across the glass, giving Jessie an odd feeling of deja vu, that brought back the dreamy atmosphere inside the car the first time she'd heard Henry's voice. It seemed like yesterday. She remembered feeling a crushing weight of grief on her chest, which the clouds had somehow lifted; at the same time her hearing had changed. But not forever, because now it was back to normal.

She yawned and cracked the window a couple of inches for fresh air. "I don't know why I'm so tired," she sighed, laying her head back, keen on the vibration of the engine, a steady, peaceful rhythm, lulling her.

Seaborn was waiting for a news report, to tell him if he and Jessie were missing yet. He avoided the gridlock traffic of the turnpike and took the narrow back streets, along with the techno gypsies on their motorcycles burning ethanol. He took stock. He had enough H_2 to get them beyond Virginia. Then they'd have to find a fuel station. He had a good working heater and a couple of blankets. Food was a problem. He had some raisins and a full case of spring water in the back seat, and Jessie's pound cake, although she was possessive of it. Jessie seemed to be grappling with hunger like a bear who'd been in hibernation. After they got through the recycling checkpoints, he'd get on the turnpike and put the pedal to the metal and get far enough away so it might be safe to stop at a restaurant.

Seaborn put his NONE sign in the windshield and drove on through the checkpoints which were spaced every ten blocks or so.

"What's that for?" Jessie asked.

"It's unlawful not to recycle your materials and compost your garbage," he answered, tired from all the explaining, but trying not to show it. "People bring their refuse to the checkpoints and get chits that get credited against their taxes. The landfills got full and nobody wanted any new ones near where they lived, so recycling has become a global imperative. We're groping for global order, Jess. There's no place else to live."

"What about other planets?" She remembered people used to talk about colonizing other planets– Seaborn's own father had been on a list to go to Mars.

"Takes years to get to the nearest one and it's not even habitable. There are probably thousands of technological civilizations in our galaxy, but they're too far to get to. Earth is our only home. People have finally realized that. When we get on the highway, we can take these wigs off and get more comfortable. Seaborn reached in the backseat, "here, eat some raisins." he said, tired of talking.

Seaborn is a good enough man for any world, Jessie thought, feeling more love for him knowing how hard he always tried. She savored the raisins but was almost too sleepy to chew. The motion of the windshield wipers was hypnotizing her, greasing the wheels of the windmills in her mind. She sundered deeper into memories of her old life and recalled riding in a convertible with Kate. It was like being airborne. She saw squirrels, cats and peacocks flying in the air above them. She let the dream fog roll in remembering a cozy little town with bungalows called Casadega.

Seaborn concentrated on his driving. He turned the radio up when *"Windmills Of Your Mind"* played unexpectedly on the oldies station he was tuned to. Dusty Springfield's version, his favorite. His thoughts wandered over the years during which time Jessie had been like an explorer to him, colonizing death with her traveling consciousness, and he had been right beside her. She had seemed so close at times, so into him, like they were one. But now he didn't know. If she hadn't really been awake or aware during those years, if she had little memory of them, wasn't it like he'd been hugging a shell? He felt a cold wave run up his spine. This was possibly a new Jessie beside him, one he was beginning to feel he didn't really know, sort of like an old girl friend from high school who could make you go shy.

He pulled his wig and neb piece off, tossed them into the back seat and reached in his pocket for the aroma therapy Jane had given him. He sucked on a couple of anise drops, and put the basil inhalator over the visor, ready to take breaths from it, if he felt tired.

He wished he could call Frank or Jane and talk to them, but he didn't want to chance waking Jessie up. She had fallen over in the seat. He'd eased her head around, so it rested on his lap and slipped the wig and glasses off. Her dark shiny hair fell across his legs and reminded him, as if zapped by a time warp, of the trip to Florida when Henry died. Was the Jessie he knew then, and still remembered, coming back to him? He glanced down at her, deep in sleep, making a little snore, and wondered what she dreamed about.

At the same time over in Manhattan, Jane gave a signal, and from different positions in the underground parking lot of One World Trade, five blue Land Rovers, nearly identical, except these were not the original paint jobs, with couples made up to look like Seaborn and Jessie inside them, went off in five different directions.

37
The Reverend Thinks It Through

At the Reverend Thackston's CATHEDRAL FOR THE LORD studio in suburban Atlanta, all the lines were tied up with shocking reports from The Reverend's disciples: Jessie Pettengill was first rumored, and now it was confirmed; she was "missing." Eli and Smithy were offering a hefty reward for her "safe" return. Seaborn and Jessie were believed to be headed south, possibly to Atlanta.

In his inner chambers, The Reverend Thackston sat with a seraglio of young, pretty assistants working on various parts of his itchy body, massaging, manicuring, while he digested the startling reports, and labored on his next sermon, as well as his bludgeoning personal agenda. This last included phone meetings with select members of a secret group called The Christian Militia which he helmed. He'd sweet-talked Desmond into joining, and even recruited Jessie's own two brothers, although they were less than active members, a disappointment.

The Militia numbered in the tens of thousands, with lots of surprising members. Its stated purpose was to restore the authority of the Bible. Under this egis, the Reverend had a right to vanquish anyone who opposed old-fashioned Bible babble. Life had to have dominion, for the Bible said...*and death shall have no dominion.* Why that little chippie Jessie Pettengill was just a latter-day oligarch and he would show her a thing or two about true religious rhetoric, so strong it could paralyze snakes. Babble indeed! He admitted to himself he had not been able to shut her down, for which he had an overwhelming sense of failure and shame. It was just like the helpless feeling he had when as a young boy he'd been bullied for his fox red hair.

The Reverend had done as the Bible commanded him in Mark 16., to take up serpents. He raised his gledgy eyebrows and peered over his desk at the cages, wooden boxes with screen wire lids. His snakes were packed in there like soup. He had rattlers, moccasins, copperheads and even a batch of brown tree snakes, hungry and fierce with the quickening spirit of God. But his prize snake was a huge Indian python he got from a snake handler; it was always starving.

He'd tried whiskey, marijuana, cocaine, but nothing got him higher than taking up serpents. He jerked spasmodically just thinking about it. He felt heat in the crotch of his pants; the keychain on his belt swung from side to side. "Whew! he expelled a plush tuft of wind and laughed a squeezing laugh. "Hit's a spirit 'at moves in ya alright!"

His assistants, all performing various tasks about the room gazed at him snakelike, and he felt the need to speechify, a sermon bubbling up to the surface:

"America was founded in Jesus Christ's name-ah," he began, "other Christians may see abortion-ah and homosexuality as the main enemies of Christianity, reasonable minds may differ-ah, but as for me and my flock-ah, we shall excoriate this she-devil, she is the true enemy of the Lord-ah." He liked the way he'd trained his arms to rise naturally with his voice.

When he took on a more confidential tone, his eyes naturally squinted: "This Jessie is a philistine who is defiling the Church of God-ah. Forget due process; she's like unto a wicked whore! STONE her-ah, the way the Bible says, stop her-ah, she cannot be allowed to cross our borders!"

He'd been sounding the alarm for years—why won't everyone join in? He slammed his fists down on the desk, ruining his manicure, and waited for applause that came only in his own mind.

"Did you get all that?" he snapped to the pretty assistant perched at a computer terminal beside him. She nodded, waiting for him to erupt with the rest of it.

He kicked back with his water bottle full of rum and Coca-Cola, sucked on the plastic nozzle, and thought about the flow charts, and the ratings. He grimaced. He practiced his facial expressions in a hand mirror– the three C's: charm, charisma, and coercion. And then, through a little chink in his armor, the bitter spite he had been corking leaked through. He felt it hotly. His presumption of piety had let him down, like it wasn't working anymore. His proud air of righteousness had been damaged by the inglorious acts he'd been driven to, just trying to stay in the Jesus game.

He had gone from on high, to eating Jessie's dirt, and no one seemed to appreciate him anymore. It was one thing to keep firing up his flock, but he wanted his own revenge on her now, needed it, to set things right again. He had usually been able to derail anyone with fear, shame, or guilt. These had always worked to keep his flock in line. This is what kept all of society's members in line, mankind's old sin-nature. But it hadn't worked on Jessie and her bunch. By all that was holy, she had to be brought down.

One of the assistants saw his distress and she quickly moved to relieve him with a deep neck massage. Another assistant flipped on the music he liked so much that he might relax. He liked how most of his assistants lived in fear of his irascible mood swings. Except the ones that had joined the heathens of the #MeToo movement and come up against him with lawsuits.

In a few minutes, he had removed his clothes, his MEN WILL BE BOYS T-shirt, and his BVD's, and was having his feet anointed with almond oil, his favorite submission.

So! Eli and Smithy were offering a big reward for Jessie's return. He shook with a giggle, rejoicing. And she's coming down through my neighborhood. My people are everywhere. There's no way she can get through the Bible Belt alive. I could ransom her to Eli and Smithy... or... I might give them a corpse. But what if her corpse started talking? He shuddered to think she might could tell on him. Only a thought. He ran his eyes down at his limp sexual organ. Have to get rid of all this doubt; it's worse than guilt, the devil's work. He shrugged it off with his round, pink shoulders and sat tall and proud again. He was a Christian soldier. The assistant massaging his neck pummeled his shoulders back down until she restored his characteristic look of humbleness that fooled everybody. He groaned with pleasure. Ahh the lord has placed a heavy burden on me.

There is only one way to burn out this tumultuous hatred I feel: I've got to bring her to her knees. The thought gave him an unexpected euphoria. He began singing along to "The Duke Of Earl," one of his all-time favorite songs. He felt it had been written for him.

To all his assistants The Reverend roared: "It's time to blow things asunder!"

"Massage my cock now hon," he said to the assistant with the almond oil.

PART FOUR

38
Divorcement

Seaborn had put about 6400 kilometers between them and Hoboken, keeping his eye on the rear-view mirror and on the sky, as well as the road ahead. He was traveling southwesterly on Interstate 81 having long, whispered conversations on the car phone, first with Jane, then Frank, and now he was back on with Jane again. Jessie was still asleep. The scrambler was engaged, so there was a delay, and everything took twice as long to say. He didn't mind. He was in for about seventeen hours of driving time no matter what. Talking on the phone made it go faster.

He paid attention to his driving. Car-phone accidents were greater than DUI accidents- there was news you shouldn't get at 70 miles an hour. He'd gotten the news that everyone knew Jessie was missing by now. And they were being hunted by professional news hunters in P.H.'s equipped with special kinds of radar/sonar, and by satellite trucks from most of the networks. Seaborn's heart raced. The media monster had grown gigantic, and the melee always included unknown quantities of followers and fans, short for fanatics, some of them half a bubble off level. Most of all he was worried about The Reverend Thackston, and his Christian Militia who lived all over the southern route they had to take, which was called the Bible Belt.

Jane let him have a sample on the Rover's little TV screen of what was happening outside on the square at One World Trade. The crowds were agitated, angry, chanting: "We want Jessie," over and over, till they were dry-mouthed, and glazy-eyed. It gave Seaborn cold chills. She'd be dead meat if a crowd like that ever...well, he didn't want to think about it. He found nothing amusing about fame. He'd learned the hard way that it was a dangerous game of scarce rewards, commanding nearly absolute power over a person's life, and everyone else around them. It always bothered him how the courtship of fame seemed to be Chuck-Pete's favorite sport. Such a waste to chase something that could kill you, and that you could never hope to control. Fame was like a poison and colorless flower.

Jane promised to keep coming up with new defense ploys. "I've already told enough white lies to ice a cake." She told about sending out the blue Land Rovers to act as decoys- they were all on different highways—how she'd managed to find them was a long other story. She rabbited on, hardly taking a breath, "I also sent out those two look-a-likes we've hired before a time or two, in a brown van, and passed the rumor that you were going to a safe house on Prince Edward Island. So, some of the media headed for Nova Scotia following the van with you and Jessie in it. The Indian trackers didn't buy that Jeri dying around the same time that you and Jessie disappeared, especially when she woke up on the Staten Island Ferry and surprised everyone. They can't be fooled so easily—no such thing as coincidence to them, that's just white man talk. They think coincidence is God's way of sneaking in little miracles. I have to give up on linear plotting, too. They see right through it. So, the word is pretty much out now that you're headed South in your blue Land Rover. But so are five other blue Land Rovers. The Indians might know right where you're going. Let's hope nobody else does. All these years we never let anyone near One Wing. Hopefully, they've all but forgotten about it. Golly day, I wish your license plate wasn't registered in your name." Jane had talked herself out and finally took a breath.

Seaborn looked up and saw a few small P.H. flocks, but they were not the Indians. Why did Jane dwell on the Indians so? Then he realized she didn't want to talk about the real danger, which was The Reverend's people; she didn't want to worry him with that.

"One more thing," Jane hesitated, "Desmond did another interview with Chuck-Pete- supposedly to make up for the way he ambushed him that last time. If Jessie's still asleep, I'll play it for you. It's pretty bad though."

Seaborn looked over at Jessie, who appeared to be sleeping soundly, and he switched on his monitor. "Okay, I'm ready," he said, adjusting the picture and the volume.

There on set was Dr. Desmond in a leather chair, sitting across from Chuck-Pete, who was looking handsome, smiling, giving off rancor and charm in contradictory doses as usual.

Desmond opened with: "Mr. Monroe, your sister seems to be suffering from a protracted case of death denial. Is there anything that...?"

Chuck-Pete held up his hand, interrupted him: "She's not my sister anymore." he said, grinning matter-of-factly.

"Oh...yes, well, uh, what we want to talk about here, today, is how someone can be changed by who and what they love, sometimes to the point of losing their own identity."

Chuck-Pete shifted in his chair. He looked puzzled, cagey.

"Did you notice in your sister's childhood any, uh..."

"She's not my sister, I told you." Chuck-Pete's face dropped, "You said you wanted to interview me."

"Yes, of course, I do," Desmond said quickly, "but you are related genetically, right?" He leaned in closer toward Chuck-Pete, gingerly touching his trousered leg.

Chuck-Pete yanked his leg away. "Whaddaya mean?"

"You had the same parents, didn't you?" Desmond smiled, waiting.

"No, I'm an orphan... or she is. I choked the goose that laid her egg. Ha ha ha..." Chuck-Pete yoicked, slapping his knee, enjoying his own little joke. What the hell, this was all a farce anyway. But this time, by Jesus, he would NOT lose his temper. He drifted off in a memory of being out in the back yard with the geese when he was only five, and Jessie was a cute little toddler, and he'd felt so much love for her that he squeezed her too hard and she cried. Then a goose started pecking at her legs, tormenting her, making her cry even more. He wanted to protect her, so he'd chased down that goose and squeezed his neck until he felt the goose go limp.

Desmond studied Chuck-Pete, encouragingly, then drew him out of his reverie: "Did you really choke a goose? Tell me about it."

"I wanted to choke her, so I choked a goose instead. Ha!"

"Oh I see...mhmm... Mr. Monroe, do you suppose some primitive chemical is stored in both you and your sister's chromosomes, and it's being stimulated to, uh..."

"She is not my sister anymore. Don't you listen?" Chuck-Pete snorted. The vein in his neck began its terrible bulge. The camera found it.

"Uh, this comes as a big surprise, Mr. Monroe. I wasn't prepared for you to denounce your own sister." Desmond fingered the solid gold coil on his Bollo tie, waiting.

Pent-up anger lifted Chuck-Pete from his seat, and he punched the air like a boxer, "She's just another puffed up maniac, you know? Can't you see I'm getting cheated here?"

There was a dreaded silence, and a merciless close-up on Chuck-Pete's face as he fought to hold his temper. After a moment, the director gave up waiting for it to happen, and cut the interview off; then cut to a news bite about the missing Jessie, and then to a commercial for Pepsi Cola, with a voice-over that sounded just like Jessie's.

Seaborn switched the TV off. He whispered to Jane, "They ambushed him again. I don't see why they even ran it in the first place. It's awful."

"Because Chuck-Pete and Tom filed for a divorcement between siblings. It's some new kind of legal move, and it ties in with Tom being the attorney who is leading that class-action suit against Jessie, remember? It's big news when a family starts crumbling. It's shameful, in a biblical kind of way, you know. Great day, Frank is going to hate this, it was bad enough they were outcast, now this. He hates family dissension."

Seaborn didn't like it either. If the crimson cord of bloodlines meant nothing to Jessie's brothers, what did? he wondered. In Jane's lingo, Jessie and Frank had both been PNG'ed: and labeled personas non-grata in their own family. He'd forgotten about Tom representing all those people who wanted to sue Jessie for mentioning their dead relatives' names. Jessie's lawyers had so far prevented the suit by suggesting that Jessie made all those names up, as in fiction. Everyone thought that would upset Jessie, but instead she laughed, said it was okay as a defense. Tom kept various nonspecific lawsuits going that he meant to shape up as soon as she committed some actionable crime. He had a problem charging libel because it was defined as a statement that defamed a living person. Invasion of Privacy and False Light were more promising– they were endlessly arguable. The worst was the sui juris challenge where Tom claimed Jessie wasn't capable of handling her own affairs. And what about that goose? He wondered if it was true. It would explain why Jessie never liked being around geese. She practically hyperventilated. Having brothers like that was like having an appendage that was useless but might someday develop a disease that could kill you. He drove on, chomping on raisins while he thought peevishly about all of it.

This divorcement was one more thing he'd have to try to shield Jessie from. It would break her heart. Deep down, she had to know how her brothers felt; when for years they wouldn't take her calls, and only called her with insults and blame; then telling everyone they no longer wanted anything to do with her. She tried her best to cover up how much her brother's rejection hurt. She taught Seaborn never to underestimate the power of denial.

Back on with Jane, he changed the subject, "How're Eli and Smithy taking our disappearance?"

"They're the ones hired the Indian trackers. They want their property back. Ya'll walked on a contract. But, great day, they sure are wallowing in all the publicity this is getting."

"Who knows about One Wing?"

"Far as I can tell, just some Indians. Eli and Smithy told them. Maybe The Reverend. I believe the media are taking south to mean Atlanta, or Silver Lake, where we buried Henry and Doris, and maybe even Casadega."

Jessie stirred and sat up. A strong aroma had ruptured her dreams. "I smell chocolate," she groaned, feeling waves of nausea, something rhythmic inside her flipping over and over...

"Stop the car quick!" she gasped.

Seaborn reacted, pulling over on the median. "We just passed Hershey, Pennsylvania," he said. "They're cooking up the chocolate..."

But Jessie was already out the door, retching in the ditch beside the car.

Seaborn went to her aid, leaving Jane squawking on the car phone: "What's a matter? What happened? Great day!"

Afterwards, when they were back on the road, Jessie felt much better. She slugged down water, while they talked again with Jane, who asked about Jessie's nausea and her ankle.

"You might have a little motion sickness, take one of those capsules labeled "On The Road" for it. It's a blend of ginger and licorice with a dab of cayenne—and it works. I'm really sorry about those high-heels."

Jessie didn't reply, but when they had signed off with Jane, she started talking a blue streak about her dreams and newfound memories: "Where is Kate? God, I miss Kate so. I want to see her and find out about Casadega. She took me there. I'm starting to remember things: how Daddy talked to me, convinced me that we had a mission, and how much I wanted to make a new peace with my brothers after he died, but I could never get close enough to them. I don't know why."

Seaborn gave her a sympathetic shrug. He put his arm around her and drew her close to him. It was cold and dark outside, even the stars looked cold in the pitch sky. Jessie shivered, and Sea turned up the heat.

They skirted Harrisburg, and by Chambersburg both their stomachs were grumbling. The capsule had calmed Jessie's nausea, as Jane said it would. Seaborn still hadn't spotted anyone tailing them on the road or in the air. He saw pottery shops, then a Japanese "Park n' Blow." He pulled in and parked the Rover under one of the drive-in canopies. Quickly they put the wigs and glasses, and neb-pieces back on. But when he blew, nobody came out. They would have to go inside.

He cautioned Jessie, "Now don't use my name and I won't say yours. We shouldn't speak at all. Let's pretend we're the people in these clothes, Okay? Frank says you have to believe in the pretense yourself for it to work."

"I'm so hungry I'm not going to say one word, all I'll do is eat," Jessie promised, pulling her wig down so low that Seaborn laughed. Luckily, no one knew about their disguises as far as he knew,

He adjusted the wig, lifted the glasses, and looked deeply into her tender blue eyes. She was his Jessie still; he saw her there in her eyes, trusting him. It was Jessie, now rootless, without her anchor bearings, a brotherless orphan, who knew deep down that she'd been PNG'ed.

39
Moisture

They took a booth by a window, positioned so they could watch the TV set hanging over the bar. The customers who were sitting at the bar watching robotron units prepare Sushi all turned and looked at Seaborn and Jessie when they came in, then went back to their engrossment with the robotrons.

Seaborn pushed a button on their tabletop and heard the menu read out in English. Wet rolled towelettes were set down by a wait person with deftly automatic movements. Seaborn greeted her by putting his hands together and nodding.

Jessie pushed the button again and got the menu in Japanese, and again, in Esperanto. Seaborn clamped his hand over Jessie's and glared at her.

"It talks three languages, is all," said the wait person with a cockney British accent, even though she looked Japanese.

"Oh, I was just curious," Jessie said, then covered her mouth quickly, sorry for speaking.

Seaborn cleared his throat, coughed.

The wait person set down silverware, chopsticks, and printed menus as well. She waited.

Jessie picked up a warm towelette: *oshibori,* she thought, wondering how she knew that word. She wiped her hands, grateful for the civilized custom, accidently dislodging her glasses and wig, but straightening them out quickly.

"Why don't you take those off, and relax," the wait person suggested.

"Oh no, there's a blemish I'm covering," Jessie lied, tittering, pointing, demurring to look at Seaborn. It was impossible not to talk.

"What would you like then?"

Jessie ordered Spinach Goma Ae, Chicken Teriyaki, vegetable tempura, a house salad with ginger vinaigrette, Jasmine tea and a large carrot juice. She pointed to what she wanted on the menu, instead of speaking, and the wait person repeated each item back as she wrote it down.

Seaborn's jaw dropped. "I'll have the braised fish with sticky rice." He said, ordering light, and breaking his own rule about not speaking. He'd probably have to help Jessie eat all she had ordered; her eyes were bigger than her stomach lately.

When the food came, Jessie ate like a savage animal. She inhaled the Goma Ae before Seaborn could even get a bite. It was like she was trying to fulfill all her hungers of the last five years at one sitting.

Someone changed the channel on the television, and reruns of "The Life of Death Show" came on. Some diners watched, and others ignored it. Often, they turned and stared at Jessie and Seaborn with curiosity. The announcer interrupted the show twice with live updates on the missing Jessie Pettengill, and her manager/husband, Seaborn—So far, they'd been spotted in Hoboken, Toronto, and Baltimore. Seaborn began to get nervous.

Then Jane Thrower came on with a special appeal: *Please feed Jessie Pettengill if you see her, because her homeostasis is out of whack, and she won't get hungry and eat on her own. She could starve to death. She doesn't cycle on a twenty-four-hour period like a normal person.* Jane went on and on, exaggerating wildly, trying to throw people off.

Seaborn couldn't help smiling in admiration of her performance. He speared a piece of Jessie's chicken off her plate—no way she could eat all that.

Jessie watched Jane on TV and hunkered down on her food. She was cleaning up the last dish when the wait person came back over.

"What's your name, then, dearie?" she asked Jessie right out, startling Seaborn so he sat up quickly.

"Lucy," Jessie said, plucking a name out of the air, and trying to steel herself into the lie the way Frank said.

The wait person's small, narrow eyes widened into surprise when she saw how much food Jessie had polished off. "Ah, Lucy," she said, now winsome, "that's an unusual name. You don't hear it much anymore. My name's Jade. That's an old classic too. I named my daughter Skylar, after the first P.H., the Sky King model, very nice. Did you want any dessert?" she asked doubtfully.

Jade was chattering as if she was just working on a good tip, but Seaborn knew better. He watched her when she walked back to put in Jessie's order for green tea ice cream. She shook her head at the bar-side patrons and Seaborn read her lips: "This one ate too bloody much." They all laughed, then turned and looked toward Seaborn and Jessie's table one last time, disappointed.

Back in the car, Jessie burped so loud she blushed. Then she took out a cigarette and started to light up.

Seaborn yelped, "Where'd you get tobacco?"

"Lying on the table. I thought I'd smoke in the restaurant to get in character, but I forgot."

Seaborn peeled away from the Park 'n Blow into the darkness, just as a school of P.H.s, full of hungry news hounds, landed on the other side of the building, like jelly-fish swarming under a boat. He wasn't sure if he got away before they saw him.

"You better just go on forgetting," Seaborn said, picking up speed, "that's the most enslaving habit ever known to humankind. It will kill you slowly, from the build-up of little causes long continued. They leave them on tables now, trying to hook people because hardly anybody will buy them anymore. You finally quit smoking years ago, don't you remember?"

Jessie had the sheepish look of a reformed cigarette addict.

"We had to give you lots of vitamins and hot and cold baths and water and juice flushes to get the nicotine out of your system. The withdrawal was torture. Then one day you finally forgot about smoking, like you'd been set free—you were so happy. Don't you remember?"

Jessie shook her head. What a talker Seaborn was. She did remember that. But how did she not remember quitting smoking?

She thought about smoking and then she saw an image in her mind: "There was something blocking me from smoking," she said, "I can see thousands of cigarettes all lined up like soldiers, waiting for me to smoke them; but one little soldier-cigarette is in front, blocking all the rest, and if I smoke it, I'll smoke all the rest too. Jane planted that mental picture, I remember; it was the whole secret of quitting. Just now, I guess I wanted to challenge that one little soldier, you know?"

"Well, smoke it if you want to." Seaborn opened the glove compartment. "Looky here, I've got this hammer, and if you want to, you can take it and put your fingers on the dash and slam that hammer down on them, hard as you can, make 'em bleed."

Jessie laughed, but a part of her still wanted to smoke the cigarette. She rolled it between her fingers, like an object of fascination.

"I think I'm picking up where I left off many years ago. Life hasn't happened to me the same way it has to you and Jane and Frank. I've got memory, but it's in bits, fragmented—like I remember a certain word I used to hear constantly."

"What word?"

"Moisture. People talked about the moisture in the air, on their faces and skin."

"Sure, it's always on the weather news—the Dew Points—they tell you the humidity and the barometric pressure, as if everyone understands what that means."

"I haven't heard the word once since I woke up. I wonder what happened to moisture. Oh, Sea," Jessie stroked his cheek, mocking an old commercial, "Your skin is so soft and moist, whatever do you use on it? Tell me your secret."

Seaborn grinned. After a thoughtful silence, he said, "I guess the Earth just got moister, and the fixation went away. We stopped polluting the air and waters so much, for one thing. It wasn't profitable anymore. Clean-up cost more than the companies were making on their products. We've stopped destroying the rain forests, they were erupting virus's– virus's come from the earth, not the waters, not the air. They make their way into a person's soft membranes, penetrate a person's body, like it's earth."

Jessie looked puzzled. "What about the AIDS virus?"

"They can arrest it, but not eradicate it. Prevention is starving it out; the epidemic is being managed. Medicine, ecology and economics are tied together, no more pyrrhic profits. Human rights are tied to Earth rights. The Earth is the first organism."

The picture-phone beeped. "Seek higher ground," Jane's face flashed on the monitor.

Seaborn turned on the scrambler and spoke, "That was a great dissemble Jane, perfect timing. Jessie had the feedbag on just as you were broadcasting, and they jumped on it like a duck on a June bug. How'd you know?"

After a long delay for the scrambler: "I thought it was about time for you to stop and eat. Where will you refuel?"

"Still got plenty of fuel. We'll make it to Roanoke easy, maybe Boone. And by the way, the Rover registration in my name is worrying me too—anything you can do about it?"

"Oh, Lordy, I'll try, just don't use biometrics to charge anything."

"What are biometrics? Jessie asked.

Seaborn said: "A thumb print, a voice or retinal reading."

"Using cash attracted a lot of damn attention, too. Those people in the restaurant acted like we just got out of jail."

"There's a sign." Jessie said, pointing out the window, "we just crossed into Maryland."

Seaborn looked at the dark sky; against a lid of clouds he saw a flock of P.H.'s—Indians? He couldn't tell.

"I've got a choice coming up in about an hour; I can stay on 81 or take the Blue Ridge Parkway," he said, thinking out loud.

But he knew what he'd do. The Blue Ridge Parkway was an old Indian trail he knew well. Besides, it was dangerous for P.H.'s to fly in the mountains at night, even Indians. Mountain peaks were unlit and would be treacherous to try to navigate in the air in total darkness, even with good instruments. So, they weren't likely to follow him.

"How're you feeling, Jessie?" Jane asked, changing the subject.

"I'm fine, thank you, except I've got a craving for a cigarette."

"Great day," said Jane, "you quit years ago after many false starts—fight it off girl."

Seaborn signed off with Jane, then switched on the radio looking for music or comedy and found The Reverend's Christian Crusade instead. He started to change the station, but Jessie stopped him. It was a new variation of his usual backwater sermon:

"This Jessie is not a Christian! She scorns the Bible's teachings-ah. What kind of prophet is that? NONE! NONE! I say to you, she cannot be allowed to cross our borders-ah. We must rid the world of this harlot who sins among us, who worships the BEAST-ah-MACHINE-ah."

Jessie cringed at the idea that people she didn't even know were sitting in judgement of her. She was being pilloried over the airwaves, and she couldn't do a thing to stop it.

Seaborn switched it off. The hatred in The Reverend's voice had deepened, his humor had decayed. He was a scary bugger.

40
Tunnels

An hour later they were the hottest news item on the airwaves. Seaborn watched the small TV screen, as a news reporter standing in front of One World Trade told how Jessie had been sighted in Canada, in the Lincoln Tunnel, on the Tappan Zee Bridge, even atop Lookout Mountain in Tennessee. He had the sound down low– Jessie had dozed off again.

Chaos! Great! he thought, speeding up a little. He'd always loved chaos, but as he'd matured he recognized that it was a disguised desire for pure order, which was hard to get. Reminded him of one of his favorite messages from Jack Kerouac, a prolific messenger: *Now I realize my fascination with anarchy was a craving for stability.*

Another TV reporter interrupted the broadcast with a news item she'd just that minute received: *Seaborn and Jessie are headed south on 81 near Chambersburg. A sky copter news hunter has picked them up on his lightning tracking radar screen.*

Seaborn looked up and saw the news hunter in his P.H., slathered with the station I.D. He knew he had to start heavy evasive action right then. The party was over. He called Frank, turning on the scrambler and the ECM which was louder. Frank had equipped all their phones with Electronic Counter Measures. Seaborn's voice verged on panic:

"SOS, he's right here, over my visor..."

Jessie groaned, then sat up, wide awake.

After a long delay for the ECM., Frank answered, "Yeah, I hear you and I have a picture. The only way they can intercept you is if they can stop you, so that's what they'll try to do– probably with illegal roadblocks. But they don't know about my capabilities." Frank bragged a little just trying to reassure Seaborn, "I have a satellite picture of both ridges coming through those mountains. There are basically two, maybe three paved roads, and lots of dirt roads. They won't have enough personnel to block all of them all of the time, so we'll dither between the roads. But don't use the G.P.S. system because our enemies will pick you up on it."

Frank thought about his satellite feed. He was always afraid some nutcase would fly over and shoot it out– like throwing poison in a well– the most un-American thing he could think of. He had not come up with a way to effectively defend the dishes, though he was working on it.

To Seaborn, he said casually, "About time for you to take the Parkway, isn't it? Anyone else after you?"

"Yeah, I don't know. Jane says Eli and Smithy hired a bunch of Indian trackers."

"Watch out for them. They fly the bat. It's the best sonar. They can get through those mountains in pitch black. Gibbous moon up there tonight, Seaborn, fairly dark, that's in our favor." Frank tried to sound cheerful.

"Feeling poetic, are we?" Seaborn said. "So what are you going to do about this tail?"

"You worry too much. Have a little patience, my man, watch and wait."

Just then, the sky copter news hunter veered off and headed back away from them in a big hurry.

"Hey, what'd you do to that guy?" Seaborn yelped.

"I messed with his computer, so he thinks he's losing fuel, took a few minutes, but he got the return to base signal."

Frank whistled a little snatch of "Windmills."

Jessie was so surprised to hear it that it jolted her memory. "Oh Frank, I've missed you so much." Her voice trembled, as memories of Frank began to flood her mind.

Frank came back: "Me too, glad to see you're on the way home. This place needs a woman's touch."

"How are your little pigs?" she asked.

"They grew up to be big ole hogs." Frank was surprised that Jessie remembered.

"And how's that lil' Baby Beast?" she said, and Frank's cat at that moment meowed, giving everyone a much-needed laugh.

"She sleeps right here on the console all the time, likes to stay by me." Frank stroked Baby Beast, and they heard her purring.

Seaborn saw the sign and turned onto the Blue Ridge Parkway. Instantly the view became majestic, sweeping.

Jessie looked at the dark mountains ahead and felt nauseated. She had eaten too much. She was unused to her body, and it was tough learning how much food she needed. It was hard for her to kick back and relax into it, but she knew that's what she had to do, or else she'd always feel at sixes and sevens, like now.

"You okay?" Seaborn said, "You remembered Frank's cat, that's really good."

Jessie nodded, holding her mouth tightly shut.

Seaborn turned up the sound on the TV. This newscaster had a tinge of a Latin accent:

Today META filed charges against The Life of Death Show for interfering with astronomers' efforts to contact intelligent life in outer space. META charged that the show's million channel receivers are causing too much static on the airwaves. Jessie Pettengill, as you know from earlier reports, is still missing and the LODS is unavailable for comment.

"What does META stand for?" Jessie wondered out loud.

"Great day," Jane chirped, "It stands for Mega Channel Extra Terrestrial Assay, and believe it or not, these guys don't consider spirits extraterrestrials."

"Oh boy," said Seaborn, "we've got a four-way going. You still there too, Frank?"

"On higher ground than META," Frank said. His face appeared on the monitor, then morphed back to the newscaster's face. "They think every disruption in communication is our fault. Solar flares on the sun's surface—you know, those little storms—they cause static and interference, too. When solar radiation strikes the ionosphere, hell, everything blinks. The whole world blinks, but it's our fault."

"Hey Frank," Jane said, intimately.

"Hey Jane." Frank matched her intimacy.

Jessie and Seaborn exchanged a puzzled look.

"I'm going to have to fuel up soon," Seaborn said.

"Roanoke's not a good idea, Sea," said Frank. "Do you like Kudzu Blossom, Jane?"

"I love it. In fact, I think of Jessie every time I catch a whiff of it around here," Jane said.

"I'll make you some cologne too," said Frank.

"Would you? It's so spectral, like magic to the mood. No one else has it yet, either."

"I know, 'cause I've got the name and essence tied up and registered," said Frank.

"You're so smart," Jane said.

Jessie and Seaborn looked at each other and smiled a knowing smile. They listened while Jane and Frank went on and on, Seaborn thinking how easily this could digress into phone sex, among his other stray thoughts. What happened to that gaping six-year difference in their ages?

Eventually, Seaborn had to cut in, to report sighting the Indians, and Jane signed off.

"I think they've been following us since before we got on the Parkway. Man, they fly like swifts."

"They're more like yellow jackets," Frank answered. "Remember, they can pester you and chase you, but they can't keep you from leaving the room."

"It's pretty dark out here, but I can see seven of them, green lights flickering– they look like lightning bugs. They like to dive and buzz us every couple of miles."

Seaborn peered out over the Shenandoah Valley, so vast, so heaven-reaching. Even in darkness it was brightly bussing the clouds, and he could see how clean and streamlined autumn had left it. He saw the bare trees in the valley and wished he was under their branchy cover, however sparse. He recalled Henry telling him once that Shenandoah was an old Algonquin word meaning *bright daughter of the stars.* When and where had Henry learned Algonquin?

Frank said, "Now listen to me, in case we lose touch, momentarily. You're coming up to the Craggy Flats tunnel..." the radio-phone buzzed with static, cutting into Frank's instructions, "...and there will be more tunnels, and it will get darker..." They lost him for a few seconds, then he came back, "...after you go through Waynesboro, take 64 back over to 81. You'll pick up some Charlottesville traffic to get mixed up in. Then switch back to the Parkway when you see the Natural Bridge signs. I know a guy who had stock in that bridge. Let me fax you some color maps of the whole area and some pictures of the bridge, I don't advise you to stop and see it."

The car-fax started spitting out maps, and Jessie caught them in her lap.

"Anyway, there will be traffic to get mixed up in around there, too, but not much this time of night. At Roanoke you'll be halfway here but watch out for roadblocks at Roanoke. I don't know where, but I've got a feeling. . ."

"You going non-linear on me now, too?" Seaborn asked him and drove into a tunnel.

The radiophone was silent until the Rover came out the other side and Frank answered, "Every chance I get."

"I don't like these tunnels." Jessie said, looking ahead to the next dark one coming up.

Seaborn looked at the maps, trying to spot little side roads that tied into the Parkway.

Frank signed off with a perky, "Stay in touch."

Halfway through the next tunnel, they suddenly saw three P.H.s hovering at the other end, in a V-formation, a few feet off the ground.

Jessie screamed.

Seaborn hit the brakes, cut off his headlights. There was a moment of black silence except for the whapping of the PH rotors, which came reverberating through the tunnel from the open end where they were hanging, waiting, their little green lights flickering.

Seaborn muttered, "Can't stop me from leaving the room, heh?"

He threw it in reverse and backed out of the tunnel finding the road with his brake lights. When he was out, he turned the car around and crawled down the road with his head hanging out the window to keep an eye on the edge. If he misjudged it, they'd plunge into the ravine.

He came to a narrow gravel road, turned quickly, and bumped down the rutted road under the canopy of branchy trees, dust a flying.

He broke into song, trying to take the edge off: "Like a tunnel that you follow to another one you know, down a hollow to a cave, where the sun has never come..."

It was a verse of "Windmills Of Your Mind." Jessie recognized the tune, although Seaborn murdered the lyrics.

The nausea rose. She leaned her head out the open window and hurled into the wind.

Seaborn turned on his parking lights so they had a little visibility. He doubted the Rover could be seen from the air now, under all the branchy trees. They were probably just a blip on the Indians radar screens.

But they were not even that. They were lost to the Indians, who had touched down and walked all the way through the tunnel looking for them. The Indians didn't trust the blipping lights of radar, nor did they always pay attention to them. They trusted what they could see with their own, perfect eyesight; and to them, the Rover had vanished into the dark night, like magic.

41
Crossing Borders

Seaborn sped down the rugged road for miles, their teeth rattling, hearts racing. The parking lights shone on batches of mailboxes, stacked like totems beside dark, dirt side-roads. Down those roads tiny house lights populated a mountainous shelf– the houses all but invisible yet twinkling in the blackness. Satellite dishes made silhouettes against the sky. The smell of wood smoke from chimneys spiced the night air.

Finally, Seaborn drove out onto a paved road, and it was like skating on ice. He checked his compass to make sure he was headed south on the smooth two-lanner. The darkness was less dense, the sky opened to them, clear and starlit, empty of PH's. He wondered how close they were to Frank's covered bridge, and just then saw a sign: "SKYLINE DRIVE, 12 MILES."

He segued back and forth on parallel paved roads a few times in an evasive action, and then cut over to Skyline Drive and rode the crest of the mountaintop for a while with his lights back on. He began to relax. The car was quiet. Jessie sagged against the door.

"You okay Jess?" he got no answer, but he stroked her back reassuringly. Nothing for it but to keep on going. He knew he was a good driver, loved to drive; he had his Indian connections, too. Yet his heart pounded. He repeated a mantra to slow his heart's racing. He was psyched for his ancestors' Creek Indian genes to kick in and tell him which way to go and where the traps were laid for them. He inhaled basil and sage, guzzled spring water, consulted the maps, watched the sky, and kept on driving south. At the juncture near

Charlottesville, he took 64 over to 81 and fell in with some other traffic, but no other blue Land Rovers in sight. Where were they? What had Jane done with them?

Just before Roanoke, he veered off 81 onto a narrow two-lane mountain road that meandered south between 81 and the Parkway. He saw a loose red balloon pass overhead as he breezed past the Roanoke turnoffs. He visualized the roadblocks that must be set up on both major roads, waiting for them. Penetrating lights and cameras and lots of people milling around, Honey Wagons parked nearby; a generator truck, radar, and hundreds of careless strangers hungry for a piece of them. He drove right under the natural bridge without knowing it, worrying– how could he and Jessie ever get their lives into a manageable, normal state when they were being hunted like dogs?

Seaborn felt a wave of cold, raw fear, as he plunged deeper into the Bible Belt. It would take more than magic to save them. Once, Jessie had almost caused a riot when she casually mentioned on the air that the Bible was a place where God was locked up in a book. He cringed now, thinking about the anger and hatred that had come back to her for that.

The moon was little more than half full, an October moon shrouded in clouds, and Sea craved light. He needed to talk to Frank, needed a bathroom. He could see Mars peeping through, a bright orange star. He pined for his father, John Playfair, imagining the discomforts he must be experiencing somewhere out in space, aboard a ship on the way to Mars, a two-to-five-year trip, even at ion drive speeds. Seaborn hoped he was alive and well. He'd spent his life on all kinds of waiting lists to go and finally at age 62, his name had come up. Sixty-two wasn't old in the elder culture of the twenty-first century, thanks to John Glenn who had paved the way. Seaborn took comfort in thinking about his father, whom he admired. Besides having a breathtaking gift for physics, he was a researcher into man's future and past origins in space, instead of on Earth. He was helping to give the research a Mars spin. The theory he embraced was that tiny particles were carried many light years through space and had in their genetic make-up memory of flight. Some fell to Earth into the oceans and became flying fish, from which humans were descended.

Seaborn switched on the TV and there it was, a roadblock on the Parkway, the media scene he had visualized in his adrenaline stimulated mind, except the crowds were even more pugnacious. He looked over at Jessie sleeping, and was glad she wasn't seeing this.

The on-scene anchor made pithy conversation into the camera to prepare the viewing audience for Jessie, who everyone fully expected would be coming down the road, right into their laps. The anchor's repetitions got to be hectoring; a director switched to the scene on 81, which was fermenting identically.

Seaborn heaved a sigh. So, Frank had been right about his hunch, two roadblocks, both at Roanoke. Seaborn wondered what intelligence had led to those choices. Probably the sky copter news hunter. How dumb the media were to show this to him, how monomaniacal and self-important they had become; expecting him to play ball because Jessie was in the public eye, like she was obliged, like they owned her.

Even a good distance south of Roanoke, he stayed on a dark little two-lanner, stopping once to relieve himself. He turned the TV off, not wanting to witness the disappointment and baring of teeth that would soon overtake the crowds and media, when their hungers went unsatisfied. He looked up and caught sight of the Indians, back on his trail, and he extinguished his headlights and drove in pitch black, running over onto the shoulders a few times, causing Jessie to make little yelps in her sleep.

After a while, he turned onto a road that would lead him back to the Parkway, well beyond the roadblocks, where he intended to drive directly to Boone to refuel. He'd have to lose the Indians somehow. He didn't want to bother Frank unless he had to, not until he made it to Boone, the seat of the Bible belt.

Like entering the jaws of darkness, he turned back onto the great Blue Ridge Parkway, now cast in inky fog. The sky was full of P.H.'s swooping low trying to sight the Rover. With no lights, Seaborn had to creep along slowly.

Suddenly, two-hundred yards ahead of him, all hell broke loose. Explosions lit up the sky, splitting their ears. Jessie came awake screaming. Stones and dirt flew at them. The windows clattered, close to shattering.

Seaborn cursed and swerved, speeded up on some blind impulse. At their back, more explosions sent echoes booming through the mountains. Someone in a P.H. was lobbing pineapple grenades on the road, trying to snag them– it was open warfare. "This is fucking unbelievable." Seaborn swore. He used the light from the explosions to barrel through the smoke and road hazards the bombs were creating. He zig-zagged, caroming into the guard rails, adding the head-piercing sound of steel on steel to the blasting bombs and Jessie's cries.

And then, just as suddenly, it all stopped. The sky became empty. For long minutes they drove in silence, not daring to believe it was over, still bracing for the big one. Seaborn fumed, muttered under his breath: "it couldn't be the Indians– it has to be The Reverend– or someone in his militia– only they would do something like this." Something snapped in him. He flipped on his lights and flew down the road as though they were winged. He sped toward the North Carolina line, longing for one moment that was not clotted with fear. He tried but couldn't get through to Frank or Jane. All he got was static, an earful of feedback. Had the phones been destroyed?

Jessie held onto her stomach, crying quietly, her whole body rattling inside. She wondered if she was really pregnant– or was that just a dream? How much safe ground could a simple womb be expected to provide? She was missing Henry suddenly; she felt lost without his voice. She realized she had been trying to fill the void he left with mere food. She prayed with wordless intensity for their safety, for deliverance from this awful nightmare.

At 2:30 a.m., Seaborn coasted into Boone, spotted an all-night station and straggled to a stop, desperate for fuel. He'd pushed it to the max. The aroma therapy wasn't working anymore either and he had to piss so bad his teeth ached. Driving in darkness and switchbacking between the roads had worn him down. The bombs, even though they missed, had shattered his nerves, and Jessie's too. Twisting and climbing in the high altitudes had given them both the yawns, a craving for oxygen, and sleep. Seaborn still had his mustache– he put on the wig and neb-piece.

Jessie ran into the deserted ladies' room without her mask and puked again. She brushed her teeth for a long time, getting drunk on running water, splashing her face with first hot then cold water, steaming up the mirror. She wrote across it, ANONYMOUS WAS HERE.

Seaborn fueled up at the hydrogen pipeline and bought some cheese crackers, popcorn, apple juice, whatever he could grab in the one minute he took to pay the sleepy attendant.

They cruised down the neighborhood streets of Boone with the lights off. All was quiet at this time of night; the streets were empty. They stopped at a dark house, on about a two-acre lot, with a real estate sign out front. Seaborn idled up the driveway, flashing his lights in curtainless windows. The house was vacant. He parked the Rover under the attached carport and cut the engine. They sat for a minute in silent darkness, wondering if anyone would be able to find them there.

Jessie broke the silence, "It's nice to have a roof over our heads."

Seaborn smiled. He relaxed for the first time in hours.

He tried to call Frank and finally got through. He wanted to find out where all the Indians were. He hadn't seen or heard them buzzing above the Rover since the air strike ended. "You were right about Roanoke," he said, "but you didn't call that bomb field we went through."

Frank came on very serious, "I know, I underestimated hate again. It was really bad. But did you see what happened? The Indians chased the bombers off, threatening them with the ghosts of their ancestors; phantoms were misting your car, and pelts whipping in the wind, a big red balloon following you, right in the middle of the raid."

Seaborn yawned, "How did you see all that? I could hardly see anything."

"The satellite camera on your roof. It kept on sending me pictures through the whole siege. I knew you got out, but I couldn't get you on the mobile. You did some good driving."

Seaborn yawned again. "Yeah, well, we're going to have to get some sleep now, Frank. We're beat. I think we found a good hiding place."

"Those phantoms were probably moisture, you know? Clouds and the humidity– make images sometimes. The barometric pressure is high in those Mountains," Frank theorized.

Seaborn and Jessie laughed. They let Frank who was a late-night talker go on and on, while they broke out the snacks, tumbled over into the back seat and got under a blanket, like teenagers at a drive-in. Jessie kissed Seaborn and giggled when his fake mustache tickled– she pulled it off with her teeth. After Frank signed off, they started making out. This led to a hot-blooded sexual event, a reaction to being chased, hunted, and nearly killed. They felt hidden under the carport, covered in a close, ripe darkness, under the moon, sun and nova's. They joined soul and sinew, treating each other like their own lives. It was earthy, not dreamy, and in a way, they felt like they were picking up where they had left off years before.

Several P.H.s flew over along the companionway, but Jessie and Seaborn were oblivious.

"What'll we do if the real estate agent catches us?" Jessie whispered.

Seaborn answered, "We'll just buy the house!"

What were all those enchanting sounds? they both wondered as they fell asleep.

Frank had grepped his files and found some sounds he'd been saving to lullaby them with. It was his lifelong collection of acoustic archeology, sounds that had been frozen in time, including waterfalls, animal mating calls, train whistles, and even some early Hank Williams. Now Frank played it all back softly in his own melodic arrangement, beautiful and strange.

Seaborn dreamed he was driving at a high speed, trying to get away, when he saw a tall figure in a cowboy hat, with stooped shoulders, hitchhiking. He had a guitar and sang an old Luke The Drifter song: *"...a livin' death is all that's left for men with broken hearts..."* He wanted to pick up the drifter but couldn't stop because someone was chasing him. "Maybe next time Buddy," he hollered as he sped past. But when he looked in the rear view, The Drifter had vanished.

42
In The Uttermost Part Of The Earth

The rising sun and birdsong woke Seaborn and Jessie early. Sometime in the night, Frank's melodious soundtrack had ended, they'd slept like the dead, and now they were thrown back into the reality of their flight. They washed up at a spigot outside the house, and were on their way again, moving slowly through the quiet streets of Boone, wishing they could change the color of the Rover, and the license plate. Although they didn't know it, they were well ahead of the Indians, who were still snoring in some alfalfa field miles away. Seaborn knew the Indians would have to wait for their super conductors to repolarize at an electron dump somewhere, and he had fueled up already the night before. So, his biggest worry was The Reverend and his radical Christian militia.

It was too early to call Frank, who was in a night mode, always the last to rise in the morning. Frank gave the lie to the rule that the early bird catches the worm. Seaborn called Jane instead.

"Great day, Elderculture is after you," she burst out, "busloads of them– they figured out you were headed for Boone."

"Oh, no, not them. Do they know about our disguises too?"

"I don't know how they would. No one has reported seeing you two, just the car."

"Who is Elderculture?" Jessie asked.

Seaborn didn't know where to start, to answer her question, but he tried. "They are sort of a fundamentalist music group who tour around the country in buses playing funerals and family events. They're all over seventy and have burned their candles down to the nubs, so now they're wild, nothing left to lose. You never know what they're gonna do next. They scare me to death– more unpredictable than teenagers."

Seaborn always thought The Reverend had them in his pocket, too, but he didn't say so now. "I never know when one of them sticks his hand out whether I should shake it or duck because he's going to show me he knows karate."

Seaborn drove into a strip shopping center, and parked in front of the In-Between Diner, guessing they would be safe there. His eyes rested on a sign on the entrance door which said: NO LINES, BULLIES OR BARE FEET. He started to put on his wig and neb-piece.

"Wait, I don't feel like going in yet,"

"What's the matter, Jessie?"

"Nothing... I'm just... the thought of putting this wig and the neb-piece on makes me feel sick." She was feeling safe behind the tinted windows of the Rover and didn't want to move, not even for food.

They sat for a while, sniffing an iris cap, to combat tension. The iris made them thirsty, so they took long pulls of spring water, and watched couples walk from the Cloud Nine Bridal Shop on one side of the In-between Diner, to the Gardens of Memory Funeral Home on the other side, like they were coordinating a wedding/funeral. Jessie watched this odd progression, intrigued.

After a bit, her stomach grumbled, and she managed a smile, "I feel better now. But I'm going to eat light, so I won't throw up again."

"Stay here, I'll get something to go." Seaborn said.

Just then, a huge, silver bus pulled into the lot, right beside them. They heard chanting: "Ba-wa, ba-wa, to laugh and jeer us. We are gonna take somebody near us." Jessie had no inkling that it was one of her own little sound grams thrown out from eternity, which Elderculture had picked up and used for their own purposes. A bunch of elderly white-haired people stabbed their fingers at the Rover.

"Oh, sweet Jesus, move in for us now." Seaborn was in motion in two seconds, spitting gravel in his wake.

Jessie looked back and saw "Elderculture" painted on the back of the bus in splashy red-ripe letters. She watched the bus slowly pull out of the lot, creaky under its formidable load, and come lumbering down the road, after them. She saw everyone inside the bus jumping around, and yelling all at once, spoiling the chant.

Seaborn took a sharp turn onto a country road headed west and drove way over the speed limit for a good twenty minutes. He had to stop at a JOHNSON CITY LIMITS stop sign, and just beyond it he saw a white church, THE FIRST CHURCH OF THE OPEN BIBLE. He quickly pulled off the road, drove behind the church, and hid in a parking lot filled with cars, praying silently that they would not be discovered in an enemy camp.

He planned to wait until the bus passed, then circle back to the Parkway. They sat and stared at a hologram sign that moved around the steeple of the otherwise austere white-frame church: "A day hemmed in prayer will not unravel," Jessie said it aloud, like a mantra, each time it came around.

It wasn't Sunday but church was in session. They could hear a bizarre kind of singing that Seaborn remembered from his childhood in the North Georgia mountains. It was the same eerie sound that had rattled his bones when he was a boy. "That's shape-note singing!" he said, "c'mon, let's go inside. These people aren't afraid of death– they even sing about it."

Jessie looked puzzled, but Seaborn grabbed her hand and pulled her along. They slipped into the church and sat in the back pew where they could watch the road from a window. They had forgotten their wigs and glasses, but no one noticed them, so rapt was everyone in the music: "La fa la so mi fa la so fa la so, the dead's alive and the lost is found, Glory Hallelujah, La, fa do fa re mi so..." they droned on and on. Seaborn kept his eye on the road. When, at last, he saw the big ELDERCULTURE bus chug past, he relaxed into the exotic singing without instruments. On and on the congregation thrummed in a cadence of long, deep notes; the latent language gripping Jess and Sea, and everyone else like some primal memory.

Upon the altar rested an open, cobalt blue coffin, tilted forward so everyone could see the body of a man maybe in his late sixties; the expression on his face one of unfinished business. Lying in dead repose in his lap was a small red Terrier, likely his faithful dog.

A young bride and groom in full wedding regalia stood and took their place beside the coffin. A preacher came forward and stood before them and all the congregation. Tears and smiles mingled together on all their faces. The coffin was like a member of the wedding party. Jessie stared in disbelief at the strangeness unfolding before her. She looked at Seaborn, but he looked right-at-home.

When the singing stopped, the preacher began the joining ceremony, quoting Ruth from the Old Testament about cleaving unto one another and then the old familiar do-you-takes. The bride and groom kissed.

The congregation started up singing again, more fiercely: "Do mi so mi so la do re mi so la... and we'll all shine together in that Glo-or-ry..." over and over, until the music had a noticeable drawing effect on everyone, as if a spiritual harmony had got inside them. Then the church full of people rose, and moving like one body, carried the dead man with his dog outside to the graveyard, under the big Oaks. Someone had tied a bunch of red balloons onto the casket and they bobbed around merrily, ribbons trailing the ground. The singing stopped, and the preacher began another ceremony, this time for burial. Jessie thought it was all out-of-this-world bizarre, yet it seemed to span the ages too.

"La fa do fa re mi la, the mind would feel an aching void and still want something new..." The singing went on again, rose and fell like hearts trained to beat as one. The effect on everything alive was a rising up, an ascendancy. Playing through the marrow of the sound was the hue of resolution, a peacefulness to calm the most savage beast. No longer merely human animals, the congregation was magically uplifted, sanctified, delivered from contemplating the shit on their tails.

Jessie swooned. She remembered the rappers she had heard in Hoboken; she thought of jungle rhythms and paler ones like Barbershop quartets, and the old Wiffenpoof singers she'd once been oddly moved by. She thought of Frank's music from the night before, and "The Windmills Of Your Mind," the song that had possessed her. She hoped the music would never stop because people required rhythmic singing that went on and on, in order to go on. People on earth needed the sound of human vocal cords as much as sight, touch, water, air, a need for stars. All of it fitting together for harmony's sake, for bliss.

It was the first time since waking up from her long spell, that she'd felt completely at home in the world. This was better than sleep or food. Her stifling fret and longing fell away to a manageable distance and she started to feel space again, and who she was in it, the self she might become again, given the chance.

Then came the final song, notes, and lyrics:

Plant you a rose that
shall bloom o'er my grave
When I am gone when I am gone
Sing a sweet song such as
Angels may have
When I am gone when I am gone
Praise ye the Lord that
I'm freed from all care
When I am gone when I am gone
Look up on high and believe
that I'm there
When I am gone when I am gone...

As they sang, the congregation moved, and Seaborn and Jessie moved with them, over to an arcade of picnic tables, piled high with covered dishes of good smelling food. This was the pay-off in life, Jessie thought: food, and always a last supper. She suddenly remembered the pound cake, broke away from Seaborn, and ran to the Rover, retrieving the cake from the back seat, two days old, a little misshapen but still good, she was sure. Pound cake lasted. She knew this was just the occasion she had baked it for. She tore the wrapping off and proudly placed it on the table alongside the other desserts.

She thought of the first act of Hamlet: "The funeral baked meats did coldly furnish forth the marriage table." But this was not Shakespeare's vision anymore. This was not the cold drudgery of funerals that were like the scraggly ends of parades. This was upbeat and celebratory. This food was southern, a delicious spread: deviled eggs, fried chicken, pimento cheese sandwiches, sliced tomatoes, creamed corn, pea salads, peach pies, ice-cream freezing, pork meat grilling, the whiff of barbecue, not death, not even the anguish, no one daft with grieving. It was like a joyful noise, a relief, a send-off, balloons instead of grave flowers.

Joy is a special wisdom.

Seaborn and Jessie got on line for food and filled their plates with a spoonful of each dish, while folks around them chattered and flashed them interested smiles. They sat at one of the picnic tables, breaking bread with people they didn't know, yet felt a sweet kinship with.

The bride came up when Jessie had almost finished eating. "Do I know you?" she asked, "you look so familiar."

Jessie found herself talking in letters and numbers, inexplicably, aligning them together in a mysterious configuration, like the trees made, like the shape-notes created. Then she began spouting verse: "It's not the things I didn't get that I'll regret, it's the time I didn't take but spent," The bride chimed in with Jessie, "it's the love I didn't give, the life I didn't live... "

Seaborn took hold of Jessie's arm, interrupting the recitation, "c'mon sweetie, we have to get going now." He hustled her away towards the Rover, Jessie protesting the whole way.

As they pulled out of the parking lot, the preacher saw them leaving and came over to the bride who was frozen in place, staring after them, dumbfounded. Finally she found her voice: Give me a pencil, quick." The groom produced one. On a napkin, the bride wrote the series of numbers and letters Jessie had spoken: R27, L52, R5, L10.

"Why, that was Jessie Pettengill, I'm sure of it. I think she gave me the combination to Daddy's safe. It was lost, and we were going to have to blast it open. She recited that poem Daddy always kept in his safe– I recognized it," she cried, elated, hugging her new husband, "oh, this is the happiest day of my life!"

The preacher called out, "Ya'll come back now, we'll treat you so many different ways you'll like one of 'em."

Jessie complained as they sped away, "But Seaborn, I didn't even get a piece of my pound cake. Now I'll never know if it was any good."

43
Home Free

After deregulation of Personal Satellites, Frank had been able to achieve mobile parabolics practically anywhere he wanted – expansive scale pictures, if not close-ups. He had computer friends all over the country. He had prepared for this day, for this route of escape, but the pictures he was getting now were beyond his wildest dreams.

Around nine-thirty, he'd been awakened by weird singing sounds, not exactly singing, more like an earthy chanting, soul full. He staggered over to the computer half asleep, and by rolling the cameras on the Rover was able to achieve pictures on his monitor of a white frame church, under big Oak trees, a funeral pier with red balloons bobbing on it, then movement of a bunch of singing people towards picnic tables under an open-sided canopy roof. He saw Jessie and Seaborn sitting at a picnic table eating, their plates loaded with food. Next, they were talking with a bride and groom, when Seaborn sprung up, and hustled Jessie across a parking lot to the parked Rover, and then wow, they peeled out of there.

Even after they were on the road, he could hear echoes of the strange fa-la-la-ing of that music, and the visual was like a camera riding an aerial draft on the Rover.

Frank's location finder said Johnson City, Tennessee—way off-course. Did he have satellite moves there? Frank beamed ear-to-ear at the magic.

When Seaborn found the road he wanted, 23 South to Asheville, he called Frank and sang a carpella: "Wake up, wake up, the sun is up, the dew is on the buttercup. We just crashed a funeral and Jessie got a dose of Tennessee Gothic.

It was a wedding, too, and she gave the bride a message from her dead daddy. I think Henry might be making a comeback. She's all in a daze."

Jessie looked at Seaborn and shook her head. She didn't want to disappoint him, but she didn't know where those numbers and the poem had come from; she only knew she was wide awake, feet on the ground, and it was not Henry. And she had eaten too much again, against her own better judgement, and was starting to feel like she was going to be sick. She fought the feeling. "They were just a bunch of numbers, like those shape notes," she said, wanting to put an end to it.

"Jane got rid of Elderculture for you." Frank said, marveling at the clear picture he had of Jessie and Seaborn rolling along.

"How'd she do that?"

"She sent them to Lexington, Kentucky. Told them you were headed for the Blue Grass Parkway, not the Blue Ridge, said she was with the Elderculture Welcoming Committee in Kentucky and was planning a reception for you there. She told them to call her back when the bus reached Kingsport, she'd keep them posted. You have to feel sorry for those old sports."

"Not me. They're too dangerous. Tell her to stay on 'em until she drums them into Lexington. By then we'll be home."

"You sound like an ageist, Sea," Frank laughed. But he liked hearing Seaborn say that word "home," liked that Seaborn still considered One Wing Flapping his home even after Frank had turned the place into his own personal electronics village. He and Seaborn both thought the same way about technology: it was natural, organic, gave a sense of community even. And they both served an apprenticeship to nature, why they could trust themselves with machines in the first place.

"By the way, Jane said to tell you it was too late to hide the registration on the Rover- your tag number is out there now." Frank reluctantly added this worriment before he signed off. He blamed himself. How had he overlooked such an obvious detail?

All at once, the sky was filled with buzzing Indians in P.H.'s, coasting thermals with the hawks. Seaborn knew they had their eyes on him, but also on the white-tailed deer in the valley below. P.H.'s in the air didn't bother him near as much as vehicles on the ground, even in daylight.

Seaborn looped around below Asheville and drove into Maggie Valley. Up in the sky, the Indians suddenly saw four blue Land Rovers that had come out of nowhere. One was headed into Asheville, one headed southeast toward Pisgah, one headed out 40 West toward Tennessee, and one headed south on old Highway 19. The Indians swooped off in all directions, bewildered, their rotors ruffling like feathers. One P.H. stayed with Seaborn and Jessie.

Seaborn saw them all veering off and wondered why. "I'll be damned." he said, pointing up at the sky. "Look at that."

Jessie moaned and wrapped her arms around her full stomach.

For a long time, Seaborn drove the winding road south in sweet, near silence, with only the one PH overhead. Highway 19 was a familiar trek to him. They had come so far, the first night, it was less than a hundred miles to Cowpen Mountain, and then a couple more miles winding up the mountain to One Wing.

When Seaborn crossed the line into Georgia, he noticed Jessie slumped in her seat, looking pasty. He had never known her to be car-sick before. Aroma therapy had not worked. Even the Sea-Bands he had given her to wear that exerted acupressure on the Nei Kuan points inside her wrists hardly worked. He wished he could talk to Jane, but he couldn't get through. There had been no communication from her since early that morning. He pulled a blanket around Jessie.

Jane was busy side-tracking everyone. She had jammed her scrambler, gone off-book, and sent out wildly bogus transmissions to be picked up, with the result that she was attracting other followers, fans, and media into Lexington as well. She was intent on bagging the whole lot of them. She had hired another five blue Land Rovers, as decoys, to swarm all over the Shenandoah Valley and head off in every direction but the right one. Land Rovers had not been easy to find, and the blue paint jobs had taken time– she just hoped they had all shown up and done their part.

Even Frank wouldn't risk a conversation with Jane since her scrambler was not engaged. All her circuits were tied up anyway. As far as he knew, she was still in the hot seat at One World Trade. He was worried about her. He had one emergency fax line available they had agreed to use as a last resort.

Seaborn reached Mineral Bluff in mid-afternoon, without stopping once, and with three P.H.'s on his tail. He was convinced that one of them was The Reverend Thackston. He'd caught a glimpse of that shock of red hair. But why hadn't he made a move? What was he waiting for? Were the other two the Reverend's back-up militia? Indians? or media dogs? He couldn't tell, and whenever he looked up, the sun blinded him.

Halfway between Mineral Bluff and the town of Blue Ridge, he turned onto the long, narrow road that wound up Cowpen Mountain, elevation 4149. In a couple of miles, it turned to gravel. Even though the Rover was hidden under thick pine trees, the dust he kicked up was making a trail he knew would be visible from the air.

Over the years, as the land had become available, Seaborn had added more acreage to their original holdings on Cowpen, until they owned more than half the mountain now. They were in friendly territory. A weary Seaborn began to relax.

Frank's last transmission in Mineral Bluff had declared all communication on a need-to-know-basis until they reached home. Frank was monitoring a trifecta of P.H.s following the Rover, a network-news team, an Indian, and The Reverend Thackston. Frank used the emergency line to fax a signal to Jane; she had to know the Rover was coming in now. But where was she?

Jessie took in the staunch mountain air and perked up. She recognized the ruts in the road, the vigorous smell of soughing pine, wild mountain laurel and crushed gravel all intermingling. It brought the memory of coming up this mountain road countless times, headed for sanctuary. That time didn't seem so long ago now. Seeing tulip trees, pines, and hickories again was like finding long-lost friends. The autumn leaves were gorgeous.

As Seaborn wound the mountain road, climbing higher up into the Chattahoochee Forest, the air grew cooler. All the sights and smells triggered relaxing memories for them both.

"Home," Jessie said; she loved the word, repeating it over and over, "Home, home free."

They saw the wooden mallard duck that marked their property, mounted high on a pole, with one wing flapping in the breeze. "He's gettin' it," Jessie declared as she always had before.

Seaborn felt so happy and relieved he thought he'd bust.

On the brow of the mountain stood the log cabin they loved, surrounded by pine trees. Now, behind it, three insouciant windmills churned energy and pumped water for the cabin. Dimly they could see, beyond the log house, snuggled all up in the Laurel and pines, a silvery sheen from Frank's double-wides although he had hidden them well. His energy needs were vastly greater than the log house's, and he had installed fusion generators to take care of them. Solar panels flanked the sunny side of the mountain as well.

When they crossed Frank's invisible fence and breached his security field, instead of a siren sounding, a booming Moses voice warned: BEWARE OF ATTACK CAT. Inside his trailer, Frank smiled watching the Land Rover on a monitor. He had a picture of all possible entrances around the property on a bank of surveillance monitors. His computer disclosed Seaborn and Jessie's heartbeats entering the compound. Before he went outside, Frank switched ON the electronic fences, and the monofilament aero shield to deter aerial landings. He didn't like to leave this shield on because it also discouraged the birds.

Seaborn drove around behind the house right into the open bay of a barn where the Rover would be hidden from view, as Frank had instructed him earlier. Frank called the barn an apiary because he kept two Formula One Class P.H.'s inside, which he had dubbed "The Bees," and painted them to look like bumblebees. Seaborn parked beside Frank's rare old Renault Gordini, the one he had rebuilt back in his high school days. It was the same blue as Seaborn's Land Rover.

Adjoining the barn was a greenhouse with glass sides and solar panels on the roof where Frank grew herbs, and seasonal vegetables. Beyond were the plowed terraces that Seaborn had begun, for watermelon, rhubarb, spring corn, beans, and tomatoes. He was happy to see that Frank had more than kept his promise to work the garden, to marry electronics and gardening.

Seaborn and Jessie walked out of the barn and went over to the clearing in front of the log house, stretching, looking all around, exhilarated to be home, at last.

Frank's big ole hogs, grazed in a withering salsify field, and didn't even look up.

44
One Wing Flapping Revisited

Frank came running out, and he and Seaborn hugged fiercely, nearly overcome with relief. Seaborn presented Jessie like the belle they had borne to safety, like the day had been Frank's own. Jessie tilted her head way back amazed at how tall Frank had grown. They looked deeply into each other's eyes, a look of familial love and connection.

"Welcome home," Frank said, his eyes moistening. He spread his arms wide to include all the open space of nearby mountain ranges, as well as the crisp and cloudless Autumn sky. Home was large.

Jessie caved into his arms and hugged Frank, her heart swelling. It had been too long of an absence. In her mind, she held the fond memory of Frank when he was a young boy enchanted with magnets. Now, before her, was a man. "All grown, and I didn't even get to see it." She mumbled, tearing up, sad for what she had missed.

Frank was unused to physical contact or affection, so he was a little surprised to find it was something he needed, and he hugged her back fiercely. "Hey, I'm still growing," he said.

Jessie picked up the cat who was making passes by her legs, "And this must be the infamous Baby Beast."

"My constant companion," Frank said.

"It's so good to be back in the south." Jessie gushed.

At that moment, a smoking P.H. roared up from the mountain valley below and hawked down on them so close they could read the license tag: I B 4 JESUS WHO R U 4.

Then everything seemed to change to an unreality in slow motion, as The Reverend Travis Thackston, grimacing maniacally, opened a wooden box and shook out a load of snakes, each snake wriggling free and wildly in the air, falling, and cork screwing right down on top of them. They danced around, hopping crazily to dodge the snakes. Later they would remember Thackston yelling out, a kind of triumphal warning: "Flying snakes!"

His P.H. got tangled in Frank's monofilament shield and sparks began flying around as electrical charges frotzed his motor. The Reverend had enough time to toss out another box of snakes which shattered on impact, releasing the snakes, and then take aim with a shotgun at Frank's satellite dish as well. But he missed. While trying a second shot, he veered off sharply, and began to spin. He crashed into the side of Cowpen Mountain and fell hundreds of yards down into the abyss. They heard a deafening crack-of-doom sound, like close lightning. In seconds, a malodorous smoke wafted across the whole valley.

Baby Beast shrieked and leaped from Jessie's arms, but they had all turned to watch the P.H., on fire, spinning and falling, and didn't see Baby in peril.

Jessie stared at the snakes enveloping her. She knew they would strike– it was their nature. They were as terrified as she was. A voice in her head told her: a good mystic always shows respect for physical law. She shivered, her stomach flip-flopped.

"Freeze. Don't move." Frank said in a low voice.

He and Seaborn were penned in by snakes as well; they were all surrounded by a multifarious hydra of their worst nightmare.

Then they all saw Baby Beast. They heard the crack as her head was crushed in the mouth of a huge python, and watched in horror as she was being swallowed, her body constricted in the python's powerful coils. They all felt

Frank's helpless torment as Baby disappeared into the belly of the snake. They knew she was dead, and it would endanger everyone to go for her; it was too late, they were out of their depth.

The snakes were coming around, the impact had only dazed them, except for the few that were crushed under the box. The live ones shot out their tongues, angrily tasting the air, like smelling, only more accurate. They twisted and rolled, getting the kinks out, recovering their sinuosity. The rattlesnakes were frightened, poised to strike, their rattles the only sound now in the suddenly stinking air.

Frank was ashen. He found the possibility of dying from snake bite with Baby Beast a welcome irony– except he didn't want to die. It couldn't all end here this way. From the depths of his anger and pain he threw his head back and conjured up a sound, almost as a reflex, SOO-EY! SOO-EY! SOO-EY!

Seaborn was silently identifying the snakes; copperheads, diamondbacks, moccasins, brown ones he couldn't name, the red-yellow-black banded coral snake, and that python. The Reverend had put together a congregation of evil, malefic snakes just for them. It re-amazed him what that fucking show-off would do. He wished he had a flame thrower. He remembered the Reverend saying that pit-vipers read your heart. Quickly he thought: *Snakes are eternal symbols of life because they shed their skins and are reborn.* But his good thought was too late. The fangs felt like a cluster of hot hypodermic needles. He cried out, "Ohhhhhhh Jesus!"

The next thing they knew all the hogs had come running and were rooting in the snakes, growling and snorting, jobbing them down. They put their hooves on the snake's heads and stripped them clean, taking the venomous bites like rubber tires, never feeling a one. Snake fangs couldn't penetrate hog hides. The hogs chewed the snakes up, finding them better fare than salsify. Snakes that went slip-sliding away they marked for later. Two hogs stomped the python to death.

Sensing her moment, Jessie moved to where Seaborn lay writhing in pain, his limbs trembling, his cheeks pale. Finding strength she didn't know she had, she locked her arms under his shoulders and dragged him so swiftly away Frank had to run to catch up and open the door of the cabin for them.

Seaborn was hurting bad. While Jessie propped his leg up and pulled off his boot he moaned and trembled, his head rolling. Delirious with pain, he growled, "I couldn't send my ego to its room in time." Jessie covered him with a blanket, held his head in her arms, and cried for him, and for them all. Her stomach turned. The smell of snake was in all their nostrils.

Frank came running with a snake-bite kit. He slit Seaborn's pants to the knee exposing the bite on the fleshy part of the calf, just above his sock. It was ugly, fiery hot and had already begun to swell. Frank doused it with whiskey and applied a salt and tobacco poultice which had a drawing effect. He knew that Tourniquets could do more harm than good.

"Did you see what kind it was man?" Frank prodded Seaborn, trying to keep him awake.

Seaborn's sallow face was hangdog and he groaned deeply. "A copperhead or a rattler, they both got me, only my boot took one of the bites. I saw the inside of his mouth, bleachy white man, so white...Ohhhhhhh, he moaned"

Frank saw Seaborn's face was also white, deadly white. "I'm going for help." He passed Jessie the bottle of whiskey and ran out. Medics would be at the PH crash site and he had to snag one for Seaborn.

He rode out of the barn on an all-terrain vehicle that looked like a golf-cart but coasted above ground like a hover board, except it was faster, and he shanked it straight down the mountain, fairly flying.

In less than twenty minutes he was back with a medic, a bearded mountain man familiar with snakebite, carrying a big black medicine bag.

Seaborn had gotten soused, having belted down most of the whiskey in a toasting melee. If he was dying, he was set on glorifying the moment. He recited from Cymbeline: "...as golden lads and girls all must, like chimney-sweepers, come to dust." He raised the bottle and drained it.

"Be still now," the medic said, taking a look at Seaborn's leg. "We get about two or three hunred a these venomous bites a year 'round these parts– mostly from the snake handlin' churches. And some a them go unreported. Hit's a biblical form of suicide, a gamble. You either draw energy from it or hit kills you." He was a talker. He checked Seaborn for fever and respiratory distress and went on jabbering in his slow way, made them all feel calm.

The inflammation at the site had begun to subside due to Frank's poultice. But the bite was an angry red.

Seaborn cried out when the medic squeezed it hard.

Finally, he declared: "You're a lucky devil, hit was only a copperhead."

Frank, sitting with his head in his hands looked up, relieved, a weight lifted.

"Hit's a painful bite 'cause the fangs are so big, but the venom's not very deadly to a full-grown man– hit'll kill a mouse though." He cackled as he applied Tangle foot oil to the savage bite. He gave Seaborn capsules of Feverfew, for pain and swelling. It was an herb that inhibited the production of prostaglandins, reducing inflammatory reactions.

Seaborn lazed back, light-headed, hiccupping from the whiskey. He was happy, and strangely disappointed at the same time. He smiled, closing his eyes, enjoying the idea that he was to live after all, enjoying the medics mountain accent, even liking his rough, but healing touch.

Jessie, plenty thankful for having Seaborn back from certain death, for the first time thought of Frank, and said to him gently, "That was nice Hog calling Frank."

Seaborn chimed in, "Hic, you saved our lives, man."

Frank was grateful for the hogs, and for Seaborn's expected recovery, but all he could think about now was Baby Beast. He walked outside to be alone with his grief.

"What happened to the guy that crashed?" Seaborn asked the medic.

"Burnt up, the only thing left a him was a key-chain on his belt. He had a lotta keys. Happens all the time in these mountains. They don't get enough oxygen and black out– they don't realize this mountain is the highest point in Georgia."

"Hic, I know, we used to live here." Seaborn said, mournfully.

45
A Parting Song

The network-news team that was following at the time of the crash scooped the story, reporting that the Reverend had lost control of his P.H. and crashed. Seaborn was relieved when Jessie was not mentioned in the broadcast. Was it possible they hadn't made the connection? The Reverend's P.H. was called a "CHURCH BUS," and his destination was reported as "unknown."

Sea and Jess sat together on the couch watching the newscast. Whiskey and trauma had liberated their emotions. Jessie wailed, "It's such a waste, chasing us down for nothing, losing his own life, and killing that sweet little cat, and what about all those dead snakes?"

Seaborn remembered the day when they had first moved into One World Trade, and he and Frank were watching the monitors that showed the crowds outside the building. In the middle of a mob of paparazzi, Frank had spotted a baby kitten nearly being trampled, and hissing in a courageous threat display. They marveled at how it could have gotten there. Frank ran out and rescued the little cat, brought it home to One Wing, and named it Baby Beast. Seaborn shuddered thinking of Baby's fate, and Frank's anguish at not being able to rescue her this time.

He switched off the T.V., took Jessie's hand, and held it to his damp cheek, trying to console her, and feel better himself too. They all felt bad about Baby Beast, but he was surprised to find that losing an enemy was a loss too. He would actually miss the rudely bombastic Reverend. He chalked this up to delirium.

Jessie pulled away, wiped her tears, and got up, determined to be strong. "I'm going to fill the hot tub." She turned back, suddenly angry, "All I want is a floppy place where we can live off-guard, a simple, normal life." She beseeched Seaborn: "Is that asking too much?"

He shook his head, doubtfully, filling at once with a defensive optimism. This was what he wanted, too, but her celebrity was in the way. He rose and limped off behind Jessie; now they were both limping. Out on the deck he hugged her, not uttering a word, making instead a silent promise to try and get them what they both wanted.

Jessie tossed the hyacinth bath salts she found stacked around the hot tub into the warming water, and she and Seaborn spooned together in a relaxing hyacinth bath. It was Frank's special aroma therapy meant to slow delta brain waves, and it worked. Jessie's swollen ankle hung out over the tub while Seaborn hung his bandaged snake-bit leg out over the other side. He worried about Jessie, and she worried about him. Now, they were both worrying about Frank, off somewhere, crying, and alone. They languished a bit longer in the heavenly smelling water until they were both woozy, finding in their crinkly hands and bodies something good to comfort each other with. Now they wished they could find a way to comfort Frank.

Frank stood for a long time under an outdoor shower of mountain water pumped from a spring and heated to exactly 98.6. His tears, too, were the same temperature, so he couldn't feel them falling. His whole body ached from the loss of Baby Beast, from the helpless feeling that he had because he couldn't save her, from the violation of love that her killing had been. The water was a comfort beating down on his pain. He lathered up with patchouli soap, trying to energize and calm himself. He rinsed and toweled off, rubbed sandalwood oil on his moist skin. He felt a little better, at least the smell of snake was off him.

He believed that personal and planetary rejuvenations were possible with the savvy use of scent. Lately, he'd been stretching that idea to the limits in his experiments. He and Jane had carried on long nocturnal talks by phone about scent, because one of his key projects was the development of an Aroma-Fax. He thought of how they'd compiled a list of positive-association scents, like almond, which was positive for nearly everyone on the planet, unless something bad had happened in the company of that scent. The smell of a burning P.H. was a negative scent anyway, but now he would always associate anything burning with the death of Baby Beast. He wished he could talk to Jane. He felt anxious about her– she'd been incommunicado for way too long. He worried that something had happened to her.

With Baby purring by his side, Frank had trained every part of his body to be responsive to the interaction of aroma molecules. His whole body, not just his nose, could imitate nerve impulses, and convey messages to the olfactory bulbs in his brain, where receptor cells interpreted the aroma message and transmitted to the limbic system, the part of the brain that dealt with memory and emotion. Instead of his feet smelling, he could sort of smell through his feet. Now, all of that seemed trivial to him– as did everything else, without Baby Beast.

In a cedar closet, Jessie found their old white terry cloth bathrobes. They would wait outside on the deck for Frank to come when he was ready. They lit candles and lay back on lounges heaped with towels, lotions, a scattering of flower petals and fallen autumn leaves. A jug of fresh apple cider was chilling. The fire pit was lit. All done by Frank— he had prepared for their arrival so sweetly and was looking after them as always. They slathered lavender cream all over each other, and after that, Kudzu Blossom elixir, to complete the rejuvenations. They began to feel a healing, lying out under the cool sky lit with stars, wrapped in terry cloth and each other.

In a while Frank appeared like a runaway putt, pushing a wheelbarrow, and asking them to go with him to bury Baby Beast out by the gazebo. Seaborn and Jessie dressed quickly in old jeans and flannel shirts left long ago at the log house, and hobbled along after Frank, as night fell, and the sky became a starry firmament. Frank had trained Baby Beast to come on his whistle, like a dog. When he was a boy, he'd learned to whistle from Henry, an irrepressible whistler. While he and Seaborn took turns digging the grave, Frank whistled "Danny Boy," trilling the tune like birdsong. Jessie stared into the deep hole; sadly, she tossed in Frank's slipper, the one Baby had slept in when she was a little kitten.

Baby was still inside the stomped to death python, her sarcophagus now. The hogs had not liked python meat. They all stared with whip-sawed emotions at the snake, hideously fat with the shape of Baby Beast. They felt alienated from its scent and species, still not believing what had happened, each realizing that death took different forms and would have to be understood differently. Every part of Frank wanted to pull his cat out of that snake. But instead he wrapped the python in his favorite old bathrobe, and placed it in the hole, and kept on whistling, while they pushed the dirt over it.

46
Cloud seekers

Afterwards, in the night's darkness, they went on a walk with Frank, to view some of his organic and electronic wonders, and to stay in motion and beat back some of the panicky feeling that still clung to them all. Frank had the place lit with motion sensors. He'd made many changes and additions to One Wing and he wanted to show them off, to distract from the sorrow, as much as anything else; he wanted them to see all the changes and what had survived time. They passed through the garden terraces which Seaborn had first worked, and saw the asparagus coming in from the reeds that he had planted years before. Some of the perennials he'd planted came back, year after year. Jessie wondered if the foxglove around the old lattice gazebo would come up this year. She remembered that it only bloomed every other year. Her nose twitched from the faintly comforting smell of skunk that hung in the air. Oh, this was so much better than living in a high rise. She felt a strong attachment to One Wing, to the sanctity of the land, and everything that grew on it.

They went inside one of the double-wides and saw Franks mini-TV studio where he could make videotapes to send out to the world. They viewed his computer work stations, a maze resembling a Star-Trek ship. Frank told them that he had the capability to tap into all the great tracking telescopes and radioscopes searching the skies; the NSA, National Security Agency, which tapped world telecommunications, the NRO, National Reconnaissance Office, which operated spy satellites, and MILSTAR, Military Strategic and Tactical Relay System, which was a military radio and television network. All of these agencies complained constantly that Jessie's messages interfered with their supposedly seamless systems, and Frank had to field all the complaints. He had cracked their codes and was in without them even knowing it, but he had no intention of using what he knew against them. He eschewed that kind of power game. It honestly bored him.

Frank explained that MILSTAR was just a MILITARY GAME for old Pentagon military men, a dying breed. He called them PMM's. The GAME was kept hidden from the public, the hormonal madness of it shrouded. They had launched nine MILSTAR satellites throughout the nineties, 22,300 miles from Earth, electronically linked to each other, with space sensors, just so they could play the highest priced and most dangerous RISK GAME ever invented: GLOBAL NUCLEAR WAR, the ultimate destruction game. MILSTAR had been invented as a more efficient, neater, nuclear war, mainly because too much expensive real estate was involved in the real thing.

"They're nostalgic and sentimental about the collapse of communism, like they'd prefer it had never happened," he said, "and about the Stealth Bomber, which was built at a cost of nine hundred million tax dollars for each one, to deliver nuclear warheads over the Soviet Union. When the Russians were no longer our enemies, they used them in Iraq. What use are these bombers now, except maybe to put in a museum to show how far men will go when driven by fear and raging testosterone. The Stealth wasn't even very stealthy, and way too slow, lumbering along up there slower than the red-eye from L.A."

Jessie said, "Does this game satisfy the PMM's?"

"Oh, yeah." Frank said, "and besides, they've got you to complain about now, mainly because of their fear of dying."

"How does the game go?"

"I'll show you." Frank tapped commands into the computer while he talked: "The computers run a war no single human mind could control. Robotic soldiers stalk radioactive backgrounds and the PMM's call the shots from tiny Pentagons in sky stations, or on wheels providing moving targets that speed down highways in rad-hardened vehicles, kicking ass and barking orders for warheads to be fired off from faraway secret silos. They cheat and eavesdrop on each other. Only the computer knows everything that's happening in the GAME and is able to keep the true score."

Frank stopped talking. He'd found cat hairs on the console. He was worried about Jane, and was having what she would call, *a sinking spell.*

"At least The Reverend missed our feed." He said quietly.

After tapping in a few more commands, gradually his display filled with numbers, codes, and words. The frame buffer next to it showed what looked like an animated movie in progress. The figures looked real, but their movements were simulated. Frank described what was going on: "The GAME utilizes Virtual Reality, a form of software/hardware interaction that allows the players to relate person to person and face to face over their PC's. VR makes the player feel like he's there, in three-dimensional space, since the image changes in relation to the position of his head and body. His senses range while his body stays safely behind."

Suddenly, alarms began flashing across Frank's radar screens. They heard a faint cry.

"What's that?" Seaborn whispered.

"I don't know, sounds like Mayday," said Frank.

"It's great Day!" said Jessie. "Look!"

On a surveillance screen, even in the darkness they could see a P.H. hovering above them. Frank hit the spotlights.

"Oh my God, it's Jane in a PH." said Seaborn, paling.

Frank quickly flipped the switch to the monofilament shield off. It was preventing her from safely landing.

They ran outside and watched Jane maneuver between the trees, narrowly missing them, and set her PH down on the flat roof that had a painted bull's-eye on it, atop Frank's other double-wide. She cut her engine. They all stared dumbfounded.

"Well, I'll be damned," said Seaborn.

"Yay-us!" Jane shouted, and her voice echoed across the mountaintop. She hauled herself out of the P.H. and stood tall, (all five feet of her) in a short red dress and high boots, Versace of course, flashing a grin: "Yes, yes, yes! I made it!" She shot a high-five in the air toward them all as they stood dumbly watching on the ground. She giggled up a storm. "Can I park here?" She tossed down her big bag and Frank caught it, nodding, wild-eyed.

Frank hadn't seen Jane in years except on a video monitor. Now he looked at her as if for the first time, appreciating her coppery-auburn good looks in three dimensions. A surge of emotions he was unfamiliar with made his voice sound like a rooster's waul. He tried to concentrate on the downside of his astonishment, that Jane, in his memory, wasn't a very efficient driver, so how...? "too dangerous for most good drivers," he wattled, "so how'd you get through those mountains?" When he tried to adjust his voice, it thinned out like miso soup, and he knew despite himself that he had a new respect for Jane, as well as another sort of wild-card emotion.

"No kidding, how'd you do it?" Seaborn sputtered, curious, dead serious, like he cared a lot. To his knowledge, Jane had never flown a P.H. by herself before. She was still learning.

"I just took my own sweet time, had good sonar, radar, oxygen and water– that's all! Oh, and plenty of my oatmeal-chocolate-chip cookies to give me vigor. I reckoned if the Indians could do it, I could too. I got some Indian blood." She beat on her chest. "I watched you do it Seaborn, and besides, I've been taking lessons, in fact, that's why I'm so late."

Jessie stepped up to help Jane off the ladder on the side of the trailer, since Frank and Seaborn were too astonished to move. On the ground, Jane hugged each of them, especially Seaborn who she knew she had probably shocked the most.

"I need a bath," she said. "Anybody know how to cook around here? I'm starving." She was suddenly in the mood for some athletic sex too, truth be told, but she didn't say that.

"I want to bathe in that Kudzu Blossom elixir you make for Jessie." she said to Frank looking way up at him, surprised to find him even taller than she remembered– he made two of her and was probably still growing. She smiled provocatively, having a little fun with him.

Frank was only too happy to oblige. He led Jane off toward the greenhouse where he'd built another outdoor hot tub encircled by a privacy hedge of trained kudzu. It was in a late, forced bloom, and the huckleberry-jasmine smell it produced was paradisiac. He'd always wanted to show this to Jane, and Jessie too. Somebody.

Seaborn and Jessie's mouths hung open, as they watched the two of them walk away. Jessie wished she could learn how to flirt like Jane did, it was a marvel. There seemed to be so much to learn from her. She wondered if Jane always got all the men.

Jane fell right into the enchantment of the place and as usual made much of Frank's ranginess, his wild, disparate interests, and talents. She had never been to One Wing before, so for the first time, she was seeing all the things he had talked about for years by phone, and she felt excited. "It's funny," she said, "however advanced we get technologically, there's always another logic operating in random nature. We're still at the mercy of chance and powerful unknown forces. It's exciting and fun, don't ya think?" She giggled extravagantly.

"You're not afraid?" Frank asked her, somberly.

"Not if you're not," she answered quickly, catching his eye, winking, and wondering: why is he so serious?

That's when Frank told her about The Reverend's attack with deadly snakes, and how Seaborn had been bitten by a copperhead, and Baby Beast had been suffocated and swallowed by a python. He broke down, letting go with Jane, exposing his old undefended pain over the loss of his mother, and also his grandparents, joining that pain to his new grief for Baby. And Jane held him, big as he was, rocked him and wept along with him.

Afterwards, he drew her a bath and then left her to it, lighting the pathway back up to the log house as he passed the motion sensors, walking slower than usual, yet lighter-hearted for having released so much. Frank liked Jane's comforting nature, her maturity, and sense of humor, even her giggle, which he wasn't so sure he had heard all that much before. Older women almost always possessed themselves in a way he liked and admired.

Inside the house, he found Jessie and Seaborn checking things out in the rustic kitchen, happy to be back in their old kitchen again. While they cooked they watched the Global Gourmet on TV, as he prepared a fancy feast. The Global Gourmet wrapped fresh crickets sprinkled with hot pepper sauce in sugar cane leaves and roasted them over a fire. Then he dumped them sizzling on fresh chopped field lettuces and fiddleheads and sprinkled nasturtiums on top. "Excellent source of protein," said the Global Gourmet, and Seaborn, remembering how he'd cooked crickets, agreed. Jessie watched fascinated. She did not feel up to eating crickets though, even prepared so attractively, and yet strangely her mouth watered.

At dinner, they all sat around the big old pine table and ate Frank's pan-fried trout. Early that afternoon, when communication went on a NTKB, Frank had gone fishing in the stream on Cowpen which was so chock-full of fish all he had to do was throw a baited basket in the water and about ten minutes later he hauled out enough fish for a banquet. The day before, when he knew they were coming, he'd gone down the mountain and laid in some stores from the grocery in Mineral Bluff. They were well-stocked with food, for long survival: "Let the heavens rage." Frank said now, toasting their reunion. Jessie had cooked couscous and amaranth grains together with the wild onions, sage, arugula and finocchio she'd scavenged from Frank's garden. He had frozen rhubarb and raspberries from the summer garden and Jane made a fruit crisp—a recipe she remembered that had come in from a spirit. Seaborn roasted the last of the asparagus and made buttermilk cornbread in a black iron skillet. They had fresh red wine Frank had gotten from a family vineyard in nearby Ellijay, no preservatives, so no headache, ever.

"Doesn't this taste like a great Amarone?" Frank said, introducing the wine. He was the bemused host, his first time out, keeping the wine glasses topped and urging everyone to drink, eat, dishing up seconds, slightly ahead of the need. "Confusion to our enemies!" he toasted again.

They all felt it was a special time, their first and maybe their last supper together, a brief oasis from the dangerous yet essential search for the identity Jessie urgently needed to recover. During dinner, Jane regaled them with the story of how she'd tricked Elderculture into going to Lexington, and gotten a lot of the media to follow, too. By now, they all knew they'd been duped. She told of leaving a juicy rotten tomato on top of the answering machine before she left One World Trade. "It smelled awful. You can't make an appointment with 911, so I was counting on the tomato to give me a head start, betting the juice would leak down inside the machine and short it out; and then it would automatically dial 911. The police would come and clear the penthouse out and seal it up for me." She laughed at her crazy idea.

"But it worked!" Frank exclaimed., "A while ago, I got a call from the police. When they arrived, they ran into The Reverend Thackston's men, who were in the process of getting criminally attached to bags of LODS mail– they claimed it was lost property, it had been abandoned by us and was not really ours to begin with, the old trover and conversion alibi- finders, keepers, losers, weepers. The police arrested them, and this time Eli and Smithy pressed charges for theft and trespass. And guess who was with The Reverend's men this time?"

They all looked puzzled.

"Dr. Desmond in his hounds' tooth jacket, with his arms full of petty cash and letters. He claimed he was putting it back."

"Yeah, like he didn't inhale," Jane said.

"What are they charging him with?" Seaborn asked.

"How about pandering egos?" Frank said.

"Is that against the law now?" Jessie wanted to know.

Everyone laughed.

"No, but they ought to make a special case for Desmond," Jane said.

Frank enjoyed Jane– it was all over his face. She made him feel lighthearted.

After dinner, Frank invited them to try akima, a stress reliever. It was an herb that had come from an ancient rain forest in the Mara Pampa region of Brazil. Literally translated, akima meant cloud seeker. Frank was growing his own akima and probing into the nucleatic essence of its tiny clusters. He had extracted from them a colorless, tasteless, odorless liquid which he now quickly dabbed on a plateful of Jane's oatmeal-chocolate-chip cookies and offered all around like a sacrament. Everyone took a cookie and ate it quickly because exposure to air dissipated its potency, almost as if it could disappear. It was not possible to overdose, he had tested it himself, from one up to one hundred ccs with identical effects. The akima was quickly absorbed into the bloodstream. Frank had taken akima many times and knew the effect it had on him, but he was most interested to see what it would do to Jessie, as well as Jane and Seaborn. He knew it to be an absolutely atoxic substance with no virulent properties, non-addictive, indiscernible in urine or blood tests. It was the most biodegradable substance he'd ever seen. One cc. catered a high that lasted from twelve to twenty minutes, fluctuating in temporal impact, and no aftereffects.

"I'm soaring up... into the up," said Jessie, "only the ceiling is holding me down... let's go outside to the great outdoors."

They thrilled to be outside, their senses awakening a thousand-fold, towering above the trees, floating in a soft sinew of black-velvety bliss, the night lit only by sparkling stars, and a moon little more than half full.

"Great day, I feel like I've turned into a shooting arrow, headed up, up, up." Jane said, her neck craning upward, while her feet stayed planted on the ground.

"I'm a thousand feet tall," Seaborn yelled, as though he was far away. Strangely, he felt like one of his father's flying fish in the deep end of a sky ocean.

It was an unparalleled height for Jessie too, who was also imaging lucidly. She observed herself traveling to a point on top of a distant mountain and seeing there the sleeping Indians in their P.H.'s, clinging to the mountain like raptors. She entered their dreams, woke them up with whispers, and left them flabbergasted.

"The Indians are over there," she told Frank, who was standing right beside her, "in the crevices of that mountain." She pointed into the darkness almost a half mile away.

Frank wondered how she saw them in the pitch dark. He knew she had not moved. She had to have powers greater than the average human. Frank stared at where she pointed, imagined the sleeping Indians there, in their own cozy aerie and in nanoseconds he was there too, beside them, and back again. He could not slow it down, but he was grateful his imagination had taken him, even if it was too brief to prove. He knew he had been outside his body and saw what he saw. It was like that time long ago, in Henry's hammock.

Seaborn was the first to lose the illusion of height, although his neck still craned up towards the universe. He could tell Jessie was still way up there. He felt a tinge of anxiety– maybe she wouldn't come back. He wondered if it was possible to get outside your body and not be able to get back in?

Frank put his hand on Seaborn's shoulder to reassure him.

They all watched Jessie's demeanor change, as her nearly visible essence slowly sunk back down into her body, like an act of caprice.

Much later, when everyone had gone to bed, Seaborn was feeling tanked from the wine and the pain killers he'd taken.

He tickled Jessie's back to relax her, and whispered, "I don't want you to worry anymore, I want you operating on some other level, bubbly and bouncy, like when you were around eleven."

"That would be nice," Jessie sighed.

"I want to psychically lick the underbelly of your mind, get inside there and roll your lobes with my tongue and heat up your inner ear with the music of my harp. That be okay?"

Jessie giggled wildly.

"Sush, you'll wake everyone up."

But Seaborn didn't really care. He laughed, exuberantly. Then he tickled Jessie some more with his words, made raspberries on her belly, till she giggled uncontrollably. She forgot all about Jane's allure, she had her own.

They made love in the tangled bed sheets till they were both ecstatic, lightheaded, and sleepy.

47
Tate's Hell Camp

The next morning after breakfast, everyone followed Frank around on a daylight tour of the compound and into the greenhouse where he showed off all the herbs he grew, especially proud of his sinsemillia, the female bud of cannabis. He told Jessie about marijuana:

"It's finally been separated from dangerous, addictive drugs. It was legalized for personal and medicinal use first in Colorado, Washington, Alaska, and now most other states have followed. The winds of change are much stronger now."

Seaborn broke off a stalk and held it up to Jessie's nose. "It's not a drug, it's a blissful herb." he said, "Big Pharma is fighting to keep it illegal but they're losing."

Frank went on: "The tax revenues from the sale of marijuana can be used for treatment centers for crack, heroin, opioids and other addictions that have destroyed lives. People have been scattering marijuana seeds for years; it's growing in sunny fields everywhere. That's the good kind. But as long as it's illegal profiteers will put additives in it, bad stuff like speed added to give it kick, make it addictive, and with no controls on quality. Thanks to the 2018 Farm Bill, the cultivation of hemp is no longer banned, even though it contains trace amounts of the psychoactive, THC, less than one percent, compared to marijuana's three to fifteen per cent. Almost anything made from petroleum, wood, paper, or cotton can also be made from hemp. Most people think its highest and best use is for fuel, methanol gas– it's per-acre output of methanol gas is about ten times more than corn."

"And hemp makes the best paper, too." Jane added, "The Constitution and the Magna Carta were written on it."

"Hemp has already reduced deforestation by about forty percent worldwide." Frank went on: "You're going to be flying over some hemp fields on your way south. But first, you'll fly over Tate's Hell Camp in the Florida Panhandle. It's a penal colony for dangerous criminals, killers who would have been executed under capital punishment, lifers with no parole. There are no guards or wardens. The prison is totally run by a computer, and one man. His code name is Wingnut. Guess who?"

Jessie knew: "Your mentor."

"Yes, my old friend Luke who taught me everything. You guys never met him I guess, but I called him a lot back when we were setting up the penthouse. Still do"

They all smiled, recalling those days, how they'd often joked about Frank "winging it" with Luke's help.

"He lives about fifty miles away from Tate's, on the beach at St. George Island, operating the computer for the prison, and deep-sea fishing in his down time. He's married now, has a son of his own. I'm telling you all this because Luke is going to be there to help you in Florida, he'll be monitoring your progress."

"What is this prison like?" Jessie was curious about Tate's.

"From St. George, Luke opens and closes the cell doors, herds, and monitors all the prisoners, mediates arguments, and even penalizes with water sprays and stun guns when it's necessary, all with a computer program he designed himself."

"How do they eat?" Jessie asked.

"That's the interesting part. The prisoners garden and raise farm animals. They have to provide their own living from the land. Some supplies are dropped in by P.H., things like coffee, flour, and peanut butter, along with new prisoners. But they have to cook, clean, and run their own lives by whatever survival pecking order they devise themselves. When they die or kill each other off, they have to bury their dead. They are never released, and live out their lives at Tate's, at a nominal cost to the public. They can't have visitors, no phone connections to the outside world. They have limited E-Mail, snail mail, books and T.V. It's as if they've been shipped to Mercury– and almost as hot. The joke is that Palmetto bugs at Tate's are so big they'll walk off with you standing on them. Outside the electrified fence are lots of snakes, wild boar, peccaries, panthers, bobcats, and about forty miles of wilderness swampland before you reach any road."

Frank answered the next question before it was asked: "No one has ever escaped and lived to tell about it. The penalty for helping anyone escape from Tate's is really stiff– so is the penalty for interfering with Tate's Computer Program."

Jessie was fascinated. She remembered something about men inside a prison furiously hammering on a Lexan cube. It was like the gun cube in Hoboken, only this one held a mainframe computer. They were trying to get at it, to kill its blinking lights, kill its power over them. If they did destroy it, they'd all die, one by one, like stars going out, because it was keeping them alive. And then these beaten, disheartened spirits would enter the astral world, and never soar, because badness was like weight. They must never smash the computer but struggle instead to fight off their own demons. That's what counted, the struggle, the attempt to balance good and evil. Jessie remembered a message she'd been given by an old spirit– that every good act protects your immortal soul. Everyone had the bad and the good– it was the individual's struggle to triumph over the bad that put you ahead on the ground and paved your way on the astral plane. Now, at last, here was a prison that was raw and ascetic enough to enable a prisoner to achieve enlightenment through will, effort, struggle, intensity– or else give in to darkness.

Seaborn noticed Jessie deep in thought. "Do you remember this, Jess? You had a lot to say about this when they were building it. It was a few years ago, when the immortal soul got trendy again, after a lot of people in the world had chosen to deny it. There were protests about the severity and cruelty of this prison when it first opened, and you said no, it wasn't cruel, it was a chance for redemption on earth, a chance to reclaim soul."

Jessie had a blank look.

"Oh, you don't know what you remember," Jane teased her.

"Yes...yes, I do. The message was that Time is God, doing Time is God. Something like that. Like grace, you can only have it if you can imagine it. Grace opens the chance for beauty and creativity, and it opens the heart. Crime closes off all of this. Your own imagination has to frame grace. You can't steal it, although you can kill it, and if you kill grace you must grieve it, anything less is futile." Jessie brightened. "That's what prison is for, grieving, learning to stop stealing and stop killing grace."

"A lot of people said, 'so chumping what,' they didn't get it, or didn't give a continental damn." Jane said.

"The God equals Money people, the greed heads. You said they were doing time, too. Remember that?" Seaborn prompted Jess.

She nodded, but her memory was like the shifting plates of a continent; only pieces of it were hers to capture. She wanted to recover all her memory, wanted it all back, from the beginning of the trance, and even before that. She had to retrace her steps to understand, to lift the fog she was moiled in. Her eyes teared up; she flushed with entreaty and hope.

48

A Real Good Cry

By mid-morning, they were ready to go on to Florida, to go to the places that they hoped would trigger Jessie's memory and bring it all back. Frank gave her rosemary oil, the memory herb, fresh nei kuan bands for her motion sickness, ginko biloba for energy and mental acuity. Her ankle was better thanks to Feverfew and Ashwagandha which were also herbs for Seaborn, and more tangle foot oil for his snakebite which had improved overnight.

Jane had fixed a hamper full of sandwiches, fruit juice, and some more of her oatmeal-chocolate-chip cookies for vigor. She tucked everything behind the seat of Bee One, which sat in the clearing warming up, poised for takeoff.

Earlier that morning, Frank and Seaborn had moved Bee One out of the barn. "Bee Two is ready, in case we have to come and rescue you." Frank said, "It's a fairly straight shot southwest to Tates, but a diversion because nobody expects you to go that way." When he saw Jessie was out of hearing range, picking flowers, Frank told Seaborn, "once you cross into Florida, watch out. My father is a powerful lawyer, and he intends to have Jessie committed as you know. He probably has those Christian musclemen working for him. They'll be trying to grab Jessie, ransom her to Eli and Smithy."

"Yeah, over my dead body." Seaborn said, "What's wrong with that asshole anyway?" He immediately wished he could recant his words. "I'm Sorry, man. I guess Tom was once a good father to you, but..."

Frank held up his hand, "It's okay. I understand. He's mad because I left. To him it's a betrayal, and he blames Jessie. He wants revenge. He's so old school. He thinks I worship the beast, I'm a homosexual, and every other different classification of person that threatens him. What can I say man?" Frank shrugged and began explaining about the Bee's to change a painful subject; how fast they could go, how all the extra defensive devices he'd equipped them with worked, how Bee One and Two were cast out of a compound called Unbelievium, which was virtually shatterproof.

Jane was hugging Seaborn, bolstering him up, when Jessie returned from flower picking.

It was a beautiful clear day. As Bee One revved up, a skein of geese flying in V formation sailed like an arrow across the low white clouds.

"Follow them," Frank shouted when Seaborn lifted off, raising a windy roar. He'd had to learn the instruments in a hurry.

Sitting beside him, Jessie waved unsmiling. She was mad at Jane for hugging Seaborn so much and ignoring her, not to mention having to follow geese.

Seaborn fell in behind the geese, maters for life. They knew the best route south. They were a sign that the frost would soon come, and winter with its short, perfect light would grease the wheels of change. Changing seasons always brought hope and renewal. He tried to think positive thoughts to cover the uncertainty he felt about continuing this risky trip south.

Jane stood in the clearing watching, but her thoughts were about Eli and Smithy. They were furious and threatening to sue for breach of contract among other things. They were mean when deserted. They expected Jessie to just fake it. All they cared about was money. They got on Jane's last good nerve. She hadn't told anyone about their threats, although they were weighing heavily on her. Some news is better heard over the radio, if ever at all. She would stay at One Wing now and help Frank with everything. All her public relations skills would be useful, for Jessie would have to be situated out of the limelight just as deliberately as she'd been positioned into it.

Frank and Jane stood together waving, then watched the sky helplessly as the Indians followed in hot pursuit behind Bee One, and from another mountain peak, two network-news teams, their P.H.s emblazoned with station ID's, lifted into the air like sluggish vultures.

Early that morning, a couple of media trucks had come up Cowpen Mountain Road, ignoring the NO TRESPASS signs. But they could not get past Frank's electromagnetic snare, his invisible fence, without incurring harm and damage. They had frotzed their equipment trying, and had to turn back on foot, leaving behind their electrically ramrodded vehicles. Frank had called tow trucks to haul them off.

He smiled a hackish grin, thinking about it, but when he looked over at Jane, he was surprised to see her crying.

"What's the matter?" he asked, feeling strange and vulnerable himself suddenly.

"Oh, I don't know. I'm happy I think. It's so good to be out of the city, to be here with you in this paradise. I just need a real good cry, I guess."

Frank leaned down and put his arm around Jane. He took out his handkerchief and offered it. Henry had taught him to always carry a handkerchief.

Jane blubbered, "Everything's worked so far, and I'm scared. What if they don't make it?"

Frank tilted her head back, and captured her eyes, "Look, they're gonna make it, don't you worry."

"But Eli and Smithy, and even Tom are so vindictive. They're not gonna let her off the hook easily."

"We'll figure out a way to get Jessie free of all of them."

Jane felt better after her cry. Best of all, Frank understood, which made her feel tons lighter. She turned, put both her arms around Frank's neck, looked up into his eyes and smiled the most beautiful, delivering smile he ever saw.

He lifted her up, she wrapped her legs around him, and they kissed, as though they were only creatures set down on earth bewildered and had at last found their kind. He had wanted to go to her the night before, but had stayed on his cot in his trailer, unsure of himself and her response, still aching from the loss of Baby.

Once he had her in his arms though, he held her like their lives depended on it– all the tension of deferred desire seemed to ripple up a shared spine. The same dam that had held back Jane's tears had held back her longing too, and now it was rupturing and the floodgates opening up in both of them. They were surprised and overjoyed at the feeling of connection they were discovering they had built up with each other over the years.

Frank carried Jane into the barn and laid her down on a pile of fresh hay. She kissed his face all over, mixing salty tears with the heat of her desire. To be borne up like that by a man who was taller than her jumping height now seemed like all in the world Jane had ever wanted.

Frank was only a little shy, and though inexperienced, Jane led him; it was easy to lead passion. She took his wondrous hands and worshiped them with kisses, rubbed them on her burning cheeks, placed them on her heart, where they easily found her breasts.

They undressed, uncovering the majesty and power of the deepest mystery between two people, exposing themselves in a lucky force-field called love; both of them feeling how supreme it was to be naked and natural.

They seemed to float, graceful in all their movements, like fine-tuned animals. In their single mindedness, they cantilevered the whole act up into thin air, and it held. She waited for his next thrust to find her, and she arched to meet him, again and again. She finally got it! What real mating was, the fierce strength of it. Each thrust was encoded with longings for eternal love, for possessiveness and connection.

Frank fucked with astonishment, holding nothing back, saving nothing for any future, and when orgasm began to rip away his breath, he took Jane with him and they reached ecstasy together, releasing howls, that also called the hogs.

Snorting in the doorway, sniffing, and staring, and instinctually understanding what they were witness to, the hogs brought fits of laughter from the lovers.

Afterwards, Frank talked a blue streak. If Jane thought Seaborn could talk, Lordy, here was Frank holding forth, running his mouth like a spellbinding raconteur. She was enchanted.

He talked to the Jane in progress, the future Jane. She saw that it would take her a whole lifetime to learn him.

PART FIVE

49
Paradise Revisited

Seaborn had built up about a thirty-minute lead over the Indians and the media. Bee One was faster, and he'd punched it to the linchpins. He circled their old house in Morningside, even though they no longer owned it, and swooped in low so Jessie could see. He expected to feel nostalgia for the place; but it was merely familiar. He wondered if Jessie was remembering. When he looked over at her he saw she had tears in her eyes.

When they crossed into Florida the first thing they saw from their bird's eye view were crop cuttings spelling out: SUNSHINE STATE ARRIVE ALIVE.

He flew over Tate's to get a better look at the most progressive prison in the world. Except for the electrical fences, it looked like a farm. As soon as they'd gotten in range, a monofilament aero-shield similar to Frank's snapped into place, and Seaborn received a warning. He lifted to the highest level of the companionway and signaled back to Luke the coded greeting he brought from Frank. Luke was now on standby.

On their way south to the middle of the state, they flew over thousands of acres of hemp fields. As Frank told it, Hemp provided a source of methanol fuel, and was financially saving the family farm, as well as helping release the country from a dependency on oil.

So far, he hadn't spotted anyone on their tail. He knew they would need privacy at the cemetery, the kind they hadn't gotten at Doris's funeral. He feared Jessie's reaction if she experienced the crush of the crowds that she could attract– people who would sell their pride and dignity for a picture or an autograph and tear her arm off getting it, too. The media never allowed what they were covering to interfere with their coverage of it, that was for sure.

Seaborn thought about the Indians. Although they sold information to the media, they were different. They were trackers for a living and didn't violate personal space or take advantage. They simply loved to fly like the hawks– it gave them a sense of evolving, a way to make up for the trail of tears on the ground that was their grievous history. Indians more than anyone felt like they belonged in the sky– a P.H. was a sky horse. Seaborn revered them, even while he knew their job was to report his whereabouts to whoever employed them. They had a quality he admired: they could be dignified without becoming tight assed.

Paradise Cemetery was an easy landing, since all the gravestones were flat, like the land itself and the oaks and palm trees were spaced wide apart, as were the life-sized statues of the saints. Seaborn set Bee One down on a narrow cemetery road near the gravesite and cut the motor. His rotos rustled the gravel and sent up hardy smells of the earth and grass.

He led Jessie over to Henry and Doris's grave, and then backed off himself. He wanted to give her all the space she needed to retrieve the memory of Doris's funeral, painful as it was going to be, it was crucial. He knew she had lost out on a daughter's last privilege– to mourn her mother properly. This would be like a regrieving. He wondered how much time they had, and knew he had to keep vigilant. He needed to set in motion a few real estate closings, now that he was back in Florida. It was the thing to do, finish business, follow through on half-laid plans. He leaned against Bee One, scanning the horizon, took up his phone and called the lawyers, keeping a sharp eye out. Bee One's stilled rotors ruffled in the wind like palm fronds; they joined with a song way out in the cemetery, welling from the radio of two grave diggers with a backhoe: *"When we get behind closed doors, and she lets her hair hang down..."*

Jessie heard it too, her mama's favorite song. She shivered as she walked around Henry and Doris's adjoined grave, breathing in the crisp November air of Florida which had a faint wood smoke smell from the smudge pots that protected the orange groves from frost. There had been something so off, so wrong about her mother's funeral. She wanted to remember but was afraid to at the same time. A sandy circle had been worn into the grass around the grave by the visitors and fans who came here by the thousands hoping to make contact with Henry, to see his resting place, his marriage bed in death. She knelt and gently laid the small bouquet of Sweet Annie and Mexican Sage that she'd gathered on Cowpen on the graves. Other bouquets of faded plastic or decaying real flowers were strewn around. In the litter, she saw old worn golf balls and tees. She read the bronze plaque:

REQUIESCAT IN PACE * TOGETHER FOREVER. HENRY LEE HASSETT * DORIS KATHARINE HASSETT

This is where they finished. She was beset with the aberrant thought that Henry and Doris were piled in the grave on top of each other. She shook it off, tried to think straight. But all her thoughts were inappropriate. It had always surprised her that her parents' marriage lasted, the way they fought. They never were indifferent, that was for sure. Now, here their bodies were, side by side, a couple forever. She had their model of marriage as a combative union; it had disturbed her and given her an unspoken defeatism about the possibilities of love. Yet it had shown her endurance at the same time.

Jessie dropped to her knees, disheartened. God, I have no memory of my own mother's funeral. That's so poor on my part, so poor. She wept, releasing her pent-up grief. She heard Doris reciting Dorothy Parker, not in her head like the messages, but from a childhood memory: "You will be frail and musty / with peering, furtive head, / while I am young and lusty / Among the roaring dead." Doris had loved that one, roaring herself.

In the midst of her weeping, Jessie heard a menacing whisper: *Never lay tools on lace.* It was one of Doris's "words to the wise," as she had prefaced all the bountiful advice she had barked at her children while they were growing up. Jessie experienced an old pang of bewilderment remembering *never lay tools on lace* because she had never understood what it meant. *A little bit of knowledge is a dangerous thing,* was the maxim most often given to Jessie, who had always been given to nibbling at the tree of knowledge.

Slowly she remembered the kind of day it had been, a warm, lazy, sunny, April day, just like the day of Henry's burial, barely a year before. And then she was swamped with the memory of the funeral– it felt like an hour ago; it piled in on her with all the anguish and weight of a fresh death. Her chest was strapped in agony. She doubled over, moaning. And Doris remained silent in her formidable sleep. How Doris had always loved peace and quiet. Mystics and scientists had come to the funeral, gaudy with headphones and listening devices, expecting something to happen. Doris had been wired for sound– Jessie remembered the acoustical network embedded in the blanket of flowers atop her coffin. It had all been a spectacle of expectation, a media frenzy.

She saw Chuck-Pete and Tom, grim-faced, glaring at her, angrily– and Kate, covering her face, weeping. Jane was there in her uniform, the navy-blue funeral director's suit, with the chauffeur's cap that the butterfly had landed on at Henry's funeral. She saw Jane directing traffic, insuring that none of the media trucks blocked her limo as they jousted for good parking spaces. And that was how she'd been able to rescue her. Jessie cringed now, as she remembered getting separated from Seaborn and that wild ride over the flat gravestones. Pandemonium had been loosed upon what should have been a respectful family gathering. She looked around at the balletic serenity of the cemetery. Oh yes, it had been laying tools on lace, no way to conduct a proper burial. Doris would have been unhappy with it, and Jessie had only wished to escape the media circus. Doris's cues always came too late, her fatal flaw, timing. Like her death had come, with no warning that Jessie knew of, or could remember.

Jessie recalled all the times in her adolescence when Doris had not understood her. They were so different, yet they were the same flesh. Now her thinking expanded to include all the mothers and daughters in the world, and she wondered; why are we all so afraid of being like our own mothers? Afraid of mixing ourselves up with them? And why do we always feel hostage to all their dreams and fears? Doris had been a frustrated, undeveloped actress, who became a nurse instead of pursuing her dream. Then she'd been overwhelmed with children. Jessie recalled when she first went on television as a news anchor, Doris had tut-tuted: "It's good dear, reading the news, but not exactly Broadway, is it?" And Doris had been disappointed in her for not having children, for not imitating her. She wanted Jessie to experience how children and love hold you back, wanted Jessie to appreciate her sacrifice.

Maybe Doris had spent her whole life trying to figure out her own real self, who she was. But what if it wasn't even about self? Jessie thought of a message that had come in from Allen Watts, d.1973, how did she remember this, even the date? she'd never been good with dates: *What if there is no real self to which one ought to be true? What if sincerity is simply nerve– it lies in the unabashed vigor of the pretense.* What if you made yourself up? It's a consent of your will to your own being. It isn't about ego at all, it's about echo. And the genetic payload– that has to be at least equally important; it's what you come into the world with.

She thought of another message, but couldn't recall who had sent it: *Relax, don't care so much what other people think of you. Stop the impression management. Just do your thing. Accept your life however ragged... what you must do to be happy.* Was that what Doris meant? But she had not been able to do it herself. She'd tried to be a good mother– but she had a jealous, competitive nature, which was maybe not her fault, something in her genes, or something she'd learned. What was a good mother anyway? Jessie thought of Jackie O's arch message: *If you're not a good mother it doesn't matter whatever else you do.*

She saw that Doris had deprived herself of taking pride in her own children, surely one of the rewards of motherhood. Instead, she had dwelled on how she'd missed the *"whatever else"* and felt herself a failure. Jessie rode these waves of light she knew the mother tree had ceded to her when she died, still drawing sustenance from Doris, however skewed and bittersweet.

Henry had given up his peace and quiet for a greater mission. When Jessie told Doris this, her reaction had been,

"Just like a man, but what about me?" A squawk in the dark Jessie chose to ignore– that was her own guilty betrayal of her mother. All this memory scalded her now, and she argued with it too. Henry didn't have to be a messenger– he did it because he wanted to unite this life with the afterlife he had discovered. Whitman had planted that seed: *build a bridge to the other side*. Henry was a natural born builder. He sacrificed his own tranquility so that people on earth could see the real depth and meaning of life. Doris had not been able to appreciate that.

And now he's gone, Jessie thought, and I miss him. Maybe he doesn't want to rob me of my whole ragged life. *You never know the middle of something until it's all over,* he'd told her, way back at the beginning in Casadega. Now she saw that memory could be a shelter for the organism, self-protection. Because the life force, the will to live was the biggie– to be preserved above all else. Something inside protected her from remembering everything all at once because she wouldn't be able to handle it. She was thankful for these bits and pieces that were coming back.

So many strangers at Doris's funeral– what had they all wanted from her? Jessie knew, of course. And how they'd been disappointed too. Doris's silence was a cold rebuff, even to her. She knew Doris couldn't care less, she only wanted to rest. Jessie wept freely, like she had to cry to go on living. And she cried for her father too, feeling his true absence and the cost of never hearing from him again. A cost that Doris had already paid, no song, no dance, no supper anymore. Doris couldn't live without her husband was the message she had pounded home to Jessie, and Jessie had paid her no attention.

When she looked up, Seaborn was standing over her. She wondered if she could live without him. Studying Seaborn,

Jessie experienced an overwhelming dread. She felt threatened by all that she still didn't know, and Seaborn was suddenly like a stranger. A terrible word, stranger. If Jane was his mistress, then she was a stranger too, and Jessie really was all alone. She struggled with this grudging feeling; it had seized her almost from the time when she'd awakened and first saw Jane so close to Seaborn. Whereas, entranced, she'd lacked the psychology of jealousy, or possessiveness. Now she wondered if he made raspberries on Jane's belly too.

She stood up, anger rising. "I guess Jane has fulfilled all your needs." She said.

"What are you talking about?" Seaborn shuffled his feet, alarmed at Jessie's tone.

"Your relationship with her, your affair."

He looked stunned, "you think I'm having an affair with Jane?"

"You're always touching and whispering and hugging."

"We're comfortable with each other; you might even say she's like a sister; we've been allied in the same effort to keep you alive and well."

Seaborn said it like she was ungrateful. Jessie thought he put on a good indignant act– but she was suspicious of that too.

"Something is going on." She glared at him, blushing now. She felt sick, ashamed of her suspicions, yet not ready to trust anything he might tell her.

"Jessie, are you jealous?"

"You're damn right I am. She gave you what was missing in me." Releasing this bile felt good. Why not let it all out?

Seaborn was at a loss. "There's nothing missing in you. I've never seen you like this before. You deplore jealousy and envy. You said they were the most destructive forces in the world... they killed your own mother..."

An alarm went off in Jessie's head, "What do you mean?"

"She couldn't stand it because Henry talked to you instead of her. She wouldn't even come for a visit to see you. The doctor told her to quit drinking, or she had less than a year to live. It was like a slow gun..." Seaborn stopped, afraid Jessie couldn't handle knowing all this.

But Jessie was thinking about a phone call from Doris one night when she was drunk, accusing her of stealing Henry from her. And then she was dead. And she went quickly, way, way up into the up, believing Henry loved his daughter more than his own wife, owning that sorrow, hugging it close.

"Maybe I could have done something."

"By the time we found out what was going on it was too late. No one could stop her. About like you couldn't stop messaging. She was so eaten up with envy over everything, over you, and THE LIFE OF DEATH SHOW, that she didn't want to live. It wasn't your fault Doris died, she just made it look that way."

"Is that why Tom and Chuck-Pete hate me?"

"Maybe partly, but they know better. They knew what Doris's game was, how far she'd go to get power, to get their full attention. She taught them envy."

Jessie ached with a feeling of despair for her mother's own jealous heart. And she was just like her now too. She mourned the loss of her brothers; their rejection of her was like a death. And the love she felt for them was locked tight in her heart, inexpressible. It pained her to face all of this, and yet it was freeing too.

Seaborn sensed a clarity building inside Jessie, the fruits of remembering, even if she was dead wrong about some things. She was filling in blanks. Maybe the liberation they longed for could be theirs. He scanned the sky—time was catching up.

355

"How I must have neglected you, for this...this mission." Jessie said.

"It's been hard," Seaborn looked down, picked up an old golf ball, examined it idly, tossed it aside.

"What's it all been for, anyway? Why us?"

"I don't know. Frank says it was the accident of an accident– right time and right place compounded exponentially. Any old thing can happen if all the elements are there."

Seaborn heard the fut fut of copter traffic. He spotted P.H.'s coming near. He had lost his lead. He steered Jessie quickly towards Bee One. She took a last look back at the grave site, knowing she would not return for a long time, if ever. Her knees were shambling; her heart was heavy but overlaid with healing too. She felt she had accomplished something, although there was still so much more about Seaborn and Jane that she wanted to understand.

Seaborn lifted off in a big hurry, yelling over the roar of Bee One: "We have to get to Casadega before they catch up."

Jessie studied Seaborn's hippie-like constancy, wondering if he was unfaithful, a cur-dog in disguise. She had to find out. She had to shake this feeling of shame at having been only a half-awake, half-wife to him for the last five years.

In two minutes they were over Silver Lake. Seaborn buzzed the old home place, dipping low so Jessie could see the RESERVED FOR MRS.PETTENGILL sign still hanging on the old oak. "It's still there!" she cried out. But her attention was drawn to the frame house. It was painted a purple color that took her breath away. Most of the grassy lawn had been paved over for a parking lot. A big sign said:

THE HOUSE THAT SPAWNED THE LIFE OF DEATH SHOW.

It was a tourist attraction! no longer Henry and Doris's place at all, simply a hollow mockery of what was once their home, a spook house. Jessie choked up. Who did this?

A woman came running out of the house waving up at them frantic to catch their attention. Two toddlers followed her, the littlest one's diaper dragged the ground.

Seaborn swooped low, but with no intention of landing.

"Kate? It's Kate! Hey, Kate!" Jessie opened her window and leaned way out, waving and hollering. She signed to her, over the loud, drone of Bee One: "We'll be back, we'll come back for you." She blew kisses with both hands to Kate.

Kate was signing back a message, a desperate warning: "Don't let Tom near you– he wants to have you boxed, put away." She had a lot of trouble with the word "committed", but Jessie took her meaning alright.

"Kate looks fat...or pregnant?" Jessie said over the drone, fighting back tears, "are those her babies?" She kept blowing more kisses down to Kate, and waving, as Seaborn circled.

"Yeah, she's pregnant. Again. Due this spring. She's married to a real nice guy, and they have those two little boys." He had been saving this news about Kate, but now was the right time.

"What's Kate doing here?"

That's when Seaborn had to tell her about the sui juris lawsuit, that Tom brought, claiming Jessie was not in her right mind, had diminished capacity to act. The suit had so far blocked her parents' estate from being settled. Tom liked it like that, in limbo.

"Since the house can't be sold, Tom, who your mother named as the executor of the will, painted it purple and opened it up as a tourist attraction. He gets Kate to run it for him."

"What hypocrisy!"

"He doesn't recognize the paradox. He's churning his case like he's always done, making the most of things." Seaborn wondered what Tom grossed– they were only forty miles from Disney World and Epcot.

He swerved off in a powerful glissade over the lake and took a new heading for Casadega. The sky, in just a twinkle, was swarming with rotors, thick as hornets, most of them in pursuit of Bee One. Seaborn shifted to spurt-speed and Jessie had to hold on as Bee One shot off wicked fast, leaving the other PH's breathless in its wake.

Jessie too was breathless, and mind blown. Kate sure had been busy, a husband, and two children, and another on the way! She didn't remember spending any time at all with Kate in the last five years. Was that true? Somehow, she swore she was going to get Kate back in her life.

She didn't even want to think about Tom.

50
Casadega Revisited

The Florida sun fused with Bee One's ocher glow and produced a flash of light that brought everyone in Casadega out of doors. The live oaks in autumn were blazing gold. The window-rattling sound of the P.H. got absorbed in the bright light. Instead, everyone heard a balalaika playing da da da da da da da da da da da da da da, an old familiar melody to Jessie, who was instantly filled with remembering. Her mind scudded back almost five years to that first trip to Casadega, only it had been a warm spring day, just three days after Henry's funeral.

After that visit with George Vogel, all the roadblocks had come down one by one, and a couple of weeks later, in the middle of the six o'clock news, she'd broken form, looked into the camera, and began delivering the messages that came into her mind clamoring for outlet. She had only to jump over a tiny little lump of fear to do it. After that, it was pure radio.

And then she and Seaborn got fired, and they'd had an interlude of months; days and nights filled with strange wonderment and discovery atop Cowpen Mountain. She had learned to believe her own ears, to seek the comfort and wisdom of angels. And Seaborn had tried to grow food for their survival.

Now here they were again, in Casadega, in another season, years later. Only this time Henry was silent. And all that had happened was maybe only the merest bud of celestial promise. Jessie had a pleasant sense of having been useful, and another trumped feeling of having been *rode hard and put up wet,* to use one of Jane's expressions.

Henry's character and who he'd been in life had served to identify him, to point out his messages from among the gaggle of them that had gradually flooded her consciousness. His voice played through– he was messenger. He had brought all the messages from discarnate spirits in their own authentic language, back to their loved ones still in life. In death, he wanted to be an avatar, a go-between, a role he'd had no time for in life. And then, when they moved into One World Trade, and the place was teeming with spirits– even he had been overwhelmed.

Seaborn was first to land Bee One, a few minutes ahead of the media, in a field behind George Vogel's house. The field was already crowded with his neighbors. George's friends, men in their sixties, seventies, and eighties surrounded the house for their protection. His Peacocks acted as watchdogs, chasing anyone who got too close. George came out to meet them, hurrying them into his little house, apologetic for making the mistake of telling people they were coming.

To Jessie, George looked older, wizened, even more luminous than before. He had more crinkles at the corners of his eyes from years of smiling.

"So, you're all alone now." he said, leading her into the little tax-deductible room in his house where he still conducted the business of psychic readings. After a call from Frank and Jane, he had anticipated Jessie's arrival and knew she was there to recapture memory– to understand all she could about spirits and find out how to catch up after a five-year trance. If only he knew.

Seaborn hung out nervously by a window in the hallway while Jessie was in with George. He had a good view of a gathering throng of people, wild-eyed fans, two media trucks, even an Elderculture bus had pulled in. A flotilla of News P.H.s came whopping down, roaring everyone. The peacocks scattered, screeching. Bee One had been quickly surrounded. People were climbing inside and sitting all over it, like vultures sucking on a possum. He scratched his itchy snakebite. They would need help to get out of this alive. He could hear Jessie crying. Again. In the past years she hadn't cried hardly at all—now though, she was making up for it.

Jessie was at a critical juncture with George: "Why didn't my mother ever talk to me?" she pleaded.

"Are you sure she didn't?" George asked her gently.

Jessie dropped her head. "She didn't send messages." She rubbed away hot tears with the back of her hand. "Why didn't she even try?" She knew she was pressing him like a child and felt ashamed, but what else could she do?

George handed her a box of tissues, "What I believe is that being dead is something like dreaming, it's a little hard to control where you go. Your mother was afraid, and what you are alive, you are dead. A lot of people, after they die, the subsequent proceedings just don't interest them. It's like a still-death, a chance for the rest they've always craved. They conducted their lives reasonably, without much input from the unknown, from what we sometimes call the soul; they expect to conduct their death the same way and do. It's their right."

He smiled and waited for Jessie to take his meaning before he continued. His voice lowered, became confidential:

"As I understand it, your mother, Doris, died at a time when she was self-medicating with alcohol. That could have dulled her capacity also, don't you see?"

Jessie nodded. She remembered a message from a spirit telling her husband to die sober so he could get through.

George grew more speculative: "People really know more than they think they know, but they don't believe in it; and they know less than what they're cock sure of, but they still rely on that instead. You know what I mean?"

Jessie nodded again, dabbing her eyes. But she felt like she knew nothing at all, like she had no personality, no idea who she was anymore.

"Besides, Doris didn't believe in it, did she?"

Jessie recognized the plain truth of that. She blew her nose, and sighed, ready to change the subject: "I feel so angry, and I'm jealous. I cry easily. I've never been like this before. I'm fearful, and I have all these gloomy suspicions. I'm like a middle-aged child on the verge of some sort of emotional tantrum."

George said: "After all, you're once again just an ordinary woman with normal feelings and reactions, and you'll have to deal with that now. You'll have to accept the temporary, imperfect nature of your gift. Maybe someday you'll enjoy being on a peak spiritual journey again. So, you have that to look forward to, you see?"

George patted her hand. "Meanwhile, don't worry, pain makes you genuine. You earn life with it, and then life will turn around and make you smile again."

Jessie blurted, "Oh, I don't know why I'm like this. I should be happy to be alive, to be normal again, and I am, but... now I miss my father so, and mama's gone too, and I feel like an old orphan."

"You're grieving, finally. And you've been given back your life too." George said.

"But I'm nearly forty-two years old." Jessie's shoulders lifted plaintively.

"Yes, well...Sleeping Beauty was over forty when she awoke, too, I think." George crinkled his eyes in another smile– he had a whole vocabulary of them, "there's still time."

Jessie could only smile at that.

When they were saying good-bye, George pressed a little book about the possibilities of reincarnation into Jessie's hand. He winked, "this will help you in future."

She thanked him for everything and hugged him like the tree of life that he was to her. He turned her towards the window with a cautionary tenderness that suggested she take courage for the danger she was about to encounter outside, earning her life again.

Jessie cringed at the sight of the engulfing mob lying in wait for them. She had received comfort in Casadega from George, as well as enlightenment, both times. It was a special place with a rarefied atmosphere of spirits, living and dead. But she knew, after all, it wasn't home. One Wing was her home now. How she longed for its piney scent, the clay earth, and rainbows and sunshine. Looking out at the wild crowd, she didn't see how they would ever get back.

Frank had outfitted them with offensive belts that were made of bubble-wrap and instructed Seaborn in how to use the belts to activate a noxious force field in a crowd situation. Seaborn popped a few bubbles on his own and Jessie's belts. George had to take a step back. They all got a hot whiff of the rank smell of polecat.

Seaborn placed nose clamps on himself and Jessie and told her to breathe through her mouth. A howling wail rose from the crowds as she and Seaborn appeared in the open doorway. George's friends formed a protective pathway and tried to hold people back, but they were taking a beating for it. The bodily surge coming towards them terrified Jessie. Seaborn wrapped his arm around her and aimed them towards

Bee One. The sounds and faces of the crowd were a mix of friendly and hostile; it was impossible to read the mood of each person.

Seaborn tore at their belts with the titanium tip of his Victorinox, slitting whole rows at a time. The fumes rose as they plunged deeper into the fray.

Faugh! People grabbed for them and then sprang back, bespattered, repelled, firing questions, then covering their noses, suffocating, not staying put for the answers, popping off haywire pictures.

One lady tore Jessie away from Seaborn, grabbed her around the throat, and talked urgently, up in her face: "My dead son, please, he's a Phi Beta Kappa, summa cum laude, with an M.A. from the University of Alabama, I have to know, does he talk to you?"

"Let go of me, I can't anymore." Jessie said, pushing the woman off her. The woman recoiled, hawking and spitting, overcome by the skunk fumes from Jessie's belt.

Jessie saw t-shirted, Muscle Men for Christ, holding chains up over their heads moving towards them, amazingly slow, overconfident, as if the hubris of possessing bodies like these made showing them off the first priority.

But where was Seaborn? She spun around searching for him and spotted him curled up in a ball on the ground being trampled by Elderculture, all in matching red t-shirts. Her heart leapt; she felt a rush of adrenalin; then she was screaming, her voice so shrill it caused just enough shift in the startled crowd so she could get a grip on Seaborn, pull him to his feet, and hustle him towards Bee-One. Hunched together they staggered through the clawing mob, getting pummeled to a fare-thee-well.

When they reached Bee-One, it was suddenly like there was a fox in the chicken coop. All the trespassers scrambled out and fled, yelping like kicked dogs, tripping and piling up on each other. From St. George Island, Luke, who was witnessing everything on satellite video, had activated a high-pitched SOUND-BOMB, which made a painful, earsplitting shriek, worse even than Jessie's scream. Once they got inside the PH, Luke quickly disabled it.

Then they were lifting off, with Jessie at the controls. Seaborn was slumped over in the passenger seat. One of the Muscle-Men-for-Christ was hanging onto the door. He'd managed to get his arm and chains around it and was holding them back. Jessie glared at him. The motor revved-up, strained, made a sound like an Oldsmobile throwing a rod.

Luke turned on the surface shock-assault, and the entire outside of Bee One was electrified like the fence at Tate's. The Muscle Man let go of the door and fell back, burned and screaming in pain. Jessie sent his chains groundward, tossed their reasty skunk belts out the window too, as she lifted off.

Levitating a moment above George's house, Jessie saw a shimmery moiré' of rainbow unveiling. She steered into this pool of color and felt her heart move. In that moment, Jessie let go of all that was past, let go of Henry and Doris, finally surrendering her hold on them, and theirs on her, and felt a liberation of all their spirits at once.

George Vogel, watching out the window, saw the splendid rainbow. He thought he saw gossamer particles swimming in the air around Bee One, enabling them. As he watched, the yawping rotors took the form of angel wings, rosy-red ones. At that very moment, the light reached a crescendo and was eclipsed by an unearthly red-black absence of light; Bee One was wrapped in undiscoverable darkness.

George was in awe, reflecting on how special Jessie had been and how ordinary at the same time. Because of her and

Henry so many people had been encouraged to go on with better quality lives. In a sense, Jessie herself had died and been reborn. Lots of people die but are not reborn to their old lives. They messed them up too bad. Lots of people die for other people, and for other people's sins too, but they don't get an eclipse when they do it.

Inside the media trucks, reporters anxiously told what had just happened as they saw it: One reporter blurted over the airwaves: *It's like the fucking end of the world!*

Another reported: *A cordon of protection seemed to be surrounding them, an invisible wall, rumored to be an Asian shield... but, uh... an Indian contingency is also claiming it... then it got dark... dark and red...*

Still another reporter stretched to describe what he'd seen:

A brilliant RED eclipse! Historically, the last time there was a red eclipse like that was during the crucifixion of Christ!

All the reporters began making wild observations. While on the ground people were holding their noses, moaning in agony, clamping their ears, coughing, vomiting projectily, and bumping into each other in the blood red darkness that had overtaken them. No one was reporting on all of that.

In Bee One, it was just a sunny autumn day, traveling at breakneck speed.

"How'd you know how to fly this thing?" Seaborn wailed over the noise.

"I watched you. If Jane can do it, so can I. It's almost as easy as driving a car."

Seaborn groaned. His whole body felt like one big bruise. He scratched his always itchy snake bite, and called Frank to report in.

"It worked," he gruffed into the phone before he'd even given the password or turned on the scramblers. "What'll we call this new invention of yours, Frank?"

"How about Skunk wall?" Jessie said, with a laugh, "you can market it for people who have to cope with fame all the time."

Frank was exultant. "A rose by any other name still smells the same. I found a fresh dead skunk and got the idea to harvest his gland and synthesize it, made it about a hundred times stronger. But the suffocating ambrosia had to be contained airtight, it was so pungent– makes your eyes smart, don't it?"

Jane came on, sounding possessive of Frank: "He used the plastic bubble method, since he was already making kudzu-bubble-wraps, which I love."

"A classic hack," Seaborn said, "worse than mace—and that sound bomb works too, it's painful man."

Jessie made a cringing face into the picture-phone.

"Extreme measures for extreme circs," Frank said.

"In case you guys haven't noticed," Seaborn said, "Jessie's piloting Bee One."

"What's the matter with you Sea? You sound rough."

"I got a little mauled out there, but Jessie saved me, AGAIN!" Seaborn looked all hangdog at Jessie. Thank Luke for us, will you? He saved our butts too.

Jessie said: "We're making a little detour to go get Kate, and then we'll be home."

Seaborn set the course for Silver Lake, then closed his eyes and passed out.

Over the airwaves, everyone who heard this unscrambled transmission scrambled to find out who the hell Kate was and where she was at.

Jessie slowed down to cruising speed, settling into her flight plan. She took some deep breaths, trying to clear her mind. But she couldn't stop thinking. Fame was like snake handling, so dangerous you couldn't control it—so why would Chuck-Pete seek it? She wondered how she would ever reach Chuck-Pete. How to reach Tom? She remembered Henry's words, long before she understood the need for them: *You will have to learn to forgive your brothers for whatever they do.* But would they forgive her? Tom can have the Silver Lake house she decided. She would always wonder how he had become so hard-hearted, and why he had turned on her, and even on his own son. Most of her questions had been answered, or rested, and maybe enough of her memory had returned. She had a sense of fait accompli, of catching up, oddly, by letting go. She was free, coming back to herself. Yet she felt antsy– something still bothered her, and it was ugly and dark.

She looked over at Seaborn often, checking on his breathing which was labored—he had been traumatized. Her heart swelled in her chest, full of feeling for him, however conflicted.

Thirsty and hungry, Jessie reached behind the seat for water, and Jane's legendary oatmeal chocolate chip cookies.

51
Home

"You've got to do it," Seaborn repeated, taking a strong stand, trying to convince Jessie. Why was she being so damn stubborn? She sat on the couch, balking, dead set against him. They had returned from Florida late the night before and gotten very little sleep. Jane had doctored his wounds, but he was still hurting from the beating he took at Casadega. He'd been trying to talk Jessie into doing the right thing since breakfast. She wanted to skirt the whole issue, but Seaborn knew better.

"Can't we just let it all blow over? Say I'm taking a personal day... for the rest of my life."

Seaborn said, "It's not gonna just blow over. You have to say you're not an oracle anymore, no more messages, you lost the gift. You have to show that you're just an ordinary person now, who woke up from some kind of extraordinary trance," his voice rose, "you have to finish this Jessie, or they'll never leave us alone."

"Why? I don't owe anybody anything." she persisted.

"Yes you do. When you get famous, you owe. That's what fame is. People look up to you. Now you must give them a way to look at you differently, to get along without you. They depended on you, to fill a certain void."

"Haven't I given enough?" Jessie hugged a pillow wretchedly. "just about five years of my life." She wanted to attack his vim. "You've given away all our money buying houses for people."

There was silence.

She looked into his kind brown eyes, unable to stop herself: "Frank told me all about it. All those real estate closings you and Jane go off to with bags of money, signing over deeds to total strangers—you love that righteous feeling it gives you, don't you?"

Seaborn looked stricken. "You sure have changed. No one used to be a stranger to you. And it was your idea to give away houses in the first place, to put a dent in homelessness. "Donate big! One on one." you said, "instead of impersonal acts of philanthropy that barely scratched the surface."

Jessie tried to remember that.

He paced, limping in pain; he could feel a knot forming in his throat, taking his voice down deep. "I don't think I even know you anymore."

Jessie heard sarcasm in Seaborn's tone that she hadn't ever heard before. Why was he trying to control her like this? It made her feel rigid, wooden as a bowsprit—yes, she felt exactly like she had been nothing but a wooden lady, for years. Sea must have gotten bored of himself with me, she thought miserably. He must have liked Jane better, liked how she pulsed with life, instead of death.

Jessie's eyes welled up, her voice broke, "Oh you're good Seaborn, buying houses for poor people, you and Jane. But you're imprisoned in virtue, like I am in fame." Jessie's accusation emboldened her, "I remember when you told me there was plenty of housing, there just weren't enough able buyers, so you supplied the money and created buyers out of yearners. You were so smart! You said the desire for a home and family was one of the strongest drives in a human, right up there with food and sex."

"Well, it is." Seaborn dropped his head. This was hurting him. All these new, raw feelings stood around them like ramparts, blocking their progress, cheating their happiness.

"Why can't you just trust me on this?" he said. Jessie had started crying big crocodile tears. He couldn't believe how much she could cry now. He eased up, lowered himself on the couch beside her, took her hand, talked softly:

"You've probably got normal hormones now honey, and sometimes they can take you on a ride. You're just feeling the little insecurities the average woman feels, that's all..."

Jessie shot up and bolted out of the cabin. Seaborn started to go after her, but he felt too tired. He sunk deeper into the couch, weak, confused, dejected. Maybe it was time to quit, to just give it all up.

"Damn," he muttered. His thoughts rambled; she'd never been a shirker; what was happening to them? She wasn't herself at all. She'd never resisted him like this before. He'd always been her champion. The strain of all that they'd been through had taken its toll. He didn't feel like himself either. He felt dragged out and dizzy. His heart was beating too fast. He felt like he would pass out. He closed his eyes for a few minutes.

When he opened his eyes again, a ghost was standing over him smiling, sublimely holding out her fur stole, like an offering. He stared at her. His lips moved involuntarily, "*mother*?" In all the years of Jessie's messaging, he'd listened carefully to every message, but his mother had been silent. He looked at the stole. It had a little weasel face with brown button eyes at one end, tiny feet, and a white-tipped tail at the other end. Then it came back to him, how she had called it *my Stone-Marten,* just as she had called him *my Seaborn,* and he had thought it was her pet's name. He was four and a half years old, crying wretchedly in his bed. He'd crept downstairs in the night, dragged a chair over and climbed up so he could put Stone-Marten in the coffin with her, so she wouldn't be lonely. Although he wanted to stay by her more than anything, he knew he couldn't, because he couldn't keep still like she and Stone-Marten could. As soon as he put the pet in with her, his tears dried, his sadness and grieving ebbed away. The act had been swaddled in his memory, warm and comfortable. He'd grown up happy, his heart full of her love and immanence, and now he realized that she had been with him all this time, accompanying him everywhere he went. But what was she trying to tell him now? He looked at her kindly smile and felt the word *COURAGE* grow like one of those magic sponges. He closed his eyes and rested, letting all the lassitude go, surrendering himself to a wonderfully deep and restful sleep.

Jessie was crying again. She ran through the greenhouse and the garden, out to the very edge of Cowpen mountain, to the viney old gazebo where they'd buried Baby Beast. She remembered going there when she had to get away. Above the entrance was a new sign, carved in wood: "Chid' invidia campa disperato muore" she knew the Latin: "Who lives in envy dies in despair." But she had never seen the sign before. Had Frank put it up? Seaborn? She sat down on a bench and looked out through the lattices. She knew she was once a good person, a kind person. Now she was in the most heart-mangling despair she'd ever felt, dogged by hideous feelings she couldn't even name, and lashing out because of them. Confrontation was the only way to clear the air—she had to confront them both. Why did she dread it so? How could she have seen Jane as a faithful friend for years, and now suddenly see her as a rival for Seaborn's love, arousing more jealousy than she ever thought it possible to feel? Her pulse raced hotly. She could feel the jealousy becoming rage, no part of it love. Where was love?

At that moment, Jane walked up. Even as she was approaching Jessie, Jane felt the bitter alchemy all around her.

"Want some company?" Jane asked, hesitant.

Jessie was so surprised she blushed and slid over quickly without saying a word to the last person on earth she wanted to see at that moment.

Jane sat down softly beside her. After a bit of silence, she decided Jessie needed cheering up. She started talking. She like to burst with ideas about the kitchen, bed, and bath arrangements. But she caught a flash of anger in Jessie's eyes, and knew it was time to think of something funny, quick. At first, nothing sprung to mind, then she thought of her dead grandfather who could always make her laugh.

Jane slapped her knee: "Whoo-eee, I sure do get a kick out of all these preachers nowadays using that phrase `laid to rest.' My old granddaddy who was in the funeral biz told me how that phrase came into use. He said in the old days everybody said `bury' and `put under'– and he decided they needed a friendlier term. So, he thought and thought, now what do folks like best? getting laid right? and what else? resting. So, he came up with `laid to rest' and durn if it didn't stick."

Jane laughed, delighted with herself, expecting Jessie to laugh too, but when she looked over at her, Jessie looked back with distaste.

"You know a lot about getting laid don't you." Jessie said coldly.

Jane was stunned. "What do you mean?"

"You seduced Seaborn, didn't you?"

"Don't do this, Jessie."

"I know what's been going on. You can stop trying to fool me"

"Unt uh, I don't think so. You don't even know who I am anymore. You don't want to know me."

That's when Jessie reached out and grabbed a hank of Jane's hair and pulled it hard.

"Hey, wait a little minute!" Jane slapped Jessie's arm away, and then the hissy fit began.

They stumbled out of the Gazebo slapping each other with open hands like they were making bread. They locked on each other's wrists and twisted till they both fell sprawling to the ground, pulling hair and anything else they could get a hold of. A good-ole-girl fight.

"I'm sick of you touching him!" Jessie screamed, rolling Jane over, pinning her down.

"He needs cherishing," Jane shot back, "I do the cherishing, somebody has to!" She'd started crying, surprising her own self, and Jessie pressed her advantage, rolling Jane's limp body over and over until they were perilously close to the edge. They both looked down into the abyss where The Reverend Thackston had met his end.

Fear suddenly helped Jane recover her strength, and despite her small size, she pitched Jessie off her, away from the edge, pinned her arms down, and yelled in her face: "The man is a goldarned saint! He's TOO moral. Know what he told me? He said the thing about morals is they never just go away. He's true blue, but you're too blind to see it! He told me you two sometimes woke up holding hands. He's such a romantic! The most dangerous thing for a man to be!"

They studied each other's faces and grew very still. Jane released her hold on Jessie, got off her, and sat up in the grass, brushing herself off.

"Besides, I'm in love with Frank. He was not just a roll in the hay. I always have been, only I didn't know it. You should know that Seaborn and Frank both have a certain receptor gene. Men who have it make faithful husbands and fathers."

Their eyes locked; they were flushed and panting for air, yet they both were strangely exhilarated.

"So, you never...? I thought you must be the one fulfilling his needs..." Jessie hesitated, "Maybe I was just like a mechanical bride?"

Jane wanted to laugh but she didn't dare. She shook her head, amazed. She looked deeply into Jessie's eyes hoping she wouldn't see any more crazy ideas there.

"I was like the sister he never had." She said.

Jessie swiped the grass off her arms and said, "I don't know how out of it I was, maybe I didn't...you know..."

"Oh yes you did Jessie," Jane interrupted her, "in fact, that synesthesia you have makes you very passionate– he told me– and after lovemaking, the messages poured in. Where is all this coming from?"

"What a nightmare..." Jessie buried her head in her hands. She threw back her head and hollered, "I don't know!" and it echoed off the next mountain over.

They looked at each other keenly. Suddenly, `I don't know' sounded like the funniest joke they had either one ever heard, and they fell back laughing in echoes.

When they recovered, Jessie sighed, "Oh Jane, now I see who you are. You've been like a Shaman to me and Seaborn, haven't you? You're wise and loyal, and I've misjudged you awfully. Can you ever forgive me?"

Jane swallowed hard. She knew her own worth and Seaborn's and Jessie's worth as well and had never suffered any doubts.

"You sure you're over this green thing?"

Jessie nodded earnestly. She had felt it fall off her.

Jane said, "I guess we worked it out then. You know my granddaddy used to say 'leave it lay where Jesus flung it.' Good advice, don't you think?" She giggled.

Jessie nodded, giggling with Jane. She longed to have the fresh simplicity Jane had. She felt a sweet deliverance now from the ugliness of jealousy, her darkest nightmare laid to rest.

Now she had to make up with Seaborn. She had misjudged him badly. She wanted the earth's kiss again, and as she touched her belly, she hoped she had it. She looked at Jane with a blissed-out smile and confided: "I think I'm pregnant."

52
A Message for Seaborn

When Seaborn opened his eyes, Jessie was standing over him with a calm expression and brand-new resolve. She chewed her bottom lip, mustering up the courage to apologize, and talk about what she wanted and needed for both of them, and most of all to clear the air between them. She took a breath and poured it all out rapid fire, her voice quavering:

"I'm sorry for attacking you, I'm glad about all the houses you bought for people, I really am. It's just that I want us to have a home, too, and I don't want fame to plague us anymore. I love you so much. Oh Sea, I know I was wrong about you and Jane, and I hope you'll forgive me. I never learned to trust love. I've lost my brothers, and I don't want to lose you, too. But I can't go back to that penthouse, Sea. I'm sorry. I can't go back to our old life doing the news either. I can't go backwards at all, anymore."

Seaborn stood up, "Is that what this is all about? You think I want you to go back to New York?" He looked at Jessie, incredulous.

Jessie broke down crying, "But how can I get out of this without going back?"

Seaborn pulled her close, "You don't have to go anywhere Jess. One Wing is our home now. All I ever cared about is living each moment we have, together. I'll stay by you. You're like my own life. We're gonna grow old together. I've saved enough money for us to live a long life—I didn't give it all away."

He held her out at arm's length and looked into her teary eyes. "You can tell the world you woke up from right here. Don't you remember the little TV studio in Frank's trailer? One more broadcast—it won't suck us back in, I promise you. It will get Eli and Smithy off our backs, get us out of all that psycho-legal junk with your brothers, too. Slip all the hoodoo off us so we can get on with our lives. We'll build a bigger log house and take peacocks to raise." He held her chin up, "Remember how you liked those peacocks at Casadega?" As he saw Jessie coming around, her smile beginning, Seaborn started to feel like his old self again too.

"I have something to tell you, Seaborn," Jessie said, with more weight in her voice than when she had delivered a message from Sukerov. She took a step back.

"What Jess? Just say it honey, what? What is it?"

"I'm pregnant."

"Oh, sweet Jesus."

For once, Seaborn was the one enraptured. He looked like a man with a vision. His eyes glowed, his face flushed with joy. In that instant, he felt their new life begin to begin. He felt like dancing a Tarantella.

"Are you sure?" he whispered, gently regarding Jessie. To Seaborn, a baby in the womb was a lot like a spirit in the Universe, miraculous.

Jessie nodded, "Jane gave me a pregnancy test."

Seaborn carefully sat Jessie down on the couch like she was fragile now, and he danced around her, hooting like the Indian he was, and laughing wildly.

He knelt before her and took both her hands:

"I will love you until all the stars disappear or kingdom come, whichever happens first." And he covered her hands with kisses, moving up her arms until she giggled wildly.

The bemused ghost of Doris, who was witnessing all this, curled her lips and uttered a universal question: *Why on earth is the female always reluctant to tell the male she's pregnant?*

53
Jessie's Denouement

After setting up in the trailer, Frank stood beside his aunt Kate to watch his aunt Jessie make a clean sweep. They had all missed Kate and were happy she and her family were with them now. Kate had picked a box full of Persimmons at Silver Lake, to bring to One Wing, and their autumnal fragrance filled the trailer.

Seaborn had two video cameras at different positions on Jessie who sat in an easy chair, looking uneasy. She wore her mountain clothes: jeans and a sweater. Seaborn would edit the takes himself and send the same product to all the networks equally. Frank would send a version out on all the social networks to go viral. Seaborn enjoyed being a camera operator again– it was tactile and visual, requiring skill, like a carpenter. Directing came natural to him. He screwed his Mr. Pettengill ball cap around to the side and looked into each camera, in turns, making adjustments.

"Just relax and be yourself," he coached, "we're rolling...anytime now..."

Maybe this was the first time ever that Jessie felt free of the wear and tear of impression management, free to be herself without thinking about it. She sat looking down at her handles. Instead of Henry though, she thought of Doris, who she now felt living on beneath everything she did, knowing their connection was the womb, as it always had been.

Jane stood next to Jessie, beaming, ready to sign.

An Esperanto translation would be added later to scroll across the bottom of the screen.

Jessie looked up and began to talk, tentatively, like a greenhorn, "I want to tell you that after all this time...I woke up..." (In her days as an anchorwoman she had fought a nervous edge in her voice, a feminine excitement, almost a squeak. It was reminiscent of Natalie Wood or Elizabeth Taylor in the movies of the late nineteen-sixties. Now that squeak was back, bigger than ever. It served to make her more vulnerable, like a regular person.) "...from what seemed like a dream. I'm retiring now, to start a family." The babe leaped in her womb as she held her belly with both hands and smiled in a cringing, hopeful way. "I must have been under some sort of a spell. Anyway, the messages have stopped. I'm just an ordinary person now..." She went on up talking; it was unanchorlike, fraught with a fresh amateur iffiness. "Forgive me for abandoning you in this mystery. It's a mystery to me, too. For all the people who believed and for all who didn't, let me just say, I had a hard time believing myself, and still do."

She suddenly went quiet. She was remembering the car trip south, just days ago, listening to an interview Chuck-Pete did with Dr. Desmond. Seaborn thought she was asleep, but she wasn't. She heard it all. Her brother said he choked a goose, and the memory of that flooded her mind now. The goose had attacked her little legs when she was two years old, and she had squealed, and Chuck-Pete who was only four had caught the goose and rang its neck. He saved Her! That's what really happened.

Seaborn said: "Jessie, you okay?"

Now with tears flooding her eyes, Jessie finished with mea culpas.

"I'm sorry... to my family, to my brothers for all the trouble I've caused you... please forgive me. I love you, and I forgive you... for everything."

She hadn't planned to say all that. But in her heart forgiveness was a delivering reflex for what she couldn't stand knowing any longer.

A warbling of the old musical theme came up: Frank's whistled rendition of "Windmills," and Seaborn called out "that's a wrap!"

Jessie sank with relief into Kate and Jane's open arms, heaving one of Jane's little whistle-sighs, "Whoo-eee." This Jessie did not love the camera.

"It's okay, you were charming, don't worry." Jane reassured her, wondering where all Jessie's professionalism had gone to.

"Let's go make some persimmon jelly." Kate said.

Frank had recorded his own whistled rendition of "Windmills of Your Mind" for the denouement. He credited words and music to Michelle Le Grand, Marilyn and Alan Bergman. Were they all still in life? Frank didn't know, but the music was still alive, that he knew. Frank was musical like Henry. Like Henry, he possessed a wilderness of ever-growing talents.

It was to be an epiphanous spring on Cowpen Mountain. Frank began composing his own musical score for Spring, with a working title, "The Great Day Overture."

54
Desmond Borked

The funeral for The Reverend Travis Thackston had been poorly attended. No one had even bothered to wire him with microphones, before or after he became a box of ashes. The media coverage was sparse and what there was got bumped on the airwaves in favor of Jessie's farewell, which flashed by satellite into most of the world's households– including jails.

Dr. Desmond, the person who perhaps might grieve the most for The Reverend, could not attend. He was in jail in New York at the time of the funeral, fuming, "Those bastards at the LODS turned the tables, arresting me on a Goddamn grand theft larceny charge. Those sanctimonious scumbags, Eli and Smithy. Why'd she have to go and wake up, anyway?"

He'd called Tom Hassett down in Florida for his one phone call that first night. He almost couldn't get him to accept the charges. He had to beg. Tom acted like he didn't know him anymore.

"You better g-get yourself a New York lawyer. I only p-practice in Florida." Tom told him.

"But I only get one phone call a day. Can't you call someone to get me out of here tonight?"

"You got yourself in there." Tom said, with a little chuckle.

Desmond started thinking Tom had no respect for him, he'd only used him. He decided to try another tactic: "You know Tommy, Jessie said she forgave you for everything. But she might not know about those papers we drew up..."

Tom cut him off abruptly: "Who asked for her f-f-forgiveness?"

Now that she was awake, Tom knew he'd have to drop his suit. She was capable of coming to court now. But he knew how to churn, as long as he remained detached and cold, he'd never have to settle Henry and Doris's estate. Jessie wouldn't dare push him. He had control of everything, as usual, so long as he let nothing kill his deadness. Ha! Desmond was a wild card he'd already played.

Go fly a kite, was the gist of what he communicated to Desmond.

Like a lizard, Desmond crawled up into the darkest, dampest corner of his cell and apoplexed. He was habituated to despise things that were terrible and uncomfortable. It was four more days before he secured bail and got out of jail. But by that time, he had a megalo depression. Everything was lost.

It was not that he loved The Reverend so much, but more that he needed the engaging domination of his Lucifer, to whom he could always feel superior. He didn't know what to do without The Reverend leading the war against Jessie Pettengill– a war that had kept him working in the reflected limelight. He should have taken up golf instead. Now, all that was left to go up against her was the extreme lunatic fringe. The rest of the Christians had been turned by some damn red eclipse, and they had all deserted leaving him in the lurch, forgotten.

It started being for him now a major miscalculation of events, of the efficacy of Jessie, and her preposterous claim to fame. He had believed that she was just a cultist on a psycho-tech reality show, and he was waiting for her to buy off on her own con. But not like this. Her recent unbosoming on television was more than he could bear. Just a normal woman indeed! After years of cashing in on a block busting psychosis, why was he the only one left holding the bag? His practice was shot. His reputation was sludge. He'd sacrificed everything for her. He'd been on the wrong side and now everything seemed to be rolling down on top of his failure. He idly wondered if he could get another interview with her brother Chuck-Pete and stir something up again. People loved to see Chuck-Pete go flooey.

What he thought was free-floating anxiety, a little agoraphobia, changed in days to a full-blown depression. Too much acetylcholine and not enough serotonin. It was simple he knew, but he could not adjust himself. Whenever he added serotonin it was like he'd taken a dose of LSD- he curled up in the fetal position, tried to assume room temperature and communicated like someone with autism.

For weeks, he fought this depression.

His taste in clothing plummeted. He woke up on the couch in his office one day to find himself too lazy to live, wearing a grey cottony shirt that had the texture of tripe or brain material and a compost-colored, sheeny suit, wrinkled beyond belief. Where, oh where, was his mind? What he craved was a mental carminative, that was all. He looked in the mirror and saw that his hazel eyes had become brown puffy s'mores, the pupils dark as the inside of a black cat. His gold coil was gone, hocked like everything else of value, to pay the lawyers, to get up the bail to get out of that hell-hole jail.

He'd lost his own appetite for scandal, and now the media was goring him, portraying a characterization of loucheness for him, so clearly defined he even believed it. The F.B.I. had Travis's diary and claimed it contained evidence that Desmond, had been plotting for years, along with The Reverend, to kill Jessie Pettengill; they had been responsible for the would-be assassins who'd shot at her. The F.B.I. was going to indict him, and he'd have to face the music alone. It was a big lie, he'd only played along. Why would HE want to kill Jessie? She had been his meal ticket.

An inquiry was begun, by the Christian Alliance, into alleged homosexual trysts between The Reverend Travis Thackston and various C.A. members, including him, especially him. Video had surfaced of calamitous acts of sodomy, that showed him and Travis in flagrante delicto. That finished it, the coup de grace. After all he'd done for the cause, and for that white-trash lunatic. Would they leave him nothing?

He gripped his withering member for comfort. Thank God, he'd always been mendicant to the body's pleasures. He began slowly stroking, while he watched himself in the two-way mirror that fronted his video camera. He couldn't get off. Soon he was beating himself with manic scurrility. He accidently tripped the switch and video-taped himself being obscenely abusive. He saw in the mirror that he was the picture of self-disgust, of middle-aged longing and regret, and he laughed viciously. His life as he'd known it was over. All that was left was pain, and comeuppance.

He had a sudden flash of insight: Death was not the brick wall that all his patients feared, but a tenuous veil, a thin raiment. It would be so easy to pass through to peace. Like that Morrie guy she had on who said by the time he died he had such an understanding of death that he merely passed through the thinnest of veils to get there.

The Bible preachers were always predicting that the Apocalypse was soon to come. If I had a gun I could get out of here first, he thought, just take me a dirt nap.

He looked at himself closely in the mirror. The truth came over him along with a wave of gastro-intestinal turbulence: He hated his face, hated everything about it. The face is plastic after death; as the facial muscles cool and contract, they draw the face into many shapes. He palmed his cheeks, violently displacing his features. He punched himself in the face. Not hard enough. He tried again and again and found it impossible to hit himself hard enough. His nose bled though, and he smiled. Sometimes the dead smile. He looked intensely into the damnifying back-at-you mirror. He punched at the mirror harder and harder until shards of glass were embedded in his bloody fists, yet he felt nothing.

55
Renascence

In early spring, right around the sixth anniversary of Henry's death-day, amidst a building boom atop Cowpen Mountain, the curtain was rising on a wedding. There were guests from down the mountain, most notably Luke, his wife, and their young son. The Forrest Ranger whom Seaborn and Frank had befriended had come, and he would perform the ceremony. Kate's family was all there; they now lived on Cowpen in one of the new log houses built especially for them. Their nanny who was also a midwife was present. She would be kept very busy in the days to come. Two bulldozers were parked for the day on the far side of the mountain where they were grading for a proper nine-hole down-hill course. But to everyone in this family the game of golf reflected an uphill tendency of life.

The wedding party was not bothered by the fut fut of hovering P.H.'s full of news hounds, nor by any fans. They had all gone on to other exploits. Jessie was all but forgotten in the press, no longer in the conversation. She was merely the exemplar for other Televisionary's. A whole new coloratura of pretty parvenus from the mystic echelons of California had surfaced, messages engulfing them, as they competed for staying power and their own shows with the networks.

The newly expanded porch on One Wing was bedecked with yellow daffodils, purple crocus, lavender, all the early spring flowers that could be found on Cowpen, and ivy, the Olympic climber—*why don't we cheer?* A large horseshoe arrangement of red roses stood upon a stand with a sash across that said, "GOOD LUCKS." On the way to Mars, John Playfair Pettengill had gotten the news from Seaborn that Frank and Jane were tying the knot. He sent the same arrangement for all the major events in life, birth, graduation, marriage, death. There would come another "GOOD LUCKS" when his first grandchild arrived. He was not about to break a streak.

Homemade root beer, fresh orange juice, St~Germain Elder flower, and bottles of a good Veuve Clicquot from Reims chilled on ice in an old claw-footed tub on the porch.

Frank's new musical score, "Great Day Overture," seethed with glissandos in the spring breezes. In the yard, Peacocks bobbed their heads at each footfall, in time to the music.

All were assembled on the big, wide porch, waiting for Jessie, the matron of honor. Kate was wearing petal-pink because she was thinking pink. She didn't know she was carrying another boy, the third prince of serendipity. She was overdue, and so hugely pregnant it hurt her to stand. So, she sat in a rocking chair resting her delicate nosegay of wildflowers on her full-term belly, hoping not to go into labor until after the ceremony. Her husband, a patient, good-natured fellow, prematurely bald, stood behind her, keeping her rocker in motion. Every now and then he broke off to go check on his two little boys who were running around the yard chasing big red balloons and a sudden influx of butterflies. Kate and her husband were a bit embarrassed about having a third child since zero population was the ticket, but having children was something they were good at. To Kate, nothing was more real than flowering. She wondered if this was the serendipity George Vogle had promised her at Casadega all those years ago.

Glowing with the blush of fresh love, Jane looked sublime. She had arranged Tussie Mussies for all the women—nosegays of kudzu flowers, snapdragons, lily-of-the-valley, buds of love-lies-bleeding she found growing wild, and ivy of course. She tied the little bouquets up with pretty trailing ribbons. She demonstrated tucking a Tussie Mussie into the bosom of her dress, so that her body heat unleashed the aroma of the flowers. It was an old-fashioned Southern custom she knew about from her old aunties.

Along with vintage black cutaways, the men in the wedding party were wearing round, red clown noses, to counteract the weightiness of the ceremony. These were causing the children to run wild and giggle, a sound everyone was fond of, a sound that promised an exuberant Universe and a carefree eternity. Angels and ghosts were in attendance, but Frank was the only one who seemed to notice. In particular, he was watching a mute, diaphanous, angel, who kept getting mixed up in the red balloons and then deliquescing in wavelets. He was no longer troubled by the painful memory of his mother's death. It had slipped away, been deleted in this new, populous nest. Jane had a lot to do with it. She too was newly pregnant, they had become betrothed, and today was the day their love would encircle them.

Frank heard his grandmother Doris's voice in his head: *You men are all alike, all you want to do is knock women up. Look at you now, you've become clowns and magicians.* He smiled. He liked who they had become. He liked how he could knock Jane up, so she could give life. He told Doris this silently, his voice hidden in the light of his thoughts. He told her that she was welcome to hang around with her grandchildren and he knew that was why she was there. Frank wanted to stay in Doris's good graces, now that she was sober and seemed to have her old Norman Irish energy back. He had decided that men's roles were too limited and counter intuitive. He wanted to expand into nurturing and maybe his grandmother and that red balloon angel could help him with that. He was a quick study. He felt excited about the babies that were coming, and about the chance to develop his own nurturing and comforting faculties the way women did. Seaborn had always had a well-developed female inside him—so did Kate's husband, and even his friend Luke. Frank was eager to unfurl his too, even if it was an added responsibility. He was ready for it. Jane had helped him realize that his handles were a special, creative force in his body, capable of describing to a certainty what was in his mind. He wanted to pass them on, along with all Jane's talents. He'd always liked bringing something up from seed.

Up on the porch Kate said, "I'm about ready to pop," and just then a balloon in the yard popped and everyone jumped, laughing.

The light was soft and otherworldly out in the jasmine-covered gazebo where Jessie sat reflecting. She knew everyone was waiting, but she needed a few moments to herself before the ceremony. The foxglove was all abloom, big clusters of purple bells, with tiny black spots ensouled within. The birds were in full song. Henry was gone, but she wasn't sad. She'd come to realize that when a person is really gone, they're with you forever.

Diehard fans had sent lots of beautiful wedding dresses, as well as the old vintage tuxedos. Many of the dresses were lacy antiques that had been worn by beloved ancestors who had messaged. Jane had chosen a lacy ivory one with a diaphanous veil held with a bridal wreath of sweet pea, lily of the valley and a bit of baby's breath. She was gorgeous. For

Jessie, her matron of honor, one dress ultimately surpassed all the others. It was the pale color of fresh lemonade, a fine, sheer organdy lawn, simple yet elegant, with a low scooped neckline, capped sleeves, and a full ballerina length skirt with appliques of white organdy butterflies fretting in it. The kind of dress Jacqueline Kennedy might have worn to a garden party in Newport many years ago. Jessie wore a wreath of wildflowers and baby's breath that Jane had fashioned for her.

She was feeling wonderfully lackadaisical crowned with flowers and her embosomed Tussie Mussie. She rose and walked to the edge of the mountain and stood in a dazzle of spring light nearly blinding to the eyes. Spring had laid a whammy on the winter bourne brown, transforming it almost overnight to lusty green. The rich red clay earth of the mountains was dowsed with purple heather and the glamour of sprouting buds. The ice had melted, creating freshnets of new trout. The garden was thriving. At the wedding party, they would feast on the first Silver Queen corn, Big Boy tomatoes and roasted mountain Trout. She encircled her pregnant bump, smoothing it with both hands, and thought of how lucky they were to be alive, how close they'd been to death in all they'd been through. She looked out at the land from which she drew her energy and opened her arms wide to embrace it all. Among other things, she'd learned that love was not just a feeling, it was an ability. Seaborn had mastered that ability more than anyone she knew, and she loved him for it.

Dragonflies mated in thin air in front of her eyes, filling her with delight. She felt a rush of pleasure, of gratefulness. As with all pleasure, all you have to do is receive it. In the distance, she heard a dog barking; it sounded just like Ibsen. Then she heard the Wedding Singers voice: *Oh, my love, my darling, I hunger for your touch...* It was the same voice she'd heard long ago when Henry had told her *Music is the heart of the invisible.* She turned and saw Seaborn coming for her—it was time. The time for belonging is now. He didn't seem to be walking at all but was being borne along by the same magnetic force that had always attracted and held them together, through all the sea changes. *...a long, lonely time... are you still mine? I need your love, God speed your love to me...*

Henry Lee Hassett didn't talk anymore, although every now and then he kicked. He had no idea where he was, only that he was reposing in a balmy bed of ease and it smelled delicious.

THE END

ACKNOWLEDGMENTS

Many thanks to all my book loving, book clubbing friends, especially Erasue Kahn, a natural born leader and sugar pumpkin. To my garden club, my close neighbors, Joy Rousso and Max Alligood, and Krista Russell, a fabulous writer. I love being in all of you all's orbit. Thanks to the good people in the Ryland clan, my bubble, who have sustained me and shown me what boundless family love is. Thanks to Madeline and Phil Van Dyck, savvy readers, joyful and constant lights.

Thank you to Joseph and Leslie Bird Torre. You are my rocks. You live in the intersection of spirituality and technology. To Nicole Torre who gave me grand girls, Camille, and Chloe, Thank you all for holding me close and scattering joy in uncountable ways. Thanks to the constant givers of solace, Jackie and Peter Martin, and their children. And to all the Noonies, my infinite family, gate openers all.

While we will always grieve what once was, I wish everybody in the quantum universe the currencies of love, laughter, and light.